BLIND CONVICTION

A NATE SHEPHERD NOVEL

MICHAEL STAGG

Blind Conviction

A Nate Shepherd Novel

For more information about Michael Stagg and his other books, go to michaelstagg.com

Want a free short story about Nate Shepherd's start as a new lawyer? Hint: It didn't go well.

Sign up for the Michael Stagg newsletter here or at https://michaelstagg.com/newsletter/

❀ Created with Vellum

STONE

1

They found Abby Ackerman at seven a.m., lying twisted among the rocks at the bottom of the abandoned stairs. I'd like to say it was because the lifeguards were so diligent, but really, it was because one of them had snuck over to the far side of Century Quarry to burn a cigarette before his shift started and had noticed the glint of gold on her wrist.

It was at least forty feet from the top of the stairs down to the water's edge. Fortunately, Abby had gotten wedged between the rocks, which kept her from slipping into the deep water of the Quarry itself. Those same striated rocks almost hid her though, blending in with her reddish-brown hair and her boots and her blood so that, if it weren't for the flash of her bracelet in the sunlight, they might not have found her that morning at all.

The lifeguard was a lifeguard after all, so he tossed the cigarette, rushed down the stairs to the cement pad at the bottom, and scrambled over the rocks to check her. Then he got on his radio to call for help and, within minutes, the rescue squad was there, trying to figure out how to get her out.

It took a few more minutes before they could move her. When they did, they saw that one side of her face had been smashed and that the bones on the outside of one eye had been collapsed. The chief paramedic had seen plenty of slip and falls in her day and she had seen plenty of blunt force trauma, so she decided that they had better call Sheriff Dushane.

The Sheriff arrived quickly and did what sheriffs do. He cordoned off the area, found evidence, and was zeroing in on a suspect by the end of the day. He agreed with the chief paramedic that Abby had sustained blunt force trauma and believed her attacker had used a rock but, given that the scene was literally a stone quarry filled with rocks submerged in water, he never found the one that was used.

That didn't matter though. Sheriff Dushane found plenty of other evidence, which he methodically collected, then turned over to the prosecutor. After that, he made an arrest.

I learned about the attack on Abby Ackerman a week after it happened. By that time, everyone else had a huge head start. I soon found that the case was a lot like the crystal-clear water of the Quarry itself.

It distorted the view of the bottom. And it was a lot deeper than you think.

2

The case didn't start out like the mess it became, but then, I suppose it never does.

No, this case started when Olivia Brickson stuck her head into my office and said, "Morning, Shep."

I was surprised, not at the shock of bleached white hair or the half-mirrored sunglasses because those were typical for her, but because she was there. It was eight-thirty in the morning, a time when she was usually working at her gym.

"Hey, Liv. Don't you have a dawn death march class to teach or something right now?"

"It's a morning boot camp and Cade's covering it for me. Can I come in?"

"Of course." Olivia owned a gym with her brother Cade. She was also an investigator and we'd worked together on my biggest cases. If she was here, it was serious. "What's up?"

She sat. "I have a potential case for you."

"Shoot."

"It came from a friend of mine at the gym. Her fiancé has been accused of attempted murder."

"Okay."

"He didn't do it."

"Shocking."

"I believe her."

"Alright. Do you have names and info for me?"

"Actually, I have the accused's parents."

I blinked. "What do you mean you have them? Here?"

Olivia nodded. The glasses always made it hard to read her expression, so there might have been a tinge of "I'm sorry" to it, but I couldn't be sure.

"Well, I guess I'd better talk to them then. No promises though."

She nodded. "That's what I told them."

I went out and saw that there was a couple waiting in the main conference room. I grabbed them each a cup of coffee and Olivia motioned that she'd stay outside. As I passed her, she whispered, "Alban and Susanna Mack." I nodded thanks and went in to meet them as she shut the door behind me.

They stood and we shook hands. I handed them the coffee as we introduced ourselves all around. Mr. and Mrs. Mack looked like they were in their sixties and in reasonably good health. Mr. Mack sat down and took off a baseball cap with a logo that read "Mack Farms," revealing a bald head with a ring of hair that was still mostly brown. Mrs. Mack's hair had a bit of white in the front that fell around sharp, focused eyes, and she carried a small spiral notebook and a pen.

"Mr. and Mrs. Mack, Olivia tells me that your son has been accused of attempted murder."

"It doesn't make any sense, Mr. Shepherd," said Mr. Mack. "None at all."

"Our Archie wouldn't hurt a woman," said Mrs. Mack. "And he certainly wouldn't hurt Hamish's Abby."

I was suddenly swimming in a sea of "A's."

"I'm sorry, Mr. and Mrs. Mack. Hamish, Abby, Archie...I have no idea who everyone is."

Mr. Mack nodded to his wife.

"Our oldest son is Archie, Archie Mack," Mrs. Mack said. "He's accused of attempting to kill Abby Ackerman."

"Okay."

"Abby is the fiancée of our youngest son, Hamish."

Mr. Mack shook his head. "That's why it makes no godd—" Mr. Mack got a sharp look from Mrs. Mack. "That's why it makes no sense," he said. "They've always gotten on great."

"And who told Olivia about this?"

"Bonnie," said Mrs. Mack. "Bonnie Price. Archie's fiancée. She works out at Olivia's gym."

"Alright. How is Abby?"

"Not great," said Mr. Mack. "Her hip was shattered and her head was banged up so that she broke her"—Mr. Mack looked at his wife—"Orbit bone?"

"Orbital bone," said Mrs. Mack.

"Right, her orbital bone here." He indicated the side of his face.

"I see. And they're accusing Archie of being the one who attacked Abby?"

"He didn't do it," said Mrs. Mack.

"Even Abby says so," said Mr. Mack.

"I see," I said again, although I absolutely didn't. "Do you know what happened?"

Mr. Mack started to speak, but Mrs. Mack raised her hand and said, "Abby was attacked by someone last week after the Big Luke concert. They think our oldest son Archie did it. He didn't."

"What does Abby say?"

"She agrees Archie didn't do it."

Which was an interesting way to put it.

"Then why was he arrested?"

Mr. Mack waved a hand. "Sheriff Dushane said some nonsense about video and blood."

"I know Sheriff Dushane. He's not going to arrest someone without evidence."

Mr. Mack waved again. "It's circumferential."

I decided not to get into a discussion about the nature of evidence and the measurements of circles. Instead, I said, "So how old is your son?"

Mr. Mack looked at his wife the way husbands do when they've stored information in the other half of their marriage.

"Thirty-nine," she said.

"Then, Mr. and Mrs. Mack, I need to speak to your son about this."

Mrs. Mack looked relieved. "That's exactly what we need."

I wasn't at all sure this was a case I wanted to get involved in, so I said, "Olivia told you about me?"

"At first. Olivia told Bonnie and Bonnie told us, but we go to church with Judge French so we asked him about you. He agreed you were the man to call."

I swore in my head. I'd just finished a murder trial a couple of months ago in front of Judge French. His opinion meant a lot, and I didn't want to turn down a case he'd recommended me for, but I still needed to sort through this cluster a little more before taking it.

"I'll need to talk to your son. He's the one who has to engage me."

"We run the same farm," Mrs. Mack said. "The money all comes from the same place."

"I understand. He still needs to be the one to hire me though."

"The point is, our son had no reason to hurt Hamish's girl," said Mr. Mack.

"You mentioned that."

"And there's no reason for our boy to be in jail," said Mrs. Mack. "And Judge French said you'd know how to get to the bottom of it." They looked at me expectantly.

There was one more potential out.

"This kind of case is expensive."

"We run a large farm, Mr. Shepherd," said Mrs. Mack. "We know all about lawyers. How much?"

I told her.

To their credit, Mr. Mack didn't blink and Mrs. Mack just nodded her head before saying, "You'll have it in the morning."

I raised a hand. "I haven't taken the case yet. I need to talk to your son and to Sheriff Dushane. After that, I'll circle back around to you."

Mrs. Mack opened the notebook, and I saw her write down "Shepherd," underline it, then write down a numbered column of "1. Archie" and "2. Sheriff Dushane."

I felt instantly accountable.

Mrs. Mack snapped the cap back onto her pen. "Thank you, Mr. Shepherd. You're just what Archie needs."

"Maybe."

"Right, right." She waved a hand and gathered her things.

We all stood and Mr. Mack picked his hat up off the table. I shook Mr. Mack's hand; it was hard and worn from a lifetime of work. Mrs. Mack's was just as firm. I smiled and walked them to the door with promises I'd be in touch soon.

Daniel Reddy, my associate, came out of his office as they left.

"Where did Olivia go?" I asked.

"She said she had a class to save from Cade. What was that about?"

"Did you hear about a woman who was attacked after the Big Luke concert last week?"

"That was out at the Quarry, wasn't it?"

"I think."

"I did. Are we representing her against the Quarry?"

"No. Their son is accused of attacking her. We might represent him."

Danny stared at me.

"Allegedly."

Danny leaned his long frame against the doorway and sighed. "I just got back from Petoskey, you know."

"So you should be well rested."

Danny looked at the ceiling in what can only be described as a look of infinite patience.

"Nothing official yet," I said. "I'll go find out what's going on first."

"I can't wait."

I left Danny to his daydreams of Petoskey stones and better bosses and headed out.

≈

MY OFFICE IS IN CARREFOUR. If you've never visited us before, Carrefour is a small city that sits right on the border of Michigan and Ohio, not too far from Indiana. According to the Macks, the attempted murder had happened at Century Quarry, which is on the Michigan side of the line. That meant that the investigation would be under the jurisdiction of the Sheriff of Ash County, Michigan, Warren Dushane. The Sheriff's office is in the town of Dellville, twenty minutes north, which is also where the Ash County jail is located. I decided to visit the sheriff first. I'd called ahead, so he was waiting for me when I arrived and showed me straight back to his office.

Sheriff Dushane was a cinderblock of a man. In his early sixties, he was still thick-armed and barrel-chested, with the only indication of his advancing age being the loosening of one extra notch on his gun belt. He was dressed as a Michigan sheriff—brown wide-brimmed hat, a brown shirt with yellow borders, and khaki pants. He had a blunt face and a salt-and-pepper mustache and was just as comfortable with the gun belt around his waist as he was with a coach's whistle around his neck, which was how I'd first met him when he'd coached me and my brothers and my friends in pee wee football.

"How's your dad?" Sheriff Dushane said as he dropped into his chair.

"Good. It's morning, so I imagine he's still on the water."

Sheriff Dushane nodded. "We caught a good run of perch last weekend. How does Tom's team look?"

Tom was my older brother and the coach of the Carrefour North High School football team. "You know you can't trust a coach in August. If you listened to Tom, you'd believe his whole team has broken legs and scurvy."

Sheriff Dushane chuckled. "True enough. Guess I'll have to find out with everyone else."

"How about your granddaughter? Is she playing volleyball again?"

He nodded. "J.V. Middle hitter."

"Outstanding. My niece is too. I'll look for you."

"I'll be running the scoreboard." He smiled and rubbed the side of his face. "I've been told that it keeps me occupied."

It was my turn to chuckle. I've been a sideline witness to Coach Dushane's enthusiasm. The scoreboard seemed like a good idea.

"So what can I do you for, Nate?"

"I had the parents of a potential client come to see me this morning. I wanted to check around before I took the case."

Sheriff Dushane leaned back. "Did I arrest him?"

"I'm guessing you did but I don't know for sure."

"Okay." Sheriff Dushane turned toward his computer and put a hand on his mouse. "What's his name?"

"Archie Mack. Archibald, I think."

Sheriff Dushane straightened, took his hand off the mouse, and turned back to face me before folding his thick hands in front of him. "Yes, Nate, I certainly did."

"For an assault at Century Quarry?"

"For an attack that left a young woman nearly dead at Century Quarry."

I nodded. "What can you tell me?"

Sheriff Dushane stared for a few seconds before he said, "We have to turn square corners on this one, Nate. It's a bad case."

"That's why I asked what you can tell me. Nothing more."

Sheriff Dushane stood. He walked out of the room and, a short time later, returned with two cups of coffee. He sat down, sipped his, thought a moment more, then said, "Big Luke played a concert at Century Quarry last week. A woman named Abby Ackerman attended. The morning after the concert, she was found on the rocks, by the water, barely alive."

"Where in the Quarry?"

"You know it?"

"I worked there in high school."

Sheriff Dushane nodded. "At the bottom of the abandoned stairs."

"The stairs on the closed side?"

"Exactly."

I thought. "It's dark there. Or used to be."

"Still is. That's why they didn't find her until sunrise the next day."

"So did she say who did it?"

Sheriff Dushane looked to the side. "No."

"Give you a description?"

"She's says she didn't get a clear look."

"What about—"

Sheriff Dushane raised a hand. "I agreed to talk to you, Nate, not be cross-examined."

I smiled. "Habit. Sorry."

"That's okay."

"Can you tell me about her injuries?"

"Broken hip. Shattered pelvis." He stopped.

"I hear she had a facial fracture too?"

He looked at me.

"I haven't seen Archie yet. His parents told me."

He nodded. "Yes, a facial fracture, right on the side of her eye. They had to do emergency surgery to evacuate the bleeding and swelling."

I nodded and thought. "I've been told she's the fiancée of Archie's brother. That makes him an unlikely suspect, doesn't it?"

"His brother didn't think so."

"What do you mean?"

"They fought in the hospital right before we arrested him."

"Argued?"

"Not words. Fists."

"About?"

"You'll have to ask your client."

"I will. So if the victim didn't ID Archie, why did you arrest him?"

Sheriff Dushane appeared to think before he said, "There's blood and there's video."

"Of the attack?"

"Of your client at the scene."

"My potential client. Anything else you can tell me?"

"That the investigation is ongoing and that I'm sure there will be more evidence by the time of trial."

"Seems a little light."

"Damning blood, damning video." Sheriff Dushane paused. "And a damning scene." He stood, which was his polite way of saying he'd reached his limit.

I finished my coffee. "Coming out to the lake next weekend?"

He gave me a snarl that was twenty percent serious. "That didn't get you out of laps when you were ten, and it's not getting you more information now."

I put a hand to my heart. "I was just asking if my father's best friend was going fishing on our lake at a time when small mouth bass abounds."

Sheriff Dushane pointed, but he smiled. "Out."

I waved. "Thanks."

"We'll see."

I left the Sheriff's office, finding my way through a small warren of plexiglass windows, metal rails, and painted steel doors, and came out right across the street from the Ash County Jail.

I jaywalked over to see Archie Mack.

Cade Brickson met me in front of the jail. I'd called him on the way up and my meeting with Sheriff Dushane had given him time to get here and arrange for us to see Archie Mack.

Cade wasn't hard to find. He was about six foot four and two hundred sixty pounds. He had black hair, cut short on the sides, and wore black wrap-around shades because, of course. His black t-shirt strained to contain huge shoulders and he looked exactly like what he was, the most fearsome high school wrestler Carrefour North had ever produced. By all reports, he'd only grown more dangerous since then.

Cade was a bail bondsman, among other things. I didn't get up to Dellville as often as he did, so I'd asked him to see if his connections could get me in faster to see Archie, the tradeoff being he'd get the bond business. It turned out they could and, a short time later, after metal detector searches and the removal of all things weaponizable, we were in a room with Archie Mack.

Archie was average size, maybe leaning toward the broad side, but it was hard to tell because he was sitting down. The orange jump suit was short-sleeved, so you could see that he had large forearms and blunt, sawed-off hands. He was bald with brown hair around the fringe and he had that curious tan-line that comes from wearing a baseball cap, running right across his cheekbones so that his forehead was pale and his chin and cheeks were tan. His eyes stayed on Cade, which was a typical reaction, until I said, "I'm Nate Shepherd. Your parents want to hire me to represent you. I told them that decision had to come from you, so that's why I'm here."

"And him?" said Archie.

"Cade Brickson is here to make arrangements for your bond once the judge sets it."

"How much is that?" said Archie.

"Expensive," said Cade.

"Of course," said Archie.

Cade shrugged. "Bond for this kind of case isn't cheap. I understand your parents have a farm. You'll probably need to use it as collateral."

"Get in line," said Archie.

Cade put a "Brickson Bonds" card in front of Archie. "You can give that to Nate when he leaves. Let him know if you want me to help get you out of here."

Archie nodded distractedly, but it looked like bond was one more thing than he could think about right then. Cade walked to the door, smooth and quiet for such a big guy, and buzzed to be let out. The guard came, Cade nodded, and he left.

"I didn't do it," said Archie.

"That's what your parents said."

"I could never hurt Abby. She's family."

"I'm glad to hear it."

"I mean it."

"So do I. Do you want me to represent you?"

"Bonnie said my parents picked you?"

"They came to my office."

"And Judge French recommended you?"

"So I've been told."

"Then yes."

"There's a fee and a retainer."

Archie waved a blunt hand. "My mom handles the books on the farm business. Did she say it was okay?"

"Yes."

"Then it's fine with me."

"You've got yourself a lawyer then. So tell me what happened."

"I went to the Big Luke concert. I went home. I found out about Abby the next morning."

"Who did you go to the concert with?"

"Myself."

"So no easy alibi? No one who was with you all night?"

He shook his head.

"Why did you go by yourself?"

"Is that a crime?"

"No. But it makes it harder to prove you didn't commit one."

"Bonnie and Abby and a couple of their girlfriends had tickets and were sitting down at the front. I bought mine late and was standing in the back."

"Bonnie your fiancée? She went to the concert with Abby?"

Archie nodded. "They've become good friends."

"Did you see them there?"

"From a distance. They were having a girl's night so I didn't want to interfere."

"Did you see anyone else there? Anyone who knows you or would be able to say when you were where?"

Something flashed across Archie's face, but then it was gone and he shook his head. "I left alone and was alone back at my house. I didn't see Bonnie until the next day. Listen, Mr. Shepherd—"

"Nate."

"Nate, I didn't do this. I could never hurt her. They're saying I tried to kill her!"

"I know. Are there any other easy things you can give me? Anything that'll show you didn't attack her?"

"I didn't even see her after the concert! I just went back to the farm and..." His eyes widened. "Nate, am I going to lose the farm?"

"One thing at a time, Archie."

Archie was about to ask me for a bunch of things I couldn't promise him yet, like an assurance that he wasn't going to spend the rest of his life in jail, and I didn't have enough information yet to tell him how that was going to go.

Instead, I said, "Our first job is to post bond and get you out of here. Then we'll start putting together your defense."

Archie leaned forward. "I did not hurt Abby. And I would kill anyone who did."

I wasn't crazy about that phrasing but decided that was a battle for another day. It was enough that Archie was adamant that he wouldn't hurt Abby and, right then, he seemed sincere and believable.

Of course, if you know my recent past, you know I'm not always right on that score. More digging was in order.

"Fine," I said. "Do you want out of here?"

"Yes."

"I'll tell the guard to start the process and you can talk to Cade."

"The big guy?"

I nodded. "He'll handle the arrangements for your bond."

He nodded then, and I buzzed out.

I wanted to do a little more diligence on this. I went outside and checked the time. It would take half an hour or so to get back to Carrefour. I decided to stop at the Brickhouse on the way.

~

THE BRICKHOUSE WAS an old warehouse made entirely of used brick that sat near an abandoned sidetrack of railway. Olivia and Cade Brickson had renovated the warehouse into a gym complete with weight equipment in one part, cross-training equipment in another, and fighting equipment in a third. It was all brick walls, cement floors, and iron bars with the only soft thing being a mat in the back used to toss people on. It was a no-nonsense, no-frills gym designed for sweat and hard work, an attitude which emanated directly from its owners.

A new guy was working the desk.

"Is Olivia here?" I asked.

"I can give you membership information," New Guy said.

"Thanks, but I need to see Olivia on business."

New Guy glanced at the tie and the white shirt before he said, "She's in back with a kickboxing class."

"Poor bastards."

The comment appeared lost on him. He *was* new.

I made my way through the weights to the area of heavy bags, ropes, pull-up bars, and speed bags. There were about a dozen people on those, along with stations for jumping rope and shadowboxing. Olivia Brickson stood off to the side, a phone in one hand. She was dressed in her usual workout attire—black tights and a red tank top that showed a tattoo that trailed down her left shoulder into a sleeve that covered her from elbow to wrist. She wore half-mirrored sunglasses and a sinister smile that ticked up as she saw me coming and yelled, "That rope isn't hitting the cement nearly fast enough. I can hear you loafing!"

I might've imagined it, but it seemed like the "tick-tick-tick" of the jump ropes hitting the concrete floor sped up.

"That's better," she yelled. "Faster now, faster!"

Her phone beeped. "Time! Rotate! Clockwise! Thirty

seconds." I saw a dozen people jog to a different piece of equipment, some with hands clasped over their head, breathing hard. A few had their hands on their knees, panting.

Right on cue, Olivia yelled, "No leaning, no bending over, no fatigue faces! Stand up straight, hands over your head if you can't catch your breath. Smile or pretend to. Don't let anyone know if you're hurting."

They all straightened, and if they didn't look happy, most of them at least made an effort to take the pain off their faces.

"That's it now, that's it," Olivia said. "Five seconds—and 3-2-1, go!"

Ropes spun, bags bounced, and people pulled themselves up. One particularly eager soul did muscle ups over the bar instead.

"Hey, Liv," I said.

Olivia glanced at me. "You're not dressed for work, Shep."

I looked down. "That's exactly what I'm dressed for."

"You call what you do all day work?" She teased her bleached white hair down around the left lens of her glasses. "We have to get you out here more."

I sighed. "I'm taking the Mack case. I'll need some help with the investigation."

"Alright, let me finish here first."

She turned and barked at a man who'd gotten stuck halfway up the salmon ladder, advising that salmon who didn't make it upstream never spawned.

Yeah, so, that.

I watched Olivia cajole, curse, and credit the class's effort for another two rotations. It was fairly amazing. I swear there were things she picked up on when she wasn't even looking, like when a group behind her stopped doing double-unders and she let them have it without even turning her head. I enjoyed watching her in her element and, when the class was over, I stood by my usual excuse to her—I wasn't nearly man enough to take her class.

When time was up, she gave the class a chance to get water. Then she brought them in for five minutes of wrap up, letting them know that they were better for having done the class and that today was a victory over themselves of yesterday. I smiled at the Olivia-ization of a quote from the greatest swordsman who ever lived. As her class wandered off to commiserate, collapse, or die, one woman stayed behind. She was a little shorter than Olivia, with a blond bob and a sunny smile that seemed unaffected by what had wrecked most of her classmates.

As I approached, the woman said, "You must be Nate Shepherd."

I blinked and smiled. "I am."

She extended her hand. "Bonnie Price. So can you help my Archie?"

I took it and said, "I'm going to try."

"There's no way he did it."

"So I've been told."

"Abby and I are too good a friends."

I pulled out a card and handed it to her. "If you want, text or email me your contact info, I'll be in touch to talk to you about what you know."

She took the card and nodded. "When will he get out?"

"Cade is working on it as we speak."

"Good." Bonnie wiped at her neck with a towel. "Look at me, sweating it out during a business meeting. Thanks, Nate. I'll email you. Tomorrow, Olivia?"

Olivia nodded. "Iron motion. Noon."

Bonnie smiled and left.

"Talk?" I said.

"Sure," said Olivia and we went back to her office.

Olivia's office could only be described as eclectic. An old

battered desk that looked like it came from a phys. ed. teacher's office sat in front of an elaborate computer setup including three monitors, a printer, a scanner, and two laptops. One wall was covered in pictures of her many students, all of them orbiting one picture of her with Arnold Schwarzenegger and another of her with Royce Gracie. The opposite wall was filled floor-to-ceiling with books that were almost all workout, strategy, or philosophy related.

She offered me a water, I declined, and we sat.

"Cade and I saw Archie. I'm taking the case."

She nodded. "Cade handling bond?"

"Once it's set. Can you handle the research?"

"Bonnie's already convinced me to get involved."

"Is she always that cheerful?"

"Unrelentingly." She turned to her computer screen. "Who do we start with?"

I checked my phone. "I represent Archibald Mack. The victim is Abby Ackerman. She's engaged to Archie's brother, Hamish."

Olivia typed. "Bonnie mentioned that."

"Apparently Abby and Bonnie are friends. Has Abby ever come in here?"

"No. What else do we know?"

"Parents are Alban and Susanna Mack. They all somehow work on or own Mack Farms."

She clacked the keys. "Got it. What do we know?"

"Abby was found at Century Quarry the day after the Big Luke concert. They're charging Archie with attempted murder or something similar."

"That bad?"

"Dushane said she was left in pretty bad shape. Sounds like serious pelvic injuries and orbital fracture. I think they had to do emergency surgery to save her eye."

Olivia paused for a moment then kept typing. "Did they?"

"That's unclear right now."

"What does she say happened?"

"According to the Sheriff, she doesn't know who did it."

Olivia stopped typing and turned to face me. Her half-mirrored glasses often made it hard to read her expression. This was not one of those times. "Who did?"

"I don't know."

"Seems kind of important."

I nodded. "A friend of mine just brought me the case this morning."

Olivia smiled. "Sounds like you need better friends."

"I was thinking that."

Olivia went back to typing. "Typical starter package?"

I nodded. "Background on all of them."

"Done. I'll have it for you in a few days."

"Thanks." I stood.

"Working out?" she said.

"Have to get to the office."

"Don't let the day get away from you."

I smiled. "I'll catch it, Coach."

She shooed me. "Thanks for the work."

"Always."

As I left, I smiled as I saw about half of Olivia's class still scattered about the gym in various states of exhaustion.

They'd already caught the day.

4

I started the next day with a trip to Century Quarry. The land surrounding Carrefour has its share of sandstone and gravel so there are quarries scattered throughout the hills and woods, some working, some abandoned, and some, like Century Quarry, developed for another purpose entirely.

Century Quarry had been mined out long ago, leaving striated rock cliffs around a wide pool of beautiful, filtered water. The water was as much as fifty feet deep and so clear that it looked no more than five. It was scenic enough that an enterprising family had bought it in the 1970s and turned it into a public swimming spot. Soon, people were showing up in droves to swim so they added diving boards and a zip line and rafts so that it could accommodate hundreds of people on any given weekend. That was so successful that the owners eventually, in the ultimate irony, hauled in tons of sand to build a beach down near the water's edge on one side.

As time passed, the family realized that the public access spot where the trucks used to load up gravel was actually a great location for an outdoor amphitheater. Within three years, they built a permanent stage that they could use to bring in musical acts during the summer. It took off. Soon during the summer, Century Quarry was packed with swimmers every day and with concertgoers every weekend night. That's where I went now.

As I pulled in, the electric sign out front announced the month's concert schedule, showing that Big Luke had played a couple of weekends before. A crowd of people was waiting by the gate. I checked the time and saw that it was a little after ten, which was normally when the Quarry opened. I parked my Jeep and walked over, making my way through a crowd filled with swimsuits and coolers and all manner of folding chairs and inflatable fun. Since I was wearing a tie, people assumed I wasn't cutting in line and let me pass. A college kid who—judging from the tan, the bleached hair, and the red tank top—was a late-season lifeguard, stood at the closed gate. As I neared the front of the line, I heard him announce, "It'll be just a little longer. We'll probably open about a half-hour late."

There was a collective moan. The lifeguard looked at me. Kirby wasn't expecting me, but I thought I'd give it a whirl.

"Nate Shepherd here to see Kirby Granger."

The kid looked at me with caution and a distinct lack of curiosity. "Kirby said no reporters allowed."

"Good. I'm not one."

Which was true.

"I'm not supposed to let anyone in."

"I'm a friend of Kirby's."

Which was also true.

That was as much of a security check as the lifeguard was interested in performing. He nodded his head, unlocked the gate, and waved me in. There was a brief surge from the back of the crowd, which was quickly cut short by the clang of metal and a click.

"Thanks," I said.

"They're on the north side," the lifeguard said. I didn't know who "they" were but decided it included Kirby and headed that way.

On the other side of the gate was a large, central courtyard. I walked to the right, past the concession stands that were just opening for the day and two buildings that were combination locker rooms/bathrooms. I followed the path around the upper edge, looking down at the water below. After a couple hundred yards, I came to a hard metal stairway that led down about sixty feet to "the Beach," a huge area of sand about the size of a football field that gave swimmers access to the water. I skipped this stairway and kept walking around the top of the quarry to the far end.

Eventually, I came all the way around to the other side of the water, directly opposite the courtyard entrance, to another stairway. Like the one that led to the Beach, these stairs went all the way from the top of the Quarry down to the water. Here, though, rather than sand at the bottom, there was a square cement pad with large rocks on either side. As I arrived, I saw the reason that the front gates were still closed. Four sheriff's deputies were working at different spots on the stairs. A bald man wearing a bright yellow shirt was watching them. Kirby Granger.

Kirby was a few years older than me and had worked at the Quarry all of his adult life. He was a little shorter than me and a little wider and his broad shoulders now offset a prominent belly. He was tan, as always, and his bald head, which had been that way for fifteen years, made it impossible to tell whether he was thirty or fifty. He looked worried as he stood, hands on hips, watching the deputies.

"Hey, Kirby," I said.

He jumped, then smiled when he saw it was me. A moment later, the smile vanished as he said, "Jesus, is Abby suing us already?"

I stared at him for a moment before I realized what he meant. "No, no, Kirby. I'm not here to sue the Quarry."

Kirby looked unconvinced. "You're not?"

"I'm not."

"Well, that's something, I guess." He went back to watching the deputies. "I have enough problems today."

I watched the gears click on Kirby's face. 3-2-1...

"So why are you here then?"

"Investigating."

"For who?"

"For the man accused of doing it."

"Attacking her?"

"Yes."

Kirby's face twisted. "Scumbag."

"I don't think he did it."

"Don't you have to say that?"

"The family doesn't either."

"You haven't talked to Hamish then."

"You have?"

"He's right pissed." Kirby shook his head. "His own brother—"

Kirby's attention was pulled back to the deputies. He seemed distracted.

I tried to pull him back. "Is this where she fell?"

"Where she was pushed? Yes." He pointed to where the second deputy was working on the stairway. "They said she tumbled about halfway down before she went off the stairway into the scrub over there. I think that saved her life."

"How so?"

"If she'd stayed on the stairs, she would've kept hitting her head on the metal and then the cement pad."

"Hmmm," I said. A non-committal grunt seemed like the best way to keep him going.

Kirby shook his head. "I passed right by here to go to the back parking lot when I closed up. I didn't see a thing."

We both looked down the stairs. The Quarry's top ridge was lower here, so we were only about forty feet above the water. The quarry wall was different too; rather than a straight cliff, it was more of a gradual slope with a sandy surface that allowed vegetation and even small saplings to grow. I could see a line of broken stalks on the right that started about halfway down the stairs. I followed the flattened weeds down to a collection of dark, mossy rocks that lined the water's edge. One of the deputies was there now, crouching down carefully.

I pointed. "Is that where she ended up?"

Kirby nodded.

I looked at the water. I'd swum here since I was a kid. "It's sixty feet deep at this end, isn't it?"

Kirby nodded again. "They never would have found her if she'd gone in."

There was nothing to say to that.

One of the deputies climbed the stairs, not touching the railing that ran down the center of it. He glanced at me, then said, "We're about done here, Mr. Granger. You can let your swimmers in now."

"Great," said Kirby. "Do you remember how to get out? The back entrance is that way."

"We know. Thank you. Do you have the rest of the video for Deputy Phillips?"

"Oh, right, right. No, I still have to download that, Officer. How should I send it to you?"

"I can arrange for a pick-up."

"Sure. Tomorrow?"

"End of day today would be better, Mr. Granger."

It looked like the deputy had just put the second to last straw on Kirby's back, but the manager smiled and said, "Okay. I'll call."

The deputy nodded. "Thank you, sir."

Kirby started hustling back toward the front. I went with him.

"There's video?" I said.

Kirby nodded. "We've put in a camera system since you worked here."

"Did it have a view of the old stairs?"

Kirby shook his head. "No. It's not a high traffic area." He winced. "It didn't seem important."

"Can't predict everything. Can I get a copy too?"

Kirby stopped. "It's good to see you, Nate. But Abby's my friend."

"I understand. But I get anything the Sheriff does. This just lets me get it sooner."

A steel Kirby didn't often show entered his shoulders. "Then you can get it from him."

That was as far as this was going to go. "Okay." I pointed at the front gate. "Been busy?"

"Always," Kirby said, nodding, but he was barely hearing me now as we re-entered the central courtyard area. He focused on the crowd and went straight over. He raised his hands and said, "Thank you for your patience. We had an inspection this morning. We'll let you in in just a moment."

"You better not be charging us full price for a day pass, Kirby," said a woman.

Kirby shook his head. "You are just shameless, Macy. It's barely even ten-thirty and you know we don't charge half price until after three."

"Well, when are you going to open up?"

"As soon as the lifeguards are in position. Go ahead, Tyler," Kirby said to the lifeguard. "You and the others can set up now."

Tyler sauntered off.

The woman, Macy, did not look remotely satisfied due in part to the fact that she was juggling a cooler, a chair in a bag, and a pink plastic inflatable inner tube with princesses on it, all while maintaining a grip on an eight-year-old girl who did not seem at all interested in being contained.

Macy's gaze fell on me. Her eyes lit up and she said, "Are you done, Inspector?"

I'd left my jacket in the car, but I was probably the only person in a half-mile radius wearing a tie, so she wasn't totally off base. I smiled at Kirby and said, "Well, Mr. Granger, my inspection is done so I see no reason to keep these good people waiting any longer."

Kirby looked like he wanted to strangle me, but then a whistle blew three short blasts.

"There we go," he said. "The lifeguards are all set. Welcome to Century Quarry."

Kirby opened the gates and we both stood aside as the crowd rolled in. I waited until the main rush was through, felt a twinge of jealousy for a day spent entirely on that beach and in that water, then climbed into my hot car to drive to the office.

5

If you haven't been there before, my office is in Carrefour, on the Ohio side of the line. It's not one of those romantic old buildings or modern high-rises, it's just part of a suburban office complex made mostly of glass and stainless steel that houses small groups of lawyers and doctors and accountants. I had a small suite on the third floor that had one office for me, one for my associate, Daniel Reddy, and a third one where we kept our optimism. Besides the conference room, that was it. I didn't have a secretary because there was less need for one now in these days of automated voice answering and electronic filing, and, more importantly, because when we had started out a year and a half ago, I really couldn't afford it. I probably could now, but I was still reluctant since we were getting by without one.

"We really need a secretary," Danny said as I entered the office.

"Yeah?"

"Yeah. I'm spending way too much time answering the phone and filing."

I nodded. "I'll take it up with the management committee."

"I'm serious," said Danny.

"Me too."

He sighed. "I have the police report. I put a request in for the file materials with the prosecutor's office."

"I haven't been up to Ash County on a criminal case since we started here. Who is it?"

"A guy named T. Marvin Stritch."

"Sounds delightful."

"He might be a perfectly wonderful guy, Nate."

"Your optimism is infectious. Keep after them for the disclosures. I have Olivia doing background on everybody."

"Good."

I took the police report and started toward my office, then stopped. "Did you tell Jenny we have a new case?"

Danny nodded. "I told her we'd be busy."

"How's she doing?"

"She said we should have stayed in Petoskey longer."

"A good move for anyone."

"And she wondered if we were always going to be defending murderers."

"No. We're defending attempted murderers too."

Danny's smile was strained.

I'd deflected him, but this really wasn't what we'd planned to do when we broke off from our old firm. "You know how litigation is. The types of cases can ebb and flow and we can't always be choosy. You okay?"

Danny nodded. "Oh, don't worry, Nate, I'm fine. She was just asking and I thought it was a valid question."

"It is. We'll try to use these cases as a jumping off point to broaden our horizons."

"Sounds good."

In fairness to Danny, investigating a crime scene and having an existential conversation about the nature of work wasn't how I'd seen my morning going either, but there you go.

I sat down and reviewed the police report from the responding officers:

Call received at 7:06 a.m. from Century Quarry indicating an injured woman found. First responders arrive followed by deputies and additional rescue personnel. Victim appears to have fallen down stairs to rocks at water's edge. Injured woman identified as Abby Ackerman from ID and wallet. No purse or cell phone found. Scene secured while rescue personnel extricate victim. Victim alive for transport but unconscious. Severe hip and head injury. Bleeding significant. Blunt force trauma suspected but no weapon found. Rescue efforts supported.

The report went on.

Quarry personnel, including manager interviewed. Investigating officer determined that Quarry has security video. Portion of video of previous evening briefly reviewed to determine that recording for time frame at issue exists. Copies of video requested and Sheriff Dushane notified of need for potential criminal investigation.

The original responding officers had obtained brief statements from Kirby and from the lifeguards who had found Abby Ackerman. They basically said just that—that they'd come in to work and found her that morning. Kirby had seen her before the concert when she picked up her tickets, but no workers had any recollection of seeing her after the concert the night before.

An addendum had been added a week later:

Suspect in custody. Responding officer's involvement concluded. Investigation taken over by Sheriff and prosecutor's office.

There was nothing in the report that connected the dots to Archie.

My office line rang and showed a number I didn't recognize.

"This is Nate Shepherd," I answered.

"Mr. Shepherd, this is Abby Ackerman."

I straightened. "Ms. Ackerman, I don't think we should speak right now. I represent Archie Mack and his interests are different than yours."

"Well, how am I supposed to tell you that he didn't do it if we don't speak?"

"Ms. Ackerman, my client is accused of attacking you and—"

"I know, Bonnie told me all about it. That's how I got your number. There is no way that Archie did—"

"Ms. Ackerman, let me stop you for just a second. Do you want to talk to me about Archie?"

"I called you, didn't I?"

"So here's what you need to do. I'm going to give you the name of a lawyer who specializes in victim's rights—"

"I am not a victim."

"I understand. But she can protect your interests in any conversations with me."

"My interest is in telling you that I don't think for a minute that Archie would hurt me, no matter what Hamish says."

A red flag flew up. "Ms. Ackerman, you really need to contact this lawyer. You can tell her what you want to tell me and then we can all get together."

"We need two lawyers to have a conversation?"

"You need someone to protect your interests. That's not me. Once you have somebody, you can tell me whatever you want.

I heard a sigh. "Fine," she said.

"Great. Do you have a pen?"

"Is that a joke?"

I felt a surge of embarrassment at the automatic question. "I'm sorry. Is your vision still affected?"

"My vision? No, I'm leaning on crutches and balancing a phone between my cheek and a shoulder. Isn't that enough for you?"

"I'm sorry, Abby. That was thoughtless of me."

"You didn't push me down the stairs, Shepherd. And neither did Archie. Hang on."

A moment later, another voice came on. "Nate? This is Bonnie Price."

I blinked. "Archie's fian—I mean, you're there?"

"I'm helping her get settled back at her house."

"Isn't that awkward?"

"Not for us. Do you have a name?"

I gave her the information for Ronnie Hawkins, a lawyer who'd been recommended to me before that did this type of work in northern Ash County. There was a pause from Bonnie as she wrote it down, then said, "We'll call him right away."

"Her."

"Really? Well, that would have been embarrassing. Thank you. Do you want me to put Abby back on?"

"Please don't. Just have her call Ronnie and then she can get in touch with me so that we can meet."

"Is all this really necessary?"

"Yes, it is."

"When is Archie getting out?"

"Bonnie, I can't discuss this with you while you're sitting right next to the victim of Archie's alleged attack."

"But—"

"Bonnie. Have Abby call Ronnie. Then Ronnie can call me."

Bonnie seemed to understand and we hung up.

It was no more than half an hour before the phone rang again. I answered.

"Mr. Shepherd, this is Ronnie Hawkins."

I chuckled. "That was fast."

Ronnie chuckled back. "Ms. Ackerman is persuasive and she insists on speaking with you right away. I can't do it today, but do you have time tomorrow?"

"I do."

"Great. I'll meet with her first and then the three of us can have a chat."

"Excellent."

"My office okay? I'm in Dellville, but that's also a little closer for Abby."

"That's just fine."

"I appreciate you making sure she has representation. There can be a lot of conflicting interests in these family situations."

"No problem. Seems standard enough."

"You'd be surprised. I'll see you tomorrow afternoon. Two o'clock?"

"Sounds good. Thanks, Ronnie."

I hung up and thought. There was nothing in the police report linking the attack to Archie and the victim had just called me to say Archie didn't do it. I was obviously missing key evidence, maybe a lot of it.

I decided to tack a second meeting onto the one with Abby Ackerman tomorrow. I made a call and arranged it.

6

The next day I drove to Ronnie Hawkins' office up in Dellville. It was in a small, squat Tudor-like building of brick, stucco, and stained wood that screamed, "1970!" Inside, a small sign informed me that Ronnie shared space with an insurance agency and a surveyor. I walked down the hall, found the door to Suite C, and went in.

I entered a small common area and as I shut the door behind me, Ronnie came out of one of two rooms. She smiled and extended her hand.

"Mr. Shepherd, please come in. Good to meet you."

Ronnie looked young for a lawyer. Her formal handshake and the "Mr. Shepherd" made me certain of it.

"Nate, please," I said.

Ronnie smiled. "I meant what I said earlier, Nate. I appreciate you calling me in on this. Turns out the situation's a little complicated."

"It seemed like there were more connections than I was going to be comfortable with."

"There are."

"Then I'm glad you're involved."

"Me too." She waved me in. "Come meet Abby."

I entered the small conference room to find Abby Ackerman seated at one end of the table, a set of crutches leaning against the wall behind her. She wore jeans and a button-down shirt and she was looking down so that her reddish-brown hair hung forward.

"Good afternoon Abby," I said.

Abby's head ticked up, revealing a horrible bruise on the left side of her face that surrounded an eye that was swollen and blood-filled. "Pardon me if I don't get up, Shepherd." She flipped a hand at her crutches. "My giddy-up is busted."

"Of course. How are you doing?"

She put out her hand and I shook it. "Either you really mean that or Archie's got himself a great lawyer."

"I really mean that."

"Hmphf. Well, I'm alive, so I can't complain."

"Really?"

She shrugged. "I have a busted hip that's ended my figure-skating career, but I'm making up for it with a dent in my head."

Now that she said it, I saw what she meant: the bone that framed her left eye was dented in. I focused on the crutches instead. "Should you be up and around?"

"You know, Hawkins here asked me the same thing and I'll give you the same answer—how's a body supposed to get better in bed?"

"The doctor might know what he's talking about," said Ronnie.

"Pfft," she said.

I realized I hadn't seen anyone else in the office. "How did you get here?"

"Bonnie drove me. Hamish would never have let me come."

"That's part of the dynamic I was talking about, Nate," said

Ronnie. "I wanted to talk to Abby by herself, without Bonnie or Hamish or anyone else, and hear what she had to say."

"Which we should get to," said Abby. She gestured at her face. "Archie didn't do this."

"Who did then?"

She shook her head. "I don't know. But it wasn't Archie."

"Did you see the person who did it?"

She shook her head again. "I never saw the chicken-shit full-on."

"What do you mean?"

"I mean it was dark when he bashed my face in."

"Why don't you just start at the beginning, Abby," said Ronnie.

"You're bossing me again, Hawkins." Abby sighed in irritation. "But okay."

Abby turned toward me and when she did, the dent in her eye socket was pronounced. I focused on her other eye as she said, "So I went to the concert with Bonnie and Heather and Kayla because Heather is a super fan and she was sure that Big Luke was never going to play Carrefour again, which is probably true. Kirby hooked me up with tickets for all four of us."

"How do you know Kirby?" I asked.

"I went to the Quarry a lot when I was in high school and worked there on and off for a couple of summers after. Anyway, I knew it would be packed, so I parked in the employee lot and then came through the back gate. I picked up the tickets from Kirby, met the girls in the courtyard, and went to the concert." She shook her head. "That boy can tear it up."

"Did you see Archie at the concert?"

Abby shook her head. "No."

"Not that you remember," said Ronnie.

"Right, that I remember. I do remember seeing Hamish there, though."

That was new. "You didn't go to the concert with him?"

"No, it was a girls' night and I didn't think he was interested. He said afterwards that it was a last-minute thing. So the girls and I were in line for a drink after the concert and I saw Hamish from across the courtyard and waved. He was leaving out the back too and I wanted to say 'hi' real quick so the girls and I said we'd meet at HopHeads and they went out the front to their cars and I went out the back to see Hamish."

"Did you catch up to him?"

"I did."

"And?"

"We talked."

"I see."

"A little more than that, actually."

"Oh?"

"Hawkins here might not want me to say it, but we fought like cats with our tails tied together."

"Okay. Fought or argued?"

"Well, isn't that a lawyerly question. We yelled at each other, Shepherd. Hamish never laid a hand on me."

"So then what?"

"So then I was still worked up." She smiled. "You may have noticed that I tend to get a little animated."

"You don't say."

"It's true. So I took a seat on the old stairs for a bit to calm myself and I sat there for a few minutes and then, when I stood up, somebody grabbed me and said, 'Hey!'"

"What did you do?"

"I cussed and jerked back. And that's when I took my tumble."

"Did you see anything?"

She shook her head. "Not a bit. So next thing I know, I'm lying on the rocks and I'm dizzy and I can't really see and when

I try to move, it's like someone jammed a cattle prod into my hip."

I nodded. "And then?"

"So then, I'm pissed and I call for help and I hear footsteps on the stairs and I think whoever the jack-wagon is that grabbed me is coming to help."

"Then what?"

"So I hear him and I see someone on the cement pad, but its dark and my vision is crap and all I can see is his outline against the sky. And he comes toward me and I tell him he took his sweet time, and then I see this guy rise up and, bam!"

"Bam what?"

"I wake up in the hospital."

"What happened?"

"I'm not sure, but they tell me that the jack-hole smashed me in the head with a rock."

"That's what the doctors think," said Ronnie.

I pointed at my eye. "That's what this is from?"

"Charming, ain't it?" said Abby.

I thought. "And Hamish isn't the suspect?"

"I'm sure there's a reason," said Ronnie.

"Sure there is," said Abby. "Neither of them, Archie or Hamish, would ever hurt me."

"Do you remember anything else?" I said.

Abby paused, then said, "It sounds stupid."

Ronnie put a hand on her arm as I said, "Nothing in this sounds stupid."

"I know that, Hawkins. I mean the guy was stupid, it made no sense."

"What's that?"

"What he said right before he brained me."

"Which was?"

"He said, 'More gas than the Albion Skip-N-Go.'"

"What?"

She shook her head. "I know, right?"

"'More gas than the Albion Skip-N-Go?'"

"Like I said, it doesn't make any sense. And who wants to go to Albion anyway?"

"Good point." I thought. "Was it Archie's voice?"

"I don't think so."

"Abby," said Ronnie.

Abby sighed. "I can't say who it was or wasn't. But it couldn't have been Archie."

"So you don't think Archie did it, but you can't describe the person who did?"

"Listen, Shepherd, I don't know if you've been able to talk to Archie yet—"

"I have."

"But he would never do this. Never. He's devoted to his family and he's devoted to Bonnie and he would always look out for me. There's no way he would hurt me."

"Abby feels pretty strongly about this," said Ronnie. "She'll comply with any subpoena, but she's not going to cooperate with the prosecutor."

I nodded. "That's my next stop." Abby shifted and winced and then pushed the look off her face. I realized the pain she must be in and stood. "I've kept you long enough, Abby. Thank you for seeing me."

"You have to make him drop this, Shepherd. Archie shouldn't be in jail. And it's damn near killing Bonnie."

"It's good to know how you feel about it, Abby. Thanks again for telling me."

Abby stuck out her hand and I shook it. Her grip was surprisingly strong as she said, "I mean it."

"I can see that. I hope your recovery goes well."

"You and me both."

I stood and Ronnie walked me out. Once we'd left her office, Ronnie said, "I'm not getting any sense that she's being pressured by anyone in the family to say this. The opposite in fact."

"What do you mean?"

"I mean Hamish is convinced his brother did it."

"Why?"

"I'm not sure, he won't tell Abby. I'm sure Stritch knows though."

I nodded. "I'm going to go see him now. I'll let you know what he says."

"Good."

I looked back at the room. "Abby seems to be on her way back."

Ronnie looked at me then, hard. "Recovery is a long path, Nate."

"Sorry, I didn't mean it wasn't."

"Just because someone presents as fine doesn't mean they are."

I nodded. "Like I said, Ronnie, I'm glad you're involved."

She smiled then. "Thanks."

We said goodbye and I left Ronnie Hawkins' office to make the short walk across the street to the Ash County Courthouse and the office of prosecutor T. Marvin Stritch.

7

T. Marvin Stritch was a lot like the Ash County courthouse itself —a no-nonsense dispenser of rigid steel justice clothed in shades of brown. He was a career prosecutor who had spent two-and-a-half decades in the job, first under the current judge and now as the chief. He was one of those lawyers who got better and better at the practice of law as he aged because his focus became narrower and narrower until it was really impossible for him to have a conversation about anything without bringing it back around to the law. He had brown hair and wore dark brown glasses that sat above drawn cheekbones that made it look as if the law was slowly sucking the life out of everything about him except his animated eyes.

He was kind enough to see me the same day that I called and I saw that his office was a lot like him too—brown paneled walls, a square metal desk with a laminated wood finish, with his lone luxury being a plush, brown leather rolling chair.

"Come in," he said politely enough and gestured to a wooden-framed, upholstered chair. "We haven't met, have we?"

"We haven't."

"Are you new to the practice here in town?"

"No, my office is down in Carrefour."

The light in his eyes tempered a bit. "Ah. An Ohio guy then?"

"No, I actually live in Ash County on the Michigan side. Voted for you in the last election."

The light came back. "Well, thank you. Nate Shepherd, Nate Shepherd." He tapped his desk a couple of times before he pointed. "That's right, you're the attorney who handled the billionaire murder a few months ago, right?"

"Alleged murder," I said. "Turns out it was just an unfortunate heart condition."

"Of course. I read about that. Interesting case." He shook his head. "I don't think I ever would've brought that prosecution."

I nodded. "It was a little attenuated."

"Doesn't make any sense to bring a prosecution if you're not going to win it."

"True enough."

Stritch's eyes narrowed. "So, are you taking a case up here?"

"It's looking that way. If the case keeps going that is."

"Oh? Have charges been filed?"

"Yes."

"Here?"

"Yes."

"Then it will keep going. What I said before, you know?"

"I see."

"Which case?"

"The Archie Mack case."

Now Stritch's eyes really lit up. "The assault at Century Quarry."

I nodded. "That's the one."

"Well, I'm afraid that one's not going away, Nate."

"Are you sure? I just came from a meeting with the victim, Abby Ackerman."

"Oh?" His eyes hooded and I had the distinct impression of an owl waiting to swoop.

"And her attorney, Ronnie Hawkins."

That surprised him. "She's represented?"

"Seemed prudent given the family dynamic in this. Anyway, Abby's convinced it wasn't my client."

"I see. Can she say who it was?"

"Only that it wasn't Archie."

I saw the slightest hint of relief.

"That's consistent with her statement to the Sheriff then. It doesn't change my thinking."

"Really?"

"Really." Stritch shook his head. "This is as bad a case as I've seen, Nate, without an actual killing. Pushing her down the stairs then trying to finish her off with a rock? You know that, right? That he tried to finish her off with a rock?"

"I heard someone did."

Stritch frowned at the connotation.

"Do you have the rock?"

The eyes hooded again. "Not at this time, no. We have plenty of other evidence though."

I kept a straight face. "What evidence is that?"

"Evidence that puts him at the scene at the time of the attack."

"Evidence of attempted murder?"

T. Marvin Stritch smiled. "I don't have to tell you, Nate, not yet, but I will because you'll find that I'm very upfront about things. We have security video and blood. I'll give you those right away."

He stood, walked across the room to a beige file drawer, opened it, went straight to the fourth file from the right, opened that, took out a brown envelope, and emptied its contents into his hand. He replaced the envelope, put back the file, shut the drawer, and came over and handed me a thumb drive. "That's the video. I'll email you the blood work. It's only typed right now; the DNA is still pending."

I took the drive. "Thanks. Any eyewitnesses to the attack?"

"No. Not yet. Still, we think we have this locked up pretty tight."

"What about Hamish Mack?"

"What about him?"

"Wasn't he with the victim shortly before the assault?"

He nodded. "So I understand."

"So why isn't he a suspect?"

"What you're holding in your hand. And the victim's testimony that Hamish left the scene, among other things."

"Those being?"

"What?"

"The other things."

"We're still running those down."

We'd apparently ended the upfront portion of the discussion so I stood.

"Well, thank you Marvin—"

"—T. Marvin."

Of course.

"Sorry, T. Marvin. I appreciate you taking the time to see me."

He smiled a perfectly functional smile. "We're a small legal community up here, Nate. We may be adversarial, but we always try to be reasonable with each other."

"It certainly seems that way. Thanks."

I was walking out when I noticed three plain wooden shelves on the back wall. The first two were filled with small model antique cars. "Car buff?"

"I am. The old ones."

"That's quite a collection."

"The internet is a wonderful thing."

"I bet."

I was leaving when he said, "I buy one every time I win a case."

"That's quite a fleet."

"I haven't lost since I took over as chief prosecutor."

"Impressive. Congratulations. Thanks again for seeing me."

"I look forward to seeing you soon," said T. Marvin Stritch and went back to work.

I headed back down to Carrefour and my office. The hope I'd held for a dismissal after talking to Abby had dissipated now that I'd talked to T. Marvin Stritch. He seemed convinced that the man he was prosecuting was the guy.

Given my encounter with T. Marvin, I suspected that was a common occurrence.

8

When I got home, I grabbed a plate of leftover chicken and vegetables out of the fridge and set up at the counter with my dinner and my tablet. I put the thumb drive in, downloaded the program I needed to run it, and took a look at what T. Marvin Stritch had given me.

A simultaneous feed of four cameras popped up on the screen. I fiddled around with it and soon realized that I could go to any individual picture/video and make it fill the screen or I could watch any combination of them rolling in sync. I decided to run all four at once at sixteen times speed to get a sense of what I was dealing with.

There was one camera positioned in the front parking lot, one on the entrance/courtyard area, one on the concession stands and bathrooms, and one focused on the surface of the water of the Quarry itself.

I started the video at eight o'clock on the morning of the concert. There was an early rush of people through the gate to swim in the morning and, after that, it was just a steady churn of people, in and out, like ants in a hill.

The concert had started at eight that evening, so I slowed

things down to eight times speed at around six o'clock. By then, there was a steady migration of swimmers going out of the Quarry and concertgoers coming in. The concertgoers milled about the courtyard, ordered drinks and food, and generally hung out before going into the open amphitheater.

I didn't stop to see if I could pick out Abby or Archie before the concert and instead went straight to the end. I slowed it down to two times speed and watched the flash of fireworks as people started to file out. Because I knew where she had to end up, I didn't watch the crowd in the middle of the courtyard camera. Instead, I focused on the concession/bathroom camera, which was the last camera on the way to the walkway around back. After almost an hour of video time, I saw a woman in a white shirt, jean shorts, and cowboy boots that screamed summer country music concert. She was jogging and raising her hand as she left the frame. It seemed to me like she was trying to get someone's attention.

I rewound and paused. It was Abby.

Now that I knew where she was, I rewound and followed her backwards and then let it play. I watched her come into the view of the courtyard/patio camera as she filed out of the amphitheater with her friends and the crowd. I saw her and Bonnie, along with two women I assumed were Kayla and Heather, divert out of the stream of people and talk. There was some gesturing and laughing and, at one point, singing, and then the four of them walked out of view of the courtyard camera. A moment later, they entered the view of the concession stand camera and the four of them got in line. They crept forward a place or two at a time when Abby gestured, slid out of line, and went into the bathroom. A few minutes later, she emerged. She started back toward the girls when I saw her look in the other direction, toward the back of the Quarry. She shouted, waved, then looked back at her friends and pointed toward the back. Then she waved again and jogged out of the frame.

Knowing the Quarry layout like I did, I knew she was jogging toward the path that led around the Quarry's edge.

First to the Beach, then to the abandoned stairs.

I knew there were no more cameras in that direction, so I focused on upper right corner of the concession camera view, the part that led to the back path. It was hard because there were people milling around it and people crossing over and back in a jumble. The crowd gradually thinned though and people started to leave.

I realized I hadn't been watching Bonnie and her friends, so I rewound a little, saw them wait in line, get bottles of water, then stand around for a little while longer before leaving out the front entrance.

None of them showed the slightest sign of being worried about Abby.

There were fewer people now, and it was easier to keep track of the comings and goings. I ate dry, cold chicken and watched.

Then I saw him enter the concession camera view. From the back path. From the direction Abby had gone.

He was the only one I had seen coming from that direction in a while. He was wearing a black baseball cap with some sort of yellow writing on it, along with jeans and a short sleeve checked shirt, none of which was surprising at a Big Luke concert. That's not what caught my attention.

It was his left hand. There was a bandage on it. And blood.

I froze the picture and expanded it on the tablet, but that just made it blurry. The technology of refining and making it clear on this program was beyond me right then so instead, I rewound the video. I saw the man walk backward out of the frame then let it run forward again. He walked into the picture and across the concession view but he was still a little far away, at the top edge of the screen, as he left the concession view.

A moment later he walked into the frame of the courtyard camera, closer, closer. I stopped it and this time he was close enough to make things out.

I had a clear view of the bandage. It was dark and stained. The bill of his baseball cap covered his face, but I could make out the yellow logo on it now.

It said, "Mack Farms."

I couldn't see his face, but I knew I was looking at Archie. I might not have been able to magnify the earlier views right here in my house, but I knew the Sheriff could at the station. I looked at the time code, 11:39 p.m. My guess was that matched the time of the attack too.

Archie walked quickly through the entrance area and out of view until the parking lot camera picked him up. He walked to the furthest section of the lot then out of view since the camera didn't pick up the whole lot. A minute later, I saw a series of trucks leave the lot. My guess was that one of them matched Archie's.

I kept watching the concession camera then, even though I knew Abby wasn't coming back. At 11:59 p.m., the video stopped. I was going to pull the thumb drive out but then I realized there was another folder. We had a portion of the next day too, it looked like until noon.

I clicked it open and started the video rolling at the beginning, at midnight. By 12:30 a.m., the place was pretty well cleared out except for a smattering of cars in the front lot that were the usual side effect of people having too much to drink. The lights in the Quarry stayed on, I assumed for security. Eventually, around 1:00 a.m., I saw Kirby make his rounds, locking the front gate and the concessions and the bathrooms, and throw away a couple of cans. Then he took a last look around and walked through the concession stand view toward the back path to go out the back gate.

I kept watching. I couldn't help it. Up until now, I'd ignored the fourth camera, the one pointed at the water. Other than the occasional reflected light and the sliver of a quarter moon, that screen was pretty dim. I thought I could see the ripples on the black water, but I couldn't be sure on my tablet. I fast forwarded then but I kept watching. I increased the speed.

We were on daylight savings time, so sunrise was later. Still, at 5:30 a.m., the water of the Quarry began to gray into light.

By 6:00 a.m., from the water camera, I could see her. Her brownish hair blended into the rock, but I could see one pale leg and one arm draped between the stones, fingers in the water. I clicked to real time. She didn't move. Not once.

I saw the lifeguards arrive in the front at 6:30 a.m., unlocking the gate and dithering around in the concession stands. I willed them to go to the water. They didn't. The sun was almost up and I could see her clearly now. But of course, I knew where to look. She still didn't move.

Finally, at 6:52 a.m., a young man who had been arranging chairs on the courtyard side looked up, startled. He looked around, behind him, then finally, across the water. A lifeguard was on the cement pad next to Abby, waving. I could see the guy on the pad point to her before the guy in the courtyard sprinted over to the concession stand. A moment later, two lifeguards were running out of the frame toward the back path and the abandoned stairs. I looked back at the concrete pad on the far side of the water. I saw the two figures: one scrambling over the rocks, the other, still.

T. Marvin was right. They had video. They were going to have blood.

And I had a big problem.

9

I met Olivia early the next day at the Brickhouse—and by early, I mean I was there at seven in the morning and she had just finished leading what I assumed had been an hour-long class. She waved me back and smiled when I handed her a coffee.

"Bless you," she said.

"How'd the class go?" I said.

"Better than the first one. This group was on it."

"The first one? As in before this one?!"

She took a sip and nodded. "People have to work. It's not so bad once you commit to getting up. Especially after breakfast."

"I find that hard to believe."

"You should join me. The Cast Iron Kitchen."

"Over on Hill?"

"That's the place. You can get your own breakfast skillet."

"What time do you go?"

"Four-thirty."

"See, you're just showing off now."

She didn't say she wasn't but she didn't deny she was either. Instead, as we went into her office, she said, "I know your bond hearing is today for Archie. I finished some preliminary research and wanted you to have the info before you went."

"Really? These hearings are usually pretty routine."

She nodded. "I think the Judge might consider some of it with the bond."

"Okay. Shoot."

She clicked a few times and a satellite photo popped up on the monitor.

I leaned forward a little. "What am I looking at?"

"The Mack farm. They own a whole section."

"Like a literal section?"

"Yep."

A section is six hundred and forty acres. That's one square mile, a mile on each side. Much of southern Michigan is laid out that way, in sections. The farther out you go into the country, the more likely it is that the only roads were the section roads, and it was pretty rare to have one family own the whole thing.

"That's impressive."

"It is," said Olivia.

Judging from the satellite photo, it appeared they maintained tree lines here and there to fight erosion and to mark off fields, but most of the land had been cleared. A creek or a drainage ditch ran diagonally from one corner to the other across the property.

"Now, here's the part that's relevant today." Olivia clicked her mouse and yellow lines were superimposed across the screen so that the square was divided into three rectangles.

"Are those equal?"

Olivia nodded. "Two hundred thirteen and one-third acres apiece." She pointed from left to right. "Hamish lives here, Mr. and Mrs. Mack here in the middle, and Archie on the other side."

I bent closer and Olivia zoomed in, knowing what I was looking for.

There were three clusters of buildings on the acreage. In the center was Mr. and Mrs. Mack's. I could see the house and a couple of outbuildings, which I assumed were for equipment, and two old silos. The driveway from the section road was not long, probably no more than twenty-five yards or so, and the buildings were clustered neatly together.

In the center of the rectangle on the right and a little farther back, was another cluster of buildings. Again, it looked like a house and a couple of barns.

"Archie's place?"

"Yep. And this is Hamish's."

She pointed to the left rectangle. A white house sat back squarely in the middle of the property which, if you were keeping track, would make it at the end of a half-mile drive. I made out a couple of buildings, one smaller and one larger than those on the other two, a pond, and the light blue rectangle of a pool. From above, it looked more like a McMansion than a farm.

"Interesting," I said. "So do they each own their piece?"

"Just what I wanted to know," said Olivia. "So I pulled the Ash County property records. Electronic records went back to the 1950s. Mr. Mack's parents, Evan and Betsy Mack, owned the entire section back then. Evan and Betsy eventually died and passed the whole section on to Alban and Susanna Mack. They owned it all until ten years ago when they transferred the one-third sections to Archie and Hamish for nominal fees."

"A living inheritance maybe?"

"Maybe. Shortly after that, the boys built their homes."

"Mortgages?"

"Big ones. On all three properties."

"I see. So what did you want me to know today?"

"Two things. The mortgages will be an issue if Archie needs a lot of collateral for a high bond."

"Did you tell Cade?"

"I did."

"So that's handled. What's the other?"

She faced me directly so that I could see my reflection in her glasses. "Nate, if Archie did this, you're asking the Judge to let him go and live in the middle of nowhere next to a house Abby frequents."

"Does she live with Hamish?"

"Bonnie says Abby technically has an apartment in Dellville but spends more nights at Hamish's than not."

I looked at the farm with just three houses in a square mile at the farthest reaches of the county.

"I don't think he did this."

"I don't either. That's why I'm working on it. But the Judge might not see it that way. And the prosecutor certainly won't."

I nodded. "I see your point. Abby's convinced Archie didn't do it. That has to count for something, right? I'm sure we can come up with some restrictions that assure her safety for the judge."

"Maybe. But don't forget the other side of it."

"What's that?"

"What's Hamish going to do if the man he believes tried to kill his fiancée is back home, right next door?"

I stared at the isolated farm.

"What would you have done if your neighbor had tried to hurt Sarah?"

It had been a while since my wife had passed, but it wasn't hard to picture that situation. I swore.

"Exactly." Olivia stared at me a moment with those half-mirrored glasses then turned back to her screen and started closing windows. "I didn't want you to be blindsided today."

"Thanks. Can you send me the links?"

"Already did."

"Thanks, Liv."

"Forewarned, forearmed, and all that."

I checked the time. "I have to get up there."

"See you later."

I was to the door when she said, "Shep?"

"Yeah?"

"We need to find the miserable sack who did this."

Olivia wasn't looking at me as she said it. She was facing her computer screen, bleached white hair swooped down covering part of her face, her sharp jaw set, her arm flexed a little harder than it needed to be to type.

"I agree," I said. "My first duty is to Archie though."

"What better way to fulfill it than to find the actual coward who did it?"

I nodded. "You're a good person, Liv."

"Don't let word get out. I've got a gym to run."

"Don't worry. No one would believe me."

She made a suggestion about how I could pass time on my way to Dellville. I thanked her for the encouragement and left.

10

Judge Eliza Jane Wesley held her own bond hearings. Word was she liked to get a first look at the case and let everyone know how things were going to go. Archie's bond hearing was the first time I'd met her.

It did not go well.

Judge Wesley was a formidable presence behind the bench. She had wide shoulders and wore her long black hair piled up on her head, held in place with two silver-tipped black hair sticks. She had an easy smile and a disarming manner that brought her thirty years of experience to bear in a flash. She had been a prosecutor in Ash County for almost twenty years before her predecessor had retired and she had won a hard-fought race for her seat against a local powerbroker. One didn't do that by being shy and no one had ever accused Judge Wesley of that failing.

I stood at the counsel table along with Archie. T. Marvin Stritch stood alone at the prosecutor's table.

As Judge Wesley leafed through some papers, she said, "I see from your filings that your office is in Carrefour, Ohio, Mr. Shepherd."

"It is, Your Honor."

"What brings you away from your home state?"

"This is my home state, Your Honor. I live in Ash County. My office just happens to be in Ohio."

"So do you just happen to spend most of your time practicing outside your home state?"

"I always have cases going here in Michigan, Your Honor, but it's true that most of my cases are in Ohio."

"Our rules are different here, Mr. Shepherd."

"I understand, Your Honor."

"I expect you to follow them."

"Yes, Your Honor."

"I expect you to refer to things by how they're known here, not by their Ohio counterparts."

"Absolutely, Your Honor."

"We're not terribly fond of Ohio here."

"I see that."

"You have the internet in your office?"

"I do."

"And a smart phone in your pocket?"

"Yes, Your Honor."

"Which is turned off, I trust?"

"I saw the sign, Your Honor."

"Then our local rules are available to you twenty-four hours a day."

"Certainly."

"So there will be no excuse for running afoul of any local procedures. If you do, I will know that it is completely and utterly your fault."

"That would be my assumption too, Your Honor."

"I expect you to abide by them all."

"Without fail, Your Honor."

"Very good." She smiled. "Then welcome to our court. Mr. Stritch, do you have a bond recommendation?"

"No bond, Your Honor."

"I see. Mr. Shepherd?"

"If Mr. Stritch believes Mr. Mack should be free without bond, I have no objection, Your Honor."

Stritch smirked. Judge Wesley set down her paper. "Mr. Shepherd, that's exactly what I was talking about. 'No bond' might mean free without bond in Ohio but in Ash County, *Michigan,* we use that to mean the defendant should not be eligible for bond and should remain incarcerated until trial. Do you want your client to remain incarcerated until trial?"

"I do not, Your Honor."

"What do you request then?"

"That Mr. Mack be released on his own recognizance."

"On an attempted murder charge?"

"Mr. Mack has no prior convictions and his status as a farmer makes him a minimal flight risk."

"Farmers can't get in cars or hop on planes? Interesting theory."

"A farmer's life is tied to his land, Your Honor. His home, his income, his debts. Mr. Mack's family has been on the same section for more than one hundred years and Mr. Mack has a harvest to get in."

The last one seemed to register with Judge Wesley. "Mr. Stritch, your thoughts?"

"That may be true, Your Honor, but the victim here is Mr. Mack's brother's fiancée. She comes to his home frequently, often for the night. Allowing the defendant to reside on property in that same section puts her at risk."

Judge Wesley looked at me.

"Ms. Ackerman doesn't think so, Your Honor. She doesn't think Mr. Mack was the attacker."

"All the more reason to protect her, Your Honor," said Stritch.

"The farm is divided into three distinct properties with the parents' farm between Archie and Hamish Mack, Your Honor," I said. "Perhaps if Mr. Mack were restricted to his own property?" I looked at Archie. "If I understand correctly, Mr. Mack will be spending every waking moment between now and the trial in his fields."

Archie nodded.

"Not allowing him to do so will create a significant financial hardship."

"Trying to murder someone tends to do that," said Stritch.

"Mr. Stritch!" said Judge Wesley.

"My apologies, Your Honor. If I may—"

"You may not," said Judge Wesley. "Bond is set at five hundred thousand dollars. Terms will include restrictions to his home with work privileges which, if I understand you, Mr. Shepherd, will also limit him to his property. Mr. Mack will not be permitted to go to his parents' family home, come within two hundred feet of Abby Ackerman, or otherwise communicate with her. Is one of the Mack parents here?"

I nodded. "Yes, Your Honor."

"One of them will sign on to their acknowledgment of the no contact provision if the defendant is to be released."

I pointed to the back of the courtroom where Mrs. Mack sat next to Cade. "Mrs. Mack is prepared to do so, Judge."

Judge Wesley nodded. "The rest will be typical terms, including our electronic monitoring plan which will be conducted according to our standard *local* procedures. Any questions?"

"No, Your Honor," both Stritch and I said.

"Then we are adjourned." Judge Wesley nodded and the bailiff called the next case.

A sheriff's deputy came over to take Archie back to the jail. Before he did, I said, "Cade will process the paperwork with you and go over the terms. We should have you out by the end of the day."

Archie looked stricken. "I don't have five hundred thousand dollars."

"You need fifty. And collateral for four hundred and fifty thousand dollars."

"I don't know if I have that either."

"Cade will work through it with you."

Archie's face didn't change as he nodded and the deputy led him away. Cade and Mrs. Mack followed them out.

I walked out of the courtroom. T. Marvin Stritch walked with me.

"We have more video," Stritch said.

"From the Quarry?"

"From a gas station right after. It's damning."

"How can that be?"

"Not the slightest bit of remorse. He'd just smashed his future sister-in-law's head in and left her to die and he just goes to a gas station and cleans up afterwards as if nothing had happened."

"That sounds like a more likely explanation."

Stritch blinked. "What does?"

"That nothing had happened."

"I don't see the evidence that way."

"I'm just saying, you keep hearing zebras instead of horses."

Stritch stared at me for a moment then shrugged it off. "Speaking of horse power—"

"Were we?"

"I have my eye on a Rolls Royce Phantom."

"On a prosecutor's salary?" I remembered his office. "Oh, you mean the car models."

"They're replicas."

"I'm sure that's a very important difference. The meter's running on my Jeep. I'll talk to you later. You'll send me the new video?"

Stritch smiled. "When the prosecution's evidence disclosure is due under our local rules, yes."

"I see. Thanks for the heads up."

"Of course."

Stritch turned down the hall toward his office. I went downstairs to go see about Archie's release.

～

It took a few hours, but Cade eventually had Archie processed and out. It turned out he'd been able to come up with the fifty thousand but, when the little equity he had left in the farm, equipment, and harvest wasn't enough collateral for the rest, his mother stepped in and pledged her retirement account. As we stood in the parking lot, Cade and I both warned him one more time that he was to stay put, work, and avoid any family gathering with Abby or he'd end up right back here. I think he got it.

Mrs. Mack straightened, gave Archie a look that I'd wager hadn't changed in thirty-some years, and said, "And you'll stay away from your brother too. Call your dad or me if you need to change out any of the equipment."

Archie pulled down on the brim of his Mack Farms baseball cap and nodded.

As we watched the two of them drive off together, Cade bunched his shoulders together and then jerked to the side, cracking his back, before he said, "Olivia doesn't think he did it."

"Me either."

"Know who did?"

"Not yet."

"What about the Sheriff?"

"They think they have their man."

"You best get cracking then."

"Very helpful. You going to the gym later?"

"Probably not 'til late tonight."

"Do you have to post another bond?"

Cade shook his head. "I have to collect one."

"I take it that's all I want to know about that?"

"Yep," was all Cade said.

"Excellent. Good luck."

"Not necessary."

The two of us went to our cars. As we separated, he said, "That was good advice about avoiding the brother." Before I could respond, he climbed into his truck and shut the door.

I did the same and went back to the office to finish out the day while Cade went...well, I guess it's best all-around that we don't know what Cade went to do.

EARTH

11

A couple of days later, I was sitting at my office conference table with Danny and Olivia.

"I want to attack Archie's case a couple of ways," I said. "I'll run with the physical evidence—blood, DNA, fingerprints."

"You mean the fun stuff?" said Olivia.

"Not at all. I'm already used to the science and Sheriff Dushane will be more likely to tell..." I saw her smile behind her sphinx glasses. I sighed. "One point you."

"Of many," she said. "What about us?"

"I'd like you to dig into motive, Liv. Archie doing it doesn't make any sense. By all accounts, this is a pretty harmonious family."

"It seems that way," said Danny.

"Appearances can be deceiving," said Olivia. "What did you have in mind?"

"Two thoughts. First, dig deeper on the background check on all of the Macks and Abby. See if there are any priors for any of them, any calls, red flags, anything. Nationwide. Then search through the local land records—title work, banking, all that stuff. The land is the biggest asset they have, so it could be the biggest potential motive."

Olivia gave me a thumbs up. "So look for any needle in the haystack."

"Exactly." I looked at Danny. "Two things for you. First, do a business records search. I expect they've incorporated or done something to run their farm. Let's start seeing how the operation fits together."

"Okay. That shouldn't take too long."

"It won't. Then I need you to start breaking down the video. All of it. First, follow Abby through the whole thing and log where she is when and in what camera. We know Archie is in there too. Look for him and do the same. Then the same for Hamish."

Danny gave me a look that I didn't think I'd completely earned. Well, maybe a little.

"Then go over all of it again and look for anyone or anything else that's significant."

"All of it?"

"Yes."

"For anything that's significant?"

"Yes."

"Which is what, exactly?"

"Significant things, I expect."

I believe that Danny's regular church attendance was the only thing that prevented him from swearing at me.

I smiled. "Any questions?"

There was silence for a bit before Olivia said, "Seems dry."

"What do you mean?"

"I mean, someone sent Abby down a flight of stairs, smoked her with a blunt instrument, and left her to die. Land use and corporations seems like a pretty dry place to look for a motive for something like that."

"I'm open to suggestions."

"Domestic abuse orders? Personal protection proceedings?"

"Search away. Check any files you need to."

"Okay."

Olivia and Danny were coordinating their searches between each other when Olivia turned and said, "So what are *you* going to do?"

I smiled at Danny.

"I'm going to track down some more video."

∾

I PULLED into the Ash County Services parking lot and called the county receptionist. She said Sheriff Dushane would be there any moment. I thanked her and waited for about twenty minutes until Sheriff Dushane rolled up in his patrol Jeep. As he parked, I got out of the car and was halfway to him by the time he opened his door. When he saw me, he sighed and rolled his eyes.

"Chrissakes, Nate, I haven't even gotten to my office yet."

"Where are my manners? It's barely noon!"

"We're working splits right now, so I'm actually early."

"Right. Got a minute?"

"For you, yes. To talk about your case, no."

"Not exactly the case. But sort of."

Sheriff Dushane stared at me for a moment before he shrugged. "I'm at least going to have a cup of coffee first." He gave me a wave. "Join me. Then I'll kick you out."

We went into the office and poured hot coffee into cardboard cups. I dropped a couple of dollars into the can in appreciation.

"Come on back, big spender," said Sheriff Dushane, and we went into his office.

The Sheriff's office was an institutional-looking building that had been built in the 1960s or 70s and shared a look with many Michigan courthouses and patrol buildings—there was a lot of brown metal and tan walls and the occasional orange rail highlight. Sheriff Dushane's office was the biggest one, which really wasn't saying too much. There was room for his desk and two chairs and a computer that looked like an afterthought. I plopped into a chair and sipped the coffee as he logged in to his computer. When it flashed on, I said, "Have you considered you have the wrong guy?"

"On the Mack case? No."

"The victim, Abby, doesn't think he did it."

Sheriff Dushane shrugged. "Domestic cases make for difficult situations."

"But she didn't ID him."

"She didn't need to."

"I know Stritch feels that way. He sent me his initial disclosures."

"Good for him."

"I saw you found blood."

"We did."

"On the handrail?"

"Yes."

"DNA back yet?"

"I'm sure Stritch will give it to you when it is."

"I didn't see the warrant to take my client's blood to match it."

"Then you didn't look very hard. It's in there."

"Were the fingerprints in the same spot as the blood?"

"That's in the report."

"Is your department going to enhance the Quarry video?"

"No."

"Really? Why?"

"Because we already have."

"By we, I assume you mean one of your deputies?"

Sheriff Dushane smiled. "Exactly."

"Didn't seem like a clear ID in the video."

Sheriff Dushane shrugged. "How do you think we got the warrant for the blood?"

"Stritch said there's more video."

"From the Quarry? I haven't seen it."

"No. From somewhere else. A gas station, I think."

"You don't say?"

"I didn't. He did."

"Then I guess he'll be getting that to you shortly."

"You'd need a warrant to take it from the station itself, though."

"Hmm."

"I didn't see one filed."

"Well, you did miss the one for the blood."

"You wouldn't need one for the video from one of your eye-in-the-sky units though."

"No, we wouldn't."

"I imagine you might want to post one near an event like a Big Luke concert."

"That's a great idea. I'll have to keep that in mind."

"And it seems to me that a complex at the corner of Century and Stone that has a gas station, a liquor store, and a Taco Bell all in one location would be a likely spot."

"It does sound like the Holy Trinity of late-night trouble."

"So I think I'd like to make a public records request for the footage from your eye-in-the-sky unit at that location from the night of the concert."

"I'm sure the video elves would be happy to take your FOIA request."

"Down the hall?"

"Second window on the left."

I stood. "I'd say thanks, but I don't think you did anything."

Sheriff Dushane lifted his cup. "I provided good company *and* coffee."

"I suppose so." I lifted my own back. "Thanks."

"See you around, Nate. Say 'hi' to your dad."

"I will."

"When you do see it, Nate? The video?"

"Yeah?"

"It's your guy. And he acts guilty."

"Huh. Not a crime to gas up a car, Sheriff."

"No. But I'd be interested in why he was hiding a bloody bandage."

"I guess we'll see then."

"I guess we will."

"You're not sitting on anything else?"

"That's not enough?"

"That wasn't my question."

"That's my answer though."

I'd really gotten as much from him as I could expect. "Thanks for seeing me, Sheriff. Keep an eye out for the real attacker."

"We think we have him."

"I know. Still."

"Bye, Nate."

I left.

12

I was driving back to my office when my phone buzzed. Olivia. I hit the console and put her on speaker.

"Miss me?"

"Never," she replied. "Are you still at the Sheriff's?"

"Just left. Why?

"It would've made things easier is all."

"Did you find something already?"

"I'm not sure. I started with a criminal background check, police reports, that sort of thing."

"Uh-oh."

"No, not an 'uh-oh.' More of a 'hmm.'"

"This conversation has devolved."

"So let me finish. I didn't find any criminal convictions on anyone in the family, no indications of domestic abuse of any kind going in any direction."

"No indicators that Archie had a history of violence?"

"Right."

"So why talk to the Sheriff?"

"About four years ago, they filed a police report about vandalism on the farm."

"They? Meaning the whole family?"

"Yes."

"What happened?"

"That's what's hard for me to tell. If I'm reading this right, they claim that someone snuck onto their farm while they were out of town and applied fertilizer to their crops without their permission."

I thought I misheard her. "They *applied* fertilizer?"

"Yes."

"Doesn't that help?"

"That's what I thought, but I'm not a farmer. I thought if you were still there you could ask Dushane."

"Huh. Anything ever come of it?"

"Not that I can see."

"I'll ask Archie about it. Anything else?"

"Besides eliminating a criminal history for everyone involved and finding that the Macks were the apparent victim of an ambiguous crime? No, I haven't done anything else this morning."

"Well, I have this friend of mine who says that you have to push yourself, so let's get at it."

"'Let's?' As in 'let *us*'?"

"I'm traversing the county in search of justice as we speak." I thought for a second. "I'll give Archie a call and see what he can tell me."

"Okay."

We hung up.

I told the phone to call Archie Mack. After asking me if I wanted to call Angie McVeigh then Archer, Elaine, I realized I'd entered him into my contacts as Archibald Mack.

It took me two cursing miles to figure it out, but the phone eventually rang.

A woman's voice answered. "Hello?"

I had no confidence that my virtual, cloud-based assistant had dialed the right number. "I'm sorry, I was trying to reach Archie Mack."

"Oh, Mr. Shepherd, this is Susanna Mack. Archie's in the field. He'll be out there all day. He doesn't come in at all during the day given...given what's going on. Can I help you with something?"

She probably could but my conversation with her wasn't protected, so I didn't want to say too much. "No, Mrs. Mack, I need to speak to Archie. When do you think is a good time?"

Mrs. Mack chuckled. "We're farmers, Mr. Shepherd. Probably about half an hour after the sun sets. You know, I was just over here putting together some dinner for when he gets in. Why don't you stop in?"

"No, really, that's okay."

"Are you married, Mr. Shepherd?"

I paused. "No."

"Then I'd be willing to bet that nothing you could make tonight will be as good as my baked chicken."

"No, I don't suppose it could."

"Then come up here and eat and ask Archie your questions."

I decided that it wouldn't hurt to take a look at the farm and see Archie's setup there. Baked chicken put it over the edge. "Okay. I'll be there."

"Perfect," Susanna Mack said. "We'll see you tonight."

We hung up. I rarely felt like city folk, but knowing that I'd have to check my phone to find out what time the sun set, well, that seemed like a personal failure.

I needed to gas up if I was going to the Mack farm tonight. I knew just the station to use.

⁓

I WENT to the station on the corner of Century and Stone, the same place where Archie Mack had stopped right after the concert. I filled up my tank, paid at the pump, then went in and bought a bottle of water and a pack of gum. As I paid, I asked, "Is the manager in?"

"Gary?" said the attendant.

I had no idea. "Sure."

"He's back in the storeroom by the restrooms doing inventory."

"Thanks," I said and went back to the storeroom. I knocked on the door, which was open, and saw a man bending down with a clipboard and pen, filling in blanks on an inventory sheet.

"Gary?" I said.

The man looked up. "The restroom's next door," he said, pointing. He bent back over his clipboard so that his long brown hair hung forward over his black glasses.

"I wasn't looking for the bathroom. I was looking for you."

He glanced back at me, then straightened. "Sorry, we weren't expecting anyone from corporate until next week."

The tie did that sometimes. "No, I'm not from corporate. I have some questions about the Mack case."

Gary looked at me blankly and shook his head.

"From the night of the Big Luke concert?"

Gary's eyes cleared. "Right, right, right," he said. "But I already told that deputy everything I remember."

Bingo.

"Sure. I just wanted to ask a couple of questions for my own report."

Gary looked at me, looked at the rolls of toilet paper he was in the middle of tallying, and was clearly torn between which he preferred to do.

Flattering.

"I only have a minute," he said finally.

"That's all it'll take. Who was on duty that night?"

"I was. Freaking RJ called off."

"That sucks."

"No shit. On a Friday night too."

"So did you see him come in?"

"The dude with the hand? I did."

"How did you remember?"

"The bandage. His hand was bleeding right through it and he actually dripped in a couple spots." Gary shook his head. "I had to do the full biohazard protocol to clean up, gloves, disinfectant, the works."

"What happened?"

"He went into the bathroom and cleaned up his hands. I expected to find a bunch of bloody paper towels in there but there weren't any. I figure he must've taken them out. Hiding his tracks, you know?"

"Did he still have the bandage on when he came out?"

Gary shook his head. "No. Well—wait a minute, I guess he did have a bandage on, but it must've been a new one. I remember it wasn't dripping at all because I was glad."

"What did he do when he came out?"

"He bought a Tall Tea and some beef jerky, puts them on the counter, then he thinks about it and goes back and buys a twelve pack of beer. 'One of those days?' I asked him. I found it's better to engage the odd ones right away to see if there's trouble, you know? And the guy just kinda clenched his teeth, pulled down on his cap and said, 'One of those years.' And I said, 'All we can do is keep plugging, right?' And he just kind of nodded and didn't say anything else, like he was thinking of something. And then he paid, and he left."

"Anything else you remember?"

"Not really. We were pretty busy with the concert traffic."

Gary pushed his long bangs out of his face and then gestured at the stacked toilet paper. "Do you mind? I have a ways to go."

"No, I'm sorry to have kept you. Thanks."

"No problem," said Gary, and went back to his inventory.

As I left, I added hiding bloody bandages to the list of things I needed to talk to Archie about tonight. Great.

I was almost to the office when the phone buzzed and the car announced, "Call from, Olivia." I answered. "You do miss me."

"I need you to get over here, Shep."

"Where's here?"

"The gym."

"What's up?"

"It's Cade. Pearson's here to question him."

"Don't let him say anything. I'm on my way."

13

When I entered the Brickhouse, Mitch Pearson, Chief Detective in Charge of Serious Crimes for Carrefour, Ohio, was standing in front of the desk. Cade and Olivia were on the other side. Pearson was tall, blonde, and wore a slim fit suit that made the gun under his arm and the badge at his belt all the more obvious. He looked like a stereotype of everything he was, a former quarterback, a triathlete, and a complete pain in the ass.

"Pearson," I said. "You're far from home."

"Thought I'd try some barbecue." He pointed at the Railcar across the parking lot and then shook my hand, trying as usual to crush it. "As long as I was here, I wanted to follow up on a new case."

I nodded. "See, by far from home, I meant out of your jurisdiction."

Pearson shook his head. "So suspicious. This is a courtesy call. I know Mr. Brickson does a lot of bond work in our Ohio court, so I wanted to follow up on a complaint right away."

"What do you mean?"

Pearson looked around. "Can we take this to your office?"

Rule number one—never voluntarily let the police into any part of your house or business.

"Right here is fine," I said.

"Isn't this a place of public accommodation?"

"The gym is. The office isn't. We can go outside if you prefer."

Pearson shrugged. "Suit yourself. I was just trying to save you any embarrassment."

"How's a courtesy call embarrassing?"

Pearson pulled out his phone and poked here and there on the screen. "Cade, did you bring Travis Kopcek in on a skipped bond yesterday?"

I raised my hand to Cade. I didn't need to. He stood there, his arms folded.

Pearson sighed as if our distrust was the weight of the world. "Fine. Kopcek made a complaint that you assaulted him when you brought him back."

Cade, Olivia, and I had a contest to see who could out-sphinx the other.

Pearson poked the screen a few more times and, when he had what he wanted, looked up and said, "Assuming this six foot four, two hundred sixty pound man in a black t-shirt with black wraparound sunglasses is you—"

Cade stood there with his arms still crossed, all six foot four, two hundred sixty pounds of him, wearing his black wrap-around sunglasses and a black t-shirt.

"—Then this footage that a doorbell video system caught might interest you."

Pearson put his phone on the counter, flipped it toward Olivia and Cade, and gestured. I stepped closer and leaned around so I could see too.

Olivia hit play. The video showed a view of a driveway with two trucks parked in a line on one side. Three men were standing in the bed of the front truck, apparently installing a toolbox. A black Expedition pulled into the driveway on the other side and Cade got out. There was no audio with the video. All three men straightened and one, with a cut-off flannel shirt and sun-bleached hair, stepped forward and gestured back. There appeared to be a discussion, with Cade standing there and Flannel Boy gesturing more and more. One of the guys hopped off the far side of the truck bed.

He had a flathead hammer in his hand.

I couldn't tell if the Cade in the video could see it from his angle. I glanced up at Cade now. I didn't see any hammer marks, so took that as a good sign and looked back down.

The third guy was braver. He hopped down on Cade's side but then appeared to hesitate when he found that, on level ground, he was about six inches shorter than Cade. From where the man was standing, with his back to the camera, I could see a screwdriver sticking out of his back pocket.

Pearson pointed. "See now the guy staying in the truck bed, Kopcek, was a no-show for court last week. You'd posted his bond."

Silence.

"He doesn't appear to be interested in going in."

Kopcek began to gesture more as the guy with the flathead hammer snuck around the back of the pickup bed to come at Cade from the other side.

Cade didn't move. Kopcek gestured more wildly, pointing and waving now. Cade tipped his head toward his car.

Then everything happened at once. Kopcek jumped off the far side of the truck and yanked open the driver-side door. The man with the flathead hammer ran up on Cade and swung. The man with the screwdriver whipped it out of his back pocket.

What happened next was almost too fast to follow. Cade spun toward the man swinging the hammer, caught his wrist with one hand and struck him square in the chest with the other, spinning him around and slamming the back of his head into the side of the truck. That made the man with the screwdriver hesitate, which allowed Cade to bring an elbow back, smash the man's face, and wrench the screwdriver free as the man crumpled to the ground.

Cade followed the momentum of his elbow strike, ripped open the passenger door of the truck, and lunged in. It was hard to see inside the cab, but then Cade straightened and pulled Kopcek straight out of the cab by both wrists. Cade side-stepped and twisted Kopcek's wrists and a handgun tumbled onto the driveway. As the gun skipped across the cement, Cade rabbit punched Kopcek behind the ear, then yanked him to his feet. A couple of zip-ties later, Kopcek's hands were behind his back and he was tossed headfirst into the back seat of the Expedition. Moments later, Cade pulled out of the driveway, leaving the other two staggering and tool-less.

Pearson reached over and hit stop.

Cade stood there, silent. The speed with which he'd taken the three men down was breath-taking, so fast that it had seemed choreographed, like a movie. It wasn't though. Cade had done it in real life in real-time. I reminded myself to be nicer to him.

"Kopcek has made a complaint for assault. It seems to me, though, that three people jumped a bail bondsman with the contents of a small hardware store."

"That seems about right," I said.

"See, was that so bad?"

"You never know."

Pearson ignored the comment. "Do you want to give a statement, Mr. Brickson?"

"No," Cade said.

Pearson stared at him, then shrugged. "We'll turn the video

over to the prosecutor. We don't see any evidence of an assault here, but I'm sure they'll want to look into it."

"No evidence of assault by Cade," said Olivia.

"Right," said Pearson. "Well, I guess that's it for me. How's the family, Shepherd?" He looked at Olivia and Cade as he said it.

"Fine, thanks," I said.

My friends ground their teeth.

"Give them my regards," said Pearson.

"Goodbye," said Olivia.

Pearson gave half a wave and left.

Olivia turned on her brother. "I thought you said you didn't have any trouble?"

Cade shrugged. "I didn't."

Sweet Jesus. "I'll get Danny on it," I said.

"No need," said Cade.

"Someone needs to mind it, Cade," said Olivia. "If they file charges, it could put your bail bond business in jeopardy. Let him do it."

Cade shrugged. "I'm going to get a lift in," he said and walked away.

Olivia watched him go. "You will have Danny keep an eye on it?"

"Absolutely."

"Good. I don't trust Pearson."

"You shouldn't. Hey, turns out I'm going up to the Mack farm tonight. Did you find out anything else?"

"A little. The Macks are mortgaged to the hilt."

"Bad?"

"From what I can see, it's more than the property is worth."

"It must include an interest in the machinery and crops."

"And animals," said Olivia. "Bonnie tells me that Archie runs some pigs too."

"I understand that's normal for farmers. The mortgages, I mean."

"It is but...I don't know their books, but it sure seems like one down year could drive them under."

"I hear that's normal too. Farm bankruptcies are way up, especially for family farms. I'll add that to the list when I talk to him tonight."

Olivia nodded and looked away. "Bonnie was in today for a class."

"Yeah?"

"She said Abby's improving. Had another procedure to repair her orbital bone."

"That's good news."

"It takes a special kind of scumbag to do that, Shep."

I nodded. "I agree."

"The worst." She looked at me. "We have to find the guy who did this."

Olivia was always diligent. This was extra.

"I agree. We can't let it get in the way of representing Archie, though, Liv."

"Seems to me finding the real attacker is the best way to represent Archie."

I know a losing argument when presented with it. I pointed out at the gym. "What do you have going now?"

"Time to make some people feel guilty about feeling unmotivated to work out."

"You're a terrible person."

"So I've been told. Call me if you learn anything interesting?"

"Will do."

I left and checked the time. Then I cursed and checked my smartphone for what time sunset was that night, did the math, and killed a couple of hours before heading up to the Mack farm for dinner.

14

It was still early when I got to Mack Farms, so I decided to drive around the fields a couple of times as the sun set.

A square-mile is bigger than you think. If you've never been to Michigan, or any of the other Midwestern states, then you might not have ever seen square-mile sections before. In a town, they can be hidden by side-streets and development but, out here, the layout was clear—four county roads running in straight lines forming a perfect square marking off six hundred and forty acres. I arrived at the intersection on the southwest corner of the farm, turned so that the Mack fields were on my right, and just drove along, taking right turns, keeping my eye on their property.

The first time around, I got a sense of the land itself. It had some hills to it but more gentle rolls than steep changes. I could see the creek that ran through it because it was lined by a thin stand of trees on both sides that I assumed served as a windbreak and a warning. As I turned and passed the center of the farm, I saw a tractor in the field—if I was oriented right, that would be Alban Mack, the father, working on his part of the farm.

I took the circuit again. This time I focused on the houses. There were two gravel driveways on the south side of the square about two hundred yards apart. The first was set about fifty yards back and dead-ended into a large barn with a house offset to the left. Archie's place. Two hundred yards later, right up next to the road, was a yellow farmhouse with white trim and a large porch. Mr. and Mrs. Mack's house. Their barns were set a little farther back but not much, which was more what I'd expected from an older farm.

I had trouble finding the drive to Hamish's house. It took me two laps to realize that it was on the opposite side, the north side of the square, and that his house was set all the way back in the middle of the property, almost half a mile from the road. I saw a cluster of lights but the view was obstructed by trees and the gloom of gathering dusk. All in all, the whole thing seemed like a normal farm, whatever that means, no different than any other farm you could see driving down the highway or on the back roads of Michigan.

For the record, the sun set at 8:19 p.m. that day (admit it, you didn't know either). I pulled off to the side of the road, around the corner from Archie's place, and waited so that I pulled into his driveway at exactly 8:49 p.m. I got out of my Jeep and made my way up the porch stairs. The house was newer, well-maintained with light green siding and dark green trim. The deck of the wrap-around porch was a composite, the kind that would last for years without signs of wear.

Archie Mack opened the door before I could knock. He wasn't wearing his hat so his mid-face tan-line stood in stark contrast to his bald head.

"Nate," he said. "Come in. I was glad when Mom said you'd called."

"Thanks, Archie. I won't take much of your time."

"No problem. We're going to eat first though."

"I know your mom mentioned that, but it really isn't necessary."

Archie put his hand on my shoulder and grinned. "You can explain to my mom that she shouldn't have made extra, but I'm certainly not going to. Come on."

Archie led me to the dining room and I'm not sure what I was expecting, but it wasn't this. It wasn't rustic and country and it wasn't a modernized farmhouse either. It was hardwood floors and a sturdy oak table and a series of ceiling fans that, when combined with open French doors, made for an incredibly pleasant breeze on a warm August night. Mrs. Mack had a large serving plate with a couple of chickens on them that were crisped to a golden brown and smelled delicious. The rest of the table was filled with vegetables and salad and fruit and what looked to be marvelously spiced red skin potatoes. The smells hit me like a wave and my stomach growled. I'm not kidding, it literally growled.

"Right on time, Mr. Shepherd," said Mrs. Mack. "You can tell a lot about people by when they arrive." She waved. "Sit, both of you." She went back to the kitchen and returned with a handful of serving spoons.

I sat. There was a pause, then Mrs. Mack said, "We say grace."

"Of course," I said, and bowed my head.

Mrs. Mack said a brief prayer, thanking God for the day, requesting healing for Abby, and blessing this food as nourishment to the body of this lawyer that it might give him strength to work tirelessly to deliver her son from false accusations of wickedness. Then she began taking plates to dish out food.

So, no pressure.

It didn't seem appropriate to delay a guy who'd been working out in a field all day from eating, so there was a brief interlude as chickens were carved and potatoes were scooped and vegetables were dished out. When plates were filled and forks were flying, Mrs. Mack said, "So how's my son's defense going?"

"Fine," I said. "I can't talk about the details with you, though, Mrs. Mack."

"By fine, do you mean you've found the person who actually did it?"

"I can't discuss it with you, Mrs. Mack."

"I see," said Mrs. Mack. She clearly did not. "My son can't go to jail, Mr. Shepherd."

"Mom," said Archie.

"I'm doing everything I can to prevent that, Mrs. Mack."

"Are you?"

I looked at her squarely. "Yes."

"Well, then I guess that's all we can ask."

The dining room was filled with the sound of forks on plates for a few minutes before I said, "I do have a question for you that might help me."

"Anything."

"I was doing some background research on your farm and found something I don't understand."

"What's that?"

"There's a record of a complaint of vandalism and criminal damaging on your farm a while back."

Mrs. Mack looked at me blankly. Archie seemed intent on a chicken leg.

"You all called the sheriff saying that someone had ruined your crop by putting fertilizer on it."

Mrs. Mack's face cleared. "Goodness, yes! That was terrible."

"So someone destroyed your crops?"

"No. Yes. Not exactly."

I smiled.

"I suppose it *is* confusing. Archie?"

Archie waved a fork that she should go ahead and kept eating.

"Do you know anything about organic farming?" said Mrs. Mack.

"Assume I don't."

"So to be an organic farm, you can't use certain fertilizers and herbicides on your land for three years before your first crop. After that time passes, you can be certified as organic."

"And get the better price at market," said Archie as he paused long enough to carve out a chicken breast.

"So five years ago, as a family, we decided to make that transition. We'd been struggling and we all agreed to give it a shot. It was hard because we had to relearn everything we had ever done. Farm technology changes but not that much. The seeds and fertilizers and things have evolved, but a lot of the techniques for planting have been consistent, you just have more computers and better equipment to help you do it. My Alban has a pretty good feel for what works and my boys"—her pride was apparent in her words—"well, they're very good at it too. When we made the change though, without being able to use our usual products, we were flying a little blind. They had to learn a new system of crop rotation and new techniques to minimize bugs and disease without resorting to spray. Corn and soybeans were mostly what we grew before, so now we were looking at different seed options and maybe adding in some other crops too. It was a lot to take on."

"So how did it go?"

"Year one, five years ago, was a little rough. We were learning, we were transitioning, and yields were way down. We didn't cover our loan for the year, although we were close."

"Year two was better. We made adjustments to the planting schedule, and got a better line on stock and seed. We covered our loan and our deficit from the year before, even without being able to sell as certified organic. We could start to see that, with the premium, this was going to work."

She shook her head. "And then we had year three. Once we got through that, we would be certified the following year. We got everything planted that spring and the weather conditions were just about perfect for once. We felt good. The crops were planted, there were no infestations, and we felt just fine about going for a long weekend to a family wedding in Wisconsin. The boys drove the normal way, down around Chicago, but Alban and I decided to drive to Ludington and take the ferry across Lake Michigan with the car."

She sighed. "It was fantastic. We had a great time and barely thought about the farm at all, which is pretty rare for us. We got back Sunday night. It was late so we didn't notice anything and just went to bed. So then Monday morning, Alban, he's up before the sun and I usually don't see him until lunchtime at the earliest. And he comes back half an hour later just as the sun is coming up. He doesn't say anything to me, just motions and takes me out to his truck."

Mrs. Mack handed me a dish of potatoes and stopped talking until I put some more on my plate. Then she said, "So Alban puts me in the truck and we start driving around our section and pretty soon we see a fertilizer sign. And then another fertilizer sign. And another. Every fifty yards. All the way around the section."

"So I just looked at him and I said, 'Do you think it's true?'"

"'It's either true or it's a sick joke,' he said. 'We'll test.'"

Mrs. Mack pursed her lips. "It wasn't a joke. We tested the soil and pretty much our whole section had been hit with pesticide and fertilizer. So after that year, we had to start the three year clock all over again."

"What did it do to the crops?"

"That's why it was hard to answer your question. People use

fertilizer because it works. Between the perfect growing conditions and the fertilizer on top of that, we had the best year we'd had in a long time."

"That's good, anyway."

"Maybe. But it still put us three years away from premium crops again."

I did the math. "And now you're in the final year again?"

"This is it," she said. "We just need to get through this harvest, and avoid sabotage of course, and we can start growing organic next year."

"So no out-of-town weddings?"

"No, we've been sitting tight to make sure nothing bad happens..." She trailed off and looked at Archie, who had stopped eating and looked at his plate.

"Well, we've been sitting tight," she said.

"How is Abby, Mom?" said Archie.

Mrs. Mack brightened. "Good! She's using a cane now!"

"Already?"

"You know Abby. She's not going to tolerate crutches for long and a cane for less."

Archie looked pained. "You saw her?"

Mrs. Mack nodded. "I was over there last weekend; Hamish had bought tickets to one of those casino fund raiser trips he favors, for the Future Farmers, I think this one was. Or maybe the Dellville softball team, I'm not sure. Anyway, he wasn't going to go, but then I offered to stay with Abby, and she insisted that he go win her some money, so I went over and Abby and I had a grand time."

"Doing what?"

"Well, that's none of your business, Son, now is it?"

Though his mom's tone was light, Archie didn't smile. "I suppose not." He tapped his fork on his plate. "And her eye socket?"

Mrs. Mack's smile turned forced. "Better. I think the last procedure helped. She could see well enough to trounce me in rummy, I can tell you that."

Archie's face looked stricken. "Mom, I didn't..."

Mrs. Mack put a hand out and grabbed her son's arm. "I know, Son."

"I just don't want you to think—"

"I don't. That's why we hired Mr. Shepherd. He's going to prove you didn't."

I took a bite of my favorite dish—chicken with a side of expectations.

"Well," Mrs. Mack tapped the table, "I know you boys have things to discuss and I can't listen to them, so I'm going to get your dessert and be on my way."

I looked at the wreckage of chicken bones and vegetable stalks on my plate and couldn't think of what else there might be. "Mrs. Mack, I'm stuffed."

"Not before the strawberry shortcake you're not."

Archie smiled and stood up with his plate. "We'll clean up while you get it, Ma."

Archie and I cleared the plates, and I was following him into the kitchen with an armful of them as his mother said, "I'm just putting the leftovers into the...oh, dear."

Headlights flashed across the kitchen window and before I knew it, Archie was heading for the back door.

"Mr. Shepherd," said Mrs. Mack and, judging from her tone, I hurried out the back after Archie.

Archie had stopped on the back porch, gripping the rail. A blue Dodge truck had stopped in front of the barn and a man climbed out. In the porch light, he looked about the same age as Archie, a little stockier, a little shorter, and with a full head of red hair where his brother was bald. He stopped short of the porch, spit, and said, "I have to use the Hopper Topper tomorrow."

Archie was rigid. "I thought Dad was going to pick it up for you."

Hamish Mack—because it had to be Hamish—glared, then looked away and shrugged. "He's running with the lights on tonight. I have to set up for tomorrow."

I stepped forward, not because I had anything to say, but so that I was between them on the stairs.

Hamish Mack turned and spat again, then tucked his tongue into his lower lip in the classic gesture of a man packing a dip before he said, "You must be the lawyer."

I did one of those circular nods that meant "yes," "no," and "what the hell?"

"Why didn't you just call, Hamish?" said Mrs. Mack.

Hamish shrugged. "Knew you were here. Figured I'd be in and out while you were still eating." He glared. "Didn't know I was interrupting a legal meeting."

"We were just cleaning up," said Mrs. Mack. "Did you get the lasagna I left?"

Hamish's tongue rolled back and forth in his lower lip. "I haven't been inside yet, Mom. I'm sure Abby'll heat it up. If she can stand the pain."

There was no positive place for this to go. I put a hand on Archie's elbow and jerked my head at the house.

"Yeah." Hamish spit. "Why don't you head on in and get your story straight, Arch."

"Don't worry, Ham. All my meetings are out in the open."

"Archie, inside," I said. "Mrs. Mack, you promised to help keep them separated."

"Boys," was all she said.

Archie turned and went inside. Hamish glanced at his

mother, then at me, then clenched his fists, gave a last spit, and headed for the barn.

"I'll see that he gets the Hopper Topper and gets going," said Mrs. Mack, and hustled down the stairs. I followed Archie into the house. I handed him dishes and he rinsed them and put them in the dishwasher for a bit before he said, "We share some pieces of equipment. Helps us all reduce overhead."

"Makes sense."

"It used to." He stared out the window, jaw clenched.

I followed his gaze to the barn with its lights on and doors open. "I take it he doesn't agree with Abby? About you doing it?"

"We've had words."

"That all?"

He looked at me. "No."

"How much more?"

"I'd call it pushing more than punches."

"I see. Why would he think it's you?"

"Because there isn't a better explanation."

That was a problem.

"Which is why you have to fix this."

"That's why I'm here, Archie."

That seemed to get through. "Right, right. I just…"

"It's natural in this situation," I said. "Don't worry about it."

After we put away the last dish, Archie eyed the dessert and said, "I'd dish out the shortcake, but there are certain things my mom won't abide."

I smiled and thought of my dad and his Sunday barbecue. "I know what you mean."

We went back into the dining room. As we waited, I said, "So did they ever figure out who did this crop thing?"

"Sheriff Dushane never found anything. Hundreds of acres and no one saw a thing."

"Any obvious competitor's step in on the organic side?"

"Not that we could see," said Archie.

The screen door clattered and, a short time later, Mrs. Mack came out with two bowls of strawberry shortcake.

"There we are," said Mrs. Mack. "Now I'll let you boys get down to business." She collected her purse and her keys, then gave her son a kiss on the head. "He's just worried about her, you know."

"I know. I am too."

Mrs. Mack looked down at her son, her eyes filled with concern. Then she lifted her chin, smiled at me, and said, "It was a pleasure to see you, Mr. Shepherd."

"Dinner was delicious, Mrs. Mack."

She waved a hand. "Flatterer."

"Really, I can't thank you enough."

"You know exactly how to thank me, Mr. Shepherd. Love you, Son." With that, she left.

The screen door banged again, then Mrs. Mack's truck fired up, and we heard the crunch of gravel as she left. Archie gestured and I dug into the strawberry shortcake.

Now I'm not much of a dessert eater but I have to tell you, eating strawberries picked fresh from a field outside your door and served on top of homemade shortcake was enough to make me change my mind. We spent the next five minutes appreciating that fact until I finally said, "We need to talk about some things."

Archie was still concentrating on the shortcake. "That's what we're doing."

"You went to a gas station after the concert."

Archie nodded. "I filled up the tank."

"You also went in and cleaned up a bloody bandage on your hand."

"I did."

"Why?"

"Because I was dripping blood."

"Why?"

"I had a cut."

"From what?"

"Earlier in the day. Ham and I were working on a drainage tile. Cut it pretty good." He held up his hand. The cut was healing but it was still there, a slash right across the center of his palm.

"Will Hamish testify to that?"

Archie shrugged. "You'll have to ask him."

"Did you have a spare bandage with you?"

"Yes."

"Why?"

"In case it broke open or seeped. Which it did."

"Why didn't you just throw the bandage away in the bathroom?"

Archie looked up. "And make some poor kid clean up my mess?"

I met his gaze. "What happened, Archie?"

"I took the bandage with me."

"Not at the gas station. In the Quarry."

"Nothing."

"I've seen the video from the Quarry, Archie. You walk toward the back of the Quarry, toward the old stairs, ten minutes after Abby. You come back. Abby never does. And you go straight to a gas station and clean blood off your hands. Blood they also found on the railing. What happened?"

He shook his head. "I never saw her."

"But what happened?"

"I never saw her."

"You said that. But why did you go back there?"

Archie shrugged. "It doesn't matter, I didn't see her."

"Of course, it matters! I have to explain it."

Archie looked at me. "I was just clearing my head and letting the traffic clear. Nate, if I'd seen her, I'd have been the first one to help her. But I didn't."

"I need more than that."

"Nate, I didn't see her, I didn't talk to her, I didn't throw her down the stairs and I certainly didn't hit her. None of it."

I decided to try another tack. "Who'd you go to the concert with?"

"No one. Just me."

"Why?"

"I originally wasn't going to be able to go. My schedule freed up, but Bonnie was already going with Abby and their friends and I didn't want to horn in on their girls' night."

"So you went by yourself?"

"I like Big Luke."

"We all do. But by yourself?"

Archie looked up. "My first wife left me four years ago."

"I'm sorry."

"Don't be. She thought she was marrying a rich farmer. She wasn't."

"What does that have to do with Big Luke?"

Archie smiled a little. "'Good Riddance.' 'I Get the Dog.' 'I Found the Bottom of the Bottle But You're Still You.'"

"I stand corrected." I thought. "Why did you follow Abby around back?"

"I didn't follow Abby. I didn't know she'd gone back there."

I stabbed the last elusive crumb of shortcake and ate it before I said, "Attempted murder carries a life sentence, you know."

"So I've been told."

"I need to explain to the jury what you were doing."

"I told you, I was clearing my head. And I never saw Abby."

"Archie. There's a video putting you at the scene of the

attack, at the time of the attack, and walking away with a bloody hand. I need to explain it."

"I don't know what to tell you, Nate." Archie chased imaginary crumbs around an empty bowl and ignored me as the silence grew. "I didn't see Abby back there. I didn't see anybody."

I believed Archie when he said he didn't see anyone. I wasn't getting the same feeling about why he went back there. I suppose it could have been to kill time. But I wasn't all the way there and I didn't think a jury would be either.

I'd had enough for the night. I stood and put my bowl in the sink. Archie stayed seated. Before I left, I said, "You know, if I didn't do it, I'd want someone to find the person who attacked my future sister-in-law."

Archie flashed. "I do."

"I need all the information you have about it."

"I've told you everything I know about the attack, Nate. Which is nothing."

I left then. Archie didn't see me out.

15

I'd never heard of a strawberry shortcake hangover but I swear I had one the next morning. It took me a few extra minutes to get moving and, by the time I got to the office, Danny was already there. That in itself wasn't unusual.

Olivia being there was.

The two of them were holed up in the conference room and, the minute I opened the door, Danny came tumbling out.

I saw Olivia behind him, grinning.

I set down my tablet. "Look at you two plotting and conspiring already this morning."

"More like searching and discovering," said Olivia.

"What do you mean?"

She waved me in. Danny jerked right, decided on left, then lurched in front of me. I smiled, put one hand on his back, and gently guided him into the room ahead of me. As I sat, Olivia teased her hair down around her glasses and said, "So remember when I said the first thing we would check were banking and land records?"

"I do. You figured out that the property had been divided and said the Macks were drowning in debt. They've pretty much admitted that to me by the way."

Olivia nodded. "Right. We all thought that was common for farmers."

"Isn't it?"

"It is, but I wanted to check to be sure. So Danny and I started looking at filings for the surrounding farms."

"And they had similar mortgages?"

"A lot of them. Revolving lines of credit mostly."

Olivia paused again and the two of them grinned.

I nodded, confused. "Good job?"

"Don't be snide, that was good work. But that's not all we found."

"That was sincere, not sarcastic. Are you going to make me ask?"

They kept grinning.

"Geez, you two, you're acting like you found diamond mines or oil wells or something."

Their smiles vanished. "You knew?" said Danny.

"That there are diamond mines in Ash County? No, I did not."

"No. Oil wells."

"There are?"

"So you didn't know!"

I sighed. "Would you two please just explain it?"

Olivia leaned forward. "We looked in the Ash County Register of Deeds for records of the surrounding properties, hoping to get more information on what's typical for farmers up there. We found oil wells."

"What do you mean?"

"A company, Hillside Oil & Gas, has been quietly filing leases for the right to drill for oil and natural gas on farms in northern Ash County and the surrounding counties for years."

"I haven't heard about that before. Have you two?"

They both shook their heads.

"How many?" I asked.

"Sixteen that we've found so far," said Olivia. "I'm sure there are more. We're going to keep looking and map it out. They're not too close to Mack Farms but they're scattered about enough to be interesting."

"What do you know about Hillside Oil & Gas?"

Olivia turned to Danny. "He knows we just found out about the wells last night, right?"

"He does."

"And he's asking about the oil company?"

"He is."

"Is he always like this?"

Danny nodded his head and sighed. "It does get wearing sometimes."

Olivia turned her glasses back on me. "We came in early today, before certain others, to follow up on that."

"I'm beginning to think that having the two of you work together wasn't a very good idea."

"It's a perfect idea," said Olivia. "We have to get this fine young man out in the world away from his troll of a boss. I'm betting he's going to have a gym membership by the end of this."

"Jenny was thinking about taking a boot camp class," Danny said.

I had to get in front of this burgeoning insurrection. "Danny, print out the property owners who have oil and gas leases and let's put them on a map so we can see the layout. Olivia, if you have the time, and don't mind, and would be willing to, pretty please, do some research on Hillside Oil & Gas, I would certainly appreciate it."

"Maybe. If you ask nice."

"I'll try. Oh, and Liv, Pops is having his Labor Day cookout Sunday. Are you and Cade in?"

"Wouldn't miss it."

"How about the Reddy family, Danny?" I said, although I knew the answer.

"Sorry, Nate. Our church is having a potluck after services."

"You're always welcome if your daughter wants to swim after."

"I know, Nate, thanks."

I stood. "Alright, if that's it, I'll leave you to it." I stopped. "Last night, Mrs. Mack said Abby's improving. Heard anymore from Bonnie?"

"Just that the doctors are encouraged and that she's starting to have less pain getting around."

Danny shook his head. "It's terrible."

"It is," I said.

Olivia nudged Danny. "Let's get to work."

I considered asking who the ogre was now, thought better of it, and let the two of them get back at it.

Olivia left at noon for the gym and I told Danny to leave early to get a jump on the holiday weekend. I spent the rest of the day doing lawyer stuff, which was no more fun to do than to write about, so let's just say that by the end of the day I was done and I left the office and I didn't learn anything more about Archibald Mack or the Mack farm until Sunday afternoon at my parents' house.

16

My parents have a place on Glass Lake, just north of Carrefour. My mom loves water, my dad loves fishing, and they both love their grandkids so, now that they are retired, their place on the lake gives them easy access to all of that. Pops has a cookout every Sunday afternoon, but he pulls out all the stops on the big three—Memorial Day, the Fourth of July, and Labor Day. On Labor Day, he likes to add a fish fry to the mix and burn through, or I should say fry through, some of the inventory he relentlessly added to every day.

Now if you've been to one of the Shepherd barbecues before, you know that there are all sorts of people running around and that it can be hard to keep track of who's who. On this particular Labor Day, my older brother Tom and his wife Kate were running a little late because Tom is the varsity football coach for Carrefour North and had to finish his film study in the morning so he could be with us in the afternoon. Tom and Kate and their daughters Reed, Taylor, and Page, along with little Charlie, would come later.

When I arrived, my other brother Mark and his wife Izzy were already there. Their three boys, Justin, James, and Joe, were down by the water's edge, wrestling a kayak and two paddle boards from the shed to the thin strip of beach. Justin and Joe were each taking an end of a board and walking it down while James carried two paddles. James was limping, but didn't seem to be in any pain. My mom and Izzy were down by the water, supervising. I saw my mom start to help James but Izzy reached out, touched her arm, and shook her head. My mom stopped but she didn't look happy about it.

I joined Mark and my dad next to the smoker. "James is looking good," I said to Mark. James had had a terrible break of his leg a few months before.

Mark nodded. "It doesn't hurt as much. It's mostly the stiffness that's causing the limp."

"Still in therapy?"

"Some. A lot of it's at home now. Tom lets us into the high school weight room sometimes too."

"Any word yet on the growth plate?"

Mark shook his head. "We just have to wait until he starts really growing. We'll find out in the next year or so."

I shifted focus to the smoker. "Do you want some help with that, Dad?"

My dad was always a weathered hickory plank of a man but here, at the end of summer, he was exceptionally tan with a shock of white hair and a smile that gleamed most often when he was on the water. This was a close second, though, and I could see his enjoyment as he tapped the black smoker lid with the bottom of a beer can. "No need, Son."

The wafting smell of hickory smoke and spices convinced me that was true. "Ribs?"

"Yep."

"Are you going to wrap them?"

"It depends on when Tom gets here." He flashed a smile. "You can't rush these things, you know."

The three of us watched Justin and Joe get the boards into the water while James climbed into the kayak. After a series of hollers and tilts, they all started paddling. As they headed for a small group of ducks minding their own business, I said, "A bunch of the guys at the plant live north of Dellville, don't they?"

My father was a retired tool and die maker from one of the big three automakers. My brother Mark had followed in his footsteps and now worked at the same Dellville plant.

"Sure," said Mark.

"Have you ever heard anything about a company coming in and trying to buy oil and gas leases up that way?"

"Not me," said Mark. He reached into the cooler and pulled out two more beers and shook the ice water off before handing me one. "Why?"

"I just heard about it, about the drilling. I didn't even know we did that around here."

My dad took a beer from Mark, cracked it, and said, "Now that you mention it, I did hear that Ben Newton's boy got lucky a few years back on a piece of vacant property he had up-county. Something about getting a cell phone tower and a well on the same piece of crappy land. Want me to check?"

"No. I just hadn't heard anything about it. Wondered if you guys had."

"Is it related to a case?" said Mark.

"Maybe. I'm not sure."

My dad stared out at the lake. "How is the Ackerman girl?"

"Improving."

"Pretty awful if her own brother-in-law did it," said Mark.

"She's not married into the family yet." That sounded bad as soon as I said it. "And I don't think he did it."

"You have to say that."

"No, I don't."

"Is Olivia helping you with that case?" said my dad.

"Quite a bit. She found the oil leases."

He nodded. "You having her do a lot of computer research?"

I stared. "That's what she does. Why?"

My dad shrugged. "Just curious."

I don't think my dad had asked me a question to satisfy his own idle curiosity since my junior year in high school when he'd asked just how I thought I was going to get to Zach Stevenson's house without a car or a bike or any other mode of transportation for the next two weeks. I was distracted from any other questions, though, by the slam of a car door, and then another. A moment later, Cade and Olivia rounded the corner of the house; Olivia dragging a raft, Cade with a full cooler on his shoulder, and both wearing sunglasses.

Olivia went down to the water and gave my mom and Izzy a hug before yelling at Justin that he needed to dig deeper with the paddle if he wanted to catch that duck. Cade sauntered over to us and set the cooler down with a heavy slosh indicating that it was already filled with ice and sundries.

"You look good, Cade," said my dad. "Losing weight?"

Cade looked down at his bulging arm before he could help himself.

Mark nodded. "About time you tried to slim down. Carrying all that weight can't be healthy." He raised his beer in salute. "Good for you."

"Work does make it hard to get to the gym, doesn't it?" I said.

Cade's mouth twitched. "Hi, Mr. Shepherd." He nodded at me and my brother. "Turds."

The party, as they say, had started.

∼

AT THE END of the day, Olivia and I were sitting on plastic chairs at the edge of the water. The air was warm and the sand on the beach was cool as we soaked in the last rays of the sun, which was still above the woods on the far shore of the lake.

"Why'd Tom and Kate have to leave so early?" Olivia said.

"He got a call from his quarterback," I said. "Something happened with his father."

"That can't be good."

Speaking of fathers reminded me of mine, and what he'd asked about. "We're going to be chin deep in this Mack case for a while. You don't have to do the research all in one day."

"Work doesn't bother me, Shep. Stupid questions and wasted light bother me."

"I just mean you seem pretty focused on it."

She turned toward me. "How is that a problem?"

"It's not."

"Then why are we wasting this sunset?"

I smiled and tipped my can to her but I didn't look away.

She did instead, straightening her glasses and facing the sun.

I looked from her to the setting sun and back.

"I'm just saying we have plenty of time—"

She faced me again. "Margarita me."

As I opened the cooler and filled Olivia's glass from an icy pitcher, she said, "Speaking of work though, Danny and I mapped out the leases we've been able to find so far."

"You're not seriously going to ruin a sunset with work, are you?"

"No, you did. There's actually a bit of a pattern to them. They fall in a line from the northwest to southeast, kind of a diagonal running right through three counties. It's not completely straight and they're scattered about, but it definitely seems like a pattern."

"All the same company?"

She nodded. "Hillside Oil & Gas. I'm not sure if it matters though."

"Why is that?"

"The Mack place seems outside the line by quite a ways so I don't know that it's relevant."

"Can you guys send it to me tomorrow?"

"Danny saved it into your system already under 'Research.'"

"Great. Thanks."

"Don't shut that lid, Shepherd!" Izzy slid into the chair next to Olivia and held out her own glass. "Fill me up and explain why you couldn't find the time to go with Mark and me on our casino trip two weeks ago."

"Sounds like you had plenty of people go."

"We did but it wound up being an odd number. *Shayne* was certainly disappointed."

"I'm sure you all had a good time."

Olivia smiled. "Is our boy ducking out on fun again, Izzy?"

"Only if you consider a charter trip with a group of friends that involves going to a casino for a diamond hunt, dinner, and gambling fun, Olivia."

"It certainly sounds fun."

"And if you wouldn't do it for fun, it seems like you might do it to raise money for your nephew's baseball team."

"It certainly does."

Izzy shook her head. "I'm wondering if he even remembers the half-assed excuse he gave me or if he's going to make up a new one now."

I smiled. "There are no diamonds in Dowagiac, I'd only lose money gambling, and I still donated to Justin's team."

Izzy fluttered her eyes. "There are diamonds in Dowagiac. But even if there weren't, you'd get to spend the day with your loving family and new friends."

"My new friends? Or a particular friend?"

Izzy shrugged. "Who knows?"

"Seems like we won't," said Olivia.

"It's a damn shame."

"Shouldn't you be checking on your kids?"

"Cade and Mark are playing with them," said Izzy.

"That seems like deflection," said Olivia.

I spent about another orb's worth of sunset deflecting my sister-in-law from my dating decisions before kids' laughter saved me. Cade was walking down to the beach, Justin hanging from one arm, James from the other, with Joe wrapped around one leg laughing his little blond head off every time Cade took a step. Mark hustled past them and flipped a blanket onto the grass. Once it was open, Cade stopped, said something about how the mosquitos on this lake were getting out of control, and tossed Justin and then James and then little Joe to Mark, who caught each one and deposited them into a laughing heap on the blanket. Proclaiming himself free at long last of annoying insects, Cade pulled up a chair next to me and maxed its capacity when he sat. I added twelve ounces to it for him. The chair held.

My mom came down a moment later. I pulled a chair over for her and she sat down with a sigh. "Cade, Liv, I put two containers of ribs and potato salad on the counter. Make sure you get it on the way out."

"Thanks, Mrs. Shepherd," they both said.

She patted Olivia's knee then sat back and turned to me. "Now where is your father?"

A few minutes later, just as the sun touched the treetops, my dad joined us. He brought a lemonade-based cocktail to my mom and stood next to her, one hand on her shoulder. While normally in motion, he was now perfectly still.

We didn't say anything then. We sat there together, and we soaked in the last of the summer sun, and watched it set behind the Grove on the far side of Glass Lake.

17

I trudged into the office on the Tuesday morning after Labor Day because, honestly, how else are you going to go in. True to her word though, I found the illustration Olivia had mentioned in the e-file and my morning picked up steam. I opened it and, sure enough, it showed a scattershot of oil and gas leases running in a diagonal line across several counties. They had cross-referenced it so that I could click on any individual well and a graphic would pop up so that I could see the name of the property owner, the name of the company getting the drilling rights, and the date of the lease. None of them listed the price the company paid for the lease, though; they just stated that it was for a confidential amount for a certain number of years so I didn't know what kind of money we were talking about. It seemed to me that the oldest lease had been filed eight years ago while the newest had been about eighteen months.

Liv was right about another thing—this didn't really seem relevant to the Mack farm, which was a little south and a lot west of the scattershot pattern. Still, for completeness, I clicked on each graphic and checked out each lease.

All of them were with Hillside Oil & Gas.

I followed the line of wells up to the far northwest corner, to what appeared to be the oldest of the leases. The language was the same as the others—it granted an unlimited drilling right in a designated area on the land with no permanent ownership of land itself—but there was an exhibit attached to this one that wasn't part of any of the others. I blew it up and saw that it looked like some sort of geographical map, showing types of rock and strata and land formations for all of southeast Michigan and northwest Ohio. It made no sense to me.

At the bottom, I saw an acknowledgment—"Courtesy of LGL University Press, Professor Elias Timmons."

I stared at it for a while, but eventually my takeaway was that the geology of the land was important to the leases and that Professor Timmons' map showed something about it.

I thought for a moment then picked up my phone and called Archie Mack.

"Archibald Mack residence, Susanna Mack speaking."

I smiled. It reminded me of calling my grandmother when I was young.

"Mrs. Mack, it's Nate Shepherd."

"Well, good morning, Mr. Shepherd. What did you think of the strawberry shortcake?"

"I think I'm going to be representing you soon, Mrs. Mack, because that shortcake was criminal."

She chuckled. "Mr. Shepherd, you will turn my head. Do you want me to leave a message for Archie?"

"I have a question about the farm. Maybe you can answer it."

"Probably. What about that confidentiality stuff though?"

"I don't think it would matter for this. My guess is you all know it. Has your family ever been contacted by Hillside Oil & Gas?"

"Some time ago, yes. Why?"

"I'm not sure. Do you remember how long it's been?"

"At least two, maybe three years now."

"What did they want?"

"Drilling rights of some sort. We weren't interested."

"Why is that?"

"We want to farm the land, not mine it."

"Do you remember the name of the representative who talked to you?"

"Goodness no, but I can probably find his name if it's important."

"Would you mind?"

"Not at all. Will it help Archie?"

"I don't know yet."

"Only one way to find out then. I'll send you the information, Mr. Shepherd."

"Thanks."

We hung up and I found myself staring at the diagram. Geological maps, oil wells, and organic farms. I had no idea what it meant. But from the outside looking in, it didn't seem to have anything to do with the attack on Abby.

Nothing did. Which is what was driving me crazy.

~

A LITTLE AFTER LUNCHTIME, I received an email from Mrs. Mack with the contact information for Will Wellington of Hillside Oil & Gas. Honest, that was his name. I hopped online and found a bare-bones website for an independent agency which could represent you in all of your sales and acquisition needs related to oil, gas, and aggregates. Judging from the picture, Will Wellington appeared to be a man in his early forties projecting in all earnestness that he truly did want to buy or sell your oil rights.

I thought about it and decided there really wasn't a downside to calling him. So I did.

I got an automatic operator that encouraged me to press two if I wanted to speak with Mr. Wellington, which I did and got the voicemail of Will Wellington of Hillside Oil & Gas who was anxious to reconnect with me just as soon as he was available. I left a message saying who it was, that I was a lawyer, and that I was calling about some property acquisitions.

My phone buzzed three minutes later. I answered.

"Nate," he said. "This is Will Wellington of Hillside Oil & Gas. I don't think we've met before."

"No, I don't think so, Will."

"So what can I do for you? Are you representing a seller or a buyer that I've been dealing with?"

"Neither actually. I was researching a matter for a client and I saw from the title work and deeds that you've secured drilling rights on a number of sites in and around Ash County over the last few years."

"I have." Will's tone was still warm but even through the phone I could hear his caution. "We've been fortunate enough to work with folks all over southern Michigan."

"None of them mention price terms though."

"No, we aren't obligated to file those numbers. That's pretty sensitive information as you might imagine."

"I can. Can you tell me what some of the standard terms are?"

His tone cooled. "I'm sorry, Nate, I can't discuss anything about any of our partners' deals or interests or negotiations."

"How about whether a site was a potential acquisition site?"

The phone became downright frigid. "That information is even more sensitive." Then he warmed up. "Unless you represent a landowner in the area? I'd be happy to take a look at their site or come out and walk their property to get a feel for it."

I wasn't prepared to go that far yet. Plus, it wasn't true; I didn't represent the Macks on this. "No, I'm sorry, I don't. I was just doing some research on another matter."

"Then I'm sorry, Nate, the oil business is a tough one and the lease acquisition business is even tougher. I can't talk about any deal before it's done and even afterwards I still can't talk about it."

"I understand."

"You're a local guy though?"

"I am. My office is in Carrefour."

"Well, if you ever have a client who wants to sell oil rights or if you need someone to assess them for you, please keep my number and give me a call. I'd be happy to help anytime."

"Thanks, Will. I appreciate it."

"No problem. Sorry I can't be more help."

We hung up.

I hadn't learned much from that at all. I was feeling like a spaghetti flinger, standing in the middle of my office whipping noodles around.

I decided to keep on flinging. I got back on the computer, printed out what I needed, and made another call. After being passed from a receptionist to a secretary to a grad assistant to a personal assistant, I was able to secure an appointment with Dr. Elias Timmons, LGL University Professor of Geology and the man credited with creating the illustration that was attached to the lease filing that Olivia and Danny had found.

I got in the car and headed to the University.

18

I don't know what I was expecting in Professor Timmons' office —dusty rocks, a carving hammer, antique maps. It was nothing like that. Instead, I found a neat, well-lit space with sleek metallic furniture, a glass top desk that was almost entirely clean, and a three-monitor computer setup that an air traffic controller would envy. He sprang up from his desk and came around, offering his hand.

"Mr. Shepherd, please come in. So nice to meet you."

Professor Timmons was in his late forties. He wore tan pants and a blue patterned blazer that appeared to be made of finely tailored wool. He was lean and his hair was a neatly trimmed brown. Like the office, he was not what I was expecting. He looked more like a company president than a man who taught students about the composition of rocks.

"Nice to meet you too, Professor Timmons," I said. He gestured and I took a seat in front of his desk. "I'm surprised you could get me in today."

"Are you kidding?" he said. "I'm a big fan."

That, as you might imagine, is not something a lawyer normally hears. "Really?"

"Of course. I followed the Braggi case and the Vila case. Matthew Beckman is a colleague of mine here at the University, so it was interesting to follow his testimony."

"That's right Dr. Beckman's office is in this section of campus, isn't it?"

"It's a couple of buildings over but we run into each other from time to time. So," he leaned forward, eyes bright. "What can I do for you? Are you looking for an expert on something?"

"Nothing so glamorous I'm afraid," I said and pulled out my copy of the diagram. "This was attached to some documents I reviewed recently. I don't know what it means and I saw your name on the bottom. Since you're right here in town, I thought I'd see if you could tell me about it."

I saw what I took to be disappointment in his face, then curiosity, then a moment of hesitation as he pulled out a set of no-frame reading glasses and put them on. He frowned and squinted for a moment before his face cleared and he said, "This is an illustration from one of my textbooks."

"I see. So you didn't make it for a particular landowner?"

"No, no, this is from a text about the geology of the State of Michigan. Are you familiar with it?"

I shook my head. "I'm afraid most of my higher education went toward reading and useless Socratic reasoning skills."

Professor Timmons smiled. "It all depends on the arena we know, doesn't it? I'm sure Mr. Braggi was glad that he didn't have a geologist defending him."

"So this is an excerpt from your book?"

Professor Timmons nodded. "It is. It's actually part of a series of illustrations where we dig down layer by layer through Michigan's strata and substrata. See, what this doesn't show you are the moraines closer to the surface. The Kalamazoo Moraine extends from Hastings, southeast through Marshall, over to Devil's Lake where it connects with..." He took off his reading glasses and looked a little sheepish before he grinned. "I find moraines to be terribly interesting."

I smiled. "My dad always told me that you should never apologize for your enthusiasms."

"He sounds like a wise man." Professor Timmons pointed at the illustration with his glasses. "Anyway, this one shows layers that are deeper down, that were created by the plate tectonics of the area. Far older. Like I said, not really as interesting as some of the other areas, more important as a knowledge base for my students than anything else." His brow furrowed. "What was this attached to again?"

I chose my words carefully. "I was looking at a property description for a client. This was attached to a lease description and I didn't know what it meant, so I didn't want to make a decision without knowing what exactly it was doing in the title work."

Professor Timmons nodded. "I'm not sure why they would've attached this. What this shows is the types of formations that are typical for the area. It shouldn't matter at all for your metes and bounds or other surface measurements."

"I see. So this was just a form that someone used from your book?"

Professor Timmons cocked his head to the side. "A lawyer might say that it is a piece of my intellectual property that someone stole from my book and used without paying me."

"That lawyer would be right. People are pretty lax with copyright these days."

Professor Timmons shook his head. "The Internet's only made it worse."

"That's the truth. So you didn't do this as a special project? Someone just took your illustration?"

Professor Timmons nodded. "For whatever good it would do. Like I said, the moraines are more interesting. I see more people who want to learn about those so they can find places to search for diamonds or pan for gold."

"In Michigan?"

"More than you would think but less than would make it worthwhile."

"Right." Which summed up my day. I stood. "This was very generous of you, Professor Timmons. I really appreciate you taking the time to see me today."

"Anytime, Nate. May I call you Nate?"

"Of course."

He pumped my hand. "Any geology angles in your current cases?"

I thought. "It doesn't look like it."

"Well, if you ever need an expert on rock formations—"

I pointed at him. "Or moraines."

He smiled. "Or moraines, you know who to call."

"I certainly do. Thanks, Professor. Take care."

"My pleasure. You too."

I started to leave then held the diagram out to him, offering it.

"Good Lord, no," he said. "I have fifty students buying that book this semester alone. Keep it."

I waved it. "Thanks," I said, and left.

Yet another noodle had fallen off the wall.

I sighed. It was that awkward spot that was too early to go home and too late to go back to the office, so I set out for the Brickhouse.

~

WHEN I WALKED into the gym, Olivia was standing behind the front desk. She looked up, a slight smile on her face. "A little early, isn't it?"

I shrugged. "I worked really hard today."

She smirked. "I bet."

"Don't tell my dad I said that."

"No promises."

"I saw the map that you and Danny put together. That was a lot of work."

"Like you'd know."

"Probably not. Thanks anyway."

"You're welcome. Did it help?"

"Some. You know that illustration that was attached?"

"To the old lease? Yeah."

"I went and saw the guy who made it."

Olivia was curious so I described my visit with Professor Timmons. When I was done, she said, "You're thinking."

"What makes you say that?"

"I smell smoke."

"It's not me. Probably just the brimstone from when you left home this morning. No, I'm thinking about what Abby told me her attacker said before he hit her. Something about gas and the Skip-N-Go."

Olivia nodded. "The man said 'More gas than the Albion Skip-N-Go.'"

I raised an eyebrow.

"It was in the report too."

"She mentioned it to me when I met with her. I'd discounted it but now there seems to be some gas interests around the farm so..."

"So maybe there's something related. Good point."

"As long as I'm flinging pasta, I might as well check."

"What?"

"Never mind."

She shook her head and waved. "Go work out, would you?"

"Going to coach me?"

"No, thanks. Just ate."

"What if I need coaching?

"Pick a heavy thing up. Set it down. Repeat."

"What was that last step?"

"Goodbye."

I finished my workout an hour later. I didn't see Olivia puke at the sight of it, but I can't say that she didn't either. By the time I was done, though, I'd decided what to do next.

I was going to Albion.

19

Albion is a small town that sits right on I-94. It's west of Jackson and east of Battle Creek right before you hit Marshall. None of that means a thing to you unless you're from southern Michigan. If you are, you probably know that Albion is a small town whose main industry is Albion College, home of the Britons. If you're not, it's enough to know that it sits on a major US interstate that's forty-five minutes north of Carrefour and that there's no direct route between the two.

I drove through country that was mostly rolling hills, woods, and farmland on winding roads that seemed to have no intention of taking me directly anywhere. I was traversing the western edge of the Irish Hills, which meant that there were lakes everywhere, forcing the roads around them. As always, I had to be careful of deer, although, frankly, there wasn't much to do about it if one shot out on the road.

I followed one back road after another until I hit Business I-94 and took that to an offramp of I-94 itself. There, at the Albion exit, I pulled into one of three gas stations, the big truck stop that advertised two restaurants, showers, and the lowest diesel prices anywhere.

The Albion Skip-N-Go.

I wove through the rows of diesel pumps and long parking spaces filled with trucks to one of the regular pumps and gassed up. When I was done, I pulled forward into one of the parking spaces by the store and went in to get some coffee. A woman with a lot of earrings and a healthy scorn for my age and life choices took my money. I grabbed a seat at a table, drank my coffee, and looked around. It really didn't look any different from any other all-service gas station that could be found anywhere along I-75 from Michigan to Florida.

I sat there and finished my coffee and didn't have an epiphany. I wasn't sure what I was expecting, maybe a big sign with an arrow that said, "Clues to Attempted Murder Here," but I didn't see one. I got up, bought another coffee, and was making my way out to the car when I saw a rack of brochures. It was the typical faux wood holder containing brochures for all sorts of local attractions, ranging from Stagecoach Stop to a mysterious location of visual contradictions where water flowed uphill. I saw brochures to the Michigan International Speedway, a local carry out, a bait shop, and a boat rental agency. Filling up the entire top row were applications for Skip-N-Go cards. There was one for everyone—The Trucker Pay-Back Program, the Frequent Fueler Program, and the Coffee Rewards Program, which gave you a free coffee for every ten you bought. I picked up the Frequent Fueler application and opened it. I saw an ad for all of the amazing things you could buy with your Skip-N-Go points and a list of gas stations where you could earn them. It looked like there were six or seven different brands, all of which had some derivative of "Go" in them, but that's not what caught my attention. What caught my attention was the line at the bottom.

Skip-N-Go. Part of the Hillside Oil & Gas family of companies.

I stared at that for a moment. Then I tapped the brochure on my hand and left.

I had more work to do. It was time to dig deeper into the Mack farm and the time Hillside Oil & Gas had tried to put a well on it.

OIL

20

The next day at the office, I told Danny about my trip to Albion the night before and the potential link of the station to Hillside Oil & Gas. Then I said, "We have two big problems that I can see."

"That's less than usual," said Danny.

"Funny. First, we have no explanation for what really happened that night. None. Abby can't identify who pushed her and Archie has admitted that he went to the concert but has no explanation for what he was doing back in that part of the Quarry where Abby was attacked. The video has to give us a clue. Have you found anything yet?"

Danny seemed pained just by the mention of it. "I'm about a third of the way through."

"That's all?"

"Four cameras. Thousands of people milling around. Looking for any little thing. Yes, Nate, that's all."

"I just thought you'd be farther."

I watched an act of supreme will happen before my eyes. "That's as far as I've gotten, Nate."

"Fortunately, we still have some time before trial. I'll help."

Danny brightened. "Reviewing the video? Good, that'll cut the time in half."

"No, I mean I'll help investigate that side of it. I'm going to arrange another meeting with Abby and her lawyer."

"That's cruel."

"What?"

"Never mind."

"We also need to focus on Hillside Oil & Gas."

"What's its role?"

"That's just it, I'm not sure. But we know it's been buying up leases in Ash County, it offered one to the Macks, and it owns the gas station Abby's attacker mentioned."

"So what does that mean?"

"I don't know. But there has to be a connection."

"So what's next? Other than me sitting in a sunless room ruining my eyes."

"I think I'm going to see the Macks again."

"That sounds like you're going to go drive around and talk."

"I am. It's very difficult."

Danny stood. "Well, I'm not going to go nearsighted just sitting here. I'll be in my office."

"Thanks. I'll give your regards to the great outdoors."

"Talk to you."

I made a call and then, just after lunchtime, I was on my way to see Mrs. Mack.

∾

MRS. MACK OPENED the screen door of the Mack home before I could knock.

"Mr. Shepherd," she said. "Come in, come in. Now I hope you like coffee because I just put some on." She kept talking as she guided me in. "People always ask, Susanna how can you drink coffee in the afternoon, doesn't it keep you awake? But I think that just means one of two things; either you're not waking up early enough or you're not working hard enough. How about you, Mr. Shepherd?"

"I'm pretty much a coffee all day kinda guy."

"I knew I liked you," she said. "And how are you with cookies?"

"No. Thank you, though."

She tsk'd. "That's probably because you buy them in a plastic box at the grocery store. What about real cookies?"

"I'm sorry, Mrs. Mack, I'm just not much of a cookie eater."

She led me into what I'd think of as a traditional farmhouse —original wood floors, authentic plaster work—but bright, with plenty of light from windows that allowed a view of the fields. I saw a combine running not fifty yards away, which I assumed was Mr. Mack. "Now you have a seat and I'll be right back."

I sat.

Mrs. Mack walked out with a cup of coffee for me (hers was already on the table) and a plate of the thickest, most fragrant chocolate chip cookies I'd ever been around. The chips looked like they were still melting.

I smiled at Mrs. Mack. "It appears that I am just prejudiced against store-bought cookies," and took one.

Mrs. Mack beamed. "That's better." Her face turned serious. "I'm glad you called, Mr. Shepherd. Before we start, I have to say I'm very concerned."

"About Archie? That's totally normal in this situation."

"Of course, about Archie, yes. No, I meant I'm concerned about what's happened with his case."

I searched my mind. "Nothing's happened with his case, Mrs. Mack."

"That's my point, Mr. Shepherd. That's what concerns me."

Mrs. Mack wasn't my client. But my client's family needed a

little assurance. "I know it doesn't seem like it Mrs. Mack, but there is. When I say nothing's happened, I mean there haven't been any court filings. This is the stage when we're investigating. It may not seem like a lot, but we are running down every angle on this thing."

"Are you?"

There's no way Mrs. Mack would know so, as frustrating as it was for me to hear, it was a fair question. "Yes."

"I don't know that the farm will survive without him, Mr. Shepherd."

"I understand."

"And I don't know that he will survive without the farm."

"I understand, Mrs. Mack."

Mrs. Mack held her coffee cup in two hands and took a sip. When she lowered it, her face was back to that of a cheerful friend serving cookies. "So what can I do for you?"

"I have some questions about the farm."

"Okay."

"You mentioned that Hillside Oil & Gas approached you at one point about putting an oil well on the farm?"

"Right."

"Do you know exactly when that was?"

Mrs. Mack frowned a little. "Oh, I want to say it was about three years ago."

I did the math. "So the same year that someone sprayed the fertilizer on your land?"

"I guess it would have been, yes."

"Was the offer before or after your crops were sprayed?"

Mrs. Mack thought. "Well, the wedding was in June, Wisconsin is so beautiful in June, and I want to say that Hillside approached us right as we were going into the harvest. So it would have to been after. Why?"

I ignored her question. "Who did the oil company talk to?"

Mrs. Mack straightened. "I handle the business side of the farms."

"Did you ever think seriously about accepting it?"

"The drilling lease? Not really. Not by harvest time anyway."

"And Will Wellington was the man you dealt with?"

"He was," Mrs. Mack chuckled. "Once I saw the card I remembered. A man looking to lease drilling rights for oil wells named Wellington. It tickled me at the time. Still does."

I smiled. "Why didn't you think about accepting it? Weren't you in trouble with the organic problem?"

"At the beginning of the season, we thought so. It wasn't clear then how we were going to make it. And honestly if Archie and Hamish hadn't put in so much extra time for us, I don't know if we would have. But because of the weather, and because of their work, we had our best crop in years and really didn't have to think about taking the oil money by the time harvest rolled around."

"Was Hillside offering a lot? You don't have to tell me the amount, just relatively speaking."

"Certainly enough that we wouldn't have had to worry about our harvest that year."

"So why not take it?"

"When you farm for generations, Mr. Shepherd, you don't just dump it because of an offer from an oil salesman."

"But the money..."

"Can't buy organic food unless someone grows it."

I smiled. "I suppose that's true. Did you meet with Mr. Wellington often?"

"I want to say three or four times over the course of a couple of weeks? He was insistent, but once he saw we weren't really interested, he let up. Probably didn't contact us more than once a month or so after that."

"He still kept in contact though?"

She nodded. "For the better part of a year. And then it sort of trickled away and I didn't hear from him again."

"Do you know if any of your neighbors signed a lease with Hillside?"

Mrs. Mack shook her head. "Not that I know of. But it only takes up five or ten acres of space, so we might not notice it."

"Do you have any documents that show when he was contacting you?"

"Well, we never saw an agreement or anything like that."

"How about emails or letters? That show the discussions were happening."

She thought. "I do believe I received a couple of emails confirming times for calls. And maybe one appointment over coffee."

"Would you mind printing copies for me?"

"Not at all. Mr. Shepherd, does this have something to do with my son's case?"

The look Mrs. Mack gave me wasn't just a concerned mother asking after her son; it was a shrewd businesswoman who managed a multi-million dollar concern assessing a contractor.

I decided to be blunt. "I'm not sure. But I think it might."

"Then I'll get what I have. It won't take but a minute. More than enough time for another cookie. Come on."

She led me into the kitchen where there was a small nook with a table and cubby holes built into the wall like the teachers' mail slots at a school office. It was neat and it was organized and looked to be filled with papers. She sat down, went into her email and within moments a printer started.

"Looks like I had three," she said. Moments later, she was handing them to me. "Here you go."

"Thanks, Mrs. Mack."

"I hope it helps." There was a deep concern in her eyes, but that was all she said.

I held up my empty cup. "And thanks for the coffee." I started to rinse my cup in the sink.

Mrs. Mack smiled. "I'll wash that, Mr. Shepherd. But my compliments to your mother. Now,"—she pulled out a covered plate of cookies—"I've packed these up for you and I don't want to hear any objections."

I heard a screen door clatter shut and just then Hamish Mack walked into the kitchen. A good-natured smile turned into a scowl and a puffed chest as he saw me, stopped, and said, "What are you doing here?"

"Don't be rude, Hamish," Mrs. Mack said.

"What's he doing here, Mom?"

"Talking to me."

Hamish looked at the papers I was holding. "Wait, you're *helping* him?"

"What do you want, Hamish?"

"You need to go," he said to me.

Mrs. Mack practically slammed the plate of cookies into my gut. "Last time I checked, this is *my* house."

"You shouldn't be helping this lawyer help Archie."

"The land *I* gave you for your house is a quarter mile up the road. Go back to it."

Hamish adjusted his No Weed Seed hat and clenched his jaw and looked ready to throw a punch all at once. "Why can't you see it?!"

"I'm not the one with the vision problem, Son. Go."

"You don't understand. If you'd heard…" He bit off the last words, adjusted his hat, and said, "I need Dad's pump."

"It's not in this kitchen."

Hamish turned and left.

"I'm sorry, Mr. Shepherd."

"Don't worry about it."

"He's so angry."

"I would be too."

"He really believes Archie did it."

"I can see that."

"They fought that very first day at the hospital when Archie came to visit. Security had to take Archie away, it was terrible."

I'd heard about the fight but made a connection I hadn't before. "Wait, the first day at the hospital?"

"Yes. She was still in surgery, I think."

"Why did they fight?"

"Because Hamish thought Archie had done it."

"Right, but why? How could Hamish know to be mad? Archie hadn't been arrested yet."

Mrs. Mack shook her head. "I don't know. It must have been something the police said."

I nodded, but it didn't sound right. I held up the cookies. "Thanks, Mrs. Mack."

"You can keep the plate."

I said goodbye and left. I took the scenic route home.

I didn't notice any oil wells on other farms around the Mack property.

21

I called to check in with Danny on my way back.

"We got some news today," he said.

"That doesn't sound good."

"It's not. The DNA came back on the blood."

"And?"

"It matches Archie."

"That's the blood from the railing?"

"Right at the top of the stairs."

"That's pretty damning."

"It is."

I thought. "In some ways though, it doesn't change anything. We already have the video showing him coming and going."

"Except the blood proves he went right where Abby went down."

"As opposed to?"

"As opposed to just walking by and not noticing the stairs at all."

"You are one optimistic guy."

"I learned from the best."

"You're also right."

"I learned that on my own."

"Good thing you're a self-starter, it'll come in handy with that video you're watching."

There was a mutter at the other end before we hung up. I'm sure it was just our connection.

I decided it was time to compare notes with Olivia.

~

I STOPPED by Olivia's office at the gym on the way back. I told her about what Mrs. Mack had said about the offer from Hillside Oil coming in just a couple of months after the crop sabotage.

"That can't be a coincidence," Olivia said.

"It does seem a little too fortunate. My guess is that Hillside knew the Macks were struggling and knew they might resist putting a well in. So they have someone sneak in, knock the Macks' plans off by a couple of years, maybe even force them under. Now they're willing to deal on the oil lease, maybe even for a lower price."

Olivia nodded. "Except that it doesn't work out that way."

"Right. The oilman doesn't know that the Macks are having a perfect growing season and that the chemicals just put them over the top. And he doesn't know that Hamish and Archie will work their asses off to make sure their parents don't go under."

She was right with me. "So, Hillside makes the offer, but now instead of a position of weakness, Mr. and Mrs. Mack are in a position of strength and can tell him no."

"And it doesn't get the well."

The two of us sat there, thinking.

"It would have to be a pretty big find for the oil company to risk all that, wouldn't it?" Olivia said after a while.

I shrugged. "I suppose you have to drill where the oil is."

"That's just it." Olivia turned toward her monitors. "It doesn't seem like there's any there."

"What do you mean?"

She clicked away and pulled something up. "I've been checking that end of it too, so I looked for a map of oil wells in southern Michigan, just to see."

"Didn't you already do that?"

She shook her head. "I looked up leases. This time I looked up the wells themselves."

"Did you find something?"

"I'm not sure." She clicked, then pointed. "Here."

I came around the desk and Olivia scooted her chair to the side and tilted her monitor toward me. It was a map of Michigan with oil and natural gas wells marked on it, a green dot for an oil well and a red dot for gas. The first thing that jumped out was a huge slash of red across the upper part of the state. There were so many red dots that it looked like a broad redline stretching from Traverse City to Alpena.

I pointed. "So that's natural gas?"

"Yes."

"I had no idea we had so many."

"Me either," said Olivia. "But look at this."

She pointed at a thin green line of oil wells with red dots of natural gas scattered about it. It ran diagonally through three counties in the middle of southern lower Michigan.

I oriented myself. "That's north and east of the Mack place," I said.

"By some miles. So it doesn't seem like the Macks are part of whatever that is. And see all this white space around it? I think it's empty."

"So looking at this, it doesn't seem like the Mack place would be a candidate for an oil lease at all."

"Right."

We stared.

"So what does it mean?" Olivia said.

"I'm not sure," I said. "But I know someone we could ask."

I pulled out my phone and scrolled to a number that I'd only used once, but which the man had insisted I take. Surprisingly, he picked up right away and said certainly he had time to see me, how about this afternoon? I said that would be just fine, hung up, and said to Olivia, "Professor of Geology Elias Timmons would be happy to see me today."

"I'm going too."

"I'll drive."

"Let's go," she said, and we left.

~

WHEN WE ARRIVED at the office of Elias Timmons, his secretary led us straight back and, as we walked through the door, he was already standing, hand extended.

"Mr. Shepherd, it's a pleasure to see—"

Professor Timmons stopped dead. I'm around Olivia so much that sometimes I forget the effect that a fitness fanatic with spiked, bleached-white hair, half-mirrored glasses, and a tattooed sleeve running down the length of her left forearm has on people.

I chuckled. "Professor Timmons, I hope you don't mind, I brought an associate of mine, Olivia Brickson. She's been helping me with some of my research."

Professor Timmons smiled and extended his hand. He was dressed once again in a fine wool blazer and slacks, this time a checked blue, that still seemed more like someone out of the corporate world than the collegiate one. "It's my pleasure, Ms. Brickson. Please, please, come in. Did Sheila offer you anything?"

"I'm fine, Professor Timmons, thanks," I said.

"Me too," said Olivia. "Thanks though."

"Certainly," he said. "And it's Eli, please."

I noticed that he hadn't told me to call him Eli the last time I was there.

"Thank you, Eli," said Olivia with a smile.

"So, Mr. Shepherd." Professor Timmons leaned forward, his eyes bright. "Did a case come up?"

"Not exactly," I said. "We've been looking at a map and we're not sure what it means. I told Olivia that you might be able to help explain it to us."

He smiled at her. "I certainly hope so. What does it involve?"

"Not moraines, I'm afraid."

"You can't have everything, I suppose."

"Oil and gas. We need help with a map."

He frowned. "That's not really my area."

"Mine either, but it seemed close enough to the illustration in your textbook that I thought you could help."

He glanced at Olivia, straightened, and smiled. "Well then, why don't you show me what you have."

We pulled out the full color map of Michigan with its green dots for oil wells and red dots for gas wells. Professor Timmons turned the map toward him and said, "So we're talking about Michigan again, I see. Okay. What you have here is a map from the State that shows the location of the active oil and gas wells in a given year."

"I didn't know Michigan was that big of an oil and gas state," said Olivia.

"More than you'd think," said Professor Timmons. He scowled in thought as he ran his finger over the map, scanning its contents, before he looked up and smiled. "So what did you want to know?"

"Can you tell if there's going to be oil on land before you drill?"

He smiled. "If you knew that, you'd be a very rich man, or woman, indeed. This isn't my specialty, you know my thing about moraines, but companies have become pretty good at figuring out the sort of formations that have a good chance of holding oil. Whether they actually hit it..." He shrugged. "Usually the best indicator is another producing well nearby."

I leaned over and pointed at the line of green wells that extended north and east of the Mack property. "Like this?"

Professor Timmons nodded. "The Albion-Skip-N-Go Trend. Exactly like that."

I blinked. "The what?"

"The Albion Skip-N-Go Trend."

I wasn't sure I was hearing him correctly. "The gas station?"

Professor Timmons stared at me now. "What are you talking about?"

"The Albion Skip-N-Go? The gas station in Albion on I-94?"

Professor Timmons' brow furrowed and then he laughed. "No, no, no. Albion-Scipio. S-C-I-P-I-O. It's the name of the interconnected formations that created the trend you see here."

Between names I didn't understand, trends, and maps, I was jealous of Olivia's reflective glasses. I finally just shook my head and said, "I'm sorry, Professor Timmons, I really don't understand what you're talking about."

Professor Timmons waved his hand. "Of course you don't. I'm starting from the middle. Do you see this line of oil wells?" He pointed at the green line we'd been talking about northeast of the Mack Farm.

"I do."

"That's called the Albion-Scipio Trend. It's not one big field. Instead, it's a series of narrow oilfields that run together. Most of them are less than a mile wide. When you put them all together, it creates a 'trend.'"

"So the individual fields are small?" said Olivia.

"I think narrow is a better word. Small makes you think these aren't productive."

"They are?" I said.

Professor Timmons nodded. "The first of these was discovered in the 1950s. It outproduced any other field that had been discovered in the State before then."

I remembered a recent case of mine. "Is this fracking?"

Professor Timmons shook his head. "No. That's one of the things that makes them so productive. There are hundreds of regular flowing wells along this Trend that don't require fracking at all."

"And these wells are still producing?" Olivia asked.

"I'm not sure. I think so."

"Are they still looking for new wells?"

He shrugged. "I'm sorry, I just know the rocks. I don't know how things are being developed now. You'll probably have to ask an oil man about that."

I planned on it. "Okay, so from a rocks perspective, is this Albion-Scipio Trend limited to what we can see here?" I pointed at the green line.

Professor Timmons pursed his lips and studied the map. "My understanding is that its area is pretty well-defined. See these?" He indicated a series of yellow dots all around the Trend. "These are dry holes. You can see where they tried to drill just outside the Trend and came up with nothing."

"So what about over here?" I put my finger on the spot on the map where the Mack farm would be. "Would property here be part of the Trend?"

Professor Timmons' frown deepened and, eventually, he shook his head. "Remember, the Trend is only a little over a mile wide. You're miles away, south and west, there. That land wouldn't be part of the Albion-Scipio Trend at all. You can see the yellow dots around there too."

"But what if I were an aggressive oilman?" I said. "Would it be worth trying to drill in these areas?"

He smiled. "You'd have to ask an aggressive oilman. I'm the rocks guy."

We all stared at the map for another moment before Professor Timmons said, "So does this have something to do with one of your cases?"

I shook my head. "It doesn't look like it."

"A landowner then?"

My thoughts were on trends and dry holes and mispronunciations. "Hmm? Oh, no. I know someone who encountered some interest once but it was some time ago. Nothing recent."

"They probably found this map in the meantime. So nothing I can help with, on a case?"

"I think that's it, Professor."

Professor Timmons looked disappointed. "Ah, well. Maybe next time."

I stood and said, "I really appreciate you meeting with us today."

Professor Timmons practically sprang to his feet and smiled. "Of course. And remember if you ever need a geologist on one of your cases..."

I smiled. "I know one who is rock solid."

Oliva winced.

"You certainly do. Ms. Brickson,"—he shook her hand—"it was certainly a pleasure to meet you. I don't know if you ever need the services of a geologist, but please don't hesitate to call me."

"Thanks, Eli," she said, and Professor Timmons' smile broadened when she used his first name.

We were on the way out when Olivia stopped and pointed at his credenza. "That's beautiful. What is it?"

A polished stone the size of a fist sat on a small pedestal on his shelf. It was a stunning blue. "Ah, it's lapis lazuli." Professor Timmons hustled around to the shelf. "The symphony gave it to me for being a Premier Patron." He pointed at some engraving on the pedestal. "It's getting harder and harder for them to survive. If music wasn't written in the last five years, people don't want to hear it."

Next to the symphony gift, a rough white and gray stone was suspended in a glass case. "And what's that?" I said.

"That's an uncut diamond."

I peered closer at the engraving on the bottom. "The Diamond Mine?"

Professor Timmons smiled. "It's a casino over near Dowagiac. A man found a diamond about that size back in the 1800s."

"My brother and sister-in-law were just talking about that, said they went on a casino trip that had diamond hunting as part of the package."

Professor Timmons nodded. "When the glaciers covered Michigan, they pushed all sorts of things down here, including diamonds, so that when they retreated and the moraines were left..." He stopped, looking a little embarrassed. "I'm doing it again."

"No, it's interesting," said Olivia.

"Not to most people. My wife and I will go over for a weekend sometimes and talk to groups or show them what an uncut diamond would look like if they found one. The casino gave me that as a gift."

"Do people find any?"

"No. But they have a great time at the casino and I get to look at moraines up close. It's a fun trip. If either of you are ever interested, in the casino trip or the symphony, my wife and I would love to have you as our guests."

"Thanks, Eli," Olivia said.

Professor Timmons beamed.

"And if I ever need that moraines expert..." I shook his hand.

"You absolutely know who to call."

With that, the two of us walked out of the office and then a short time later, the Earth Sciences building.

"Rock solid?" Olivia said as we left.

"That kind of humor is the bedrock of daily interaction."

"Jesus."

"You don't have to be so crusty about it."

"You might want to save that for the geology convention."

"I'm ready to take up that mantle."

She sighed.

As we got to the Jeep, I said, "So, what do you think? Could Abby have heard Albion-Scipio instead of Albion Skip-N-Go?"

"You confused the two, and you hadn't just tumbled down a flight of stairs."

I shook my head. "I've lived here all my life and never heard that name. Who in the world besides a geologist has ever heard of the Albion-Scipio Trend?"

"I'd bet an oilman has."

I nodded. "Especially one who has negotiated leases in the area."

Olivia nodded and pulled a strand of her bangs down around her glasses. "What's next?"

"I think there's a prosecutor we want to compare notes with."

22

We went back to my office and gave T. Marvin Stritch a call from the conference room. He answered right away.

"Nate, you got my disclosure about the DNA?"

"So I've been told."

"I sent you the summary report. You'll have the full report by the end of the day."

"Great. Thanks."

"I assume you called to start discussions about a plea deal then. We can offer—"

"No, T. Marvin. I called to see if you would slow things down in light of some new information."

Silence. Then, "What are you talking about?"

This was a risk but, when in doubt, sometimes the best course is to just put it out there for the other side without any lawyer layers on it. So I did. I told him about the sabotage to the Mack's farm and the inconclusive investigation. I told him how Hillside Oil had come calling shortly after and that the Macks had rejected its offer. I told him that Hillside Oil had been able to buy drilling rights all up and down that part of the county but not in the Macks' corner.

There was more silence before T. Marvin Stritch said, "Nate, I don't see how that's relevant at all."

"Do you remember Abby Ackerman's statement?"

"Of course."

"What she said her attacker said before he tried to kill her?"

"Yes." There was a pause, then, "She heard him say 'It has more gas than the Albion Skip-N-Go.'"

"That's right."

"So?"

"So, we've since learned that there's an oil field, excuse me an oil trend, called the Albion-Scipio not far from here."

"And?"

"And it's one of the richest oil finds in lower Michigan."

"I'm still not seeing the relevance here, Nate."

"It just seems that that fact is something that a representative of an oil company, like say Hillside Oil & Gas, would know."

"There is no evidence that there was anyone other than your client on the stairs with Abby Ackerman that night."

"Actually, there's no evidence that my client was on the stairs *with* Abby that night at all, there's just evidence that he was there at some point. Look, I'm not asking you to drop the case, yet, T. Marvin. I'm just saying maybe it should slow down so you can check these things out. Just to make sure."

There was the smallest pause then T. Marvin Stritch spoke in crisp, quick sentences. "I appreciate your candor, Nate. Let me do you the same courtesy. We have video showing Mr. Mack going to and from the back part of the Quarry at the time of the attack. We have plenty of witnesses placing him at the concert, although I don't think most of them are necessary. We have blood on the top of the stair railing that matches his DNA with 99.978 certainty. We have video of him at the gas station immediately afterwards washing the blood off his hand and replacing his bandage. And I haven't had a chance to send you the last thing we've found because we're still finishing testing, but you've been up front with me, so I'll be up front with you."

Silence. Finally, I said, "What did you find?"

"Silk."

"Silk? Abby was wearing silk?"

"No. She was wearing cotton. It was corn silk."

"Corn silk?" I said. "The tufts of hair on the end of an ear of corn?"

"Exactly."

"So?"

"So, corn has DNA too. It doesn't take that much to send it off for testing to see if the silk matches the seed in corn that's purchased on a given farm. Say a farm in the northeast corner of Ash County."

"Are you saying the silk matches the corn in the Macks' field?"

"No, I'm saying it matches the corn in Archibald Mack's field."

Corn? I wasn't sure what was worse, the sudden possibility that my case was getting torpedoed by an ear of corn or the self-satisfaction in T. Marvin Stritch's voice as he said it. A thought occurred to me about how to address this new corn conundrum, but I decided to save it; it was clear this call wasn't going to make this case go away, or even slow down.

I had to admit that, in the face of all that, our theory did seem weaker. Except for one thing. "I'm still not hearing any motive, T. Marvin."

There was silence on the other end of the line. Then Stritch said, "Your client hasn't told you?"

There is nothing good that follows that sentence. Ever.

"Told me what?"

"I'm sorry, Nate, I assumed you knew. I told you, I'm very upfront about how I handle cases."

"Told me what, T. Marvin?"

"Your client called his brother Hamish from the back of the Quarry right before the attack. They argued."

"About what?"

"Seems like that's something you should ask your client. The important thing is that Abby was mentioned."

"How?"

"Again, that's information your client has."

I remembered Mrs. Mack mentioning that Archie and Hamish had fought at the hospital and not knowing why Hamish was mad. I think I'd just found out why.

I came to the original purpose of my call, but it sounded weak even to me as I said, "Have you considered that it could've been someone else?"

"I've been doing this a long time, Nate. Twenty years this coming November, ten of them working under Judge Wesley who was about as methodical and perceptive as they come. She used to say that when all the spokes lead to one place, you've got yourself a wheel and you need to roll with it." He paused. "Archibald Mack is Abby Ackerman's wheel."

"All I'm saying is that we should take a little time to double check."

T. Marvin Stritch's voice was pleasant but cold when he said, "I think we'll roll with it."

Then he said goodbye and we hung up.

23

Olivia and I were done for the day. Danny had left while we were on the phone with Stritch, so I locked up and drove her back to the Brickhouse. I took great delight in letting her shame me for not working out before pulling out my gym bag and walking in with her. She said she was glad that I hadn't completely lost my conscience and went to the back to teach one of her boot camp classes. I changed, and when I came out of the locker room, I saw that Cade was just getting going too.

It's hard to imagine that you can forget about a six foot four, two hundred sixty pound man but I had. Cade and I had worked out a lot together when we were younger, but now with our work schedules, it was a rare occurrence. I walked over to the bench he was setting up and said, "You just getting going?"

He nodded.

I pointed at the rack. "You want a partner today?"

"No, thanks. Sort of half-training somebody today."

I smiled. "Don't tell Olivia. She won't abide any 'half training.'"

Cade smiled. "She will not. Should've said more of an introduction to training."

I nodded. "You eating after?"

"I could eat."

"The Railcar?"

"You got it. About an hour and a half?"

"Sounds good. I'll meet you then."

Just then Danny came in the front door. He was looking around, a little lost. I made my way over.

"Hey," I said. "Looking for me?"

Danny looked a little sheepish. "No. I was looking for Cade."

I realized then that he was wearing running pants and a T-shirt instead of a suit. I smiled, put a hand on his shoulder, and said, "You're going to have to tell me how this happened."

"You remember that potential assault case Pearson was looking into against him?"

I don't know how I'd forgotten about my friend dismantling three men, but I had. "Yes."

"I got out in front of it and called Jeff Hanson over at the prosecutor's office. He took one look at the video and said there was no way he was bringing charges."

"Nice work!"

"Thanks."

"And this led to a workout...?"

Danny looked chagrined. "I made the mistake of telling Cade I was thinking about starting."

I shook my head. "Bad move, my friend."

"That's what I'm afraid of."

"It could've been worse."

"How?"

"You could've mentioned it to Olivia."

Right on cue, music and yelling started in the back of the gym.

Danny stared. "I think you may be right."

I followed his gaze to a couple of guys squatting a bunch of weight at one rack while two women absolutely killed an alternating box jump. I saw him thinking, so I said, "Everyone respects you for being here. Have fun." Then I smiled. "And just because you can't get out of bed tomorrow morning doesn't mean that you're excused from work."

Danny glanced at me sharply, then shook his head and made his way over to Cade, who shook his hand and then put him to work. I did my own thing, and I'd be lying if I said I didn't sneak a glance at him now and then.

Danny struggled here and there balancing the weight, which is common the first time, but he never stopped and he never quit and he did a great job.

$\sim$

AN HOUR AND A HALF LATER, Cade and I were sitting at the Railcar. It's a low brick building that sits on an abandoned section of track that runs alongside a creek that was once used to refill steam engines. It has an outdoor covered patio overlooking the water and the woods beyond and if that wasn't great enough, it was also home to the best barbecue in that part of the state. The sound of the stream and the smell of hickory smoke and the taste of the beer will almost always make you feel better about things.

There had been a time not too long ago in my life when it hadn't. Thankfully, it usually did now.

Cade and I had taken a table outside, ordered our food, and were one beer in when I said, "How'd Danny do?"

Cade shrugged, which was a fairly impressive feat with his shoulders. "He wasn't worried about looking stupid, so he didn't. And he was willing to try whatever I showed him." He smiled. "You might want to watch him when he sits in his chair tomorrow."

"You had to make him do squats on his first day?"

"What good is working out if you're not going to work?"

"You, sir, are a terrible person."

"Only mostly. He was good company though."

"Really? Danny doesn't usually say much with new people."

Cade nodded. "Exactly."

The waitress stopped by to let us know that our brisket was on the way and we ordered another beer to make it worth her trip. We were quiet for a moment, enjoying the last of the summer heat and the sound of the stream, when he said, "You and Liv were busy today."

I nodded. "We had a lot to follow up on." I told him about the day's events, which took until the brisket and the second beer arrived. As we dug in, I said, "Now it sounds like there was an argument between Hamish and Archie the night of the attack."

Cade raised an eyebrow.

"I don't know all of it yet, but I think they fought at the hospital too."

Cade set his fork down. "I'm beginning to think it was a mistake to bond him going back to the same property."

"Mrs. Mack's been running interference between them."

"Shep, if you were Hamish and you knew Archie had tried to kill Abby, what would stop you from going over there?"

That should have been enough. That should have been enough for me to put things together more quickly later, but it wasn't. Which I would regret.

At the time, though, I said, "He hasn't so far. Which makes me wonder if, deep down, Hamish doesn't think Archie did it either."

"He might be in denial."

"I don't think he did it, Cade."

Cade shrugged. "Guilt or innocence doesn't matter to a bondsman, Shepherd. Attendance and good behavior does."

I smiled. "Liv's got a different opinion about that."

"She's mentioned it."

We finished that conversation and our brisket and talked about nothing in particular until we were done.

24

They need a specific expression for farm early. I mean, those men and women hit the field rolling as the sun comes up, which means they're up and eating and caffeinating well before sunrise. Which in turn means that, if you need to meet with a farmer before he hits the field and you need to drive more than half an hour to get there, you're getting up at a downright inhumane hour that makes you question how men and women of sterner stuff could possibly do this every day.

Or so I've been told.

I caught Archie at his house the next day before he went out into the field. There were two things I needed to ask him about and I'd decided I wanted to see how he looked when he answered me.

"Coffee?" he said as he let me in the front door.

"Please."

He poured, we sat, and I said, "I know you have to get at it. I won't keep you long."

Archie shrugged. "If I want to stay on the field and out of... other places, I'll need to make time."

I nodded, took a sip of dark, bitter goodness, and said, "I talked to your mom about the offer from Hillside Oil & Gas."

Archie took a sip so that the mug was in front of his face as I said it. "And?" said Archie.

"Were you in favor of it?"

Archie sipped, thought, and said, "I wasn't against it, exactly. With the way our harvest had gone the years before, I thought we should consider anything that would keep our heads above water and the banks off our back."

"How about Hamish?"

"Hamish was against it."

"Why?"

"He wanted the farm to survive on its own. He thought we could do it. He certainly worked hard to help, even more than usual."

"More? I thought he farmed full time?"

"He does but his farm keeps him busy."

"His farm. Do you operate separately?"

"Sort of. Not exactly but yes. We each own our third but we operate together. You saw we share some equipment and we'll help each other for certain things. Hamish works most of his land himself and that takes all his effort. That summer, though, he did everything he could to help my parents survive. He spent as much time on their field as his own."

"I see," I said. "It's the timing of Hillside's offer that has me curious though. Your place gets sabotaged with the pesticide and two months later the oil company comes around offering up a lease that would solve your cash problems. That seems too fortunate to be a coincidence, doesn't it?"

Archie didn't look convinced. "I suppose."

"It didn't make sense to me at first, why they would do that. But then, the more I dug, the more I found that the oil company has just as much to gain from that lease as your family does. Maybe more. Do you know why?"

Archie looked at me. "Why's that, Nate?"

I paused. Then I said, "The Albion-Scipio Trend."

Archie stared. Not a blink. Not a twitch. "The what?"

"You know about those oil wells not far from your farm? Over in Hillsdale and Jackson and Calhoun counties?"

Archie's expression was neutral. "Not really."

I sipped my coffee, then shook my head. "I didn't either. I mean, I generally knew that there were oil wells here and there, but it turns out that Albion-Scipio is the name of a really rich oil find."

Archie's brow furrowed. "So?"

"Like I said, I'd never heard the name before this case. I heard it for the first time when Abby told me about it. She had heard the name while she was lying there among the rocks. The man who attacked her said it right before he tried to smash her head with a rock."

Archie winced at the description but then nodded. "Sounds like you should follow up on that then."

Nothing. No guilt, no recognition of the name, nothing. If Archie had heard of Albion-Scipio before, he was hiding it pretty well.

I nodded. "I will. Why didn't you tell me you called Hamish from the Quarry?"

Archie's coffee mug jerked. "What?"

"I got blindsided by the prosecutor yesterday. He said you called Hamish from the Quarry. And that the two of you argued."

"How could he know…"

"I assume Hamish told him."

It's hard to describe what happened to Archie's face next. One look after another flashed across his face. I saw puzzlement then realization then anger and then what I can only describe as a deep breath, a look at the ceiling, and a man gathering himself. Then he looked at me and said, "Well, that field's not going to harvest itself."

Archie's voice was a rusty croak, a combination of early morning and a man who spent all day by himself on a combine. It was gravelly and jagged, like a plow blade scraping across a buried rock.

"What did you argue about?"

Archie stood. "The farm."

"What about it?"

Archie dumped the last of his coffee into the sink. "Nothing that has a thing to do with Abby. Thanks for coming up."

"Archie! The prosecutor thinks he has a motive from the call."

Archie set his mug aside and pulled on his Mack Farms cap. "We argued about the farm, Nate, and it was between him and me. It had nothing to do with Abby. You can let yourself out."

And just like that, Archie left. I was still standing there when his big red barn door opened, spilling light into a world that was still half an hour away from dawn.

I poured another cup of coffee. I watched Archie prepare his rig and then make his way out into the field. I was convinced he didn't know anything about Albion-Scipio and I was just as convinced that he wasn't telling me the whole truth about his brother.

I drank about half a cup until the remainder was less scalding than I liked. Then I dumped the coffee, rinsed the cup, and put it in the dishwasher before I walked out the front door.

My mom would have been proud.

∼

I TOOK my time getting back to the office and was still there an hour and a half early, so I was on my second cup of coffee when Olivia came through the door.

"I talked to Archie this morning," I said.

She stopped. "That's early for you."

"No kidding. How do you do it by the way? I'm starving."

"I told you, the Cast Iron Kitchen. There's a spot for you at my table every morning at four-thirty."

"Good Lord."

"So, Archie?"

I shook my head. "I'm convinced he'd never heard the word Albion-Scipio before."

"Okay."

"But he reacted when I mentioned the call with Hamish."

"What did he say?"

"He seemed madder that Hamish had said something than anything else. Then he wouldn't tell me what the fight was about, just that it involved the farm." I shook my head. "There's something going on with those two. Besides our case, I mean."

Olivia crossed her arms. "I suppose one explanation is that he did it and he's afraid anything he says will provide evidence against him."

"Maybe. But I don't think so."

"Me either. I'll let you work. Danny in soon?"

"Should be."

"I'll tell him myself and see how it fits with what he's doing."

"Okay. Thanks."

Just then, I heard the rustlings of Danny entering the office and called him in. Danny staggered in on legs as stiff as stilts. Two evil people chuckled.

"Have a seat," I said.

Danny made a face, came around to the front of the chair, and started to lower himself. He made it about three inches before he winced and dropped the rest of the way into the cushions.

I smiled. "Isn't that better?"

"No."

I filled Danny in on what I'd told Olivia and, seated and intent on the case, Danny's enthusiasm returned. When I was done, I said, "Have you done any more work on the oil leases?"

Danny shook his head. "I've mostly been working on the video."

"When you need a break, I need you to look up how many oil leases have been filed since Archie and Hamish got their land from Mr. and Mrs. Mack."

"For how big an area?"

"All three counties that Albion-Scipio is in and in Ash County."

I expected a sigh but instead Danny gave me a nod and said, "I think I have most of the raw data already so I'll just have to match up the dates. Do you think it matters?"

"I'm not sure."

"So you want me to drill down on that?" said Danny.

"Like a wildcat," said Olivia.

"Very funny."

"I have a whole reservoir of them," said Danny.

"I'm sensing a trend here," said Olivia.

I sighed.

"An endless well of humor," said Danny.

"It's fracking hilarious," said Olivia.

"You can leave now, Danny." I smiled. "I'll wait."

Danny started to push himself up, winced, and dropped back into the chair. "I think I might work right here today."

"You need your computer."

He rocked forward, then stopped.

That was softness of a kind that Olivia would not tolerate.

She grabbed him by the arm and yanked him to his feet. Danny yelped—actually yelped—then nodded.

"Come on," Olivia said.

She looked back at me and smiled. She might have winked, but I couldn't tell behind the glasses. I chuckled and got back to work.

25

When we'd divided up responsibility in the case, I'd taken charge of investigating the site. I decided it was time to take another look. I gave Kirby a call to make sure he was in and drove out to Century Quarry.

It was evening late in the season so there weren't many swimmers and sunbathers making their way out when I got there. Kirby let me in and said I couldn't make a big scene around the patio because they had a fortieth birthday party going on but that I was free to check out the amphitheater and the back stairs.

I didn't think the amphitheater where Big Luke had played would tell me much, so I didn't go over there. Instead, I decided to retrace the route Abby had taken around the Quarry to the abandoned stairs.

I walked through the courtyard, past the concessions and the restrooms, and around the east side of the Quarry to the beach and the swimming area. While it wasn't dark yet, it was getting there, so I had a sense of where the gloom was and where the lights shone. The posts were evenly spaced but far apart so that there were dark areas between the circles of light, clearly a product of 1960s lighting decisions as opposed to the 2000s.

I went past a light post and around the circle toward the abandoned stairs. I was expecting to stay in darkness, but as I rounded the Quarry's edge, I found that there were two temporary camp lanterns sitting on either side of the old stairs which was cordoned off with bright yellow police tape. I figured that was Kirby's temporary solution while the owner arranged for more lighting, but that's not what I wanted to see tonight. I wanted to see what it had looked like for Abby.

I turned off both lanterns. The stairs went dark.

The light from the last post I'd passed on the path didn't reach here and the light from those in the back parking lot were a good fifty yards away. There was an overgrowth of bushes on either side and even though it wasn't fully night, the top area on either side of the stairs was concealed. I thought that a person, or two, could easily stand there and not be seen.

I went to the stairs, stepped over the tape, and descended all the way to the cement pad at the bottom. I took a few steps onto the jagged rocks where Abby had landed. She was lucky, both that the rocks had stopped her fall and that they hadn't hurt her worse. I knew the water here was clear, but at night, it would've looked like a black pit.

I stepped down off the cement pad and picked my way among the rocks to where Abby had lain. It was slippery and it was awkward and it was hard to keep your balance even when you could see.

There were plenty of fist-sized rocks around to grab.

I looked back up to the top. Forty feet. Fifty stairs. A miracle to survive a fall all that way. Then her attacker had walked all the way down those same stairs, stalked her, and tried to finish the job.

Despite everything, I still didn't think Archie was that guy.

~

NOW THAT THE case was with the prosecutor, I didn't think that Sheriff Warren Dushane would meet with me. So I decided to get creative.

My oldest niece, Reed, was playing junior varsity volleyball that year for Carrefour North. I didn't have many opportunities to see her play during the week since they usually started at four o'clock, but tonight they were playing a jamboree with matches against three different teams so I decided to hustle over and see her.

The fact that Sheriff Dushane's granddaughter was on the team and that he worked the scoreboard for their matches had nothing to do with my decision. How dare you suggest it?

The girls were in their third match when I arrived and, judging by the 23-9 score of the first game, I hadn't missed much. I looked around the gym and saw my dad's shock of white hair, standing out like a candle. I made my way over and climbed the rickety wooden bleachers to the top where my sister-in-law Kate was yelling, "Read the defense!"

"You tell her," I laughed.

Kate looked disgusted. "She keeps hitting it right at the libero! There's a huge gap on the right."

"Sounds like you failed as a mother," I said.

Kate didn't look at me and muttered something about smart ass brothers-in-law. I think worthless may have crept in there too.

If you've come to the Shepherd barbecues, you'd know Kate as the placid mother of four who manages her family with a quiet grace. Volleyball matches are another matter entirely.

"It has been wide open," whispered my dad.

"Don't you encourage her," said my mom.

I laughed, gave my mom a kiss on the cheek, and sat down

next to my dad. I realized it was just the four of us. "Where is everybody?" I said.

Mom ticked off on her fingers. "Tom went right from practice to take Taylor to dance, Page to club volleyball, and Charlie for ice cream."

"What about Mark and Izzy and the boys?"

"Justin had football practice and James and Joe are going to their first wrestling club practice."

"Really? I thought they were a basketball house?"

My mom shook her head. "James is still having trouble running. Cade apparently suggested it to Mark over Labor Day and once James was going to wrestling practice..."

"Joe wasn't far behind?"

"Exactly. It's good to have you here, though."

"I'm sorry it took so long. It's easier to make the later match."

"Are you okay?"

I looked at her. "Of course."

My mom looked at me, then patted my leg. "Well, Sarah would have loved watching Reed play."

It had been almost three years since my Sarah had passed, but it still caught me off guard sometimes. What my mom said, though, was absolutely true, so I said, "She sure would have."

My niece flowed up to the net, leapt, and hit the ball like a rocket. It hit a defender in the face and went straight into the air.

"In the gap!" yelled Kate.

My mom winced. My dad shrugged. "She's not wrong."

"I'm sure she's trying as hard as she can," said my mom.

"She can try smarter," said Kate.

The other team returned the volley and the Carrefour team bumped, set, and hit, this time in the gap, for a point.

"That a way, Jess!" yelled Kate, clapping.

I looked at the scorer's table and saw Sheriff Dushane mark the point his granddaughter had just scored.

"So, how's your case coming, Son?" said my mom.

"Fine, Mom."

"Terrible thing, what happened to that girl."

"It was."

"You must be very certain they have the wrong guy."

For the record, there's no future in getting into a discussion with your mother about the fact that, constitutionally, everyone deserves a legal defense and that we're all better off if that's the case. Instead, I said, "Hmm."

"Good. You're not working too hard, are you?"

"I'm fine."

"Well, it's nice you came. And it was nice to see Olivia and Cade the other day too."

"It was."

"I miss seeing her at the book club."

"She goes? I didn't know that."

"A few of the ladies take her morning class so she used to come every few months, but it's been a while now."

I nodded. "She is running two businesses."

She shook her head. "You all work too hard."

Just then, Reed hit and this time the ball shot straight to the gym floor on the other side of the net for the winning point of the first game. My father cheered and Kate gave him a high five. There was a timeout on the court as the girls went to the bench before they switched sides. As Reed took a seat, I watched Sheriff Dushane clear the scoreboard.

As the teams circled around their coaches, my dad leaned over to talk to Kate and the two of them agreed that Reed needed to move laterally more quickly when she was digging out serves. Then he said, "Are you going to see her tomorrow?"

"Olivia? Probably."

"Tell her I'll be by day after tomorrow to mount the TV."

I raised an eyebrow.

"She mentioned she was getting a bigger one that doesn't fit her stand, I mentioned mounting one is easy, and your mother decided that I don't have enough to do in retirement."

I grinned. "I'll tell her."

The teams came back out and Reed spent the next game on the bench as the coach played a new group but then she played the whole third game and, if she didn't hit every open spot, she hit more of them as the game went on and had a run of four service points in a row. The third game was the closest so far and had all sorts of extended volleys, but the Carrefour girls put it away with a spectacular dig-save from Reed and a monstrous spike from Jess Dushane that brought us all to our feet.

I really hadn't been around volleyball much since I'd lost Sarah and I felt a pang at knowing that she would have loved to see her niece play. Although, to be honest, the combination of her and Kate at these games might have been too much for everyone else. I found myself smiling as I clapped.

We all made our way down the bleachers and congratulated Reed. I smiled as Kate and Pops talked to her about moving her feet and hitting it where they ain't. Then I smiled, waved, and crossed the gym to Sheriff Dushane.

Sheriff Dushane was unplugging the electronic scoreboard and coiling the extension cord as I walked up. He certainly looked different without his sheriff's hat and gun belt, but he was the same blocky guy with the same smile as I approached.

"Your niece had a good game," he said.

I smiled. "So did your granddaughter."

"Thanks. She needs to slide more to the backside on defense, but she'll get there."

I smiled. "Apparently, my niece's problem is reading the defense."

His smile broadened. "So I heard. It's early yet, though. They'll improve."

"You know, Warren–"

Sheriff Dushane raised a hand. "Nate, you and I are having a good conversation about my granddaughter and your niece. Don't go ruining it by bringing up an investigation."

I put my hands out to the side. "Would I do that?"

"A cynical law enforcement officer would mention that this is the first match that a certain lawyer has been to this season."

"Thank goodness you're not that cynical law enforcement officer but, if you were, a certain lawyer might say that this was the first time they've played after seven."

"That would not change the cynical officer's statement at all."

"Fine, I won't ask you about any specifics of your investigation."

"Good. You should be directing those questions to Prosecutor Stritch anyway."

"Sure. You've known him for a while, right?"

"Years."

"Is he as uptight as he seems?"

"Seems to me like you're jumping to conclusions there, Nate."

"Maybe. Is he?"

Sheriff Dushane smiled. "Yes. But he's good to work with and a damn good prosecutor."

"It seems like he can be a little closed-minded about evidence."

Sheriff Dushane shrugged. "He hasn't lost since he replaced Judge Wesley."

I could see I wasn't going to get anywhere on Archie's prosecution with Sheriff Dushane either so I changed tacks. "Talk to you about a different investigation?"

"Is it pending with the prosecutor?"

"No."

"Then sure."

"Do you remember Mr. and Mrs. Mack making the complaint about someone sabotaging their crops?"

"A few years ago? Some."

"You didn't find anything?"

"No. It wasn't much of a priority though."

"What about Hillside Oil?"

"What about it?"

"Did you ever investigate it? Or Will Wellington?"

"Their rep? For what?"

"For the sabotage. Or...anything else."

Sheriff Dushane laughed then. "Have you ever spent any time at all with Will Wellington?"

"Not really. Talked to him on the phone once."

"Well if you had, you'd know that what you just suggested is ridiculous. Will supports damn near every organization in our county and the next, the school, the business association, the baseball league, you name it."

"The Sheriff's office?"

"Watch yourself and yes. Not my campaign but our toy drive and food drive."

"Because he has oil money."

"Of course because he has oil money! And because he's a good guy who cares about the people in our community." Sheriff Dushane looked around. "I have to get this equipment put away or the custodial team will have my ass." He shook my hand. "Your niece is a good kid. I expect to see you at more of her matches. And to go to Stritch if you have any other questions."

"Got it. Thanks, Warren."

"You're welcome."

I checked out the emptying gym and saw that my family had gone. I decided to do the same. But as I left, I thought about

Sheriff Dushane's reaction. He seemed certain that Will Wellington wasn't involved.

But from my perspective, Hillside Oil & Gas was all over this case. I just had to find the connection. Like my niece, I just couldn't quite find the open spot.

Yet.

26

The online revolution had destroyed small-town newspapers and the *Ash County Torch* (Your Beacon for News for Greater Ash County) was no exception. The paper didn't have an office to speak of anymore so I met Ted Ringel at a coffee shop in Dellville. Ted was in his early fifties and wore the local reporter uniform of khaki pants and a golf shirt. He had an easy smile and a soft frame and his face was red from his walk over as we sat down.

"Thanks for meeting me," I said.

Ted waved. "No problem. Curiosity alone was enough to get me over here; lawyers aren't usually too anxious to sit down with the press about an upcoming trial."

"Actually, I'd like to talk to you about background on a piece you did ten years ago."

"You mean back when we actually printed it on paper? How ever did you read it?" His face looked a little bitter.

There didn't seem to be a lot to say to that.

Ted raised a hand. "Sorry. It slips out sometimes. And I'd be happy to, if you'll comment on the Mack trial."

"We look forward to the trial and to proving Archie Mack innocent of all charges."

Ted stared, and I saw a hint of the hardness inside that soft frame that made him a good reporter. "How are you going to do that?"

"They have the wrong man."

"According to my sources, the evidence is pretty damning."

"That evidence does not include any eyewitness identification of my client as the assailant."

"Well, to be fair, it was dark and Ms. Ackerman was having difficulty seeing."

"She could see fine before the assault. So could the couple of thousand people at the concert with them. None of them saw my client assault Ms. Ackerman. I haven't even heard of anyone who saw him with her."

"How are you going to prove it wasn't him?"

I smiled. "That's not up to me. It's up to Prosecutor Stritch to prove beyond a reasonable doubt that it was my client. And we don't think the state will be able to meet that very high burden."

I gestured with both hands. Ted smiled. "Sure, that'll be enough. Although personally, I think you're screwed."

"Thanks."

"No problem. So what do you want to know about?"

"Back in 2008, you wrote a piece about the oil wells popping up all over the county."

Ted nodded. "I did. It was quite a local boom time."

"What drove it?"

"Do you know your local oil history?"

"Some. Enlighten me."

"The first big find in this area, the really big one, was back in 1957. Just up the road at Mrs. Houseknecht's dairy farm. Legend has it that a fortuneteller told her that there was a black river flowing underneath her property and, for the next three years, she and her uncle drilled a pipe down, section by section, until they struck oil. That became the Albion-Scipio field, the biggest oil field in the history of Michigan. The 'Golden Gulch' they called it."

"So they drill all sorts of wells and, over the course of a couple of decades, they figure out the boundaries of the thing and, if landowners were lucky enough to be inside it, they had it made."

"So what happened in 2008?"

"Technology happened. Companies started using 3D seismic imaging technology and discovering additional reservoirs."

"Was that sort of thing new?"

"Better to say it was new to Michigan. The technology has been around for a while, but nobody was really using it here in this part of the state until 2008 or so and then all of a sudden new drilling sites started popping up again. The testing wasn't always accurate, but we had a scattering of successful wells around here that had people jumping on board."

"Was Hillside Oil & Gas involved?"

Ted Ringel nodded. "They were the biggest player here. There were some other companies, but Hillside got probably sixty-five, seventy percent of the active wells."

"Why is that?"

"They were pretty aggressive. If they thought there was a potentially good site, they'd go in and offer on it even if the science was shaky. They took more of a shotgun approach than a high percentage approach."

I thought. "Were they aggressive with the landowners?"

"How do you mean?"

"If people wouldn't sell."

Ted shook his head. "It's not like that at all. The landowners aren't selling the land. They're leasing the right to drill. Most of the time, the landowners have a lot less problem with that than with selling their land outright. Plus, they like the money."

"What do you mean?"

"I mean the standard term is that the landowner gets a monthly rental payment plus one-eighth of whatever comes from the production of the well. Most of the time they were pretty happy to get a call from the HOG."

"The HOG?"

Ted smiled. "Hillside Oil & Gas."

I smiled. "I guess it is. Even farmers didn't mind drilling on their land?"

"Well, Mrs. Houseknecht didn't mind, I can tell you that. Now? It probably depends on how much acreage they have. The drilling pads can be as little as five to ten acres. You need to leave a buffer around the area, but you can still raise plenty of crops if your land is big enough. And oil is usually a more consistent producer than corn."

"What about Will Wellington? Was he working for Hillside Oil then?"

Ted nodded. "That's when he made his bones, so to speak. Will was the most aggressive agent out there. He acquired most of HOG's drilling rights for them."

"Aggressive, huh?"

Ted smiled. "By aggressive, I mean that he coaches three Little League teams, is on the board of the YMCA, has been the chair of the Ash County Business Association, volunteers at the Dellville food bank, and is a deacon at the largest nondenominational church in the area. He's at everything and he knows everyone, so when someone has a question or is interested, he's the first person they talk to."

"Have you ever heard of him strong-arming someone into a lease?"

"No. To be honest with you, that doesn't seem like his style." Ted's gaze sharpened. "Have *you* heard something?"

"I'm not sure."

"You'll tell me if you do?"

"If I'm certain it's true. I can't be a source for anything right now."

"Is this related to the Mack case?"

I shook my head. "It doesn't sound like it." I decided I didn't want to go any farther down that road. "How's the paper doing?"

"Hanging on by a thread." Ted shook his head. "We only print a Sunday edition now and it's combined with three other county papers. I post stories daily and we're getting online revenue, but it's nothing compared to what it was."

"I appreciate you taking the time to see me."

"I was working on a drain commission report. Thank *you* for taking the time to see *me*."

I bought us each coffee to go from the barista and we left.

As I drove back to the office, I couldn't help but continue to think that the timing of Will Wellington's offer was just too coincidental. The Macks had been sabotaged and Will just happens to show up with an offer for an oil lease. They had to be related and Wellington was the most logical connection.

I just had to figure out how.

27

Sometimes lawyers try to be too subtle. They skirt around the edges of a solution, trying to sneak in a clause, or find an advantage in a misplaced comma, or exert leverage from the wrong choice of conjunction. They'll ignore the direct solution because they think it's too easy, or because they're afraid they're missing a better angle when, in fact, the direct solution is the best solution because it's direct. Great, now I'm doing it.

I decided to go see Will Wellington.

I had only talked to him the one time on the phone, but I still had his card from Mrs. Mack. His office was in an old schoolhouse in Dellville, which probably lent him the air of a country boy just like the people he was negotiating with rather than what he was, which was the representative of a large oil conglomerate that counted its revenues in "B's." I parked my Jeep and walked up the accessibility ramp, which had clearly been built about eighty years after the schoolhouse itself. I glanced at the bronze plaque next to the doorway commemorating the school as a historic landmark and Hillside Oil as the good corporate citizen that had rescued it. I opened the heavy glass door that was also a more recent addition and went in.

"Good morning," said a receptionist the moment I walked through the door. "Welcome to Hillside Oil & Gas. How may I help you today?"

It's funny, in an era of computerized voices, how effective a courteous, personal greeting can be. I smiled and said, "I'm here to see Will Wellington."

"Fantastic," she said, as if it was the best thing she'd heard that morning. "Do you have an appointment?"

"I do not."

"May I tell him what it's regarding?"

"Sure. It's the Mack farm."

"Excellent. And may I tell him who's inquiring?"

It really was amazing how rare it was to run into courtesy. "Attorney Nate Shepherd."

"Wonderful, Mr. Shepherd. Please take a seat and I'll see if Mr. Wellington is available."

The receptionist picked up her phone, mentioned who I was and what it was regarding, and before I could even sit down, Will Wellington walked out an office door.

Will looked just like his card, early forties, brown hair combed over to the side, and the reasonable sort of fitness at that age which showed he moved around some but didn't make a big deal about it. He smiled and extended his hand. "Mr. Shepherd?"

"Nate," I said and shook it.

"Fantastic. Nancy said that you're here about the Mack farm?"

"I am."

"And that you're an attorney?"

"I am." This was usually where things broke down.

"Well, come on back." He waved and we went back to his office.

It was an interesting place. The windows were old and large

and two walls were covered entirely in maps. Some were of the entire state of Michigan and others seemed like blowups of areas within it. I had stared at enough oil and gas maps recently to recognize the diagonal slash across southern Michigan of the Albion-Scipio Trend.

Right there on Will Wellington's wall.

"Have a seat, Nate," Will Wellington said and began to rummage through a desk covered in papers. "Ah, here it is," he said lifting a good-sized document. "I was just going through it this morning. You'll see everything has the standard terms in it, including the lease payment and the royalty split that we discussed. It can be a little intimidating if you haven't done one of these before but we've standardized it and I can assure you this is the same deal that we've made with the folks in the surrounding counties for years. I encourage you to ask around; you'll find that folks are quite happy with it and that we are a good partner."

He held the document out to me.

I raised my hand. "I'm sorry, Will. There seems to have been a misunderstanding. I'm here about the Mack farm, but I'm not representing the Macks on negotiating an oil lease."

Will Wellington pulled the paper back and his eyes clouded. "Why else would you be here?"

"I represent Archie Mack in his criminal case."

The scowl deepened. "Hillside Oil & Gas has nothing to do with that."

"I understand. I have some questions about your negotiations with the family."

Will Wellington put the contract back on his desk and while the look on his face remained pleasant, the cheerful bonhomie of his greeting was gone. "Mr. Shepherd, I appear to have made a serious mistake. We do not comment on negotiations with landowners over lease rights. There are too many moving parts. Even mentioning it to you..." He trailed off and tapped the thick agreement on his desk. "Well, let's just say my comments this morning were enough to violate our company policy."

"I'm sorry, Will, I never said that I—"

Will Wellington raised a hand. "I know, Mr. Shepherd. You didn't. I made an assumption that was obviously incorrect and have now put the two of us in the position of having an awkward conversation in which I must ask you to leave because I have other appointments, which I thought were worth being late for when I believed you were here on a different matter."

"Sure. I'm sorry for the misunderstanding."

"No, I'm sorry," he said. "It's entirely my fault."

I stood and made to leave and, to his credit, Will Wellington came around his desk and offered to shake my hand again. "If you could keep what I said confidential?" he said.

"I'm not going to go to the paper or talk about it around town. But I can't promise you that I won't act on it for my client."

His eyes hardened and I caught my first glimpse then of Will Wellington, the wildcat oilman who was willing to take risks and make deals. A moment later, it was gone, and he said, "Sure. Nice to meet you."

"You too."

I waved goodbye to Nancy, the most pleasant receptionist in the lower Peninsula and went to my Jeep. Wellington said he'd made a mistake but what he'd said made it clear that Hillside Oil & Gas was negotiating a deal with the Macks.

Which wasn't what I'd been told at all.

～

MY FIRST CALL was to Archie. When he didn't answer, my second was to Mrs. Mack.

"I don't know what you're talking about, Mr. Shepherd," said Mrs. Mack over the speaker in my Jeep.

"I just came from Will Wellington's office, Mrs. Mack. He had a deal all set to go."

"But we haven't spoken to him."

"Could Mr. Mack have talked to him about it?"

"We don't operate like that, Mr. Shepherd."

"I didn't mean to insult you, but it was clear that Wellington thought he had reached an agreement with you."

"I'm not insulted, Mr. Shepherd, but it's exactly the opposite with us. Alban is out in the field all day this time of year. I handle the books and the business side of things. If anyone was going to have the initial conversation with Mr. Wellington on their own, it would be me. But that's not how Alban and I do things. If we were going to make a deal with him the two of us would have sat down together and discussed it."

"What about Hamish?"

"What about him?"

"Could Hamish be making a deal?"

"No."

"Doesn't he own his land outright?"

"Yes, but…It's complicated."

"Explain it to me."

"Basically, Hamish and Archie each own their own parcel of land. They'll split our parcel when we die or can't work it."

"Okay."

"Our land is adjacent, so what one person does affects the others. It's important that we all be on the same page."

"Right. Like the decision to go organic."

"Exactly. So, technically, we make all the farming decisions together, but the profit or loss from each third goes to the owner of that third."

"I'm with you so far."

"*Technically*, we make all of our farming decisions together."

This time I heard her emphasis. "And if you disagree?"

She paused. "Alban and I have a fifty-one percent vote."

"So what you say goes."

"We didn't have to give them any land while we were alive."

"I understand."

"But we wanted them to be able to support themselves, to farm before we were dead."

"It makes sense."

"And we have the most experience in making these kinds of decisions."

"Sure. And you haven't made a deal for a well?"

"No."

"Okay."

I wasn't going to say it but Mrs. Mack got there anyway. "Do you think Hamish has tried to make a deal for a well?"

I had my suspicions but said, "I don't know."

"I'll speak to him right now."

"Can you wait?"

"Whatever for?"

"I'd like to speak to him first."

Another pause. "Why?"

"I'd like to get the explanation directly from him without him having time to think about it."

"Why would you do that?"

"To get the most truthful response possible."

"Why wouldn't Hamish give you that?"

Mrs. Mack had not yet made the leap that I had. She'd get there but I didn't want to be the one who said it. "You never know."

There was a pause long enough for me to wonder if the call had dropped. Then Mrs. Mack said, "I'm not going to set up one son to save another, Mr. Shepherd."

"I'm not asking you to, Mrs. Mack. I'm asking you to give your youngest the chance to tell me what's going on in person."

"All right. I'll need to tell Alban as soon as he gets in tonight though."

"I'll go see Hamish right now."

"Thank you, Mr. Shepherd."

"Thank you, Mrs. Mack."

I hung up and kept driving to Mack Farms, to the one-third owned by Hamish Mack.

28

I timed it just about right. The sun was setting and Hamish was driving his combine into his modern steel barn when I rolled to a stop in his driveway which, unlike his parents' and brother's, was a long stretch of asphalt rather than gravel. I watched him idle the big red machine slowly through the doorway, looking side-to-side to make sure it didn't scrape on either edge. As it disappeared into the barn, I got out of the Jeep and waited on the black drive that was still giving off the heat of the day's sun.

I didn't have to wait long. Hamish came out of the barn, hit a button, and watched until the steel doors slid home and locked. He took a few steps toward his house, saw me, started to smile, then stopped.

"You're on the wrong farm, lawyer," he said.

"No. I'm looking for you."

"Oh?" He pulled a rag out of his pocket and wiped his hands. "Why would I talk to someone who's trying to free the man who crippled my Abby?"

"I don't know. I'm not that guy."

"Sure seems like it from here."

I shrugged. "I'm the guy trying to figure out who did push Abby down those stairs. I'd think you'd want to talk to him."

Hamish shook his head. "Lawyers. Always twisting things."

"Not twisting. Discovering."

Hamish snorted and I thought he was actually going to spit. When he just shook his head, I said, "Things like oil leases."

No reaction. "What about them?"

"I just came from Will Wellington's office."

Hamish began to wipe his hands with the rag again. "Oh? How is Will?"

"You know him?"

Hamish smiled. "Everybody knows Will."

"How about you?"

"Through our church and the Business Association. What took you to see Will?" His eyes were calm but his hands worked the rag.

"I had some questions about the timing of his offer for an oil lease on the farm about three years ago. It seemed suspicious to me coming on the heels of the crop sabotage."

Hamish's eyes cleared a little. "I don't blame you there. But I think Will is a pretty good guy. He just has access to a lot of information. He'd heard what happened so thought it was a good time to make an offer to the family. My parents weren't interested though. They still wanted to give the organic thing a try."

"What about you?"

"What about me?"

"Did you want to give the organic thing a try?"

"No one has helped my parents with that more than me, including Archie. I've been working their farm and mine for years."

"So why did you sign a deal with Will?"

Hamish didn't blink. "I didn't sign a deal with Will."

"Good point. Why are you about to?"

"You're barking up the wrong tree, Lawyer. My parents have a fifty-one percent vote on farming decisions for all three farms and they're not interested. I can't sign a deal."

"That's not what Will thinks."

He stopped wiping his hands. "Wish I could say it was good to see you," he said and walked toward his house.

"Why are you doing it?"

Hamish stopped. "I'm not doing anything. You need to ask my brother why he did it. Then you need to tell him to burn in hell."

"Rent and an eighth of the profits is a lot of money. More than a farm produces."

Hamish paused, then climbed the stairs to his porch and went into his house.

I waited as the sun dipped below the horizon, leaving the farm in darkness. The lights came on but Hamish didn't come back out, so I climbed back into my Jeep and left.

I thought about going to see the Macks but decided against it. If I was right, they'd find out soon enough that their youngest was trying to cut a deal to put an oil well on their property. I felt like I was missing some angles here, so I decided to call it a night and go clear my head and talk to someone else who was working through the same puzzle.

~

THE EVENING RUSH was over at the Brickhouse when I went in, but there were still a few people working out. I saw a couple of groups rotating through the weights and Cade was in back sparring with a guy who was as big as him. As I walked through, I heard a thump as Cade tossed the guy to the mat, then watched him step back and wait as the guy staggered to his feet.

I found Olivia in her office, staring at her monitors. I knocked on the open door. She glanced up then turned her chair all the way around.

"Hey, Shep."

"Who's on the mat with Cade?"

Olivia smiled. "A young guy who wants to audition for that MMA show."

"He any good?"

"Supposedly."

"Cade just tossed him."

"The two aren't mutually exclusive."

I handed her one of the two coffees I'd brought.

"Bless you," she said. "What's up?"

"There've been some developments. Do you have a second?"

Olivia rubbed her temples. "I do."

"Staring at the computer too long today?"

She straightened. "I'm fine. What's going on?"

So I told her, about my trip to see Wellington and his mistaking me for the Macks' lawyer and him disclosing that he had a deal put together to drill a well on the Mack farm, about my call to Mrs. Mack and her explanation of how she and her husband controlled the farm decision-making and that they had authorized no such thing, and about my trip to see Hamish and my suspicion that he was trying to make the deal.

"I'm telling you, Liv," I said. "There's something there. Hamish seems like the only one out of his whole family who thinks that Archie did it. But there's no way all of the rest of this is just a coincidence—first an offer from Hillside Oil right after the crop sabotage and now Hamish trying to put a deal together after his brother is tagged for attempting to murder his fiancée."

"Why isn't he talking?"

"Hamish? That seems obvious—he doesn't want the rest of the family to know about the well."

"No. I mean, Archie."

I shook my head. "I'm not sure. It has to be related."

"I wonder if Archie knows."

"About Hamish trying to sell the drilling rights? He can't, right? It would have a big impact on the organic farming that they're all planning."

Olivia nodded. "All a competitor would have to do is take a picture of the Macks' crops with an oil derrick in the background. That would pretty much scrap any healthy food claims."

A thump and a sharp cry echoed across the emptying gym. Olivia chuckled.

I chuckled with her, then said, "I'll let you know what I find out from Archie."

"Thanks." She took a sip of coffee and turned back to her computer, the monitor reflected in her glasses.

"Maybe you should knock off for the night."

"Good night, Shep."

I walked out of her office and saw that Cade and his sparring partner had put on oversized boxing gloves. They touched briefly then began to move around the mat. Cade's footwork was exceptionally smooth for his size. He flicked out a jab with a long left, 1-2-3 times before ducking a hook and tapping the man in the back of the head. I couldn't help but stop and watch for a few minutes as Cade floated lightly on his feet, tagging the man from different angles seemingly at will. Soon, I realized that he could probably knock the MMA show contender out at any time. I decided I was in the best spot when it came to fighting Cade.

Not fighting Cade.

I left.

29

Next morning, I met with Danny and brought him up to speed with everything that had happened the day before. Danny pressed his lips together as I spoke.

"What?" I said.

"You should've called me."

"I figured we'd talk about it today."

"No, I mean before you called the Macks and saw Hamish."

"Why?"

"Because I had information that would've mattered to you."

"Great. What?"

"Video of the Quarry."

"What about it?"

"Hamish was there with Wellington."

"What? At the concert?"

Danny nodded. "I'd never seen Wellington, so his face didn't mean anything the first few times I'd gone through it. Then, when we started looking at him and I went on his company website and his Facebook site, I was pretty sure I'd seen him on the video so I went back and checked. Turns out, I had."

"When?"

"After the concert."

"Where?"

"In the courtyard. He's talking to Hamish right before Hamish goes out the back."

"You're kidding."

"Nope. Then, when Abby goes after Hamish, Archie swoops in and talks to him."

"To Wellington?"

Danny nodded. "It looked animated. Then Archie disappears to the back."

"That's the video we've been focused on?"

"Right. And then as Archie returns, Wellington goes to the back."

"Toward the stairs?!"

"Yep."

"Goddammit. That means all three of them were back there?"

"Looks like it. At three different times."

I stood. "Do you have any other dress shoes here?"

"No. Why?"

"Because those are going to get dirty."

~

I'D TEXTED Archie that we were on the way to see him, but his combine was still rolling across his field when we arrived at Mack Farms. I wasn't in the mood to wait. I backed out of his driveway and drove longways around the long block to the far side of Archie's field where he was just making a turn near the road. I flashed my lights, honked the horn, then got out of the Jeep and waved. The combine stopped.

Danny and I found a narrow part of the ditch and hopped it, then made our way through a cloud of pollen and dust to where Archie stood, arms crossed, waiting.

He glanced at the sun. "I don't have a lot of time, Nate."

I nodded. "Hamish is going to build the oil well."

Archie's arms flexed and his jaw clenched. It struck me as anger but not surprise. "He might try but he can't."

"That's not what Will Wellington thinks."

"You talked to Wellington?"

"Yes. He thinks he has an agreement ready to go."

"That can't be."

"Why not?"

"Our Farm Agreement. Mom and Dad have final say in farm decisions while they're alive."

"Even on your individual farms? Yours and Hamish's?"

"Yes."

"It seems like Hamish might be operating behind your back."

"He's always operating..." he trailed off again.

"Archie," I said. "Did you see Wellington the night of the concert?"

He looked at me. "How did you know he was—?" He caught himself but it was too late.

Which, by the way, is why you never put the defendant on the stand.

"Video," I said. "Danny here watched him. Watched Hamish talk to him. Watched you talk to him. What's going on?"

Archie pulled the brim on his cap down, then looked to the side at the field. "I suspected Hamish was trying to deal with Wellington. I had no idea he'd gone so far."

"How did you know?" I asked.

"Guessed is a better word, I suppose. Things he said.

Comments he made about maximizing value." Archie shook his head. "Always with the maximizing value whether it was crop yield for the farm or betting strategies at blackjack or a trade by the Detroit Tigers, he's always talking about maximizing value. That's how we got onto the discussion of organic farming in the first place, maximizing our return for our effort. He was always harping about it to Mom and Dad and me. But I didn't realize he was willing to go around us altogether until I..." Archie stopped short.

"Until you saw him at the concert with Wellington," I said.

Archie didn't say anything. Then he nodded his head.

"What happened?"

Archie shook his head. "Bonnie and Abby and the girls had tickets up near the front. Like I told you before, I'd decided to go late so I had a standing-room single in the back. Then, as the concert was letting out, I saw Hamish leaving the amphitheater from a few aisles over. I didn't realize he was going to be there. I didn't think he was that big a fan, or I would have asked him to go with me since the girls had gone together. I worked my way over to see him but he was too far ahead of me in the crowd, so I figured I'd catch him at the gate on the way out...but then I saw him walk back the other direction."

"What happened then?"

"Hamish stopped at one of the concession areas and I figured he was getting water or some coffee for the road when I saw Will Wellington walk up to him. My brother got out of the concession line and the two began talking and it was clear that he had been waiting for Will. They talked for a while and, when they were done, they shook hands in a way that seemed excited and formal. Then Wellington went one way and my brother went the other, toward the back of the Quarry."

It was like a dam had broken.

Archie continued. "I went after Wellington."

"Why?"

"He was closer. I was angry and I, I stopped him and asked him what he was doing with my brother."

"What did he say?"

"Nothing. He wouldn't tell me anything. He kept saying I needed to talk to Hamish, that it wasn't his place to get in the middle..."

"How long did you talk to him, Archie?"

Archie looked at the sun and shrugged. "I have no idea, Nate. A little while."

"Then what did you do?"

"I went after Hamish."

"Toward the back?"

He nodded. "I went back around the Quarry, along the back path, but I didn't see him."

"That's when you called him."

Archie nodded.

"From the back of the Quarry?"

"Yes."

"You told me you were arguing about the farm."

"We were."

"Archie, you were arguing about oil."

"On the farm, yes."

He was finally talking to me so I decided not to argue. "What did you say?"

"I reamed him out for meeting with Wellington behind our backs."

"You were mad?"

"Very."

"How did that go?"

"About as you'd expect."

"Tell me anyway."

"I said he couldn't go behind our backs, he said he could do whatever he wanted, I told him Mom and Dad get to make that call, he said they didn't and that he didn't need me or Abby yelling at him about it."

I raised a hand. "He said Abby was yelling at him about it?"

"Not exactly."

"What exactly?"

"He said he didn't need either of us crawling up his ass about it."

"Did he mean that night? That she yelled at him that night?"

"Maybe. I couldn't say."

Some things came together. "You made the call from the stairs didn't you?"

He nodded. "I realized that after we hung up."

"How?"

"Because I'd squeezed the railing so hard that I'd opened the cut on my hand."

"How'd you get the cut?"

"Fixing a drainage tile with Hamish earlier that day." He shook his head. "I spent all day with him. He never said a word about going to the concert."

I stepped forward. "Listen to me, Archie. If you don't want to spend the rest of your life in a cell in Jackson, answer me honestly. Did you see Abby back there?"

He shook his head. "I wish I had."

"Not once?"

"No."

"That's all that happened?"

"That's it. After the call, I walked back out to the front lot and left."

"Why wouldn't you tell us about the oil?"

Archie looked right at me. "That's family business. And I didn't think it was part of this."

"It's part of this."

He looked unconvinced. "My parents are going through enough, Nate. Hamish being a...This'll just add one more thing."

"If you're in Jackson State Penitentiary, who's going to look out for your parents? And Bonnie? And even Abby? Are you going to trust Hamish to do all that?"

Archie thought, then said, "I suppose not."

"We need more information. Tonight."

I nodded to Danny and he listed off a bunch of background materials—the Farm Agreement, crop histories, things related to operations—nothing that would show who hurt Abby but stuff that might be important for trial depending on how things went.

When Danny was done, Archie said, "I'll get it to you."

"Archie," I said. "We can't have any more surprises."

"Good. I'm out of them."

That, of course, never reassures anyone. Still, I said, "I'll look for the materials tonight."

Archie nodded and shook my hand. "I have a crop to get in."

Danny and I hopped back over the ditch. The call and the fight with Hamish was bad but what he'd told us opened up the possibility of putting someone else at the scene. Wellington.

Hopefully, that would be enough.

∽

ARCHIE SENT the documents to us that night. I stayed up late reading them. So did Danny and when he arrived at the office the next morning, the words came tumbling out.

"Did you see it?"

"See what?"

"The pattern."

I certainly hadn't seen anything to get that excited about, so I said, "What do you mean?"

"Here, you can see it: Right before they tried to switch to organic, Mr. and Mrs. Mack were struggling on their part of the farm, right?"

"Right. They weren't covering their loan payment."

"And even though his parents were struggling, it looks like Hamish pretty much worked his own land."

I nodded. "His yields were a little better at that time. But not much."

"Right. Hamish was either preoccupied with his own survival or didn't care if his parents went under. Either way, Hamish wasn't helping them out."

"Okay?"

"Until after the crop sabotage. By all accounts, he's been working like a dog to help them ever since the crop sabotage."

I saw it then. "He started helping right before the Hillside Oil offer came in."

"Do you think he knew?" Danny said. "About the oil?"

"He's friends with Wellington. He could have learned ahead of time from Wellington."

We stared at the crop reports. I thought then shook my head. "It still doesn't explain the crop sabotage."

Danny frowned. "Wellington trying to create pressure for his deal?"

"Pressure that didn't work."

"But he didn't know that it wouldn't work."

Now I was frowning. "And it doesn't make sense that Hamish would know about the oil from Wellington but not about the sabotage."

"Or that he would know about the sabotage and then work to fix the sabotage."

Danny and I stared at the crop reports for a while, trying to make sense of something that made no sense, before I said, "You see the other problem, don't you?"

"What's that?"

"None of this tells us who attacked Abby."

Danny's excitement dimmed a bit. "What's next then?"

"I think we have one more person to talk to. And then a prosecutor."

30

Danny and I met Ronnie Hawkins and Abby Ackerman at Ronnie's office in Dellville the next afternoon. We were in Ronnie's conference room, Ronnie and Abby on one side, Danny and I on the other. A cane was leaning against the table next to Abby. The blood was gone from her eye but there was still a noticeable indentation in the bone of her eye socket.

As we sat, Abby said, "How far back did your people keep animals, Shepherd?"

I stopped. "My people?"

"Your family."

I had honestly never thought about it. "I don't know."

"Hmphf. Too bad. Pigs make more sense to me than sheep. Too much labor in wool."

"Sure." I marked that in the conversations I didn't think I was going to have today column. "Off the crutches then?"

She tapped the cane. "Still need this pogo stick but it's getting better. I started driving this week."

"That is good news."

"Nate," said Ronnie. "This is unusual, so I'd like to keep it to the point."

"Of course. Thanks for meeting with me."

"Abby insisted," Ronnie said.

"That's because Archie didn't do it."

"You don't know who did it," said Ronnie with the tired air of someone who'd said it more than once.

"But I know who *didn't*."

Ronnie smiled, but it was forced. "So why did you want to meet?"

"Let me ask first," I said. "Have you remembered anything else from that night?"

"Not a bit."

"So you still can't identify who attacked you?"

Abby speculated on certain proclivities of her attacker but was unable to say who he was.

"You told me last time that you saw Hamish and caught up with him at the back of the Quarry."

"That's right."

"You left me with the impression that the two of you argued about going to the concert separately."

"Did I? Huh."

"I don't think that's what you were arguing about. I think you were arguing about Will Wellington. Or oil."

Abby blinked. Ronnie put her hand out. "Don't say anything else, Abby." To me, she said, "I didn't invite you over to cross-examine my client. Explain what you're talking about or we're done."

So Danny and I laid out what happened that night—Hamish's meeting with Will, Archie going after Will while Abby appeared to follow Hamish back toward the stairs, Archie arriving at the stairs to find neither of them, and talking to Hamish later on the phone. Then we told her about Wellington's apparent deal with someone at Mack Farms.

To their credit, Abby and Ronnie just listened as I finished.

"Mrs. Mack and Archie both say it's not them. Can I ask one more question?"

Ronnie's hand went up again. "Maybe."

"Were you for or against the oil well, Abby?"

Ronnie dropped her hand. She seemed interested in the answer too.

"I don't have a vote, Shepherd."

"I understand. But what was your opinion?"

She flipped her hair back. "I was against it."

"Why?"

"I'm a farm girl too. I believe organic is the best way to go for the future, for all of us."

"Is that what you were arguing about that night?"

Ronnie's hand shot up. "She's not going to answer that."

I shrugged. "If she testifies, she will."

Ronnie thought about it and lowered her hand.

"Yes," Abby said.

The room was quiet as Abby raised her head and she gritted her teeth and a tear streamed from the outside corner of her wounded eye. Her voice cracked as she said, "Are you saying Hamish attacked me, Shepherd? Because I'm having enough trouble keeping my shit together as it is."

"No, Abby. All I'm saying is that Archie didn't do it."

Ronnie slid a box of tissues over. Abby ignored it and stared at me, jaw still clenched. "I don't think Hamish would hurt me anymore than Archie would."

Under her breath, I thought I heard her say, "I can't."

"I understand."

"So who did?"

"I'm not sure."

Abby grabbed her cane and smashed it against the table. "Someone did this to me! Goddammit, who did this to me!!"

Ronnie reached out. "I understand, Abby—"

"Oh? I don't see your face dented in! Just how do you understand?"

I didn't mean to hurt her. I gestured to Ronnie and got up to leave when Abby said, "No, no, no. Stay."

It was hard to explain how she looked. She didn't break down as she cried—instead it seemed as if ferocious tears of rage poured from her eyes. "Wait," she said, so I did.

It took her a moment, and then she said, "I know Archie didn't do this. I want to help him. But I need the person who did this to pay."

I nodded. I had a sense of how she'd testify now. I didn't want to, but I had one more question to ask.

"Would you be willing to tell that to the prosecutor one more time?"

"About Archie?"

"Yes."

"She's not saying anything about all this Hamish business," said Ronnie.

"No, no, I wouldn't ask her to. I'm asking if she'd be willing to tell Stritch, directly, that she doesn't think that Archie did it."

"I've already told him that," said Ronnie.

"I think it might be more powerful coming from Abby."

"Of course, I will," said Abby

Ronnie didn't look happy, but she said, "We'll see when he's in and—"

"He's in now."

"You checked ahead of time?"

I smiled. "Maybe."

Ronnie turned to Abby. "Are you sure?"

Abby gave a quick swipe to her cheeks and nodded. "I'm already here. Need to get my three-legged steps in any way." She stood and grabbed her cane.

Danny and I stood with them. Ronnie looked at us and said, "What the hell do you think you're doing?"

I blinked. "Going with you."

"No, you're not."

"If Stritch needs any other information about—"

"You can share it with him whenever and however you want." Ronnie straightened. "Abby, could you wait outside for a moment, please? I'll be right with you."

Abby looked at Ronnie, looked at me, then smiled at Ronnie. "Kick his ass, Counselor," she said. Then she concentrated on where she was putting her cane as Ronnie shut the door behind her.

Ronnie turned on me. "Listen, Nate, I know she doesn't think your client did it and you don't think your client did it, but the fact is, Abby was attacked and left for dead. Despite what she thinks, it's not her responsibility to get your client acquitted, it's yours. Now I'm going to take her over there and she's going to tell Stritch, in person, that she doesn't think Archie did it, but that's it. All of that other... stuff you said today is interesting, but it's not her concern. She needs her attacker brought to justice."

When I started to speak, Ronnie raised her hand. "I know you don't think that's Archie. So prove it. And find the cowardly shadow of a man who did it to her and make sure he's locked away so he can never do it again. But that woman," she pointed at the door, "is just now able to walk. She's carrying a visible reminder that someone tried to cave her head in with a rock. She has rights and those aren't going to be protected by talking to the state's attorney with her accused assailant's lawyer lurking over her shoulder."

We stared at each other. Then I smiled and said, "When you put it that way. Mind if we wait?"

She flashed a smile. "Not at all. I'm guessing it won't be long."

Ronnie opened the door and closed it again so that we didn't see Abby. As we sat, I looked at Danny. "Well."

Danny grinned. "Well."

"She did have a point."

"She did."

"I guess we'll see."

"I guess we will."

"We have a little time."

"We do."

"Want to do some lunges while we wait?"

"You really need to stop taking advantage of my religious beliefs."

"Religious beliefs?"

"About swearing."

I chuckled. "I suppose I should. Box jumps then?"

"Jack bag."

I thought. "Good adaptation."

"Thanks."

~

RONNIE OPENED the door to the conference room about forty-five minutes later. "I sent Abby home," she said.

"Good," I said. "Well?"

Ronnie sat, put her hands squarely on the table, and in a serious voice said, "While I appreciate your opinion on this matter, Ms. Ackerman, the state's evidence is overwhelming and we intend to proceed."

I nodded. It had been worth a try. "I appreciate the effort."

"It wasn't for you. A victim's opinion deserves to be heard, whatever it is."

"Is she going to testify?"

"Like I said before, Abby will comply with any subpoena

that's issued and give her honest recollection, and opinions, of any who ask it."

I stood. "Thanks, Ronnie. And you were right, by the way."

She smiled. "I know. Thanks for noticing."

We shook hands all the way around and Danny and I left.

As we climbed into my Jeep, Danny said, "Now what?"

"Now we go home."

"Aren't we going to go see Stritch?"

"No."

"But everything we've uncovered!"

"He doesn't care."

"Why?"

I thought. "He knows his evidence is enough to win." I thought of his saying about pointing spokes making wheels. "So he's going to roll with it."

"But Archie didn't do it!"

"I agree. So we'll have to prove it."

Right on cue, my phone buzzed. I recognized the Dellville area code and had a pretty good idea who it was. I answered. "Hello, T. Marvin."

"Good afternoon, Nate. I had the most wonderful visit today."

"Oh?"

"Ms. Ackerman came to see me, and do you know what?"

"What?"

"She's walking! Isn't that fantastic?"

"It certainly is."

"Of course, she still can't identify anyone else as her attacker, so I'll be relying on the evidence to present my case against Mr. Mack."

"I see."

"And her opinions, well, her opinions aren't based on any evidence from that night at all, are they?"

"No. Just a lifetime."

"Hmm. Which can change in an instant as I've seen far too often in my office. But listen, I'm always willing to listen to *evidence*, Nate. Do you have direct evidence that someone else committed this terrible crime? A witness? Cell phone video?"

I paused. "No."

"Ah, so perhaps your client is saying he didn't do it? I've certainly never heard that before."

"T. Marvin, Archie had no reason to do this. There's no motive. Abby knows that."

"Maybe. Maybe not. The more important thing is all the evidence points to him. And I'm going to point the jury to all of that evidence."

"You're making a mistake," I said, and as soon as I said it, I knew I had made one.

I heard the inevitable bristle on the other end of the line. "I know we're just a small town up here, Nate. Nothing like the big city of Carrefour. And I know I'll be all alone against a team of big-city lawyers who are going to charge into town to tell the good folks of Dellville how to think and how to evaluate evidence and how to judge their prosecutor's office. That's all fine, I'm sure it works in Carrefour and Lansing and Detroit all the time. But this is Dellville. I've lived here my whole life. So has the judge. At least half the jury will have too. See, you can tell me how I'm looking at this all wrong and you can tell the judge how she's weighing the evidence all wrong and you can tell the jury they're coming to the wrong decision, but in the end, it's going to come down to who the jury thinks is steering them in the right direction. And I'm not going to be steering them at all. I'm going to be pointing them to your client's picture and your client's truck and your client's *blood* that he left behind. So thanks for the warning, and when this is all over, we can revisit this and you can show me just how I went wrong. Or how you did."

I paused for a moment. Having screwed up, I came to an in-for-a-penny conclusion, then said, "Not everyone can handle it you know."

"What's that?" said T. Marvin Stritch.

"The pressure that comes with going undefeated."

"Yes. It's very hard to just win cases all the time."

"I'm not saying it's hard or easy. I'm saying that it creates its own weight and, sometimes good people, talented people, crumble under it. The 2007 Patriots. UNLV basketball. Even Dan Gable, who was the best wrestler who ever lived, got beat in his last college match by someone half as good."

T. Marvin Stritch chuckled. "Oh good, sports analogies. I love sports analogies. I prefer Edwin Moses myself. Do you know who he is?"

"I do."

"Then you know he's the best 400 meter hurdler who ever lived. He won the 1976 Olympics and then won one hundred and seven finals in a row over the next ten years. Do you know why?"

I did, but I said, "Why's that, T. Marvin?"

"Because he measured his steps. Every race, thirteen steps between every hurdle, every time. Without fail. No one else could do it for the whole race except for Edwin. And every year, every race, he just kept running, thirteen steps between every hurdle, and destroyed everyone he ran against."

T. Marvin Stritch paused. When I didn't respond, he said, "Cases are no different. You measure out the evidence and clear each hurdle until you cross the finish line."

"I guess we'll see then," I said.

"I guess we will."

"See you in a few weeks."

"I look forward to it."

I hung up.

Danny was looking at me.

"What?"

"Why would you do that?"

"I might have gotten carried away."

"Do you think that will help?"

"I seriously doubt it."

"So why do it?"

"You just had to hear him…" Finally, I smiled and shrugged. "No good reason, actually."

Danny laughed then and the surprise in his voice just about made the whole thing worth it.

31

Cade Brickson was a huge man with a huge caloric intake. To keep two hundred and sixty good pounds on that frame of his, he usually ate five meals a day and none of it was bad food. My dad used to say that Cade ate a barn-full of chickens and a pond-full of fish every day, and, as far as I could see, that process hadn't stopped.

I went to his house for dinner with him and Olivia after my meeting with Abby and call with Stritch. I had asked to meet with them and, because of the time, Cade had insisted that we meet over dinner. His dinner. Still, it was one less meal I had to make, so I didn't really mind.

His house boasted a double fridge, a double oven, and a large stovetop and he had used all of it to serve Olivia and me some sort of Mediterranean chicken dish accompanied by greens that were half delicious and half an acquired taste. He even took the time to dole the dishes out on the plates for us, saying he had to get the presentation and mix of sauces just right. It smelled great.

I told them about the developments of the last few days over dinner. As Olivia stabbed some leafy green thing, she said, "So who did it?"

"I'm not sure yet. But the most important thing is that I can put other people there at the time of the attack."

Olivia munched. "You need to figure it out."

"What I need to do is create reasonable doubt and get Archie acquitted."

"Abby deserves justice."

"Abby deserves a lot of things."

Olivia put down her fork. "Shep, that's why I sent the Macks to you in the first place."

"I thought it was because Archie didn't do it?"

"And because you'd get to the bottom of it."

"I'm working on it. *We're* working on it."

Olivia picked her fork back up and her vegetables seemed to be paying the price for her irritation. "Just make sure you don't stop."

I nodded and I watched her for a minute, then said, "My mom asked about you the other day."

"Yeah?"

"Said you used to go to her reading group?"

She smiled. "Sometimes. I don't have much time anymore."

"That's what I told her." I took a bite. "Have you been taking any time off?"

"What's that?"

As I finished my piece of chicken, Cade stood, grabbed the serving plate, and said, "We have two breasts and a quarter left."

I groaned. "He's going to kill us. So no?"

"No what?"

"No time-off."

Olivia shook her head. "I'm not built that way, you know that."

"Couldn't hurt."

She put her lenses on me. "What do you mean?"

"Nothing. Oh, and my dad said he'd be by to mount your tv."

She smiled. "Yeah. When?"

"Thurs...was that yesterday?"

"And *I* need the time off."

"Sorry about that."

She shrugged. "Pops was always more reliable than you. We're all used to it."

I shook my head. "Did you get a new one or something?"

"Yeah, got some more smart features. I was a little behind the times so I needed the upgrade."

"How's it look?"

"Still tinkering with the settings but pretty good." She stabbed a vegetable. "I mean it about finding the real attacker."

"I know you do. And I mean it about winning my trial."

"Who's more likely? Gut feeling."

I shook my head. "I don't think Hamish has it in him, even if he is being a snake about the well to his family. I think it had to have been Wellington."

"The choir boy?"

"It just makes too much sense—the timing, the knowledge, opportunity, all of it. It's right out there but Stritch just can't see it."

Olivia smiled. "That happens sometimes." She tilted her head back. "Cade?!"

"Yeah?" came the voice from the kitchen.

"Does that temple of yours allow for dessert?"

"Fruit salad."

Olivia sighed. "Coffee at least?"

"Brewing."

Olivia smiled, played with her bangs for a moment, then kept eating. A moment later, Cade arrived with a platter of still more chicken, a monstrous glass bowl of fruit salad, and a promise that the coffee was almost done.

"Abby's driving again, by the way," I said.

Olivia's face lightened. "Really?"

"Yeah, she's off crutches and using a cane."

"What about the face fracture?" said Cade.

"It seems like her vision's back, but the bone isn't healing right. It's a little...dented? I think is how I'd describe it."

Cade shook his head. "I'm still surprised this bond has worked out."

"That Hamish hasn't gone over there?" I said.

He nodded.

"Maybe he's listening to Abby," said Olivia. "Some guys do that, you know."

Cade glanced at her, then nodded.

I smiled. "You know we always listen to you, Liv."

"Right. You're more likely to show up at 4:30 a.m. for a sunny-side up hash skillet at the Cast Iron Kitchen."

"See, now that's just unfair. I'm sure I've listened to you at least once."

We talked about other things then, the gym, Cade's bail bond business, and the wanna-be MMA fighter he was sparring with who was actually pretty good. Olivia said it seemed like the fighter had been getting the better of Cade on the mat which, of course, was totally untrue but seemed to get under his skin just the same.

All in all, though, dinner with true friends is a rare thing and I knew it, so I thoroughly enjoyed the last time I went out before Archibald Mack's trial.

ASH

32

Judge Eliza Jane Wesley liked to meet with the attorneys on the Friday before trial to iron out any last-minute details. I stood at the defense counsel table along with Danny. T. Marvin Stritch stood alone at the prosecutor's table.

Judge Wesley leafed through some papers as she said, "Mr. Stritch, are you ready to proceed on Monday?"

"I am, Judge."

"Do you still expect it to take a week?"

"I do."

"Have you offered a plea agreement?"

"We have, Your Honor. It was rejected by the defense."

Judge Wesley looked back to me. "Is that true, Mr. Shepherd?"

"It is, Your Honor. A recommendation of fifteen years didn't seem like much of a bargain."

"You're aware a conviction carries more?"

"I am."

"And you're aware of the success rate of prosecutions here in Ash County?"

I smiled. "Mr. Stritch has been kind enough to fill me in."

"You don't believe it's in your client's best interests to accept a plea deal, I take it?"

"I believe that Mr. Stritch is prosecuting the wrong person, Your Honor."

Judge Wesley put her papers down. "Do you intend to present alibi evidence?"

"No, Your Honor."

"Do you intend to present evidence of the identity of the person who you believe in fact committed this crime?"

"No, Your Honor."

"Then how do you intend to prove that your client is innocent?"

"I intend to present evidence that the prosecution cannot prove that my client is guilty beyond a reasonable doubt, Your Honor."

She straightened. "I assure you that I am very aware of what the State's burden is, Mr. Shepherd."

"I wasn't implying that you're not, Your Honor. It's the same in every state."

Her eyes narrowed. "So you're going to mount a prairie dog defense."

I kept my face straight. "I'm not familiar with that term of art, Your Honor."

"It's where the defense simply pops up with cross-examinations around whatever evidence the prosecution puts on but doesn't put on any real evidence of its own."

"I don't know that I would describe it exactly that way, Your Honor."

"I suppose we'll see." She looked back and forth between us. "Is there anything else we need to take care of for Monday? I intend to hit the ground running at eight-thirty."

"No, Your Honor," both Stritch and I said.

"Very well. I'll see you then." With that, Judge Wesley gaveled us out and left.

"She's seen it all, you know," said Stritch to me.

"What do you mean?"

"She was the chief prosecutor for almost twenty years and never lost a case. She's seen every trick that defense lawyers try."

"I'm sure she has."

"I've seen them all too."

"I'm just going to put on my evidence, T. Marvin."

Stritch smiled and somehow his cadaverous cheekbones became even thinner as his eyes lit up. "Evidence belongs to everyone, Nate. Just like the truth."

I smiled back. "I have to get your fortune cookie vendor when this is over."

He blinked then said, "And we all know where that points." Which is the kind of non-sequitur you get when you have a conversation cued up in your head in advance. T. Marvin Stritch put his legal pad into a battered leather portfolio and left the courtroom.

I shrugged to Danny, who was smiling, as Ronnie Hawkins came up from the gallery to see us.

"Watching?" I said.

"I have to let Abby know we're on for next week," Ronnie said.

I nodded. "Is Judge Wesley always like that or am I just lucky?"

"Judge Wesley isn't a fan of out-of-town lawyers."

"I live in the county. My taxes go to her salary for Pete's sake."

Ronnie smiled. "As far as EJ is concerned, you're a big city lawyer swooping into her town."

"I don't think anyone calls Carrefour 'the big city.'"

"They do in Dellville. Anytime we see a letterhead with Carrefour, Jackson, or Detroit, the radar goes up."

"Great. 'EJ' by the way?"

Ronnie smiled and shrugged. "She insists on us calling her that when we're at the young lawyer mixers. Says that the constant 'Judge' and 'Your Honor' keeps her from having a regular conversation."

"I take it I can't get away with that?"

She smiled sweetly. "You haven't been given permission."

"Hmm. I assume Stritch has though?"

"They were coworkers for a long time." Ronnie's smile faded. "Stritch wasn't exaggerating about one thing, Nate. Judge Wesley was a great prosecutor and she trained Stritch in every aspect of his job. He's not going to make mistakes."

I didn't tell her that we all do. Instead, I said, "Looks like I have a fun weekend to look forward to then. Thanks, Ronnie."

"See you Monday, Nate."

∽

ONE OF THE things that's interesting about the difference between a civil case and a criminal case is the time you spend with your client. When you're getting ready for a civil case, you spend an awful lot of time getting your client ready to testify. They always have to take the stand to tell their side of the story, and you have to prepare them to be ready for any little thing the other side may cross-examine them on. That means that you spend hours together working through things and, as a result, get to know each other.

It's completely different in a criminal case. You're never going to put your client on the stand (or almost never anyway), so you don't spend any time preparing them. Instead, you spend every waking minute on the things that do matter—investigating, preparing examinations of other witnesses, and doing whatever you need to do to get an acquittal. Your client is a resource for information but you just don't have to spend nearly as much time with him to win his case.

Which can be very disconcerting for someone who is looking at the very real possibility of spending the next couple of decades in prison.

So, the last thing I did on Friday was go to visit Archie out at the farm. The trial was the week after Halloween, so it was getting close to winter in Michigan where the wind could just as easily blow freezing rain as snow right in your face at thirty miles an hour.

I found him out in his barn tending his pigs. Before I got too far in, he pointed at his shoes and back at the house. I nodded and went up to his side porch. A few minutes later, he was there letting me in.

Archie poured us each a coffee without asking and took off his hat. The tan line across his face was gone and he looked like he'd lost twenty pounds.

"How many pigs do you have?" I asked.

"About forty all told. Wish I had more."

"Yeah?"

"Yeah. I prefer livestock to crops personally."

"Is it hard to switch?"

He shrugged. "It's not what we do."

I told him then about the meeting with the Court and that we'd be going on Monday.

Archie nodded. "So it'll be over after next week?"

"It will."

"One way or the other?"

"Yes."

"Will Abby be there?"

"I assume so. I saw her lawyer today."

"How about my parents?"

"Yes. Your mom called my office yesterday asking about the time."

"Then you need to go light about any of this having to do with Hamish."

I shook my head. "Archie, I can't promise to do that at all. My job is to beat this case."

"Your job is to not kill my parents."

I thought. "I promise not to say anything I can't prove."

"Nate."

"Archie. If I can prove something about Hamish, then it's his fault. Not mine."

Archie seemed satisfied with that as he sipped his coffee. "So what are our chances?"

"Better than even."

"That's all?"

"Parts of their case are pretty solid."

"I heard that this prosecutor has never lost a case."

"That's true. But he's never tried this case before."

Archie looked skeptical.

"Just because you have rain on June 23rd every year for ten years doesn't mean it will happen next year, does it?"

Archie blew on his coffee. "No, I don't suppose it does."

"It's a new year, Archie."

He stared out the window. "I want to be here next June, Nate."

"I know."

"I don't know that I can live a life without farming in it."

"I understand."

He nodded. "I wanted you to know."

"I do."

Archie didn't seem like he was in a hurry to get me out of the house and I realized that, besides Bonnie and his mother, he probably wasn't in contact with anyone. So I took my time and I finished my coffee while the two of us stared out the window.

When I was about done, he drained his cup and said, "I'll be ready."

I finished my own. "Good. I'll see you Monday."

He walked out with me to my Jeep and we exchanged small talk about him finishing the harvest in time for the trial, which had not at all been a sure thing. I heard the faint commotion of pigs and caught a strong waft of their smell as I left.

I hoped that Archie could do the same after next week.

33

Judge Wesley didn't mess around. We started promptly at 8:30 a.m. on Monday and by 10:45 a.m., we had twelve jurors seated and ready to go. She ran through the jury questionnaires herself, asking all the basic questions like marital status, job, kids, and whether anyone had ever been accused of, or the victim of, an assault themselves. By the time she was done, we didn't have much left to ask and she wasn't interested in letting us repeat any of her questions just so we could build a rapport with the jury. In the end, we wound up with seven women and five men, which I thought was just about as good as we could do.

For the most part, I didn't have any objections. There were three that really stood out. One was a farmer who managed two hundred acres of corn, soybeans, and a decent number of cows in the far southern part of the county. I thought that he would have to know the Macks, but he claimed that he had a tendency to associate with farmers in Ohio and Indiana more than those in the northern part of Ash County. I found it hard to believe that he didn't know the farmers of six hundred and forty acres in his own county, but he was adamant.

The second was a woman who was a crisis counselor for our

local hospital system. As part of her job, she helped women who were the victims of domestic and sexual assault when they came to the hospital and supported them when the police were gathering evidence. She stayed with the women, counseled them, and helped them through what was a traumatizing, and sometimes invasive, process. Abby hadn't been taken to her hospital, so that wasn't enough to eliminate her from the jury, but I was concerned that she might be so empathetic to Abby's assault that she'd drop the hammer on Archie just to make sure.

The third was a homebuilder on the east side of the county, which normally wouldn't raise my antenna at all. The problem was that he had been about to start construction on a neighborhood when he was approached by an oil company about drilling a well. The well had hit and now, instead of building a subdivision of houses, he was collecting oil royalties. I was able to determine that his contract was with Peninsula Petroleum, a competitor of Hillside Oil's, but I couldn't delve too far into that without tipping my hand. I was concerned though that, if I did have to go there, he might be predisposed favorably toward Wellington and the oil company.

I consoled myself with the fact that I only needed to convince one juror that Archie didn't do it. One juror to convince of reasonable doubt. In theory, I didn't need those three, but I worried about the dynamic in the room and their influence on others more than their individual vote. We would have to see.

It was approaching eleven o'clock when Judge Wesley said, "Counsel, are you prepared for opening statements?"

T. Marvin Stritch looked at the clock. "Is there enough time, Your Honor?"

Judge Wesley straightened and made a show of looking at the clock. "You have thirty minutes, Mr. Stritch."

"I have been coming in around forty minutes, Your Honor."

"We've already met you," Judge Wesley said as she pulled out a brief and started marking it up. "Skip the greeting and speak faster."

T. Marvin Stritch didn't blink. He made his way up to the lectern and turned on a PowerPoint projector. A minute later, he was ready to go. "May it please the Court?" he said.

Judge Wesley didn't look up. "Twenty-eight minutes, Mr. Stritch."

T. Marvin Stritch wore a brown suit that had the same practical functionality as his neatly cut brown hair. His face looked even more drawn than it had two weeks ago, but his eyes gleamed with enthusiasm as he faced the jury and said, "Members of the jury. That man, Archibald Mack, tried to kill a woman named Abby Ackerman. He knocked her down an old stairway at Century Quarry, then went down the stairs and smashed her in the head with a rock before leaving her there to die. Thankfully, Ms. Ackerman didn't die from her injuries or from exposure or drowning. No, the good lifeguards at the Quarry and our own Ash County paramedics found her the next morning, unconscious, bleeding, and alone, with a shattered hip and a broken eye socket and saved her by fortunate chance and the grace of God. Because she survived his heinous acts, Mr. Mack has been charged with attempted murder."

T. Marvin stood in front of the jury like a veteran history teacher delivering the same lecture to students year after year. "Now, we aren't going to just ask you to believe us or make our points with clever tricks. We're going to provide you with evidence, evidence that's going to prove every bit of what we say. We're going to prove to you that Archibald Mack went to the Century Quarry last August for the Big Luke concert and that he parked his truck in the front lot. We're going to prove that to you with video that shows him doing just that."

"We're also going to prove to you that Abby Ackerman went

to the concert that night with a group of girlfriends. We're going to show that they had a grand time and that, after the concert, they gathered for a little while in the courtyard. And then Abby left the courtyard and walked toward the back of the Quarry. We're going to show you video of that too."

Stritch paused, making eye contact with each of them.

"And then we're going to show you that Archibald Mack followed her, that he went to the back of the Quarry right after her. We're going to show you the video of it so that you can see it for yourselves."

"Now why is that suspicious? Because we already know that Mr. Mack had parked his car in the front lot. There was no reason for him to walk toward the back, toward the abandoned stairway. No reason at all. Unless Abby was that reason."

He let it hang out there for a few seconds before he continued.

"Then, with that same video, we're going to prove to you that Archibald Mack came back to the courtyard. And that Abby Ackerman never did."

He shook his head.

"No, poor Abby didn't. Instead, we'll show you that Abby Ackerman was found the next morning on the rocks at the foot of an abandoned stairway, unconscious and near death."

Stritch sped up.

"Now you're going to hear from Ms. Ackerman. She's going to tell you how she was grabbed and thrown down the stairs. She's going to tell you how she lay at the bottom in the rocks, unable to move, her hip shattered. She's going to tell you how she heard someone come down the stairs, and how she cried out for help. And then she's going to tell you that that person, that monster, raised a rock and smashed her in the face."

Stritch raised one hand for effect and then drove it down with his words.

He paused, straightened his glasses, and said, "Now, it was dark and she was in horrible pain so Ms. Ackerman won't be able to identify her attacker. But the *evidence* does. The evidence will prove to you that Archibald Mack was right there at the top of the stairs. How are we going to do that? We're going to do that with his blood."

T. Marvin Stritch straightened then and pointed at Archie.

"With *his* blood that we found on the railing at the top of the stairs. And how do we know it's his? Because we tested it and it matches his DNA. And we're going to show you video of him, with his hand bandaged and bleeding, leaving the Quarry after this incident, just walking out bold as you please while behind him...Well, while behind him he left this."

T. Marvin Stritch shook his head and turned his back to the jury, walking slowly toward the projection screen, head bowed. He clicked a button and a picture flashed up on the screen for the first time. It was Abby—her body twisted among the rocks, her face bleeding, her fingers trailing in the water.

"This is how the Quarry staff found her," T. Marvin Stritch said. "Alone. Unconscious. Shattered. With nothing to keep her from slipping into the water except the sharp rocks gouging her skin."

He pointed.

"You'll notice it's light in this picture. That's because it was taken in the morning. We're going to prove to you that Abby Ackerman lay like this all night, until the sun came up. Until Quarry lifeguards found her the next day."

T. Marvin Stritch circled back around to the jury.

"And do you know the final thing we're going to prove to you? That Ms. Ackerman was the fiancée of Hamish Mack, Archibald Mack's own brother, who she'd been with for four years. And we're going to show you that Archibald Mack called his brother, angry, right before this attack. He called his brother and mentioned Ms. Ackerman in anger by name."

I kept my face straight. That was not how the call had been described to me. I didn't jot a note and I didn't move as T. Marvin Stritch shook his head. More than one of them shook their heads right back.

"We're going to prove all of this to you—that Archibald Mack followed his brother's fiancée, pushed her down a flight of stairs, and then intentionally tried to kill her before leaving her to die. And after we prove all of that, we're going to ask you to find Archibald Mack guilty of the attempted murder of Abby Ackerman. Thank you."

Stritch turned off the projector and returned to his seat in crisp, functional movements. As he sat, Judge Wesley said, "You may proceed, Mr. Shepherd. Same time limit."

"Thank you, Your Honor."

I walked over to the jury. "Good morning." I got a couple of smiles and ten stony stares. "Mr. Stritch just told you that he's going to prove that my client, Archibald Mack, attempted to kill Abby Ackerman. He says he's going to prove that Mr. Mack pushed Ms. Ackerman down the abandoned quarry stairs, hit her with a rock, and then left her there to die."

I paused.

"Hold him to it. Hold him to every word of it."

I paced a little to the right.

"Mr. Stritch just spent a lot of time telling you what he was going to prove. What he didn't say was just as important. He didn't say he had an eyewitness who will testify that Mr. Mack pushed Ms. Ackerman down the stairs. That's because there isn't one."

"He didn't say he has video of Mr. Mack assaulting Ms. Ackerman. That's because there isn't any."

"He didn't say that he had a witness or video or any other

evidence that Mr. Mack was ever at the bottom of those stairs with a rock and he certainly didn't say that he had any evidence that Mr. Mack lifted a rock and struck her and left her there to die. That's because he doesn't have any. Not a shred. He doesn't have evidence that Archie was ever at the bottom of the stairs, he doesn't have any evidence that he touched a rock. In fact, he doesn't even have the rock."

I made eye contact from juror to juror. I wasn't getting a lot back.

"Mr. Stritch also didn't say that Ms. Ackerman will identify Mr. Mack as her attacker. That's because she won't. Despite the fact that she saw her attacker, she will not identify that person as Mr. Mack."

"In fact, Mr. Stritch didn't even say that he has any evidence that specifically links Mr. Mack to Ms. Ackerman's body in any way. No, what he has is video at the concert, video of my client leaving the Quarry, and blood on a stairway railing, blood which you will learn came, not from an attack, but from a cut Mr. Mack sustained working on the farm earlier in the day with Hamish Mack, Ms. Ackerman's fiancé and his own brother."

I shook my head.

"Mr. Stritch knows all this. He knows he doesn't have any direct evidence of the crime he's accusing my client of. So I challenge him, right now, to provide you with evidence that Archibald Mack laid hands on Abby Ackerman and threw her down a stairway. I challenge him, right now, to provide you with evidence that Archibald Mack hit her in the head with a blunt instrument of any kind. I challenge him, right now, to provide you with evidence that Archibald Mack saw Abby Ackerman on the rocks by the water and left her to die."

I shrugged.

"So far he hasn't provided any such evidence to me. I would

think that he would provide it to you. When he doesn't, we're going to ask that you return a verdict of not guilty."

I turned as if to return to my seat then said, "Oh, and he hasn't mentioned why in the world my client would do such a thing to his own brother's fiancée. Listen for that too. Thank you."

As I returned to my seat, I saw Judge Wesley out of the corner of my eye. She was staring at me.

"Bold," whispered Danny.

"Members of the jury," said Judge Wesley. "We will break for lunch and begin hearing witness testimony after." Then she gaveled us out and the jury left.

"What if he has that evidence?" whispered Danny.

"Then we're screwed anyway. Why don't you take Archie somewhere for a sandwich."

"What are you going to do?"

"Get ready."

I glanced at Stritch. As the judge left, he just took his legal pad and started reviewing it, flipping through from page to page. It was clear he wasn't going anywhere.

Exactly what I would expect.

I gathered my trial notebook, my brown bag with the turkey sandwich, orange, and a bottle of water in it, and went to find a quiet corner to prepare for the afternoon.

T. Marvin Stritch was scribbling as I left.

34

Judge Wesley had us back from lunch at exactly one o'clock. Within minutes, the jury was seated and she said, "Mr. Stritch, you may call your first witness."

Stritch stood. "Thank you, Your Honor. The state calls Kirby Granger."

Kirby walked up awkwardly from the back of the courtroom. He was wearing khaki pants and a golf shirt that was having trouble staying tucked in around the edges of his stomach. He got hung up for a moment on the swinging gate that separated the gallery from the counsel tables but then made his way between us. He gave me a nervous smile and a little wave and sat down in the witness chair, clearing his throat.

After he'd been sworn in, Stritch said, "Could you introduce yourself to the jury, please?"

Kirby turned to the jury. "Hi. My name is Kirby Granger. Nice to meet you."

Stritch smiled. A couple of the jurors did too.

"And what do you do for a living, Mr. Granger?"

"I run Century Quarry."

"And how long have you run the Quarry?"

"Well, I started working there, I don't know seventeen, no eighteen, no, I think it was seventeen years ago...yes, it was definitely seventeen years ago, but that was just as a lifeguard. I started running the concession stand three, no four years later, so that would be thirteen years ago, so that means I would've started as the second manager another two years after that and then there was the time that I was co-manager with Ricky Johnson but that didn't work out so it would've been maybe eleven years now. Yes, eleven years. I think. But I wouldn't want to swear to it."

Stritch stiffened as Kirby's answer went on. "That's fine, Mr. Granger. But you know you have sworn to tell the truth, so I need you to tell the truth as much as you know it. And if you don't know it, just say so."

Kirby nodded. "Sure. I would say somewhere between ten and twelve years then. Just to be safe."

"That's just fine," said Stritch. "And as the manager of the Century Quarry, were you at the Big Luke concert last August?"

"I sure was. It was one of the biggest gates we've ever had. Acts that size usually don't come to the Quarry." Kirby's eyes grew wide. "Oh, I didn't mean it like that. I mean Luke is big, they call him Big Luke for a reason, but I wasn't talking about him. I was talking about the gate."

The jurors' smiles grew, and I lowered my head.

Stritch shifted his weight, his smile plastered on. "I don't think anyone took it that way, Mr. Granger."

"Oh, good."

"Did you see Abby Ackerman the night of the concert?"

Kirby nodded. "I did. She worked at the Quarry years ago, so I always save a ticket for her if she wants to go."

"And did she in fact go to the Big Luke concert?"

Kirby looked around, as if he were worried he was missing something. "Well, yes. Isn't that what this is all about?"

Stritch's smile didn't falter as he nodded and said, "It is, Mr. Granger. I'm just trying to establish for the jury that Ms. Ackerman was there and that you saw her. Is that true?"

"Well, yes. Sure."

"Did you give her a ticket that night?"

"I did."

"And how was Ms. Ackerman doing that evening?"

Kirby looked down, and I think he actually blushed a little. "She was great."

"And did you see the defendant Archibald Mack that night?"

Kirby's embarrassment was replaced with a panicked look again. "No, should I have? I didn't think I ever said that I did."

Stritch nodded gently. "I'm not saying that you said that, Mr. Granger. I'm just asking if you saw Mr. Mack that evening."

"No, but like I said, that was the biggest crowd we'd ever had and I spent a bunch of time running back and forth between the ticket booth and the concessions and then one of the taps broke so that I had to—"

"Thank you, Mr. Granger."

Stritch paused and I could see him reorganizing his examination in his mind before he said, "Mr. Granger, I'm going to hand you what's been marked as State's Exhibit 12. Can you tell me what that is?"

"It's a piece of paper."

"Yes, indeed it is, Mr. Granger. Can you tell the jury what's on it?"

"Oh, right. It's a map of the Quarry."

As Kirby looked at the map, Stritch put the map up on the screen for the jury to see. "Very good. And is that a true and accurate representation of the Quarry?"

"Oh, I don't know that."

Stritch's head jerked. "You don't?"

"I mean, I don't know the exact measurements of everything at the Quarry."

Stritch nodded. "I see. Leaving the exact measurements aside for the moment, is the layout of the Quarry that the map shows generally accurate?"

Kirby raised the map a little closer to his nose and stared at it and stared at it some more and stared at it a little longer before he set it down and said, "Yes. Yes, it is."

"Excellent. So let's tell the jury what they're looking at."

"Okay."

"At the bottom, right in the center, is the front gate?"

"That's right."

"What comes next?"

"Well, then, right inside the gate is the central courtyard. On the left is the path to the amphitheater, and on the right are the concession stands, bathrooms, and changing rooms."

"Great. What is that straight ahead?"

"As you stand in the courtyard, the Quarry is right in front of you."

"Which is right above it on the map? This big blue area?"

"Yes."

"Mr. Granger, we're going to be talking to the jury during this trial about different areas in the Quarry."

"Okay."

"So the water of the Quarry itself is in a rough circle, right?"

"Right."

"I want you to picture the Quarry as a clock."

Kirby's brow furrowed. "Okay."

"On the south side of the Quarry, between five and seven o'clock here," Stritch gestured at the map on the screen, "What is this area here?"

Kirby's eyes cleared. "That's terrace seating. The upper edge is about seventy feet above the water at the courtyard end of the

Quarry and there are a series of cement landing areas that stair-step down to about ten feet above the water."

"I see. Now on the outer edge of the Quarry, all around this blue circle, is there a path?"

Kirby nodded. "There is. There's a cement walkway that goes all the way around."

"So, if the terrace seating is at six o'clock, right here at the bottom of the Quarry, and I walk around counterclockwise to three o'clock, what do I find here?"

Kirby looked confused again. "You mean, if I walk from the terrace over to the stairway that leads down to the beach?"

T. Marvin Stritch smiled and it looked like it might crack his face. "Yes."

"You would find the stairway that leads down to the beach."

Stritch pointed at the map. "So right here at three o'clock on the map there is a stairway that is how long?"

"Probably about sixty feet."

"And it leads down to what?"

"To the beach."

"Describe the beach to the jury, please."

"There's a big landing area filled with sand right at the water's edge. It's probably, I don't know, one hundred yards wide and fifty yards deep."

"So about as big as a football field?"

"Is that the same size?"

"That's what I was asking," said Stritch.

"I don't know that. Not that I could swear to."

Stritch took a deep breath. "I see. And the beach leads to the main swimming area?"

"Yes. There's an embankment that's only about a foot above the water and ladders so people can jump into the water from the edge of the beach."

"Is that where most people gather during the day?"

"There and on the terraces."

"Okay, so let's go around to twelve o'clock on the Quarry."

"After going back up the stairs?"

"Yes. After going back up the stairs."

"Okay."

There was a pause.

"What is at twelve o'clock, Mr. Granger?"

"Another stairway."

"Is that stairway in use?"

"It's for maintenance purposes only." Kirby said the words slowly and distinctly, as if he had said them over and over.

"I see. And how high is the edge of the Quarry above the water here?"

"About forty feet."

"So it's lower at that end?"

"It is."

"And people don't swim there anymore?"

"Not at that end. We closed that some years ago. We used to run a zip line from the top of the cliff over here at about nine o'clock into the water below the ladder here at twelve o'clock, but we don't anymore."

"And why is that?"

Kirby looked at Stritch and then the judge and then the jury and then at me.

"Mr. Granger?" said Stritch.

"Do I have to say it?"

"You have been asked a question, Mr. Granger," said Judge Wesley. "Please answer it."

"Well, because the lawyers wouldn't let us have any fun."

There was some chuckling around the courtroom and even Judge Wesley's mouth twitched.

Stritch ran right along with it. "So there used to be a zip line that ran into this area of the Quarry?"

"Ten years ago or so, yes," said Kirby.

"And people would use these stairs to get out of the water?"

"Yes."

"Is there a beach area at the bottom of these stairs like there is at the three o'clock stairway?"

"No. It's all rocks."

"Are they sharp?"

"Well, they're rocks."

"I see. So the stairway is only used for maintenance now?"

Kirby nodded and said, slowly and distinctly, "The stairway is used for maintenance purposes only. And there is a sign there," he scrunched up his eyes, "to that effect."

"I see. And if we keep going around the clock to eleven o'clock, there is another gate to the outside, is that right?"

"There is. It's for staff."

"And there is another, smaller parking lot back here right outside the eleven o'clock gate?"

"Yes."

"Now, Mr. Granger, do you have a lighting and video system at the Quarry?"

"Yes, we do. It was installed, I don't know, about thirteen years, no, I think it was fourteen years ago now when we were—"

T. Marvin raised his hand. "The time it was installed isn't really important, Mr. Granger. Are there lights along this path that encircle the Quarry?"

"Yes. The safety of our patrons is our first priority."

"Are those lights where these posts are?"

Kirby again examined the map for a long time. "Yes."

"So again, if we're talking about this like a clock, the lights would be at eleven, one, three, and five?"

"That's right."

"So that's the lights. Where are the cameras?"

"We have cameras showing the front lot, the courtyard, the concession stand/bathroom area, and one above the terraces that's focused on the water itself."

"Were those cameras working on the night of Big Luke concert?"

"Yes."

"Have you reviewed the video from that night?"

"Yes, I have."

"Okay, we'll get back to that. How late were you there at the Quarry on the night of the concert?"

"I stayed until probably one in the morning. It takes a while to count the gate and lock up after."

T. Marvin nodded. "And which way did you leave that night?"

"I went around back, to the back lot."

And then Kirby Granger started to cry. He stopped talking, and he bowed his head, hands clasped in front of him in his lap, and his shoulders shook as he wept. Judge Wesley looked up, T. Marvin Stritch straightened, and the jury stared.

"Mr. Granger?" Stritch said.

Kirby looked up, his eyes instantly bloodshot, tears rolling down his face. "I must've walked right by her," he said. "I must've walked right by with her down there by the water, just lying there…"

Kirby broke down completely.

There was no way that T. Marvin Stritch was going to let that stop. He let Kirby cry it out as the big, sweet man took a tissue, wiped at the tears that were dropping onto his yellow shirt, then blew his nose like a trumpet. He shook a little more and I was about to ask for a recess when Kirby took a big shuddering sigh and looked up.

"I'm sorry," he said.

"It's quite all right, Mr. Granger."

"No. I'm sorry, Abby." I glanced back at the gallery but Abby wasn't there.

"Mr. Granger," said Judge Wesley gently. "You need to keep your conversation with Mr. Stritch."

"Yes, Your Honor," said Kirby. "I'm sorry, Your Honor."

"You have no reason to apologize, Mr. Granger."

Kirby nodded, took a deep breath, and looked back at T. Marvin Stritch.

I was watching T. Marvin Stritch as it all happened. His frustration at Kirby's digressions and verbal wanderings melted away and his eyes lit up over his cadaverous cheeks. "Yes," he said. "No reason to apologize at all. I tell you what, let's go to that video we were talking about a little bit ago."

Kirby wiped his eyes one last time and put the tissue in his pocket. "Okay."

T. Marvin Stritch strode back to his laptop, hit a couple of buttons, and all four of the Quarry video screens popped up for the jury.

"Mr. Granger, is this the display of your security video?"

"Yes, it is."

"So the jury knows what we're looking at, these would be the monitors for the front parking lot, the courtyard, the concession stand area, and the water, correct?"

"That's right."

"We can watch these individually or all at once?"

"Yes."

"All right, I'm going to fast-forward these a bit." He hit another button. "Mr. Granger is there a way to tell what time this video was being taken?"

"Yes, the time stamp in the bottom corner there."

"And you can synchronize these camera views so you can watch what's happening simultaneously?"

"Uhm, what?"

"You can watch what's happening at the same time?"

"Oh, yeah, right."

"Mr. Granger, I'm going to ask you to start by looking at the video of the concession stand area. Do you see that?"

"I do."

"And when was this taken?"

"That looks like after the concert."

"And we can tell that from the time stamp?"

"Uhm, right, yes."

The video showed people congregating around a concession stand in small groups when a woman with reddish brown hair, a white shirt, jean shorts, and cowboy boots separated herself a little. Stritch paused the screen and indicated with a laser pointer.

"Mr. Granger, do you know who this is?"

"That's Abby."

"Abby Ackerman, the victim in this case?"

"Yes."

"How can you tell?"

"The hair and, well, that's her."

"Very good. Let's keep going with video."

Abby made a motion to some other people in line then set out at a hurried walk for the top of the screen and disappeared out of the picture.

"Now Mr. Granger, so the jury understands what they're seeing, what direction was Abby going when she left the screen there?"

Kirby stared at him.

"Maybe putting it in the context of a clock again."

"Oh, right. She's heading onto the path that takes you counterclockwise around the Quarry."

"So, if you kept going, you'd get to the beach stairs at three o'clock, then the abandoned stairs at twelve o'clock, and the back gate at eleven o'clock?"

"Right. Exactly."

"We've just watched Ms. Ackerman set out on that path, right?"

"Yes."

"And if she ever came back toward the front, the concession camera and the courtyard camera would pick her up, right?"

"That's right."

Stritch let the video run, at double speed but still easily followable.

Abby didn't appear.

T. Marvin leaned over and paused the video.

"Now, we have not seen Ms. Ackerman appear in the frame again, have we?"

"No, sir."

"But you know, I think we've been distracted looking for Ms. Ackerman. Let's rewind a bit and look over here at the courtyard camera." He switched screens, rewound a little, and put his laser pointer on a man in a baseball cap, jeans, and a short-sleeved patterned shirt. "There we go. What do you see there?"

"A man in a baseball cap and a short-sleeved shirt."

"Do you know who it is?"

"From the video?"

"Yes."

Kirby squinted. "I can't say for sure."

"Mr. Granger, did you know the defendant, Archibald Mack before that night?"

"I still don't know Archibald Mack."

"Very good. And do you notice anything else about this man? Anything distinguishing?"

"Uhm, he's wearing jeans?"

"Certainly. Anything else?"

"His hat."

"Yes, you mentioned that. Anything else?"

"Uhm."

"With his hand perhaps?"

I stood. "Your Honor, we've given Mr. Stritch a lot of leeway here but he's leading."

"Mr. Shepherd!" Judge Wesley said.

"Yes, Your Honor?"

"Our local rules do not permit speaking objections. If you have one, make it. Succinctly."

"Objection, Your Honor. Leading."

"Sustained. Mr. Stritch, this is your witness. Don't lead him."

"Yes, Your Honor. Is there anything else you notice about this man, Mr. Granger?"

"Yes, yes. His hand."

Stritch waited a few beats. When Kirby didn't say anything more, Stritch said, "What about his hand?"

Kirby thought. "The bandage! There's a bandage on his left hand."

"Very good. Let's keep the video going." Rather than ask a question, T. Marvin just let the video run. We watched Archie walk straight across the frame of the courtyard camera, into the frame of the concession camera, and straight across that view, never looking aside, avoiding people but walking straight ahead.

He was hurrying. Right in the direction Abby had gone.

When Archie walked out of the frame of the concession camera, Stritch paused it again.

"So according to the time stamp, this is after Ms. Ackerman passed in the same direction, right?"

"That's right."

"And we have not seen Ms. Ackerman appear in any other camera view in that time, right?"

"That's right."

"Let's keep going then."

The video ran. The tension in the courtroom grew, even for me, and I knew what was coming.

Then Archie appeared in the concession camera, coming back from the way he had gone. Stritch pounced on his laptop and paused the video.

"Mr. Granger, what do you see now?"

"I see the man in the cap and the patterned shirt coming back."

"Coming back from an area that includes the abandoned stairs?"

I thought about objecting but Archie's blood was going to prove that he had made it all the way back that far. I stayed in my seat.

"Yes," said Kirby.

"Let's see what this man in the baseball cap does."

I knew, but I watched anyway. Stritch let the video run and we watched Archie walk past the concession stand but this time, his route was much closer to the camera.

"Mr. Granger, is this the same man with the baseball cap we've been following?"

"It is."

"Can you tell who it is now?"

"Now, with this view, I can see that it's Mr. Mack."

Archie's face was lit and turned up. We all could see it.

"And do you notice anything else about him?"

Kirby stared.

"Do you notice the wrapping on his hand?"

"I do."

"Do you notice anything different about it?"

Kirby scowled then said, "It's got a dark spot on it now."

"Where before it was white?"

"Yes."

Stritch let the video continue and we watched Archie pass through the courtyard and out to the front parking lot. When the video showed Archie passing out of frame to the edge of the parking lot, Stritch stopped it and said, "Mr. Granger, have you looked at this entire video?"

"I have."

"Does Ms. Ackerman ever appear in it again?"

"On the pathway? No."

"Does she appear in another view?"

Kirby cleared his throat and said, "Yes."

"Where? When?"

Kirby cleared his throat again but didn't speak.

Stritch's kind tone was belied by the light in his eyes. "Mr. Granger, you've said that Ms. Ackerman appears in the video again?"

Kirby nodded.

"You need to answer out loud, Mr. Granger."

"Yes." Kirby's voice was a croak. "Yes, she does."

"When?"

"Sunrise."

Stritch didn't say anything then. Instead, he hunched over his laptop and switched the video to a black screen that I knew was the camera view of the water. The picture stayed black, the time stamp running in the bottom corner the only indication that the video was fast-forwarding. Then the picture began to lighten and T. Marvin paused the video again.

"Show us where Mr. Granger," he said and handed Kirby a laser pointer.

All eyes followed him as Kirby fumbled with the button, found the one that created the red dot of light, and put it on the screen.

We didn't need the laser pointer, but Kirby circled anyway, just to the left of the cement pad that was at the bottom of the abandoned stairs directly across the water. An arm with finger-tips dangling in the water. A twisted body. A toe of a boot just visible over the rocks.

Stritch hit play. The Quarry grew lighter. Abby's body became clearer.

"Can you identify who that is?"

"It's Abby," Kirby said quietly and looked away.

"Is that where she was found the morning after the concert?"

"Yes."

"Did you watch the rest of this video?"

"Yes."

"Does she ever move?"

"No."

"Thank you, Mr. Granger. That's all the questions that I have."

With well-practiced modesty, Stritch took a seat. He left the frozen video of Abby on the screen.

35

I stood and pointed at the video. "Do you mind?"

"Oh, of course not," said Stritch. "My apologies." He fumbled around, longer than was necessary, then turned it off.

I smiled. "Thanks." I turned to Kirby. "Mr. Granger, just so the jury is clear, we know each other, don't we?"

"Sure, Nate," said Kirby. "Uhm, I mean, Mr. Shepherd."

"We met about fourteen or fifteen years ago when we both worked at the Quarry, correct?"

"We did."

"This camera system was installed about ten years ago, right?"

"That's right."

"By that time, the twelve o'clock stairs were no longer in use by the public, were they?"

"They were not."

"They were just used for maintenance, right?"

"That's right."

"There are no cameras that record what happens at the top of the twelve o'clock stairs, are there?"

He shook his head. "There are not."

"It's also dark there, isn't it?"

Kirby looked uncomfortable. "At night, sure."

"The lights don't reach there, do they?"

"Not really."

"Now Mr. Granger, you, personally, did not see Archie Mack interact with Abby Ackerman, did you?"

"You mean see them together?"

"That's exactly what I mean."

"I didn't."

"You didn't see them talk to each other, did you?"

"No."

"And you certainly didn't see Archie put his hands on Ms. Ackerman, did you?"

"I didn't."

"Now, you mentioned that you watched the whole rest of the video, though, right?"

"I did."

"There's no video of Archie Mack putting his hands on Ms. Ackerman, is there?"

"Not that I've seen."

"There is no video where Archie Mack and Abby Ackerman appear at the same time, is there?"

"No."

"So the jury is clear, Mr. Granger, Archie Mack and Abby Ackerman never appear on the video at the same time, do they?"

"Not that I've seen, no."

"Instead, the only video we have is of them passing the Quarry's cameras at different times, true?"

"That's true."

"Mr. Granger, there is video of you leaving the Quarry that night, isn't there?"

Kirby nodded. "There is."

"You left about one a.m.?"

"I did. A little after."

"Danny could you cue up the video, please?" Danny clicked a few times on the laptop and video marked with military time as '0046' appeared on the screen for the jury. "Go ahead and let it run, Danny."

The video began to move. "That's you at the front gate, right, Mr. Granger?"

"That's right."

"There you are locking it?"

"I am."

"It's your job to make sure the facility is secure?"

"It is."

"Now, here you're going to the concession area?"

"Yes."

"And you're pulling down the gate to the concession window and locking the door?"

"I am."

The video continued to roll.

"You are locking up the bathrooms here?"

"I am."

"And it looks like you're checking inside each one before you do?"

"I am."

"And that is to make sure no one is in it?"

"That's right. I wouldn't want to lock someone in."

"That's never happened has it?"

"No. Because I always check."

"And now you're doing the same with changing rooms?"

"Yes."

"Looking inside, checking, and then locking up?"

"That's right."

"Are you pretty thorough about going through this routine to make sure everything is secure?"

"I try to be, yes."

The video showed Kirby locking the last of the doors, checking his keys, and putting them in his pocket. Then, when he was right at the edge of the screen of the concession camera, I said, "Pause it there please, Danny."

The frame froze. "Were you done for the night now, Mr. Granger?"

"Just about. I had to lock up the back gate on the way out."

"And that's where you're going now, to the back gate?"

"That's right."

"Because the back lot is typically where employees park, correct?"

"That's right. We also used it as overflow parking on a night like this."

I nodded. "Okay, Danny, let it run again." The video showed Kirby pause at the edge of the screen and walk back into frame where he bent over and picked up a pop can.

"What are you doing there, Mr. Granger?"

"Picking up some garbage."

"So even though you're getting ready to leave, you were still inspecting the facility and the things in it?"

"I was."

"You cared enough to pick up that can?"

Kirby shrugged. "I like the Quarry to be clean."

The video showed Kirby dropping the can into a garbage bin before he kept going and left the frame.

"You can pause it there, please, Danny. Mr. Granger, did you walk directly to the back gate?"

"I believe I did."

"You don't believe you paused along the way?"

"I don't think so."

"Mr. Granger, I know this upset you earlier, but I have to ask. You were inspecting the Quarry as you left that night, right?"

"I was."

"You were looking for people in the bathrooms?"

"Yes."

"You were looking for people in the changing rooms?"

"I was."

"You were picking up things as small as pop cans if they were left out?"

"I was."

"It's dark on the path to the back lot, isn't it?"

"In spots, yes."

"One of those dark spots is the abandoned stairs, right?"

"Yes."

"It's dark there, isn't it?"

"It is."

"And you, as careful and conscientious as you are, didn't see anything when you walked past the abandoned stairs that night, did you?"

"I didn't."

"You didn't see Abby Ackerman, did you?"

"I didn't."

"You didn't see any sign that anything had happened near the stairs that night, did you?"

"I didn't."

"You didn't see any indication that there had been an accident, did you?"

"I did not."

"You didn't see any sign, at all, that Abby Ackerman was at the bottom of those stairs lying in distress, did you?"

Kirby's eyes welled up. "No."

"Mr. Granger, Abby worked at the Quarry some years ago as well, didn't she?"

"She did."

"You worked there at the same time?"

"I did."

"You consider her to be a good friend?"

Kirby nodded. "I do."

"If you had seen the slightest indication that Abby was there or that she was hurt or that there was anything wrong at all, you would have investigated, wouldn't you?"

"Of course."

"But the fact was that there, in the dark that night, you didn't see anything that let you know Abby was hurt, did you?"

"No. No, I didn't."

"It wasn't until the next day, in daylight, that Abby was discovered, true?"

"That's true."

"That's all I have Mr. Granger, thanks."

T. Marvin Stritch stood. "Mr. Granger you became emotional a little while ago when you talked about not finding Ms. Ackerman, didn't you?"

Kirby nodded. "I did."

"That's because the thought of her lying there all night torments you, doesn't it?"

Kirby looked like he might well up again. "It does."

"And the sight of her lying among the rocks? On the video?"

"Yes."

"Could you imagine leaving her down there?"

"No. Not at all."

"That's all, Mr. Granger. Thank you."

I stood. "Mr. Granger, you left Abby in the dark by the water forty feet below you because you couldn't see her as you passed, correct?"

"That's right."

"And because you couldn't hear her?"

"That's true."

"And because when you passed the stairway, you could see no sign that Ms. Ackerman had ever been there, could you?"

"That's right."

"No further questions."

Judge Wesley said, "Mr. Granger, you may step down. Members of the jury, it's almost four-thirty, so we'll wrap it up for the day. Please don't discuss this case with each other or with anyone in your home. We will get going again tomorrow promptly at eight-thirty."

Judge Wesley hit the gavel and we all stood as the jury filed out. As soon as they had left, Judge Wesley retired to her chambers.

I turned to Archie. "You doing okay?"

He didn't look it as he said, "Can I go see Bonnie?" Because Bonnie was going to testify, she wasn't allowed in the courtroom for now. Archie clearly needed some support.

"Go ahead. Be here tomorrow at eight."

Archie nodded and left.

I got T. Marvin Stritch's attention as he was gathering his things. "Who's up tomorrow?" I said.

Stritch appeared to consider it before he shrugged. "Hamish Mack and Sheriff Dushane," he said. "Not sure if we'll get any farther than that."

I nodded. "Thanks."

He nodded back and continued to gather his things.

I went back to Danny, who was doing the same thing. "Hamish and Dushane tomorrow," I said.

He nodded. "Okay."

I had known Danny long enough to know something was on his mind. "What is it?"

"Nothing."

I smiled. "It's okay to disagree, Danny. We have to be able to tell each other what we think."

He nodded. "I think that you really exposed us by challenging Stritch to produce evidence of physical contact and motive."

"I did. But it's a weakness in their case and, if they can produce it, we're in pretty big trouble anyway."

"It just sort of seems like we invited it."

"We'll see."

He frowned. "I hope not."

Mr. and Mrs. Mack had been sitting in the middle row of the gallery all day. They waited patiently for me to wrap things up before they came forward.

"What a nice man that Mr. Granger was," said Mrs. Mack. "He was so upset."

"He feels like he let her down, even though he didn't."

"He didn't see Abby the same as Archie didn't," said Mr. Mack.

I nodded. I hoped the jury felt the same way. "Hamish is testifying tomorrow."

They exchanged a glance. "Well, I'm sure it'll all come out fine."

I nodded and thought, not in a million years. "Okay. See you tomorrow."

Mr. and Mrs. Mack filed out. After they were gone, I gathered our things and we left.

The Ash County Courthouse has a bunch of narrow corridors and sharp corners, a byproduct of a 1960s addition to a 1920s courthouse. As Danny and I rounded the corner, Olivia was waiting for us by the stairs.

She was wearing a black suit with a white shirt. She seemed a little taller to me before I realized I rarely saw her in heels. She ran a hand through her spiky white hair and pulled it down around the left lens of her glasses the way she always did.

"I thought I saw you back there," I said. "You attending this one?"

She nodded. "You need anything?"

I shook my head. "We're good tonight."

"Okay, let me know." She turned and started down the stairs. She made it down three before she turned to where Danny and I still stood at the top. "You coming?"

Danny looked at me and held out the brief cases he held in each hand.

"And?" she said.

I laughed. "You'll have to excuse Danny. He doesn't know the depths of your psychosis yet."

"Don't listen to him, Danny," said Olivia. "It's a training opportunity."

We followed her down the stairs and left.

36

Hamish Mack took the stand first thing in the morning. His red hair was combed neatly and, although it had been a good month since there had been warm sun of any kind, he still had the faintest traces of a tan line running across his face, just like his brother. The similarities didn't end there—he wore a boxy blue suit similar in style and cut to the one Archie had on and it was clear that they'd both gone to the same place. Hamish showed none of Kirby's reluctance—he strode straight to the stand and planted himself.

When he was settled, T. Marvin Stritch said, "Could you state your name please?"

"Hamish Mack."

"You're the brother of the defendant, Archibald Mack?"

"I am."

"And Abby Ackerman is your fiancée?"

"She is."

"Is it difficult for you to be here today, Mr. Mack?"

He looked past T. Marvin Stritch at his parents. "In some ways," he said. He scowled at Archie. "Not in others."

"I would normally call you Mr. Mack, but to avoid confusion, do you mind if I call you Hamish?"

"Not at all."

"Hamish, how long have you and Abby Ackerman been together?"

"About four years."

"That's a long time."

"It is. It's hard to find someone who understands farming the way Abby does."

"You knew that Ms. Ackerman was going to the Big Luke concert with her friends the night that she was attacked?"

"I did. She was very excited."

"Did you have plans to go to the concert?"

"Not until the last minute. But then the day of, I got a call from an acquaintance who asked if I'd like to go. So I went."

"Who is that acquaintance?"

"Will Wellington."

I thought that acquaintance was an interesting way to put it.

"Why did he ask you to go?"

"You'd have to ask him, but I got the impression he had the tickets from his business and wanted to use them." Hamish smiled. "Since it was the day of, I'm sure I wasn't his first choice."

"So you decided to go?"

"I did."

"Did you tell Abby?"

"Before the concert? No. I didn't want to make her feel guilty about going with her friends."

"I see. So you went."

"I did."

"Was it just you and Will?"

"No, he asked a few others. I think there were seven of us altogether."

"Did you know the others?"

"No, but we were all farmers so we had a lot in common and talked some before the concert."

"So you stayed for the entire concert?"

"I did."

"And what happened after?"

"I thanked Will for the tickets and the drinks and walked back to my car."

"And where were you parked, Hamish?"

"In the back lot. Abby had worked at the Quarry some years ago and had told me about the employee lot. She'd said it was a lot easier to get in and out during big events, so I parked there."

"What happened next?"

"Well, I was partway back when I heard someone call my name. I stopped and turned and saw that it was Abby."

"I see. And then what happened?"

Hamish looked at the floor.

"Hamish?" said T. Marvin Stritch.

"We argued," said Hamish.

"About what?"

Hamish sighed. "Going to the concert."

"What do you mean?"

"That I went without telling her, I suppose."

"What happened next?"

"She yelled at me, I yelled at her, and I left."

"Why did you leave?"

"Because the concert was over and it seemed silly to be mad about how we saw it."

"Weren't you concerned about leaving her alone at the Quarry?"

"No. She was with..." Hamish's voice cracked and he paused for a moment before he said, "I assumed she was with her friends."

"I see. What did you do next?"

"I went to the back lot, got in my truck, and drove home."

"How far of a drive is that?"

"Thirty, forty minutes depending on traffic."

"Hamish, did you receive any phone calls on the way home?"

Hamish nodded.

"You need to answer out loud, Hamish," said T. Marvin Stritch.

Hamish's voice cracked again. "Yes, I did."

"When was the first call?"

"Right after I left. I was just"—he stopped and cleared his throat—"I was just pulling out of the parking lot."

"And who was that call from?"

"Abby."

"And did you talk to Abby?"

Hamish shook his head.

"Hamish."

"I didn't."

"Why?"

"I was still mad. So I declined the call."

"I see. So how do you know it was Abby who called you?"

"She left me a voicemail."

"Was it this voicemail?"

T. Marvin Stritch went to his computer, clicked the button, and Abby's voice came out of the speaker loud enough for all of us to hear:

"Baby, you're right, let's not let this wreck the concert tonight. We can talk about it tomorrow. I'm meeting Bonnie and the girls at HopHeads, but call me anyway. I love you. I'm right and you're a horse's ass. But I love you. Bye."

Hamish looked at the floor while it played.

"Is that a true and accurate copy of the voicemail message you received from Abby Ackerman the night of the concert?"

Hamish nodded, then raised his head and said, "Yes."

"Did you call her back?"

"No."

"Why not?"

Hamish looked at the gallery and then said, "Because I was still mad."

"You said you received two calls on the way home. When was the second one?"

"Just a few minutes later."

"And who was that call from?"

"From my brother, the defendant, Archie Mack."

"And did you take that call?"

"Yes."

"Why?"

"Because it was unusual for Archie to call me, especially that late at night. I was worried that something might be wrong with Mom and Dad."

"And what did Archie want?"

"He wanted to yell at me too."

"About what?"

"About the concert."

"What about the concert?"

"Turns out Archie had gone to the concert too."

"How is that a problem?"

"Going to the concert wasn't the problem. Who I went with was."

"Will Wellington?"

"Yes."

"Why was that a problem?"

"Because Wellington had made us an offer to put an oil well on our land a few years back and we'd turned him down."

"So how is that a problem?"

"Archie assumed I was trying to get things going again on my own."

"What happened next?"

"We exchanged words."

"Do you remember what those words were?"

"Not exactly."

"What do you remember?"

"I remember telling him to get off my a"—he looked at the judge—"off my butt and that I had talked about it enough with Abby as it was."

"And what was his reaction to that?"

Hamish glared at Archie before he looked at T. Marvin Stritch and said, "My brother said, 'You mean that Abby was in on this too?'"

Stritch looked at the jury before he said, "Were those his exact words?"

"Yes. That I remember completely."

"Why?"

"Because then he hung up on me and that had to have been right about the time—"

I stood. "Objection. The witness's answer is not responsive and speculative."

"Sustained," said Judge Wesley. "The witness will answer the question asked without giving additional opinions."

Hamish nodded.

"Did you hear from Archie or Abby anymore that evening?" said Stritch.

"I did not."

"Weren't you worried that you didn't hear from Abby?"

"No, I thought...I thought that she was with her friends. And I figured she was waiting for me to call first."

"When did you learn that wasn't the case?"

"When I received a call from Mission Hospital the next morning."

"How did they know to notify you?"

"We had both made each other our emergency contacts a year ago, so that we wouldn't worry our parents."

"I see. How was Abby's condition?"

"It was touch and go for a few days."

"What do you mean?"

"She had pretty serious injuries to her hip, her face. She had a few operations. She was in and out of consciousness."

"Did you talk to Abby about what had happened?"

"All the time."

"What was she able to tell you about what happened?"

I stood. "Objection, Your Honor. Hearsay."

"Sustained."

"Hamish, does your brother have a temper?"

I stood. "Objection."

"Sustained."

"Hamish, have you and your brother ever gotten into a fist fight?"

I stayed standing. "Objection. Relevance."

"Sustained."

"Have you ever seen your brother act violently?"

"Objection. Your Honor?"

Judge Wesley stared at T. Marvin Stritch. "Mr. Stritch, we've had this discussion. Questions regarding general disposition and past incidents are not admissible in this proceeding."

Stritch made a show of looking at the ceiling and pretending to think. We both knew exactly what he was going to ask.

"Hamish, did you fight with Archie in the hospital outside of Abby's room?"

I sat.

"I did," said Hamish.

"Who started it?"

"I did."

"Why?"

"Because he attacked Abby."

I stood. "Objection, move to strike, Your Honor. The witness can't testify that is true."

"Sustained."

Stritch raised his hand. "Hamish, would it be more accurate to say you started a fight in the hospital outside Abby's room because you believed he had attacked Abby?"

"Yes."

Stritch nodded. "Hamish, you said that in some ways it was not difficult to testify today. Do you remember that?"

Hamish scowled at Archie. "I do."

"Is it hard to testify against your brother?"

"No."

"Why? He's your brother."

"Because he was so angry, so angry at me. All I did was go to a concert, but he was furious and then when I mentioned Abby, well, you just had to have heard him."

"But he's your brother."

Hamish stared. "I'm sure he thinks he loves me. But he loves that farm more."

Stritch nodded and walked toward his table. When he got there, he turned and said, "Hamish, did you plant corn this season?"

Hamish cocked his head. "No. It was my turn to rotate that off my land. My parents and Archie planted it this year."

Stritch nodded. "I have no further questions at this time, Your Honor."

I stood. "So you were the guest of Will Wellington at the concert?"

"I was."

"The jury might not understand what Mr. Wellington does. Mr. Wellington is a representative for Hillside Oil & Gas, isn't he?"

Hamish nodded. "He is."

"And some years ago, he made an offer to your family to put an oil well on your farm, didn't he?"

"He did."

"Your family turned it down, didn't they?"

"We did."

"To be more accurate, your mother and father turned it down, right?"

"We all did."

"I know you say that, but your mom and dad make the final decisions about farming operations on your land, don't they?"

"We work together."

"I'm sure you do. But if you disagree, what they say goes, right?"

"That doesn't happen."

"But if it does, they win, don't they?"

Hamish stared. "They have the final say. But it's always unanimous."

"So the jury understands, your mom and dad split pieces of the farm for you and your brother so you could start farming your own land before they died, right?"

"That's right."

"They essentially gave you the land but kept control of the farming operations, true?"

"That's true."

"So about five years ago, your parents decided that they wanted to switch to organic farming, right?"

"We all did."

"That can be a lengthy transition process?"

"It takes about three years."

"And it was during that process that Will Wellington and Hillside Oil offered your parents the oil lease, right?"

"That's true. We turned them down though."

"Again, it was your parents who turned them down, right?"

Hamish nodded. "They thought it didn't fit with their image of an organic farm."

"You say 'they' thought that. Did you disagree?"

"No. It made sense."

"So when you went to the Big Luke concert with Will Wellington, what did you have to talk about?

Hamish tilted his head. "What do you mean?"

"I mean you had already decided that there wasn't going to be an oil well on your family's land. That's what the family decided, right?"

"Right."

"So why would you talk to Wellington about it?"

Hamish shrugged. "Listening isn't talking."

"And did you listen the night of the Big Luke concert?"

"Of course." Hamish smiled. "Big Luke is great."

I decided to leave that for the moment. "You testified that you fought with Abby the night of her attack, right?"

He scowled. "We argued."

"You argued enough that you left her there at the Quarry, right?"

"I didn't leave her there. She didn't come with me."

"You were angry, weren't you?"

"I sure was. I didn't think I deserved to be yelled at."

"You fought with her right by the stairs, didn't you?"

"We were not by the stairs."

"You were in the back section of the Quarry, weren't you?"

"We were. On the way to the back lot."

"Outside the view of the cameras, right?"

"I don't know what the cameras saw."

"But there's no question that you fought with her in the back of the Quarry outside the view of the cameras."

"I already told you that I argued with her and that I don't know what the cameras saw."

"But you say she called you after you left, right?"

"I don't say that, the voice message does."

"And you said it was sometime after that that Archie called you?"

"That's what my phone says."

"And Archie was mad at you?"

"He was."

"Because you were going behind your family's back to try to make a deal with Wellington for an oil lease?"

Hamish glared. "Because he *thought* I was talking to Wellington about an oil lease. Which I was not."

"Right, right, I remember, you were *listening* about an oil lease. Very different." I paused. "So what's the point of even listening to Wellington about an oil lease if your parents have control of the farming operations?"

Hamish smiled. "That's exactly the point I was making to Archie on the phone. There was no harm in it at all because our parents control the farming."

I paused for a moment. I didn't even have to look at the jury to know I was losing them with this Wellington business. I could feel it. It was time to hit them with some basics.

"Hamish, you never saw Abby with your brother that night at the Big Luke concert, did you?"

"I did not."

"When Abby left you the phone message, you didn't hear Archie in the background, did you?"

"I did not."

"Abby didn't say anything to indicate that she saw Archie, did she?"

"No."

"When you talked on the phone with Archie, he didn't say anything to indicate to you that he saw Abby that night, did he?"

"He did not."

"You didn't hear Abby in the background in Archie's phone, did you?"

"No. But it doesn't matter."

"What do you mean it doesn't matter?"

"I'm sure you can do one of those track my phone things and show that they were in the same place at the same time."

Alarm bells. "Have you done that?"

"I haven't but I think Mr.—I haven't, no."

Stritch continued to write notes on his legal pad as if he had no idea what Hamish was talking about.

"Who has told you they have?"

"Do I have to answer that?" Hamish said to the Judge.

"You do now," said Judge Wesley.

"I think Mr. Stritch has. I think it shows..."

I raised a hand. "I didn't ask you what it shows, Hamish. I asked who told you they'd done it and you answered Mr. Stritch. You, personally, you didn't see or hear anything to indicate Archie and Abby were ever in the same place at the same time that night, did you?"

Hamish thought.

"With your own eyes or ears?"

"No, I didn't."

"From your perspective Hamish, Archie and Abby got along, didn't they?"

"I used to think so."

"There was no indication of any friction between them, was there?"

"Not until that evening, no."

"Hamish, would you defer to Abby if she says there's no friction between her and Archie?"

"No."

"Why not?"

"Because she doesn't know who attacked her."

"No, she doesn't, does she?"

"No."

"She doesn't say it was Archie, does she?"

Stritch stood. "Objection. Hearsay."

"Sustained."

"Abby doesn't own any part of Mack Farms, does she, Hamish?"

"No, she doesn't."

"So any dispute Archie had about the management of Mack farm wouldn't be with Abby, would it?"

"I don't know who he would feel his dispute was with."

"Well, a dispute about Mack Farms would have to be with the people who own Mack Farms, wouldn't it?"

Hamish shrugged. "You would think."

"When you talked to Archie on the phone, he was mad at you, wasn't he?"

"It sure seemed like it."

"Because he felt that you were going behind the family's back to make a deal with Will Wellington, right?"

"I don't know that."

"Well, that's what he said, wasn't it?"

"It was. But Archie says a lot of things."

Sometimes examinations go right and other times you can feel them spin off into a place where you're doing more harm than good. I had made the points I was going to make with Hamish and now I was just arguing with him and, worse, I was boring the jury. What I had on him with Wellington, he'd just deny; I'd have to establish it with the oilman. I decided to lay a little more groundwork and get out.

"Hamish, your brother was helping you fix drainage tiles on the farm earlier on the day of the concert, wasn't he?"

"He was."

"Archie cut his hand that day removing some of the old tile with you, didn't he?"

"He did."

"We're going to hear more evidence on this, Hamish. Is it your testimony to this jury that you weren't entering into a deal behind your parents back for an oil well on your part of the farm?"

Hamish shook his head. "I was just going to the concert, Mr. Shepherd."

"Thank you, Mr. Mack."

I was pretty sure that didn't go well.

Then T. Marvin Stritch stood up and said, "No further questions, Your Honor."

Judge Wesley nodded. "You may step down, Mr. Mack." As he walked by our table, Hamish Mack glared at Archie, smirked at me, and left. Then Judge Wesley dismissed us for lunch.

I told Danny to take Archie to find some lunch. I grabbed my paper bag and my trial book and went to find a quiet corner.

I had to do a lot better with Sheriff Dushane this afternoon or we were in big trouble.

37

When we returned to the courtroom after lunch, Judge Wesley seated the jury and T. Marvin Stritch called Sheriff Warren Dushane to the stand. Sheriff Dushane ambled up from the gallery in an easy way that made it clear he was comfortable with the courtroom and himself. He set his brown, wide-brimmed hat on the rail of the witness stand and casually shifted his holster so that it wasn't pushing down on to the seat of his chair, then gave T. Marvin Stritch a slight nod to show that he was ready.

"Could you state your name please, sir?"

"I'm Sheriff Warren Dushane."

"You are the sheriff of Ash County?"

"I am."

"And have you been doing that long?"

Sheriff Dushane gave a slight smile. "Decades."

"Sheriff Dushane, in that capacity, do you have experience investigating murders?"

"I do."

"Assaults?"

"Yes."

"Have you investigated cases in which someone tried to kill someone and failed?"

"I have."

"And so do you have experience in determining whether someone has attempted to commit murder?"

I stood. "Objection, Your Honor. Extrinsic evidence, facts not in evidence, other acts, unfairly prejudicial."

Judge Wesley looked at me, let things percolate for a moment, then said, "Sustained. Counsel will limit himself to the facts of this case."

T. Marvin Stritch cocked his head but quickly recovered. "Sheriff Dushane, did you have the opportunity to investigate the circumstances surrounding the attack on Abby Ackerman?"

"I did."

"How did that occur?"

"At approximately 7 a.m., my office received a call from the staff at Century Quarry stating that they had found a woman who was severely injured."

"Was it originally reported as an attack?"

"I don't believe so," said the sheriff. "I believe the ambulance was called first."

"Was the rescue squad there when you arrived?"

"I believe we got there about the same time."

"And what did you find?"

"We found the victim, Abby Ackerman, at the foot of the abandoned stairs at the Quarry."

Stritch put the map up on the screen. "Sheriff Dushane, the manager of the Quarry testified yesterday. We've been calling the stairs right here the twelve o'clock stairs or the abandoned stairs. Are those the stairs you are talking about?"

"They are."

"Using this map as a guide, where did you find Ms. Ackerman?"

Sheriff Dushane used the laser pointer. "Here. Just to the left of the pad if you're looking from the water."

"And what was Ms. Ackerman's condition?"

"She was unconscious. She was in shock and her temperature had dropped. We didn't know the extent of her injuries, but it was clear they were severe."

"I take it your first priority was to get medical attention for Ms. Ackerman?"

"It was."

"What did you do?"

"There was some thought of stabilizing Ms. Ackerman and carrying her back up the stairs. Then one of the lifeguards indicated that they had several rafts and we decided that it would be easier to float her over to the beach area and take her up that stairway, which was wider and in better condition."

"Now Ms. Ackerman could not speak to you that morning, could she?"

"She could not."

"So when did you begin to consider that this may have been the result of an attack?"

"When we saw the streak of blood on the railing at the top of the stairs."

"And why did that indicate a possible attack to you?"

"Its placement did not seem consistent with the fall. As a result, we treated the area as a crime scene."

"How so?"

"We secured the area, limited access to the stairs, and used evidentiary protocols to take samples and investigate the surroundings."

"Did you and your men take pictures?"

"We did."

"I'm going to direct your attention to State's Exhibit 21. Can you identify that for the jury, please?"

"I can. It's a picture of the railing at the top of the abandoned stairs."

The picture flashed up on the screen. It showed a bloodied streak right at the top of the railing. "And what is this right here?"

"That's the blood I was referring to."

"And why did you immediately think that this was not related to a fall?"

"Do you see how the blood curls around the underside of the railing?"

"I do."

"That indicated to us that it was a handprint rather than an impact injury. Ms. Ackerman's hands and arms were not bloodied. Her head was. As a result, we believed that this was not from her."

"What did you do?"

"We took pictures. We took samples of the blood. We took fingerprints."

"I see. What did you do with the blood?"

"We had it tested for type and DNA."

"And were you provided with those test results?"

"I was."

"And what were they?"

"The blood was O positive. The DNA matched that of the defendant."

"That being Archibald Mack?"

"Yes."

"And the fingerprints? What about those?"

"Those matched Mr. Mack as well."

"I see. We'll come back to that. You did not know any of that yet on the morning you assisted in the rescue of Ms. Ackerman, did you?"

"I did not."

Stritch put another picture up. "Sheriff Dushane, this is State's Exhibit 22. Could you tell us what that is?"

"It is a picture of the abandoned stairway, about halfway down."

"And what is that on the stairs themselves?"

"That is blood."

"And did you also have that blood tested?"

"We did."

"And whose blood is that?"

"That is Ms. Ackerman's. It was left there when her head struck the stairs."

Stritch flipped a picture. "And State's Exhibit 23?"

"That is another stair with Ms. Ackerman's blood on it, about four stairs down from the previous picture."

"I see, and this? State's Exhibit 24?"

"This is a picture of another stair farther down, but do you see how the vegetation is smashed down next to it?"

"I do."

"That is where Ms. Ackerman tumbled off of the stairs and began to fall down the hillside of the Quarry itself."

"I see. And State's Exhibit 25?"

"That is almost to the bottom of the stairs. Do you see the strip of matted and broken vegetation?"

"I do."

"That was created by Ms. Ackerman's body as she fell. It was actually quite fortunate that she went off the stairs."

"How so?"

"Because there were no longer sharp edges of metal and concrete to hit her head on. Also, the vegetation served to break her fall and slow her down while the stairway ends in a flat cement pad."

"And why is that significant?"

"Because if she had continued down the stairway, I believe

she would have sustained additional injuries and could very well have slipped into the water and—"

I stood. "Objection, Your Honor. Speculation."

"Sustained," said Judge Wesley.

"Counsel raises a good point, Sheriff Dushane," said Stritch. "You aren't allowed to speculate or guess in court. Now you can give an opinion to a reasonable degree of probability, which means more likely than not. Sheriff Dushane, do you have an opinion to a reasonable degree of probability regarding what would have happened if Ms. Ackerman's fall had continued down the stairs to the cement pad?"

I stood. "Same objection, Your Honor."

"The question is properly phrased counsel. Overruled."

"You may answer," said Stritch.

"I believe, to a reasonable degree of probability, that Ms. Ackerman would have slipped into the water."

"Ms. Ackerman was unconscious when you found her, correct?"

"She was."

"And if she had been unconscious when she slipped into the water?"

"I believe to a reasonable degree of probability that she would've drowned."

"How deep is the water at that end of the Quarry?"

"At least thirty feet deep. In sections, it's fifty."

"Goodness, that's deep. In fact, deputies in your office do scuba training there, don't they?"

"They do. We practice recoveries. Fortunately, that wasn't necessary here."

"Indeed. And State's Exhibit 27?"

There was a sharp gasp from the jury box. Stritch sprung it on them with no warning. It was a picture of Abby

Ackerman, lying twisted among the rocks at the water's edge. Her hair was matted with blood and stuck to her face.

Stritch raised a hand. "Sheriff, I'm not trying to be needlessly graphic here, but we had Kirby Granger on the stand yesterday and he identified some video for the jury in which a woman was seen walking. So I need to ask you, when you found Abby Ackerman, she was wearing these cowboy boots?"

"She was."

"And a white shirt and jean shorts?"

"She was."

"Sheriff Dushane, I can't help but notice that Ms. Ackerman's hand is dangling in the water. Is that how she was when you found her?"

"It was."

"So she was that close?"

"She was."

"I see." Stritch left the picture up for another moment then clicked it off. "What did you do next?"

"After waiting to make sure that there were sufficient rescue personnel to get Ms. Ackerman to safety, I secured the scene and supervised the gathering of evidence such as the fingerprints and blood that we discussed."

"I see. And after that?"

"I spoke with the manager, Kirby Granger, to obtain the Quarry's security video."

"Right. Anything else?"

"I dispatched an officer to the hospital to assist in gathering evidence from Ms. Ackerman herself."

"Evidence from Ms. Ackerman? What do you mean?"

"At that point, we were not sure if she had been sexually assaulted. We dispatched an officer to the hospital to find out and gather evidence, if necessary."

"I see. And was she sexually assaulted?"

"Thankfully, no."

"And then what?"

"Over the next several days, we evaluated the security video and interviewed witnesses. This eventually led us to identify Archibald Mack as the man in the video behind Ms. Ackerman."

Stritch clicked a button. A freeze-frame from the Quarry video showed Archie. Two more clicks blew up his face beneath a "Mack Farms" hat. "Now we've gone through the video extensively with Mr. Granger. Is this the man you're speaking of?"

"Yes."

"And you concluded this is Archibald Mack?"

"We did."

"And that was confirmed by fingerprint evidence?"

"Yes."

"And DNA evidence?"

"Yes."

Stritch paused as if thinking of something. "Did you ask Ms. Ackerman to identify her attacker?"

"Not at first."

"And why is that?"

"She was unconscious after the attack, so we could not speak with her. After that, she was undergoing several surgical procedures for her injuries."

"Really? What did the doctors do for her?"

I stood. "Objection, Your Honor. Hearsay."

"Sustained."

"Where was Ms. Ackerman when you attempted to speak with her?"

"In emergency surgery the first time. Sleeping in her hospital bed the second."

"We'll leave it to the doctors to explain the mechanism of injury but it was your understanding that they were severe and required several procedures?"

"Yes. We tried to speak with her as soon as we could but it was a couple of days before that was possible."

"But eventually you were able to speak to Ms. Ackerman directly?"

"I was."

"And what did she tell you?"

"Ms. Ackerman told us that she had followed her fiancé, Hamish Mack, toward the back lot. That the two of them had spoken and argued. She told us that she was upset and sat for a time on the stairs that included a call to her fiancé. She told us that she eventually stood up and, as she did a voice said, 'Hey,' and she was knocked down the stairs."

"Was Ms. Ackerman able to identify her attacker to you?"

"She was not."

"Why is that?"

"She did not see him."

"What else did she tell you?"

"She recalled falling down the stairs and through the brush until she landed on the rocks at the bottom of the Quarry. She said the pain in her hip was so severe that she couldn't move and that she cried out. She said she heard someone on the stairs and cried for help. She heard the person coming closer and cried out again."

Sheriff Dushane paused. I knew him. He was angry.

"Then what did she report?"

"Then Ms. Ackerman reported that the person stood over her and then she saw a flash and woke up in the hospital."

Stritch shook his head. "Was Ms. Ackerman able to get a look at the man when he approached her?"

"No. It was too dark and frankly, I believe she was in too much pain at the time."

"Once you became aware of Archibald Mack's potential involvement, were you able to ask her about him?"

"I did. She knew the defendant. He is her fiancé's brother. She knew he was planning on attending the concert but had no memory of seeing him there."

"And was she able to identify Mr. Mack as the man in this video?"

I stood. "Objection, Your Honor. Hearsay."

"Sustained."

"Did you eventually arrest Archibald Mack?"

"We did."

"That's all I have at this time, Sheriff. Thank you for your long service to our community."

I stood. "Good morning, Sheriff Dushane."

"Good morning, Mr. Shepherd."

"You've been kind enough to tell the jury about the evidence that you found on the morning that Ms. Ackerman was rescued. I'd like to ask you some questions about evidence you didn't find."

"Sure."

"You never found anyone who claimed to see my client with Ms. Ackerman at the abandoned stairs, true?"

"That's true."

"In fact, you never found any witness who claimed to see my client and Ms. Ackerman together at any time, did you?"

"We did not."

"You also did not find video of my client and Ms. Ackerman by the stairs, right?"

"That's right."

"And you did not find any video of Archibald Mack and Abby Ackerman together at any point that night, did you?"

"We did not."

"You certainly never found anyone who claimed to see my client attack Ms. Ackerman that night, true?"

"That's true, although I think the evidence points to his involvement."

"I understand that you think that, Sheriff, but what I asked was whether you found anyone who claimed to see my client attack Ms. Ackerman that night. And the answer is, you did not, did you?"

"We did not."

"My client is not the only person who is seen on video heading toward the back lot, is he?"

"No."

"Hamish Mack passed that way, right?"

"Right."

"Kirby Granger passed that way, true?"

"True."

"Will Wellington went that way, didn't he?"

Sheriff Dushane paused. "I don't recall that."

"You don't dispute it if the video shows it though, do you?"

"Of course not."

"You have just as many witnesses of those men attacking Ms. Ackerman as you have witnesses of my client doing it, right?"

Sheriff Dushane stared at me.

"Zero for each of them, right?" I said.

"That's technically correct."

"That's actually correct, isn't it?"

Sheriff Dushane's mouth twitched. "Yes."

"That includes Ms. Ackerman, true?"

"What do you mean?"

"I mean that Ms. Ackerman can't say who attacked her."

"That's right."

"To be fair though, you believe that Archibald Mack did attack her that night, right?"

"I do."

"That's based in part on the fingerprints and the blood on the handrail, right?"

"That's right."

"You say that the fingerprints on the handrail match those of my client, true?"

"True."

"It would be more accurate to say that one of the sets of fingerprints on the railing match those of Archibald Mack, wouldn't it?"

"I'm not sure what you mean."

"I mean that your office lifted fifteen different and distinct sets of prints from the handrail that day, didn't they?"

"I'm not sure of the exact number."

"I'd be happy to give you the inventory. Sheriff Dushane, I'm handing you what's been marked as State's Exhibit 31. How many separate and distinct sets of fingerprints does it state were lifted from the handrail?"

Sheriff Dushane looked at it. "Fifteen."

"My client's turned out to be set number 12, correct?"

"That's right."

"One set turned out to be from one of your deputies, true?"

"True."

"You don't think he was there the night of the incident, do you?"

"No. That print was most likely left when rescue efforts were underway."

"That's sloppy, isn't it?"

"That's not ideal. But rescuing Ms. Ackerman was our initial priority."

"I see. So of the fifteen prints you took, one was a deputy's whose prints were on file, correct?"

"That's right."

"One set was my client's, right?"

"That's right."

"And you didn't have my client's prints on file, you were able to match them after you printed him the night you arrested him, correct?"

"That's right."

"And you had thirteen other distinct sets of prints on the railing, true?"

"That's true."

"So at least thirteen other people had touched the railing recently enough to leave prints, right?"

"That's right."

"But you don't know who those prints belong to, do you?"

"I do not."

"Because they didn't turn up as a match in your data base, right?"

"Right."

"Now, I assume you took prints from the entire forty feet of railing so that you could get a complete picture of everyone who had left evidence on the abandoned stairs, right?"

"No, Mr. Shepherd that's not right."

"Oh? You didn't take prints from the entire railing?"

"We did not."

"So you took them from the top half of the railing then?"

"We did not."

"From the first four sections?"

"We did not."

"Well, what section did you take prints from, Sheriff?"

"From the first section of railing, where the bloodstain was."

"I see. Mr. Stritch put up a picture from State's Exhibit 21 that showed that first section of railing. Danny, could you put that back up, please?"

The picture of the bloody stair railing appeared.

"So you only took prints from this first section here?"

"That's correct."

"That section is about five feet long, isn't it?"

"Thereabouts."

"There are approximately eight sections of railing on the abandoned stairs, right?"

"I'm not sure."

"I took the liberty of counting and I will represent to you for purposes of my questions that there are eight sections of railing on that stairway."

"Okay."

"So since you only took prints from the first section of railing, there is no way for you to know whether there were other identifiable prints on the remaining seven sections of railing, correct?"

"That's correct."

"So your office took 1/8 of the available fingerprint evidence, right?"

"We don't know if there was fingerprint evidence on those other sections of railing."

"That's exactly right, Sheriff. You don't know if there was fingerprint evidence on most of the railing of the abandoned stairs, do you?"

"We do not. We only took fingerprints from the area around the blood."

"Well, that's not true at all."

For the first time, Sheriff Dushane raised an eyebrow. I could see he had been taking all of this as part of the job, but now I had actually piqued his interest. "What do you mean?"

"Well, you and Mr. Stritch put up exhibits just a minute ago showing blood on the stairway farther down."

Danny, God bless him, put up a split screen of Exhibits 22 and 23, showing the two sections of stairs where there was blood on the runners.

I went to the first picture and pointed. "There's blood here, isn't there, Sheriff?"

"There is."

"What fingerprints were on the railing around this blood?"

"I don't know."

"How about this one?" I pointed at the picture on the right. "There's blood on the stairway here, isn't there?"

"There is."

"And this is right where Ms. Ackerman went off the stairway, true?"

"That's true."

"What fingerprints were on the railing here?"

"We don't know."

"I see. You can't say there aren't fingerprints on this railing here, can you?"

"I cannot."

"You can't say if Ms. Ackerman's fingerprints are on the railing because she tried to catch herself, can you?"

"I cannot."

"And you can't say if someone else's fingerprints are right here at this precise spot where Ms. Ackerman went off the stairway, can you?"

"I cannot."

I gestured to Danny and he put up a picture of the rail at the bottom of the stairs. "And you didn't take any fingerprints here, at the bottom of the railing by the pad, did you?"

"There's no blood there."

"No, and that's a fair statement because my earlier question was about fingerprinting where the blood was."

Sheriff Dushane nodded.

"But Sheriff, Ms. Ackerman reported to you that a man came down the stairs to her. Why didn't you fingerprint the rail at the bottom of the stairs?"

We both knew the answer, but Sheriff Dushane still looked embarrassed. "By the time Ms. Ackerman was able to tell us about that, the site was corrupted."

"How so?"

"It had rained."

"I see. Why didn't you fingerprint that area on the very first day when you were called?"

"We were focused on the area at the top of the stairs, with the blood."

"Meaning you didn't think to fingerprint the bottom of the rail, did you?"

"No. No, we didn't."

"So you can't say whose prints were present at the bottom of the stairs? Where the final attack on Ms. Ackerman was carried out?"

"No, I can't."

"Now Sheriff Dushane, you said that Ms. Ackerman was unconscious when you found her?"

"Yes."

"She had not been unconscious the entire time that she had been laying there, had she?"

"Not according to what she said."

"She reported that a man approached her, true?"

"True."

"And that she cried for help?"

"That's right."

"She also reported that she heard the man say something, didn't she?"

"She did."

"What did Ms. Ackerman tell you?"

"It made no sense."

"I didn't ask if what she told you made sense, Sheriff. I asked what she told you she heard."

Sheriff Dushane paused and he thought.

"Would you like to read your report, Sheriff?"

"No, thank you, Mr. Shepherd." Sheriff Dushane reached up, took his hat by the crown, and tapped it briefly on the railing of the witness stand. "She said she heard someone say, 'It has more gas than the Albion Skip-N-Go.'"

"I see. And how did you follow up on that clue?"

"Excuse me?"

"How did you follow up on what her assailant said? What did you find out?"

"Well, nothing."

"Nothing? Why not?"

"It didn't make any sense."

"Gotcha. Okay, did Ms. Ackerman identify whether she thought it was a man's voice or a woman's voice?"

"She said it was a man's voice."

"Now you know that Ms. Ackerman has dated my client's brother for several years, don't you?"

"I do."

"I want you to assume that she has attended every Christmas, every Thanksgiving, every Easter, every Fourth of July, and every Ash County Fair with the Mack family over the last four years. Can you do that for me?"

"I can."

"Thank you. Did Ms. Ackerman state that she recognized the voice that said, 'More gas than the Albion Skip-N-Go' as my client's?"

Sheriff Dushane tapped his hat one more time. "She did not."

"Thank you, Sheriff. I don't have any more questions right now."

T. Marvin Stritch was up before I could get to my seat.

"Sheriff Dushane, that was the defendant on the video heading toward the back of the Quarry, wasn't it?"

"It was."

"And that was the defendant's blood on the railing at the top of the stairs, wasn't it?"

"It was."

"And those were the defendant's fingerprints on the railing by that blood, weren't they?"

"They were."

"And there's no question that Ms. Ackerman was thrown down those stairs, is there?"

"There is not."

"And there is no question that Ms. Ackerman was found at the bottom of those stairs, is there?"

"Just off to the side of it, that's right."

"And we'll get more detail from other witnesses, but there is no question that your office found that Ms. Ackerman was struck with a rock on the side of her face while laying helpless at the bottom of the stairs, is there?"

"No. There is not."

Stritch put his hands behind his back and looked up at the ceiling. "Before, when I asked how many years you've been the sheriff here in Ash County, you said 'decades.' How long has it been exactly, sir?"

"Twenty-nine and a half years."

"That's what I thought," said Stritch. "I've been a prosecutor most of that time. And were you a deputy before that?"

"I was. Eight years or so."

"I see. So thirty-eight years in service to the folks here in Ash County?"

"It has been my privilege, yes, sir."

"See, you've got me by about nine years then. I always

remembered when I started because it was the year after our Dellville football team made it to the state semi-finals."

Sheriff Dushane started to say something, but Stritch waved his hand. "No, I'll save my fellow counsel the trouble of objecting, I know it's not important. It's just one of those landmarks you remember when you've lived and practiced here in this county for so long. You know, we have our own customs, and practices, and rules, and we all work within the constraints of the resources that we have. Not like some of the big cities north or east of us, and certainly not like they do things in states to the south of us."

I felt Danny tense. I smiled.

"So I have to ask you, Sheriff," said Stritch. "Why did you only fingerprint the railing around the blood?"

"Because it seemed like the most likely place where the perpetrator would have left a print."

"Did it make any sense to you at all to take prints from the entire railing?"

"At the time, no. I understand why some might want it. But no, it didn't make sense to spend the time and resources to take prints from the entire rail when we didn't know what it would yield. The area around the blood on the railing, on the other hand, seemed like it had a high likelihood of being relevant. Which it was."

"Mr. Shepherd made a big deal out of the area at the bottom of the stairs. Why didn't you fingerprint that?"

"When we found Ms. Ackerman, we thought her injuries were related to the fall. We didn't realize that an assailant had struck her again at the bottom of the stairs until we spoke to her several days later and, by then, it was too late."

"But none of that changes the fact that the defendant's fingerprints and blood were found on the first rail of the stairway, right?"

"That's right."

"Thank you, Sheriff."

I stood, but rather than approach the Sheriff, I came around the front of the counsel table, leaned back on it, and crossed my arms. "Sheriff Dushane," I said. "Dellville High School has never made it to the state semi-finals in football, has it?"

Sheriff Dushane smiled a little and shook his head. "It has not."

"After you graduated from high school, you were an assistant coach at Dellville for a little while, weren't you?"

"I was."

"From the timeframe Mr. Stritch was referring to, I'd say he was actually talking about the Dellville team you coached that lost in the regional final, right?"

Stritch stood. "Objection, Your Honor. How is this relevant?"

Judge Wesley looked at him. "I'd say it isn't except that you brought it up. Overruled."

"I expect so," said the sheriff.

"That Dellville team was good, but it had a fumbling problem, didn't it?"

Sheriff Dushane couldn't help it. He smiled. "It did."

"And for at least the last—oh, let's say twenty-five years—you've told the running backs on your youth football teams that they have to hold the ball with three points of contact, haven't you?"

His smile broadened. "I have."

"Not like a loaf of bread unless you want to fumble away a championship?"

He tapped his hat on the rail. "I may have said that on occasion."

I looked up at the ceiling. "Any boy you coached here in Ash County would have heard that dozens of time, right?"

"At least. Some needed more reinforcing than others."

"So let's leave aside for a moment where anyone's from, and what they do and don't know about our county's sports history. Can we agree that there were probably prints on the other seven-eighths of the railing on the stairs?"

"We just don't know," said the sheriff.

"Can we agree, then, that we have no idea whose prints, if any, were on the majority of that railing?"

"We can."

"Can we agree that we don't know whose prints, if any, were on the railing in the immediate area where Ms. Ackerman's blood was found?"

"We can."

"Can we agree that we don't know whose prints, if any, were on the railing at the bottom of the stairs where Ms. Ackerman was attacked a second time?"

"We can."

"Thanks, Sheriff."

Judge Wesley looked at Stritch, who shook his head. "Thank you, Sheriff Dushane," the judge said. "You may step down." She glanced at the clock. "Members of the jury, that will do it for our testimony today. Please return tomorrow at 8:30 a.m." She struck the gavel and the jury left.

"Do you know whose prints were there?" whispered Archie.

"No."

"Then why did you do all that?"

"To let the jury know that they could have been there."

Archie looked at me. "Will that help?"

"Every little bit, Archie."

He didn't look totally satisfied with the answer. I didn't blame him.

38

Abby was supposed to testify first thing the next day. When Ronnie Hawkins was waiting for me in front of the still-locked courtroom, I knew it wasn't good.

"Abby won't be testifying today," she said.

I raised an eyebrow. "Is she refusing to cooperate?"

"She can't cooperate. She had a setback last night."

"What do you mean 'a setback?'"

"She threw a blood clot from her hip injury. They're working her up for a pulmonary embolus."

A flat tire is a setback. Losing a Little League game is a setback. Having the victim rushed to the hospital to make sure a blood clot wasn't traveling to her lungs to kill her was a disaster.

"Where is she now?

"At St. Wendolin's in Carrefour getting checked out."

"So is she going to be able to testify?"

"If everything is okay. If not..." She shrugged. To her credit, Ronnie looked me right in the eye.

"Great. Are you going to tell the judge?"

"I am."

"Have you told Stritch yet?"

"This morning. I felt I owed him since he had Abby under subpoena."

"I understand." I took stock. "All right. Let's see what Judge Wesley has to say."

~

WE GATHERED in Judge Wesley's chambers: Stritch, me, Danny, and Ronnie. None of us sat. It had nothing to do with the functional brown and orange furniture, all of which was perfectly acceptable. It had everything to do with the stakes of what we were talking about.

"She's really sick, Ms. Hawkins?" said Judge Wesley. "This isn't an attempt to evade service by crossing the state line?"

"She really is, Judge," said Ronnie. "And the best vascular specialist nearby is in Carrefour."

"In Ohio?" said Judge Wesley. "That's convenient for you, Mr. Shepherd."

"I want her here as much as Mr. Stritch, Your Honor."

"So you say. But her absence does raise an issue, Mr. Stritch."

Stritch put on his poker face and shrugged. "We can prove our case without her if need be, Judge."

"How can that be?" said Judge Wesley.

"The physical evidence is overwhelming."

I shook my head. "You're going to deprive me of a chance to get exculpatory evidence from the victim?"

Stritch shrugged again. "If there *were* any, it might be an issue. But since there *isn't*—"

Judge Wesley raised her hand, cutting Stritch off. "Here's what we're going to do. Ms. Hawkins, you said there's a chance she's okay, that this might just be a precaution?"

"There is."

"And there's a chance that she'll be recovered enough to testify by the end of the week?"

"Yes, Judge."

"Then we'll keep going. If she can testify, there's no reason for a mistrial. If she can't, we'll cross that bridge when we come to it. Do you have a witness ready, Mr. Stritch?"

Stritch nodded. "Ms. Hawkins called me so I have other investigatory witnesses ready. We'll fill-in from there."

"Very well, let's go back out there."

~

THAT WHOLE DAY was spent on scientific evidence that I won't bore you with. Basically, Stritch put on a series of witnesses who said that DNA testing proved that the blood on the railing was Archie's and that fingerprint set number 12, which was found on the railing next to the blood, was Archie's too. So, according to science, Archie was at the top of the railing the night of the Big Luke concert. The jury knew all that before those witnesses testified, but it was still pretty damning when you heard it out loud.

Of course, I just told you that in two sentences, so I felt like Stritch overplayed his hand a little by spending the better part of a day on the details. I think he was losing the jury at the end, not from lack of understanding, but from too much—they understood what he was talking about in the first five minutes but then had to listen to another seven hours of it. They were bored.

It wasn't much, but it was something.

Everyone, except Stritch maybe, was glad when the day was done. As we packed up, I saw Ronnie Hawkins and Olivia in the back of the courtroom. I went over to Ronnie right away and said, "Have you heard anything?" Olivia gravitated over to our conversation.

"Good news," said Ronnie. "She has a clot in her leg, but it hasn't migrated. They put her on blood thinners, but she's doing well."

"Is she able to testify?"

"She's home, but I don't know yet if she's on any restrictions for movement. I'm going to visit her tonight and will have a better idea tomorrow." She looked over my shoulder. "I need to tell Stritch the same thing."

I nodded. "Thanks."

When Ronnie moved on to Stritch, I said to Olivia, "What did you think?"

"The jury was bored out of their minds today."

"Right."

"You made some headway with the Sheriff yesterday. You need to make more."

"That's what I thought. Thanks."

"No problem." She turned the glasses on me. "We need to prove who did it."

"Not necessarily."

"It's a lot harder to prove a negative."

"I agree."

But that's all I had at that point, suspicions and innuendo and a lack of direct evidence, so I went home to prepare for day four.

∼

THE NEXT DAY, promptly at 8:35 a.m., Judge Wesley said, "Are you prepared to call your next witness, Mr. Stritch?"

"I am, Your Honor. The State calls Gary Probert."

Gary Probert walked in from the back of the courtroom and he looked about how I remembered him from the gas station. His hair was still longish brown, he wore black glasses, but now, instead of his uniform red vest, he was wearing a short-sleeved buttoned down shirt and a tie that hung a little short of his belt.

He looked around from side to side as he walked up to the witness stand, then made his way gingerly around the platform as if he were looking for a snake that might bite him. He sat, folded his hands, put them up on the railing, then placed them down in his lap.

Stritch waited until the witness was settled, then said, "Could you state your name please, sir?"

"Gary Probert."

"And what do you do, Mr. Probert?"

"I'm the manager of the Premium gas station."

"Is that the gas station on the corner of Century and Stone?"

"It is. Right next to the Taco Bell."

"Sure. And is that a full-service station?"

"It is. We specialize in providing good, clean facilities for truck drivers who are on the road."

"Are you nervous, Mr. Probert?"

Gary Probert shot a glance at the jury. "A little."

"Well, there is no reason to be. I just need to ask you some questions about what you saw the night of the Big Luke concert last August. Were you working there that night?"

"I was. A co-worker called off, so I had to come in around nine o'clock."

"Was that before the concert was over?"

"I'm not sure, but it was before the after-concert rush at our station."

"I see," said Stritch. "So did you have an influx of people that you attributed to the concert?"

"Uhm, what?"

"Did you have a rush of people that night?"

"We did."

"Did it seem like they were coming from the concert?"

"Yes."

"How did you know that?"

"We saw an awful lot of merchandise coming through, Big Luke shirts and hats and such. Of course, it was hot that night and the concert had been outside, so we sold a lot of Gatorade and a lot of beer..." Gary Probert trailed off and his eyes widened and he looked over his shoulder at the judge. "But we didn't sell beer to any obviously intoxicated people, ma'am, that would be against company policy."

Stritch raised a hand. "No one is suggesting that you did, Mr. Probert. Did that rush eventually die down?"

"It did."

"How long did it last?"

"I'd say about an hour."

"And did you see the defendant, Archibald Mack, at any time that evening?"

"Yes, sir, I did."

"When?"

"At the tail end of the concert rush. In fact, I'd say it was pretty much over when Mr. Mack came in."

"Now Mr. Probert, you must've seen dozens of people that night."

"I did."

"How in the world do you remember Mr. Mack?"

"Well, because he bled on the floor and I had to follow our special protocol to clean it up."

The jury sat up.

"How do you know he bled on the floor?"

Gary Probert looked confused. "You mean besides watching him?"

Stritch smiled and nodded. "No, I suppose that would be sufficient. What did you see?"

"Mr. Mack came in from filling up on pump four and then

walked across the store, right in front of the cash register, to the bathroom. And as I'm watching him, because it was just him and me right then, he just dripped blood from his left hand onto the floor. Left a trail all the way to the bathroom."

"What did you do?"

"Well, our company's real clear on biohazards, so I went straight to the back and got the mop bucket and dumped in some extra chlorine bleach and cleaner. Then I wheeled it back out into the store and started mopping. I wanted to clean it up before any new customers came in if I could." He sat up straighter. "The company's real big on that, having a clean and safe environment for our customers."

Stritch nodded. "So I understand. And were you able to do that?"

"I was. I was a little surprised. I thought that Mr. Mack would be out before I was done, but he wasn't."

"What do you mean 'out?'"

"I mean out of the bathroom."

"So Mr. Mack was in the bathroom the entire time you were cleaning up the blood?"

"He was."

"So what happened next?"

"I got the blood cleaned up, and I had put out two caution signs at either end of where I'd mopped and, right about then, Mr. Mack came out of the bathroom. I went back to the cash register and watched him as he walked over to the cooler, thinking I was going to have to clean up again."

"And did you?"

"No. He wasn't bleeding at all then. He grabbed a couple of things, paid for them, and left."

"What did you do next?"

"Well, I went into the bathroom thinking I was going to have to do quite the cleanup in there too, but it turns out I didn't have to do anything at all."

"What do you mean?"

"I mean there wasn't any blood in the sink and there weren't any bandages or paper towels in the garbage. I mean, there were paper towels in there, but they didn't have any blood on them."

"I see. So Mr. Mack took anything with his blood out with him?"

I stood. "Objection, Your Honor. Speculation."

"Sustained."

"Let me put this another way," said T. Marvin Stritch. "When Mr. Mack entered the bathroom he was dripping blood on your floor, correct?"

"He was."

"And when he came out of the bathroom he wasn't, right?"

"Right."

"And there was nothing in the bathroom when you inspected it after Mr. Mack had left that had any blood on it."

"That's right."

"Thank you, Mr. Probert. That's all I have, Your Honor."

"Mr. Shepherd?"

"Thank you, Your Honor. Mr. Probert, Archie Mack walked right by you on the way into the bathroom, didn't he?"

"He did."

"He wasn't trying to hide from you in any way, was he?"

Stritch stood. "Objection, Your Honor. That's the same speculation Mr. Shepherd objected to a moment ago."

"I'll rephrase, Your Honor. Mr. Probert, Archie Mack walked right in front of the cash register on the way to the bathroom, true?"

"That's true."

"He was two, maybe three feet away from you?"

"That's right."

"There was nothing between you and him to obstruct your view, right?"

"That's right."

"No aisles, no display cases, right?"

"That's right."

"If Mr. Mack wanted to keep you from seeing him, he could have turned right at the door and walked around the rows of snacks, over along the cooler, and from there into the bathroom, right?"

"That's right."

"Instead, though, he walked directly in front of you."

"He did."

"Did you say anything to him about the bleeding?"

"I didn't. By the time I realized what was happening, he was by me and almost to the bathroom."

"I see. So you said you were done cleaning up by the time he came out, right?"

"I was."

"It's fair to describe what you cleaned up as scattered drops of blood, isn't it?"

"It is."

"It wasn't a large amount, was it?"

"It was not, it's just that, with our biohazard policy, any amount is too much and needs to be cleaned up right away."

"And you were done with that cleaning by the time he came out of the bathroom, right?"

"I was."

"You mentioned that he bought a few things when he came out, right?"

"He did."

"In fact, he bought a Tall Tea and beef jerky and put it on the counter, true?"

"That's true."

"Then he thought about it, went back to the cooler, and picked up some beer, right?"

"That's right."

"He wasn't hiding from you at all, was he?"

"That would be a funny way to do it."

"It would, wouldn't it? Mr. Mack talked to you that night, didn't he?"

"He did."

"You asked him if he'd had a tough day?"

"I did."

"And he replied that it had been a tough year, right?"

"That's right."

"And then he paid and he left, correct?"

"That's correct."

"Did he seem nervous or jumpy to you?"

Stritch stood. "Objection. Speculation."

I shrugged. "The witness is allowed to say how the defendant appeared to him."

"Overruled," said Judge Wesley.

"He did not."

"Did he seem angry?"

"No."

"Excited?"

"No."

"How did he seem to you?"

Gary Probert thought before he said, "Tired. Like the end of a long day. I assumed he'd gotten off work."

"I see. After he left, you testified that you went into the bathroom and did not discover any bloody bandages or towels, true?"

"That's true."

"Did you appreciate that?"

"What?"

"I said, did you appreciate that? Not having to clean up bloody paper towels?"

"Actually, I did. I still wiped things down, just to be safe, and to comply with our company policy, but yeah, it had been a long day and I was glad that it was easy."

"Do you have people change their kids' diapers in your bathroom?"

"Sometimes," Gary Probert said. "We have a changing station. We try to create a clean, family-friendly environment."

I nodded. "Do some families leave their dirty diapers in the wastebasket?"

"They do."

"And do some families take it out with them and dispose of them somewhere else?"

"Sometimes."

"And you appreciate it when they do that?"

Gary smiled. "I know the next customer does."

There were a couple of chuckles from the jury.

"Thank you, Mr. Probert. That's all I have."

Stritch stood. "Mr. Probert, did the police eventually come and interview you about whether Mr. Mack had been in your station that evening?"

"They did."

"And when they came to see you, was there any blood evidence for them to evaluate?"

"Well, like I said, I had cleaned up the blood."

"And there was none in the bathroom either, right?"

"There was not."

"That's all I have. Thank you."

I stood. "Mr. Probert, the police came and spoke to you about a day and a half after Mr. Mack was in your station, true?"

"Let's see," Gary Probert looked at the ceiling for a moment. "Yes. Yes, that's true."

"All of the garbage and waste from your store from two days earlier was gone by that time, wasn't it?"

"Absolutely."

"And the floors had been mopped multiple times by then, true?"

"That's true. We have the cleanest stations in the industry."

"Thanks."

"Mr. Probert, you may step down," said Judge Wesley. "Next witness, Mr. Stritch?"

T. Marvin Stritch looked at the clock and said, "Your Honor, could we perhaps take our morning recess so that I can check on the status of our next witness to make sure she is here?"

Judge Wesley looked at me.

"No objection here, Your Honor."

"Very well, let's take fifteen minutes." Judge Wesley hit the gavel and the jury was dismissed.

After they'd left, I turned to Stritch and said, "Who's up?"

"I'll let you know in a minute," he said and went out into the hallway. A few moments later, he returned. "We'll be calling Abby Ackerman next," said T. Marvin Stritch.

"Thanks," I said and returned to our table.

Archie Mack turned white.

39

I put a hand on Archie's shoulder. "You knew you had to see her eventually."

He nodded. "I just thought I'd have more warning."

I glanced at Stritch. "That's why he's doing it this way. You need to be calm and you need to be cool and you need to show nothing but concern for her."

Archie looked at me sharply. "I *have* nothing but concern for her."

"Good." I thought then tapped his shoulder. "C'mon. You're going to the bathroom."

"I don't have to."

"Yes, you do." I took Archie by the arm and led him out of the courtroom. As we walked out, I whispered, "When you see her, smile and nod."

Archie looked mildly sick, but he nodded back.

As I expected, Abby Ackerman was standing out in the lobby. She was leaning on a cane and had her other hand on Hamish Mack's arm and appeared to be listening to him, nodding. The two of them looked up. Abby smiled while Hamish scowled and puffed up a bit. I nodded, as did Archie, and we walked down to the bathroom. We used it, washed our hands, then returned. By the time we did, Abby and Hamish were already in the courtroom. We followed them in.

There were a few more spectators today. Mr. and Mrs. Mack were there, of course, in the middle row. Olivia was seated in the row right behind us. When I saw Ted Ringel of the *Ash County Torch*, though, and a woman I didn't recognize with a small notepad, I realized that Stritch must've put the word out that today was the day that the victim was testifying. Abby and Hamish sat in the front row behind him.

Archie and I took our seat at the counsel table next to Danny. Judge Wesley emerged a moment later and recalled the jury.

We stood as they filed in. One of them, the crisis counselor, spotted Abby. A series of nudges later, the whole jury was looking at her.

"You may be seated," said Judge Wesley. "Mr. Stritch, are you ready to call your next witness?"

"I am, Your Honor. The state calls Abby Ackerman."

All eyes turned to Abby.

Abby stood and, when Hamish stood with her and handed her the cane, she took it and waved him away. I saw Mr. Mack smile and Mrs. Mack nod as Abby made her way, slowly, toward the witness stand. Stritch held the gate open for her and she made her methodical way—cane, step, step, cane, step, step—to the stand.

Abby wore dark jeans along with a dark jacket and a muted shirt that was neat and strong. Her reddish-brown hair was loose and was gently curled forward a little around the side of her face. She winced as she sat and set her cane against the rail. It immediately slipped sideways and clattered to the floor.

"Son of a bitch," she said and then looked up at Judge Wesley. "I'm so sorry, Your Honor. It slipped."

Judge Wesley's mouth stayed stern but it seemed to me that

her eyes danced a little. "Yes. Both of them. Let's try to express our displeasure in a more appropriate manner, Ms. Ackerman."

Abby grinned. "Yes, ma'am."

Stritch hurried forward, picked up Abby's cane, and handed it back to her. She took it and leaned it carefully against the chair.

I looked over. Every eye in the jury was on her.

T. Marvin Stritch looked at the jury, then said in his most solicitous voice, "Could you state your name, please?"

"Abigail Ackerman."

"Ms. Ackerman, let me first ask the question we all have: Are you okay to testify today?"

Abby sat with an elbow on each arm rest, her hands folded in her lap. She lifted her chin and said, "I'm just fine."

"Well, that's very brave, Ms. Ackerman, but we can see that you're moving with great difficulty."

"I have a little hitch in my giddy-up is all."

That got a few smiles.

"Ms. Ackerman, weren't you in fact in the hospital yesterday due to your injuries?"

I stood. "Objection. Leading."

"This is a preliminary matter, Your Honor," said Stritch.

"It seems to me that this is the primary matter for which she has been called to testify and that Mr. Stritch is attempting to speak for Ms. Ackerman."

"Sustained," said Judge Wesley. "This is your witness, Mr. Stritch, so you will not lead her. Mr. Shepherd, I remind you of our rules regarding speaking objections."

"Yes, Your Honor," we both said.

Stritch thought for a moment, then said, "Ms. Ackerman, were you attacked on the night of the Big Luke concert this past August?"

"I was."

"Could you tell us what happened?"

"When?"

"Well, let's start at the beginning."

So Abby told the jury how she had planned a girl's night out at the concert, how she'd parked in the back lot, and how she'd picked up the tickets from Kirby before meeting up with Bonnie, Kayla, and Heather in the courtyard. She talked about their great seats, Big Luke's great sound, and about having a great time.

When she was done, Stritch said, "Now when the concert was over, I understand you and your friends went back up to the courtyard."

"We did."

"What happened next?"

"We got in line to get a water while the parking lot was clearing out and talked."

"Then what happened?"

"Then I saw Hamish."

"Did you know he was going to be there?"

"No. But I hadn't spoken to him that day."

"What did you see?"

"I saw him speaking to a man named Will Wellington and then I saw Hamish leave toward the back."

"What did you do?"

"I told the girls that I was going to see Hamish and that I'd just meet them at HopHeads after."

"What happened next?"

"I hustled after him."

"Did you catch him?"

She smiled. "I did. I'm pretty...I was pretty fast."

"I see. Then what happened?"

"I called out to him and he stopped and we talked."

"Talked?"

Abby nodded. "At first. Then we fought."

"About what?"

"About him not telling me he was going. And who he went with."

"What was wrong with who he went with?"

"That man has been trying to put an oil well on the Mack Farm for years. I don't much like it."

"What's wrong with that?"

She shrugged. "I don't think organic farming and oil wells mix."

"So what happened then?"

"We both lost our tempers. He yelled at me and I yelled at him and he left."

"Then what?"

"We were parked in the same lot and I didn't want to be near his sorry a—um, near him so I went and sat on the top of the old stairs and I fumed and I got generally ticked that we'd ruined the vibe of the whole night and that made me even madder. And then I thought about Big Luke's encore, he'd come out for an extra one and sang 'I'm a Duck's Back, Baby,' and I realized the two of us should know better, or I should anyway, and I gave him a call."

"What happened then?"

"He didn't pick up. I didn't blame him because I'd scorched him pretty good, so I just left a message."

"Then what?"

"Then I swore a little bit and I hummed the chorus a little bit and I decided I better head out to meet the girls."

"So what did you do?"

"I stood, and I heard a voice say, 'Hey' and I felt someone grab my arm. I was startled and I jerked away and then I tumbled down the stairs."

"All the way?"

Abby nodded. "It's pretty steep there."

"Then what happened?"

"I think I may have blacked out for a minute because I don't remember the last part of the fall. I just remember being on the rocks by the water. And being in a good bit of pain."

"Where?"

"I told you, by the water."

"No, where on your body?"

"Oh. Right. My hip. I tried to get up and I had this flash of pain and I'm pretty sure I cried out, but I'm not sure. I later learned I'd broken my pelvis and hip both."

"What happened next?"

"I realized I couldn't move so I called for help. I'm not sure how loud I was. I was afraid no one could hear me, but then I heard someone come down the steps. They're metal so they have a little ring to it when someone's on them."

"What did you do?"

"I called out for help again." She looked down. "I might've been crying too."

"I would imagine so. What did you see next?"

"Not much. It was dark and I was dizzy and I was in pain and I couldn't move. I saw someone get to the bottom, though, and I called out one more time."

"Then what?"

"I saw the person climb off the pad and slip—the rocks can be slick there—as he made his way over to me."

"Could you see him?"

"No. He was just a darker spot in the sky. And I might have been seeing double, I'm not sure."

"Then what?"

"Then he made it to me and I was relieved and actually thanked the rat bastard—"

"—Ms. Ackerman."

"Sorry, ma'am. And then I saw him swing and I woke up in the hospital."

"The next day?"

"Best I remember, it was at least two, maybe three days later."

"And what was your condition then?"

"I was hurt."

"What was the nature of your injuries?"

"I had a broken hip. A broken pelvis. A concussion. And a broken bone in my face."

"What caused those injuries?"

"The fall caused the hip and the pelvis and maybe a portion of the concussion."

"And the broken bone in your face?"

"I was told I was hit with a rock. Which made sense with what I remembered."

"I'm sorry, Ms. Ackerman, but will you brush your hair back, please?"

Abby paused then pushed the hair on the left side of her face back and tucked it behind her ear. She had a small dent in the bone next to her left eye. It wasn't huge but just enough to throw off the proportions of her face.

The jury stared. We all did.

Stritch motioned at his own eye. "Is that what caused it?"

Abby nodded. "It broke my orbital bone. It didn't heal straight." She shook her hair back down.

"And why were you hospitalized yesterday?"

"I haven't been as mobile as I was. Between that and the fractures, I developed clots in my legs."

"And was the treatment successful?"

"They gave me blood thinners. I'll be fine."

"Well, that's certainly good news. You have our thoughts and prayers."

Abby gave one of those circular head nods indicating she wanted to wrap this up.

Stritch kept the concerned look on his face as he said, "Ms. Ackerman, do you know the defendant?"

"I do."

"How?"

"I'm engaged to his brother, Hamish."

"And how often are you at Hamish's farm?"

"What kind of a question is that?"

Stritch seemed taken aback by that reaction. "Well, I, uhm, I mean..."

"Are you asking if I live with him?"

"No, I—"

"The answer is no, I don't live with him and yes, we're engaged. If you must know, I stay over at my fiancé's house sometimes but I have my own place."

Stritch looked mortified that he was being perceived as having asked a question he didn't ask. He straightened his notes and said, "So since dating Hamish Mack, you've come to know Archibald Mack?"

"Yes. Very well. We share an interest in farming and animals."

"I see. Are you close?"

Abby scowled. "I am good friends with my fiancé's brother."

Stritch, quite clearly, beat a retreat. He sucked his gaunt cheeks in, then said, "Ms. Ackerman, have you ever seen Hamish and Archie fight?"

Abby smiled. "They're brothers."

"That doesn't answer my question, Ms. Ackerman."

"Of course."

"Have they ever come to blows?"

I stood. "Objection, Your Honor. Collateral."

"We believe it's relevant to show the family dynamic, Your Honor."

Judge Wesley thought. "You have a very narrow window here, Mr. Stritch."

"Have you ever seen your fiancé Hamish and the defendant come to blows?"

Abby smiled. "That's not how I'd describe it."

"How would you describe it?"

"Scuffles."

"Scuffles then. On more than one occasion?"

"I couldn't say."

"Sure you could, Ms. Ackerman. Have you seen Hamish and the defendant scuffle on more than one occasion?"

"There might've been two."

"And what were these scuffles over?"

Abby looked around. "We're a farming family, Mr. Stritch. When we have a disagreement, we don't debate each other in our Sunday suits."

"Was one of those scuffles over your attack?"

Abby raised her head at that. "I don't know, Mr. Stritch. I was out cold for that one."

Stritch nodded but couldn't stop the smallest smile. "That's all I have, Ms. Ackerman. Thank you very much for coming in the day after your hospitalization. The State of Michigan thanks you."

Scorn came to Abby's eyes as she said, "Well, the State of Michigan subpoenaed me, so I didn't really have a choice."

I stood. "Good morning, Ms. Ackerman."

"Good morning, Mr. Shepherd."

"Do you need a break?"

"I'm fine. Let's get this over with."

"You've known Archie for about four years, right?"

"That's right."

"Ms. Ackerman, do you think Archie attacked you that night?"

Stritch leapt to his feet and said, "Objection" just as Abby Ackerman said, "No."

"Move to strike, Your Honor," said Stritch.

"Sustained," said Judge Wesley. "The jury will disregard that last answer."

But, of course, they'd heard it.

"Ms. Ackerman, let's talk about what you saw and what you didn't see that night. You did not see the person who grabbed you at all, did you?"

"I didn't."

"And you saw a person come down the stairs but could not see his face, right?"

"That's right. It was too dark."

"So the jury understands, you are not saying it was Archie who grabbed you, are you?"

"I am not."

"And you're not saying that it was Archie who came down the stairs?"

"I am not."

"And you're not saying that it was Archie who hit you with the rock?"

"Definitely not."

"You don't know who it was, do you?"

"I have no idea who that miserable son of a bitch was." She turned. "I'm sorry, Judge."

"Understandable, Ms. Ackerman. But please don't repeat it."

"Yes, ma'am."

"That's because you never saw this...person's face, true?"

"That's true."

"You did hear him speak though, right?"

"More of a mutter, but yes, I did."

"Do you remember what he said?"

"I do."

"What?"

"He said, 'It'll have more gas than the Albion Skip-N-Go.'"

"Okay, Ms. Ackerman, two things about what he said."

"Okay."

"First, you know what Archie Mack's voice sounds like, correct?"

"I do."

"Was it Archie Mack's voice that you heard?"

"I don't think so."

"Second, is it possible that the voice said, 'It'll have more gas than the Albion-Scipio?'"

Abby scowled. "Didn't we just say the same thing?"

"We did not. You said 'Skip-N-Go,' right?"

"Right.

"I'm saying 'Scipio.' S-C-I-P-I-O."

"I'm sorry, Mr. Shepherd, I'm not really hearing the difference."

"So the voice could have said, 'Albion-Scipio?'"

"Since it sounds exactly the same to me, yes."

"So the jury knows, this is not a new recollection, is it?"

"It is not."

"You reported what you heard to Sheriff Dushane, didn't you?"

"I did."

"Shortly after you woke up?"

"Yes."

"Did he ever ask you any follow-up questions about this? About what you heard?"

"No."

"Did anyone else?"

"Just you."

"Now, Ms. Ackerman, you and Hamish fought that night at the back of the Quarry, didn't you?"

"We did."

"Hamish has testified that the two of you fought about going to the concert."

"That's what I hear."

"That's not true, is it?"

Abby thought. "It's mostly true."

"How would you describe it?"

"We fought about who he went to the concert *with*."

"That would be Will Wellington?"

"Yes."

"What was wrong with Hamish going to a concert with Mr. Wellington?"

"It wasn't so much going as what it implied."

"What did it imply?"

"That Hamish was thinking about what Wellington was selling."

"Which was what?"

"Wellington puts oil wells on farms. And I don't agree with that."

"Why not?"

"Because it doesn't go with farming. I don't think so anyways."

"And Hamish does?"

Abby thought again. "I wanted to do what I could to keep him from thinking that way."

"And that's what you fought about? Putting a well on the farm?"

"The possibility of putting a well on a farm."

"Finally, Ms. Ackerman, you said that you had seen Hamish and Archie scuffle on occasion."

"I have."

"Is argue a better word?"

She thought. "Probably."

"It was usually about the farm?"

"That I saw, it was always about the farm."

"They disagreed about what to do?"

Abby shrugged. "They have different interests. Hamish favors traditional crops and maximizing yield per acre. Archie has just as much interest in animal husbandry as farming."

"You grew up on a farm, didn't you?"

"I did."

"Did you have an opinion?"

"Sure. But it's not my farm, so it matters less."

"What do you like?"

"I'm more inclined toward organic farming, the way Mr. and Mrs. Mack are."

"From your perspective, Ms. Ackerman, do you have a good relationship with Archie Mack?"

"I do. Well, until this trial anyway. Since then, Hamish and Archie couldn't go to family gatherings together anymore."

"Did you and Archie ever argue?"

"No."

"Do you know of any reason why my client would want to harm you?"

"No."

"Do you disagree with the prosecutor's decision to charge Archie?"

Stritch stood. "Objection."

"I didn't ask if it was right or wrong, Your Honor. I asked if she agreed with it."

Judge Wesley thought. "Overruled."

"Do you disagree with the prosecutor's decision to charge Archie, Ms. Ackerman?"

"Yes."

"Why?"

Abby's eyes welled up but it's not fair to say she broke down. Instead, I'd say she broke out with anger and frustration and pain all at once as she lifted her chin, tossed her hair back and said, "Because it keeps them from finding the person who did this to me."

"That's all the questions I have for you. Thanks."

Abby nodded at me as Stritch stood back up.

"Ms. Ackerman, you've testified twice now that you didn't see the person who grabbed you, right?"

"That's right."

"So you can't say it wasn't Archie that grabbed you?"

"Other than the fact he wouldn't do it, I guess not."

"And you've testified twice that you didn't see who the person was who struck you, right?"

"Right."

"So you can't say that it wasn't Archie who struck you, can you?"

Abby stared. "That right there is why people don't like lawyers."

"Ms. Ackerman!" said Judge Wesley.

"I'm sorry, Your Honor. I suppose that what you say is true, Mr. Stritch."

Stritch nodded. "Do you remember picking out what you were going to wear the night of the concert?"

"More or less."

"Did you wear clean clothes that night?"

Abby blinked. "Excuse me?

"Forgive me, but were the clothes you wore to the concert that night clean? In other words, was it the first time you had worn them since they were washed?"

She looked at Judge Wesley who gestured to go ahead.

"Yes. I mean, everything except the boots, I suppose."

"And you were not at the Mack farm earlier that day?"

"I was not."

"And did getting ready for the concert include showering?"

"Mr. Stritch, you're starting to offend me."

"I'm very sorry, Ms. Ackerman, but I need to ask, did you shower before going to the concert?"

"I did."

"And then put on clean clothes?"

"Yes."

"Thank you, Ms. Ackerman, that's all I have."

I was pretty sure I knew where Stritch was going with that last bizarre line of questioning so, unfortunately, I was going to have to look just as nosy and absurd to the jury.

I stood. "Ms. Ackerman, do you have a clothes hamper for your worn or dirty clothes?"

Abby glared at me. "Of course."

"Which is it?"

"I have a hamper."

"Does it have a lid?"

"Not usually."

"Where do you keep it?"

"Excuse me?"

"Where do you keep the hamper? Is it in your bathroom? In your bedroom?"

"It's in my closet."

"I see. That's all I have Ms. Ackerman. Thank you."

Neither Stritch nor I had any more questions, so Judge Wesley dismissed Abby from the stand. I looked over at Stritch. He gave me a half smile and nodded. That told me I had guessed right about his last set of questions.

I was concerned.

∾

J̲U̲D̲G̲E̲ W̲E̲S̲L̲E̲Y̲ H̲A̲D̲ us break for lunch and, the minute the jury left, Hamish shot to the front of the courtroom to help Abby. Mr. and Mrs. Mack went over to her too and I could hear them asking her how she was doing and what kind of medication she had to take and how they could help. Archie stood next to me, watching as his family gathered around her. He was rigid and I could feel the isolation washing over him. Stritch went over to the group, held out his arms and whispered, and corralled them out the door.

It was quiet when they were gone. As Olivia came over, Danny said, "What was that last bit at the end? About the clothes?"

"I think Stritch is about to answer my challenge for physical evidence," I said.

"How?" said Olivia.

"I think we're going to hear about corn next."

Suddenly, Archie wobbled and sat.

Danny reached for him and said, "Archie?"

He slumped forward, head in his hands.

"Archie?" I said.

His shoulders shook as I put a hand on his back and bent closer.

"Archie, what is it?"

"She's so hurt," came the muffled reply. "She's so hurt."

I realized I'd spoken to Abby twice since the attack, had studied pictures of her injuries, had read every medical record on her condition, had been immersed in everything that had happened to her.

Archie hadn't seen her at all.

The isolation from his family and the pressure from the trial had been building for months. Seeing Abby was finally too much. Archie broke down.

"Danny, make sure the hall's clear. Then we'll grab a spare room."

As Danny left, Archie's head stayed bowed. "How could Hamish think I could do that?"

"Your parents don't," Olivia said. "Abby doesn't."

Archie wouldn't hear it. He just kept his head down and cried.

Danny returned, nodded, and Olivia and I led Archie out. He could barely walk.

We found a room. Rather than prepare, the three of us spent lunch pulling Archie back from the edge so he could return to the trial.

So Stritch was successful in that too.

40

After lunch, the answer to my challenge came in the form of Deputy Sharon Reynolds. Deputy Reynolds was in her mid-forties with black hair that she wore up, round cheeks, and a pleasant smile that was disarming and comforting and I'm sure had led to numerous arrests of suspects who couldn't believe that they'd just told this nice woman everything she needed to put them away. Deputy Reynolds wasn't just a twenty-year deputy, though; she was also in charge of administering the rape kits for the Ash County Sheriff's Department.

Stritch got right to it. "Deputy Reynolds, are rape kits used for other purposes?"

"Not for other purposes but for other cases," said Deputy Reynolds. "Basically, what we do with the kit is collect evidence from a person's body and clothes."

"I see. And just to be clear, Deputy Reynolds, was Abby Ackerman sexually assaulted in this case?"

"She was not. She was attacked and almost killed. But she was not sexually assaulted."

"I see. And were you part of the investigation into Ms. Ackerman's attack?"

"I was. I followed Ms. Ackerman from Century Quarry to Mission Hospital and, in conjunction with the medical team, gathered evidence."

"What kind of evidence would you typically look for in a case like this?"

"One of the first things we look for is evidence of the attacker's DNA. In the case of a physical assault, this can take the form of blood or tissue under the victim's fingernails."

"Did you find any such evidence here?"

"I did not. It did not appear that Ms. Ackerman struggled with her attacker."

"What else did you do?"

"The next thing was to check Ms. Ackerman's clothes."

"And what did you find?"

"We found a variety of fibers and organic material."

"What do you mean by organic material?"

"It appeared from the scene that Ms. Ackerman had tumbled down a hill that was filled with vegetation. We found material from those plants on her clothes."

"Is that a surprise?"

"It is not."

"Did you find anything else?"

"Yes."

"What?"

"We found organic material that did not seem to belong there."

"You'll have to excuse us laypeople, Deputy Reynolds. What do you mean?"

"We found fibers that were not related to the vegetation that Ms. Ackerman was found in."

"And what fibers are those?"

"Corn silk."

"Corn silk? What's that?"

"You know when you shuck an ear of corn, those hairs or wispy fibers at the top that you have to pick out of the ear?"

"Yes."

"Those."

"I see. And you found those on Ms. Ackerman's clothes?"

"Yes, I did."

"And did your office run an analysis of the corn silk fibers?"

"We did."

"And what did you find?"

"That it was a type of 'no weed seed' that is planted in Ash County, Michigan."

"And as part of your investigation, did you examine what type of corn was planted by Archibald Mack this year?"

"I did."

"And?"

"He planted the same brand of seed."

"So you're saying Ms. Ackerman was found with fibers on her clothes that matched the corn that was planted by Archibald Mack this season?"

"Yes."

"Finally, Deputy Reynolds, did you examine Ms. Ackerman's wounds themselves?"

"Not all of them."

"Which ones?"

"Primarily her head wounds. I did not examine her hip and pelvis injuries."

"I see. And were you able to reach any conclusions based on those wounds?"

"Yes."

"What are those?"

"That Ms. Ackerman had an asymmetrical impact contusion on the side of her head surrounding her orbital fracture."

"I'm sorry, Deputy Reynolds, what does that mean?"

"It means we were able to see the rough shape of the object that fractured the bone next to Ms. Ackerman's eye."

"And what did you conclude?"

"That the assailant hit her in the head with a rock."

"No further questions."

I stood. "Good afternoon, Deputy Reynolds."

"Good afternoon, Mr. Shepherd."

"You're experienced in collecting DNA evidence from victims of assaults and sexual crimes, aren't you?"

"I am."

"You have collected DNA evidence that has led to the arrest of persons committing such crimes, correct?"

"That's correct."

"You did not find any of Archie Mack's DNA on Ms. Ackerman, did you?"

"I did not."

"And so the jury is clear, DNA can be in the form of skin or hair or blood or spit, correct?"

"That's correct. Any physical material from a defendant."

"And so, in an assault case like this, you'd specifically be looking for any skin or hair or blood or spit that was left behind by the attacker, right?"

"That's right."

"Deputy Reynolds, there's been evidence presented in this case that my client left blood on the railing of the abandoned stairs at Century Quarry. Are you aware of that evidence?"

"I am."

"You're aware that he had a cut on his hand the night of the incident involving Abby Ackerman?"

"I am."

"Yet, you didn't find any of my client's blood on Ms. Ackerman, did you?"

Deputy Reynolds shifted in her seat. "I did not."

"Not one microscopic drop, right?"

"That's right."

"You didn't find any of my client's hair either, did you?"

"I did not."

"Or skin?"

"No."

"People who have been assaulted often have the DNA of their attacker under their fingernails, don't they?"

"Only if they had an opportunity to struggle or fight."

"You didn't find any DNA material under Ms. Ackerman's nails, did you?"

"I did not."

"You mentioned that you found corn silk on Ms. Ackerman's clothes?"

"I did."

"You testified that this corn silk matched the brand of seed that Archibald Mack uses on his farm, am I remembering that correctly?"

"You are."

"Did you investigate how many other farmers in Ash County plant that brand of seed?"

"I did not."

"Do you know if Abby Ackerman went to the supermarket before she went to the concert?"

"I do not."

"Do you know if she had bought corn or shucked corn recently?"

"I do not. But I know from her earlier testimony that she had showered and worn clean clothes to the concert."

"I see. You know that Ms. Ackerman met three friends at the concert, right?"

"I do."

"Do you know if any of them had been around corn in the

previous twenty-four hours?"

"I do not."

"Have you ever been to a concert, Deputy Reynolds?"

"I have."

"Would you agree with me that you can bump into hundreds of people at a concert? Physically bump into them?"

"Dozens certainly," she said.

"Were you able to eliminate all of the people that Ms. Ackerman bumped into at the concert as the source of the corn silk fibers?"

"I was not."

"You mentioned that Ms. Ackerman was struck with a rock by her assailant?"

"I did."

"You never found any of my client's DNA on the rock that struck Ms. Ackerman, did you?"

"It's my understanding that we never found the rock in question at all."

"So, again, you never found a rock with my client's DNA on it, true?"

"That's true."

"Thank you, Deputy Reynolds. No further questions, Your Honor."

T. Marvin Stritch stood. "Deputy Reynolds, if a victim is surprised by an attack, she would not have an opportunity to fight with the assailant, would she?"

"If she was surprised, she would not."

"Victims of an attack do not always have tissue under their fingernails, do they?"

"They often do not."

"And just so the jury is clear, the corn silk fibers you found exactly match the seed that Archibald Mack planted on his farm this year?"

"That's what the lab tests indicated, correct."

"No further questions," said Stritch.

I stood. "Deputy Reynolds, you mentioned you're aware that Archie Mack had a cut on his left hand on the night of the incident?"

"I am."

"Yet no blood was found on Ms. Ackerman, correct?"

"None of Mr. Mack's blood, that's correct."

"So if my client surprised and attacked Ms. Ackerman, he would have had to have done it one handed, right?"

Stritch stood. "Objection. Speculation."

"It goes directly to their theory of the case, Your Honor."

"Overruled. You may answer, Deputy Reynolds."

Deputy Reynolds thought. "I can tell you that Mr. Mack never touched Ms. Ackerman in a way that left blood on her."

"Yet he was bleeding enough to leave blood on the railing."

"That's correct."

"So isn't it reasonable to assume that he never touched her with his left hand?"

"It could have been wiped off during her fall."

"Deputy Reynolds. Please."

The cheerful eyes above the round cheeks went hard. "It's reasonable to assume that he never touched her in a way that left blood that we could find."

"Thank you, Deputy Reynolds. That's all I have."

Judge Wesley looked at us and then said, "You may step down, Deputy Reynolds, thank you."

Archie leaned near me. "Is that all he had?"

I stared at Stritch, who didn't seem disturbed. "Let's see."

41

Lawyers are paranoid. If you know one, I'm not telling you anything new. If you don't, trust me, it's true. When you're around one long enough, there will come a time he—or she—becomes fixated on a phrase that you said, or sometimes just a single godforsaken word, and spend hours deciphering the accurate meaning of what you uttered as opposed to understanding what it is that you truly meant to say. There's a simple reason for this—any lawyer who's been around for any length of time has gotten pounded at some point because of the meaning of that simple word or phrase that everyone thought meant something else. It makes them prone to overkill, to leaving no stone unturned, and to reflexively driving their point home again and again and again.

I try to keep it in check. T. Marvin Stritch, though, couldn't resist doing exactly that in Archie's case. In fact, he did it twice.

First, Stritch called Officer Harold Stern of the Michigan State Police. I'm not going to spend a lot of time on his testimony because it was redundant and ultimately didn't prove anything. The reason it's important is because it shows how a prosecutor, even a good one like Stritch, can get fixated on things that, in the end, aren't all that important. Or at least not in the way that you think.

Officer Harold Stern was a specialist in cell phone tracking and, yes, he looked exactly like his name. Officer Stern spent two hours explaining how to ping cell phones and triangulation and all sorts of other location-tracing spy stuff that the police rely on when they can't get a search warrant. Or, in this case, when the suspect was a farmer who didn't use any sort of location services on his cell phone because he was paranoid about his privacy. In the end, with the help of a map and a chart and a PowerPoint graphic, Officer Stern proved conclusively and without question that Archie Mack was in Century Quarry the night Abby Ackerman was attacked.

You know, just like the blood, the security video, the ticket stub, the phone call, and everything else.

I'd had trial room courtesy drilled into me from the time I started practicing so I stood, but I didn't take the time to walk over to the lectern. Instead, I said, "Officer Stern, based on the cell phone tower configurations, you can put my client in a 1.3 square mile radius of Century Quarry between eight o'clock and midnight on the night of the Big Luke concert, right?"

"That's right."

"However, you can't pinpoint Archie Mack's location to a specific place within the Quarry at a specific time, can you?"

"Well, when our data is combined with other evidence—"

I raised my hand. "Officer Stern, I respect what you do very much and the technology you spent all this time explaining to us is very useful when you have a thief fleeing across the country or a child is missing, but let's be real clear to the jury—what you just described cannot pinpoint whether Mr. Mack was at the abandoned stairs or the bathroom or the amphitheater at any given time on the night of the Big Luke concert, can it?"

"We can place him at the Quarry."

"Well no, actually, you can't. What your technology will do is put him within a square mile of the Quarry, right?"

"The overwhelming likelihood is that he was at the Quarry."

"Based on other evidence, sure. But my client didn't have any location tracking apps or software working on his phone, did he?"

"No."

"And the police weren't monitoring him at the time, right?"

"Right."

"So all you can do is try to recreate his location from which towers his phone was pinging off, right?"

"Right."

"And all that does is give you, in this case, his location within one square mile, true?"

"Well, with the other evidence, we know—"

"I'm not interested in the other evidence. I'm interested in your cell phone evidence."

"I'm not sure how that's important."

"It's important, Officer Stern, because everyone already knows that Archie Mack was at Century Quarry for the concert."

Officer Stern looked uncomfortable, but he wasn't going to back down. He just stared back, so I said, "Okay. You can't tell us where Archie Mack was within the Quarry at any given time, right?"

"Well, if we had his location data—"

"But you don't, so you can't, true?"

Stern shifted in his seat. "That's true."

I started to sit, then stopped. "Officer Stern there were almost three thousand people at the concert that night, were you aware of that?"

"No, but that sounds right."

"Did you run your data to find out how many of them were

still in or around the Quarry between 11 o'clock and 12 o'clock on the night of the concert?"

"I wasn't asked to."

"So the answer is no?"

He stared. "I wasn't asked to do that."

"Have you ever heard of confirmation bias, Officer Stern?"

Officer Stern straightened and bristled. "I don't see how that's relevant."

One juror laughed, then covered her mouth.

I put my hands out to the side. "Well, there you go. No further questions, Your Honor."

Next, Stritch called a farming supply company rep named Scott Baden, a thin man with an enormous bushy brown beard that was second only to Hank Braggi's in ferocity. He wore khaki pants, a blue button-down shirt, and a dark blue tie. As he sat down, he gave a smile broad enough to be visible through the beard.

After getting the basics from him, Stritch said, "Where do you work, Mr. Baden?"

"At Ash County Agricultural."

"And what is Ash County Agricultural?"

"We sell farming equipment and supplies."

"What sort of supplies?"

"The whole range. Everything from seed to herbicide to pesticide to fertilizer."

"I see. How big is your operation?"

"We are the largest agricultural supplier in the Tri-County area."

"Do you sell seed corn?"

"We do."

"Do you sell No Weed Seed for corn?"

"We do."

"And do you do business with Mack Farms?"

"We do. My uncle started doing business with Alban Mack almost fifty years ago."

"Mr. Baden, at my request did you examine the purchases Mack Farms made from your company this past year?"

"I did."

"I'm handing you what's been marked as State's Exhibit 58. Do you recognize this document?"

Baden looked. "Yes. It's a printout of everything that Mack Farms purchased from Ash Agricultural over the past year."

Stritch put a copy of the invoice up on the screen. "Mr. Baden, could you explain this print out to me?"

"Sure. The first column you see there is the product. The second column is the quantity, the third column is the unit price, and the fourth column is the total price."

"I see. And it appears that this is broken into three separate sections?"

Baden nodded. "It is. Mack Farms has just one account, but they asked that we break it into three separate groups, for Archie and Hamish and Mr. Mack so they can divvy up the expenses between them. It's no trouble for us so we're happy to do it."

"I see. So the items listed under Archie were for him, the items under Hamish were his, and the items listed under Alban, that's Mr. Mack, went to him?"

"That's right."

"Mr. Baden, this shows that you sold No Weed Corn Seed to the defendant Archie Mack this year, didn't you?"

"I did."

"And he planted it this year, didn't he?"

"He did."

"And how do you know that?"

"Because they were transitioning to organic and Archie said it was the last year he was going to plant this type of corn."

"There's no doubt from your records that Archie Mack bought and planted No Weed Corn Seed, is there?"

"There is not."

"That's all I have, Mr. Baden. Thank you."

I stood. "Mr. Baden, State's Exhibit 58 shows that Archie Mack's father, Alban Mack, bought the same amount of No Weed Corn Seed as Archie did, right?"

"He did."

"And Alban Mack planted it this year too, didn't he?"

"He did."

"You've been out to Mack Farms, right?"

"Absolutely, they're one of our biggest customers."

"You're familiar with the farm layout?"

"I am."

"Alban Mack's farm is right next to Hamish's farm, isn't it?"

"It is."

"Does the wind blow in Ash County, Mr. Baden?"

Stritch stood. "Objection."

"Sustained."

I nodded. "Mr. Baden, how popular is No Weed Corn Seed?"

"It's our most popular corn seed product."

"I see. And how many customers in the tri-county area buy this seed from you?"

Scott Baden looked around. "That's proprietary. I'd rather not say, if you don't mind."

"I understand. How about this, is it more than one hundred farms?"

"Yes, it is."

"So more than one hundred farmers in the tri-county area buy No Weed Corn Seed from you. I assume that's enough to plant thousands of acres here in the Tri-County area?"

"What do you mean exactly?"

"I mean that thousands of acres in the Tri-County area are planted with No Weed Corn Seed, right?"

"That's accurate."

"So there are literally thousands of acres of corn silk scattered all across our county for someone to brush into."

"Objection," said Stritch. "Speculation."

"There are nothing but facts in that statement, Your Honor. The witness sells corn seed in this county to farmers, who grow it on thousands of acres, and it's a physical fact that someone can brush up against any of it."

"The Court is aware of how physical facts rule works, Mr. Shepherd. You will restrain yourself in your responses to objections as well."

"Yes, Your Honor."

"The objection is overruled."

Baden's head went back and forth, then said, "Yes, sir, there are."

I turned back to Baden. "Corn grown from that type of seed covers all parts of this county, doesn't it?"

"Pretty much."

"There are literally corn mazes carved out of No Weed Corn Seed within a ten minute drive of this courtroom, aren't there?"

Scott Baden smiled. "Yes. Although they have zombies at the one up in Benzie."

The jury chuckled and I decided I couldn't do better than that. "That's all I have, Your Honor."

T. Marvin Stritch didn't have any more either. Thank God. Life is too short.

~

"THE COURT IS ready for your next witness, Mr. Stritch," said Judge Wesley.

T. Marvin Stritch stood. "Your Honor, the prosecution rests."

Judge Wesley looked at me. "Do you have a motion?"

"I do."

Judge Wesley turned to the jury. "Members of the jury, we have some technical legal issues to address so the Court will send you home a little early tonight. Please be back at eight-thirty tomorrow." She warned them again not to discuss the case and dismissed them. We all stood as the jury filed out. When they were gone, Judge Wesley returned to me. "Go ahead, Mr. Shepherd."

"Your Honor, under the Michigan criminal rules—"

That was as far as I got before Judge Wesley raised her hand. "Mr. Shepherd, I believe I was very clear. You need to address the Court with the proper knowledge of Michigan procedure."

I didn't see how I could have screwed it up in the first seven words. "Your Honor?"

"We are not in Ohio trying a case under the Ohio criminal rules. We are in Michigan trying a case under the Michigan *Court* rules."

"My apologies, Your Honor."

"I'm not interested in your apologies, Mr. Shepherd. I'm interested in a concise argument."

"Certainly, Your Honor. The Michigan Court Rules state that dismissal of an action is appropriate where the State has not met its burden of proof. Here, the state has produced no evidence that my client attacked Ms. Ackerman. Presence at the site at some indeterminate time is not nearly enough. Further, the State certainly hasn't presented any evidence that Mr. Mack had an intent to harm Ms. Ackerman. For those reasons, we respectfully request that the case be dismissed."

She turned to T. Marvin Stritch. "Mr. Stritch?"

"Your Honor, we produced evidence from which a reasonable jury could conclude that Mr. Mack attacked Ms. Ackerman, attempted to kill her, then left her to die. Further, we believe the phone call to Hamish Mack is more than sufficient evidence of motive and intent to harm. For those reasons, directed verdict is not appropriate."

Judge Wesley didn't even pretend to think. "The court finds that there's sufficient evidence for the question of whether Mr. Mack committed these crimes to go to the jury. Motion for directed verdict denied. The defense starts its case tomorrow." Judge Wesley hit her gavel and left.

T. Marvin Stritch left the room. As he did, Archie turned to me and said, "Is that bad?"

I shook my head. "That's expected. We didn't think she'd dismiss the case, but we have to argue it to preserve potential issues on appeal."

Archie shook his head. "I would've liked it better if the case had been dismissed."

I smiled. "You and me both."

"What comes next?"

"Next, we present our case."

"So the witnesses should be better to listen to?"

I put my hand on his shoulder. "I certainly hope so."

42

That night Olivia joined Danny and me at the office. Because she was the guest, we'd let her pick the sandwiches. She'd gone with Cubans and, as I bit through the melted cheese and the tart pickle into steaming pork and ham, I couldn't say she was wrong.

Olivia shook her head.

"Yes?"

"Do you really eat like this every night?" she said.

"During trial."

"You need to step things up when this is done. I expect to see you five days a week."

"Four works."

"Five's better."

I sighed then broke a string of melted cheese that was refusing to let go of the bread and said, "It's not enough yet. The doubt that Archie did it. We need to show that the prosecution's evidence points to other people too."

"We have to show that someone else did it?" Danny said.

I shook my head. "We have to show that someone else *could*

have done it. The more likely, the greater the doubt." I munched. "I think I can show opportunity tomorrow. But I need to beef up motive."

After a moment, Olivia said, "You know, with all this talk of winning, we're losing track of one thing."

"What's that?"

"Who *did* do it."

I knew it mattered to her. I also knew I wasn't sure of the answer.

"That's why I took you up on your offer of help tonight, Liv. I need you and Danny to scour that video one more time. I need you to look at everything. We have to be missing something, some person some clue, some car, something. If Archie didn't do it, and I don't think he did, whoever attacked Abby has to be visible at some point on that video."

Danny rolled his eyes. "What do you think I've been doing for the last month?"

"A second set of eyes never hurt."

Olivia tapped her glasses. "I'm with you, Danny."

Danny nodded. "So, your idea is for me to just find the magic key to winning the case by sorting through twelve hours of video?"

"Exactly."

"What are you going to do?"

Olivia smirked. "This is the point where your fearless leader has to go on some vital field trip that, coincidentally, avoids the hard work."

"If by vital field trip, you mean seeing if I can raise the stakes, you're right."

"How?" said Danny.

"I think if the jury believes that a well on the Mack farm has the potential to be worth a lot of money, then they'll believe that people might've acted more extremely to get a piece of it."

"So how are you going to do that?

I stood. "I'm going to talk to a guy about some rocks."

It was a sign of the depth of Danny's disgust that he didn't even ask what I meant. He just crumpled his wrapper, went to his office, and got to work.

"I'll help him," said Olivia.

"Thanks, Liv."

"Seriously, win aside—we need to find out who did this."

"We may not, you know."

Olivia gave me a mirrored stare. "I don't accept that."

"I don't suppose you do."

I put my hand on her shoulder in thanks on the way out. She patted it once, then joined Danny.

∽

WHEN I WAS outside the building, I called the number I had used twice before.

"Eli Timmons," a voice answered.

"Professor Timmons, this is Nate Shepherd."

"Nate! Are you out front?"

"I am. Sorry it's so late."

"It's not late at all. I'll be right down."

Five minutes later, Professor Timmons was popping open the door to the Earth Sciences building and letting me in. He smiled. "We don't often have geological emergencies in the middle of the night. How exciting!"

We shook hands and he led me through hallways that were sporadically lit.

"I really am sorry about the late notice, Eli, but I need some help preparing an examination in a case and I think you're the perfect person to help."

"Well, I told you before, I'm always happy to help. When's your trial?"

"Right now."

Professor Timmons stopped. "You need my help for the Mack trial?"

"You know about it?"

He smiled. "I told you, I'm a fan. But what can I do to help with an attempted murder case?"

"Do you remember that illustration from your textbook that I talked to you about?"

"The one related to the rock formations? Sure."

"I'm going to be cross-examining a witness tomorrow. I'd like to use it and I need you to explain it to me."

We started walking again, but the look on Timmons's face was troubled. "You know, the University really doesn't like us getting involved in this kind of stuff."

"I'm not asking you to testify. I just need a little coaching on the illustration and what's important."

Timmons scowled. "How does my illustration fit in?"

"I'm examining the representative from the oil company, Will Wellington. I want to use your diagram to show that he had a motive to act, that Mack Farms is sitting on enough oil for people to do stupid things."

"You think this Wellington guy did it?"

I chose my words carefully. "I think he had the opportunity to do it."

Timmons nodded. "Do you have any other testimony?"

"Archie's brother Hamish has already testified. He puts Wellington at the scene too."

"So this Hamish Mack has already testified? And he points at Wellington?"

"Not directly, but that's the only way his testimony can be interpreted."

"And Wellington had an opportunity to commit the attack?"

"Yes."

"That's all you have?"

"That's it."

"That's not a lot."

"That's why I'm here."

We came to the junction that led to his office. Timmons looked both ways before he said, "Nate, to be honest, I thought you were calling me about a property dispute or something. I don't think the University would want me involved in something like this at all."

"All I'm asking for is a tutoring session tonight, Eli. I can't be forced to disclose an expert I don't call at trial, or his opinions. Your only involvement will be dispensing an hour's worth of knowledge to me."

"That's really it?"

"That's really it. And I would pay you for a full day's consult."

Timmons thought. "It would be quite a story, wouldn't it?"

"It would."

"All right. Come on in."

He turned the light on in his outer office and led me back. He was wearing a tan suit that I was pretty sure was more expensive than anything in my closet and a haircut that looked like it was fresh from that morning. He moved easily behind his desk, waved me to a chair, and said, "So, what do you want to know?"

I pulled a copy of the illustration, a geological map of southeast Michigan, out of a folder and put it on the desk.

Timmons smiled. *"Fundamentals of Great Lakes Geology.* Riveting, isn't it?"

"It is to me. So, like I mentioned before, I found this illustration from your book attached to a lease for an oil well."

"Okay."

"Why?"

"Because it shows rock formations that can indicate an oil reservoir."

"Which ones?"

"Here." He turned the map to face me. "See these lines here? That shows a series of syncline and anticline structures that can indicate oil and gas reservoirs in this part of the state."

I raised my hand. "I'm sorry, Eli. You're going to have to treat me like an undergrad who didn't take the prereqs for your class."

Timmons smiled. "Of course. I'm sorry. I get carried away. You know the earth is under pressure?"

"Yes."

"And that pressure can make things fold?"

The irony of that statement wasn't lost on me. "Yes."

"Syncline and anticline are just ways of describing the folds in the rock."

"Okay. And why is that important?"

"Because in this part of the state, the largest oil find was in rock formations of this type."

"The Albion-Scipio Trend?"

Timmons grinned. "You remembered. Exactly."

"Where is the Albion-Scipio Trend on this illustration?"

"Right here."

"That's in a series of anticline formations?"

"You're a quick study, Nate." He tapped it. "What makes you think Wellington had access to this illustration?"

"That lease it was attached to was one of his."

He nodded. "So you're arguing that he'd be looking to find a similar amount of oil in similar rock formations?"

"I'll be implying it more than arguing it. Is it a valid theory?"

Timmons looked skeptical. "It's possible, I guess. Do you see this area, about six miles northeast of the Trend?"

"I do."

"That's the Hanover field. It's one of the only really successful finds that isn't part of the Trend." He waved a finger over the illustration. "So where is the area we're talking about for your case?"

I made a circle. "Here, a little south and west of the Trend."

Timmons frowned, then pulled a ruler out his desk and put it on the map.

I smiled. "Ruler at the ready?"

He smiled and shrugged. "College." He moved the ruler along the map. "That spot is twenty to forty miles away from the Trend depending on which part of it you're measuring from."

"So does the illustration show that there are syncline formations here that indicate the presence of oil?"

Timmons frowned. "Not exactly. It indicates that the syncline formations are probably there. You'd have to do some sort of testing to determine whether there is actually oil there."

I thought. "So, if I have this right, this illustration shows that the conditions exist which would make it worthwhile for a company to do the next stage of testing to see if the oil is there?"

"Exactly."

"Do you know how that part works?"

Timmons sat back. "I can tell you about the rocks that form the deposit or the moraine they're part of or the estimated age of the striations of rock in that quarry of yours. But exploration and retrieval? That's an oilman's job."

I stared at the illustration. "In this twenty miles between the Trend and the farm, there are a series of dry wells. Does that eliminate the chance of a deposit on the Macks' farm?"

"These synclines are narrow, some only a mile wide. Hitting a dry spot in one doesn't mean the next one won't yield. What's the company Wellington works for?"

"Hillside Oil & Gas."

Timmons shook his head. "HOG will take its chances."

It took me a moment to recognize the acronym. "You know the company?"

"It's known in academia. We don't tend to look kindly on commercial exploitation."

"I suppose not. So Hillside Oil would know how to test this land to see if it would be productive?"

Timmons nodded. "They could move it from a possibility to a probability."

"And they would know about these rock formations before they entered the lease?"

He waved the illustration. "The proof is in the attachment."

I stared at the illustration, at the wavy lines that showed the rock formations in the Trend and the rock formations on the Mack farm. Now, having had it described to me, I could explain it to the jury.

I started to gather my things. "I've taken enough of your time, Eli. Thank you."

"Did that help?"

"You've given me exactly what I need."

Timmons smiled. "Excellent!"

"I think you must be a great professor."

He beamed.

"Please send me a bill."

"And I get paid too? Even better." Timmons seemed genuinely pleased.

I thought of something and it must have shown on my face.

"What?" said Timmons.

"An old trial rule, it's better to show than tell. I hate to impose..."

He waved at me. "But?"

"Do you have any full-size diagrams of this? I just have a

blurry black and white blow up. Do you have an electronic copy of the illustration?"

Timmons shook his head. "They're all with the publisher."

"What about a hard copy?"

Timmons frowned. "I don't think the University wants me that involved, Nate."

"I'd bring it right back."

Timmons didn't look convinced.

"I'll have my associate bring it back as soon as we're done. Tell you what, if you let us borrow it tonight, we'll go have a copy made and return it."

"This late?"

"We have a place on standby during trial."

Timmons frowned then said, "If you're using it to pin HOG, I can't complain." He went to a cabinet and pulled out a roll of laminated blow-ups. "These are from a presentation I did years ago." He unrolled a three by five map that curled under its own weight. "I do want it back. And you didn't get it from me."

"Got it. We'll bring it back tonight."

Timmons smiled. "It's a little late, Nate."

"First thing tomorrow morning. My associate Danny will meet you here."

"Fine then. Here." He handed me the map. I unrolled it and saw a full color copy of what we'd been working from that night. "Perfect. I can't thank you enough, Eli."

"You're welcome. And you really are going to have to join my wife and me at the symphony, you know."

I glanced at his lapis lazuli award from the symphony on the shelf next to the encased, uncut diamond. "That would be great."

"And your friend Olivia too."

"I'm sure she'd be thrilled."

He showed me out. "Good luck, Nate."

"Thanks again, Eli. I owe you."

He smiled and shut the door.

I hustled back out to my Jeep, confident that I had a motive tucked under one arm.

∽

IT WAS ALMOST ten when I made it back to the office. Danny and Olivia were still there, running video. Danny waved. He looked tired.

Olivia stared at her screen like a terminator.

"Find anything?" I asked.

"Nothing we haven't seen. We've been through the whole thing once and are going through again."

"Want a break?"

Danny rubbed his eyes. "Sure."

I handed him the rolled-up diagram. "Go over to Carrefour Graphics. Have them make a full color copy, preferably with a dry-erase cover so we can draw on it."

He sighed. "Can they do that without an e-file?"

"I hope so. Then, tomorrow before trial, drop the original back off with Professor Timmons. He'll be expecting you." I described where Timmons's office was and how to find him. "He wants us to keep his involvement quiet because of the University."

"Then why's he doing it?" said Olivia.

"I think he wants the spotlight but doesn't think this is the right venue for it. He sends his regards and another invite to the symphony by the way."

"Hmphf."

"I think you made an impression."

"Just different from the symphony crowd, I'd guess." She grinned. "Which means we should go."

I smiled. "I'll check my root canal schedule."

"Philistine."

"Grr. Arrg."

Danny turned his laptop off and packed up. "I'll watch this some more while I wait then just go straight up to court tomorrow."

I nodded. "See you then."

Danny left. I went to my office and worked on Wellington's cross-examination. Olivia sat in the conference room, watching video. We both knocked off just before midnight.

"Anything?" I asked on our way out.

"Too much and then not enough," she said.

I raised an eyebrow.

"At the beginning of the night, there's so much traffic it's hard to tell who's going where. At the end, it's just the stuff you already know about—Hamish and Archie and Wellington."

I nodded. "It has to be Wellington."

"You think?"

"It's the only thing that fits." We walked out to our cars. "Long day?"

"Not bad."

"That was a lot of video to watch."

"And?"

"Headache?"

"No."

"I appreciate your help."

She waved it off. "You ready to go tomorrow?"

"Just about."

"The case depends on it."

"Working on it."

She grinned. "Don't fuck it up."

"Thanks."

"Good night."

"Night."

Olivia got in her car. I waited until it started then got in mine. As I pulled out, I got a text from Danny that he was done and would drop the copy of the chart off at the office tonight so I could pick it up it in the morning. I thanked him, went home, and went straight to bed.

43

The next morning, Judge Wesley looked at me and said, "Mr. Shepherd, is the defense ready to proceed?"

I stood. "We are, Your Honor. The defense calls Will Wellington."

All eyes went to the back of the courtroom as Will Wellington walked in.

It's almost impossible to describe his unprepossessing manner. He had neat brown hair combed over to the side, was in his early forties, and had a fit but not too fit look to him. He smiled, a little shyly, and ducked his head but still managed to make eye contact with almost every single one of us on the way in. He wore a navy blue modern-fit suit, neither too loose for young people nor too tight for old, and wore a silk tie with blue and red stripes that was sure not to offend anyone. As he sat down, he looked like the most good-natured guy at the soccer banquet or the least judgmental man in church. He looked nothing like an ultra-successful wildcatter.

Or a murderer.

I swear the jury was smiling at him before he sat down.

"Could you state your name for the record please, sir?" I said.

"William O. Wellington."

"And who do you work for Mr. Wellington?"

"I work for Hillside Oil & Gas. Going on eighteen years now."

"So the jury knows, Mr. Wellington, you were subpoenaed to appear here today, weren't you?"

"I was, Mr. Shepherd. But all you had to do was ask. I would've done my duty as a citizen."

"Thank you, Mr. Wellington. What do you do for Hillside Oil & Gas?"

"I manage lease acquisitions."

"Can you explain to the jury what that means?"

Wellington smiled. "Sure. There are properties around here that have oil and natural gas underneath them. We—meaning Hillside Oil & Gas—don't want to buy or take people's land from them. Instead, we just pay them for the right to drill for oil."

"And how do you pay them for that?"

"We pay them a set rental fee and then we pay them a percentage of the revenue that the well generates."

"Is that a percentage of the profits?"

Wellington smiled. "No, too many companies try to manipulate that. We pay landowners a straight percentage of the gross or total revenue that the well brings in. It's up to us at Hillside to manage our own expenses. We want to be a good partner."

"I see. And did you acquire a lot of oil leases in nearby counties in the early 2000s?"

"I didn't acquire all of them. But I did acquire a fair number for Hillside during that time, yes, sir. Jackson, Hillsdale, Calhoun counties all had a good number."

"Did those wells produce?"

"Oh, yes, sir. Hillside Oil made a lot of money for the landowners during that time."

"And for itself?"

"Well, of course, yes."

"Mr. Wellington, does the name Albion-Scipio mean anything to you?"

Wellington nodded and smiled. "Oh, yes, sir. That's the biggest find that's ever occurred in Michigan."

"Were you involved in that find, Mr. Wellington?"

"Oh, no, sir, the first well in the Albion-Scipio Trend was found back in 1957. It was outlined and explored pretty well by the early 1980s."

"Now you said the word 'trend.' That's a type of rock formation that holds the oil, right?"

"Yes, sir. It's the most famous one in our great state."

"Mr. Wellington, I'm handing you what's been marked as Defendant's Exhibit 19. Can you identify that for me?"

"Yes, sir, it's a map of Michigan that shows the active oil and gas wells in the state."

"Olivia, could you please put that up?" Olivia, who'd agreed to sit in for Danny, popped the map up on the screen. "Mr. Wellington can you identify the wells that are part of the Albion-Scipio Trend on that map?"

"Yes, sir. See this green cluster of wells that forms a big diagonal line?"

"I do."

"Those are the wells that are part of the Albion-Scipio Trend."

"You've seen this map before?"

He smiled. "I wouldn't be doing my job if I hadn't."

"You have a map of the Trend in your office, right?"

"Indeed, I do."

I pointed to the map. "And these are the county lines here, right?"

"That's right."

"So the Albion-Scipio Trend isn't in Ash County at all, is it?"

"No, sir, it's not." He smiled. "Though we surely wish it was."

"You're being modest though, aren't you, Mr. Wellington? You went on a hot streak in the 2000s and early teens, right?"

"We did. Technology improved so that we could find some pretty good pockets of oil." He smiled and shook his head and pointed. "Nothing like that though."

"Still, it was enough for you and the landowners to do well?"

"Yes, sir, we've had that good fortune."

"But that good fortune doesn't keep you from looking for the next Albion-Scipio, does it?"

Wellington smiled and for the first time I saw a hint of the steel underneath. "Well, sir, everyone is looking for the next Albion-Scipio."

"The next Albion-Scipio would be worth a fortune?"

"Yes, sir. Yes, it would."

"Fair enough. Mr. Wellington, I'm going to ask you some questions about Mack Farms."

"Well, that would be just fine, Mr. Shepherd."

"First, so the jury can see, I'm going to put a circle on this oil well map where Mack Farms is." Olivia put a yellow circle up on the screen. "Do you see it?"

"No, sir."

I looked at him. "You don't?"

Wellington smiled. "No, sir. I see a circle that Miss Olivia put on the map. Is that the one you're talking about?"

I smiled. "It is."

"Oh, well then, yes, sir, I see it."

"Very good. Mack Farms is some miles away from the Albion-Scipio Trend, isn't it?"

"It is, yes. A good twenty-two miles from the bottom end."

"Thank you. Mr. Wellington, can you explain to the jury what all these yellow dots are between the Albion-Scipio Trend and Mack Farms?"

"Yes, sir. Those are dry wells."

"And what are dry wells?"

"Those are wells that people drilled that didn't strike anything except rock and dirt."

"So people have tried the area between the Mack Farms and the Albion-Scipio Trend before?"

"All the time."

"And no one has found anything?"

"Not in a straight line, no. There were some other wells that you can see on there scattered about, especially that grouping in Hillsdale we were talking about earlier, but on this particular line, no."

"Now, Mr. Wellington, we've mentioned the Albion-Scipio Trend a few times but the jury might not understand the scale of it. How big is it?"

"It's not very big in size, Mr. Shepherd, but it's one of the best producing oil finds in state history."

"How much are we talking about?"

"Around fifty-nine million barrels of oil since it started."

"Goodness. What about natural gas?"

"About fifty billion cubic feet."

"Mr. Wellington, was that billion with a 'B?'"

"Yes, sir, it was."

"My word. So that was quite a find, wasn't it?"

"It certainly was."

I pointed at the map. "So these other wells scattered about the area, did you procure those leases?"

Wellington nodded. "Most of them."

"So what changed between the 1980s and early 2000s? Why were some of those wells starting to hit?"

"Technology. We started using certain kinds of imaging to look below the surface for certain kinds of formations that lead to oil."

"Was this new?"

"New to Michigan. It'd been used in other parts of the world before, just never around here."

"What do you look for?"

Wellington smiled. "See now Mr. Shepherd, that's proprietary and just about as big a trade secret as there is in my industry."

"So you won't tell us?"

"I'm afraid I can't."

"Mr. Wellington, let me show you a different map." I took out the three-foot by five-foot blow-up of Professor Timmons's illustration and set it on an easel where Wellington and the jury could see it. "In the course of your work, do you have occasion to review geological diagrams?"

"I do."

"And as part of your work do you analyze rock formations?"

"I'm more of a contract guy, but yes."

"Your company does, certainly?"

"Sure."

"You see this line here?"

"I do."

"That's the Albion-Scipio Trend?"

"It is."

"And it's located in a very specific kind of rock formation, isn't it?"

Wellington shifted in his seat. "It is."

"They're identified on this map as synclines, right?"

"I'm sorry, you're getting into an area I don't feel comfortable discussing."

"Because it's a trade secret?"

"Yes."

"Well, you filed this document as part of public filing, didn't you?"

Wellington blinked. "What do you mean?"

"I'm handing you what's been marked as Defense Exhibit 38. Do you recognize that document?"

"I do."

"It's a lease for a well between you and a landowner right here in Ash County, isn't it?"

"It is."

"And you typically file this document with the county to protect Hillside Oil's interest in the lease, right?"

"I do."

"Turn to the first attachment, please."

He did.

"Is that a copy of the illustration we have blown up here for the jury?"

He licked his lips. "That's not supposed to be attached."

"Is that a copy of the illustration we have blown up here for the jury?"

He flipped to the front. "This was my first lease."

"Do I have to ask a third time?"

Stritch stood. "Objection, Your Honor. This is completely collateral."

Judge Wesley looked at me.

"Judge, the assailant's words made this relevant. Further, Mr. Wellington was present the night of the attack and these issues are related to conversations that occurred that night."

Judge Wesley thought. "I'll allow it, but bring it around soon, Mr. Shepherd."

"Go ahead, Mr. Wellington," I said.

"I can't," said Wellington.

"Your Honor, could you direct the witness, please?"

"Mr. Wellington, Mr. Shepherd is asking you about a publicly filed document. There is no trade secret protection for that. However, Mr. Shepherd, your questions in that regard should be limited to the document itself."

I nodded. "Mr. Wellington, is that attachment to your lease a copy of the illustration we have blown up here for the jury?"

We'd talked a lot about rocks. Wellington looked like he wanted to crawl under one as he said, "Yes."

"This illustration shows rock formations known as synclines running the length of the Albion-Scipio Trend, don't they?"

I watched him work out how to answer the question. We all did. Finally, Wellington said, "The illustration shows that."

I circled an area on the illustration. "Mr. Wellington, would you agree with me that the area I just circled on the illustration also contains syncline formations?"

"The illustration shows that."

"Would you agree with me that none of the area immediately surrounding that circle contains syncline formations?"

"That's what the illustration shows."

I flipped a clear plastic overlay over the illustration. The overlay had the county roads marked in black and Mack Farms marked with a red square.

Mack Farms fit entirely within the circle.

I tapped the red square. "That's the location of the Mack Farms on the illustration, isn't it?"

"Mack Farms isn't on the illustration."

"Well, by my count, you've filed eighteen leases in this area of Ash County over the last ten years. If you want, we can take the jury through each one of the leases, put them on the record, and show where those leases are in relation to the square on the map."

Wellington shifted his weight. "That location looks about right, approximately."

"The Mack farm is located over a syncline rock formation?"

"According to the illustration, yes. I can't say that's actually true."

"Fair enough." I left the map and the overlay there, the red square like a beacon. "Mr. Wellington, I'd like to talk to you now about your dealings with the Mack family."

"Certainly."

"When did you first approach them about an oil lease?"

"I'd say it was about four years ago."

"And why did you contact them?"

"Because I thought the discussions might be productive for both sides."

"And you thought a well would be productive?"

"I thought there was a good chance."

"Why?"

Wellington smiled. "That's back to the trade secret, Mr. Shepherd."

"Sure. So you made an offer for a drilling lease on the Mack property?"

"I did."

"When you made the offer, were you aware that the Macks had had a setback so that their transition to becoming an organic farm had been delayed?"

"I was."

"Were you aware that someone had actually sabotaged their fields by putting pesticide on them?"

"I knew they had had a setback. I wasn't aware of all the particulars."

"How did you learn that? Or is that another trade secret?"

"Not at all. Dellville is a small town. I had heard about it either through my son's baseball team or church, I don't remember which."

"And having heard about it you wanted to see if you could capitalize on it?"

Wellington frowned. "I don't like that term at all, Mr. Shepherd."

I shrugged. "What would you call it?"

"I would call it helping someone in need in our community who might view it as a good time to have another source of income."

"I see. But you weren't just going to give them money, like a charitable donation."

"No, not at all. We would make lease payments and pay them an additional percentage from the well's earnings."

"You wouldn't make that offer unless you thought there was a chance the well would hit, would you?"

"We always hope they hit."

"But you had special knowledge here?"

"We are coming back around to areas I can't talk about."

"I see. So the Mack farm was sabotaged and a short time later you made an offer for a drilling lease on their property."

"I did."

"And how did the Macks respond?"

"They turned it down."

"Who turned it down specifically?"

"Mr. and Mrs. Mack."

"Did they give you a reason?"

"They said that they did not think it meshed with their plan for organic farming."

"Did you have any dealings with Hamish or Archie Mack at that time?"

"No. I understood that Mr. and Mrs. Mack made all the decisions related to farming."

"Did you follow up at all? Ask again?"

"I did."

"How many times?"

"Once a month for a few months right after, then every couple of months after that."

"Why?"

Wellington shrugged. "Circumstances change. People change their minds."

"How long did that go on?"

"About a year I would say. Then I stopped calling. We would run into each other here and there and I might mention it casually, but I stopped contacting them directly about it."

"So did there come a time this summer when you contacted Hamish Mack?"

"I did."

"Why?"

Wellington shrugged. "It's just good business to keep in touch with potential contacts."

"But tickets to the Big Luke concert? That seems like more than just a casual contact."

Wellington smiled. "Hillside Oil has a generous entertainment allowance. I invited a few friends."

"By friends you mean other farmers who have oil wells on their property?"

"That's right."

"That wasn't a coincidence, was it?"

"What do you mean?"

"That you invited Hamish on a night when you were entertaining other farmers with oil wells."

"Heck no, Mr. Shepherd, that wasn't a coincidence at all. That's just good business."

"Why did you do that?"

"I wanted Hamish to be able to talk to other farmers."

"Other farmers who had allowed Hillside Oil onto their land?"

"Other farmers who had partnered successfully with Hillside Oil."

"Did you talk about the possibility of an oil lease on the Mack farm that night?"

"We did."

"Even though Mr. and Mrs. Mack had told you no repeatedly?"

"Hamish was giving me the impression that the situation might've changed."

"How so?"

"Hamish told me that under the terms of his deed, Mr. and Mrs. Mack controlled all the farming decisions. He had recently received an interpretation that drilling an oil well wasn't a farming decision. So I believe his thought was that he had the authority to agree to put a well on his own land."

"What did you think?"

"I thought it was worth looking into."

"How did you feel about that?"

"I was excited."

"Because you thought it could be a big find?"

"I wasn't sure but, like I said, I was hopeful."

"Where did you leave it with Hamish?"

"That we would both have our lawyers look at it, but if it worked out, Hillside Oil would be more than willing to move ahead."

"We've seen video of the two of you talking in the courtyard of the Quarry after the concert. Is that where the two of you left off your discussions that night?"

"Yes."

"What happened next?"

"I said goodbye to Hamish and he left."

"Did you see which way he went?"

"No, sir. Like I mentioned, I had some other guests there that night and I was going back to say goodbye to them."

"What happened then?"

"Then your client came up to me."

"What happened?"

"He asked what I was talking to his brother about."

"What did you say?"

"I said we were talking about Big Luke."

"So you lied to him?"

"I did not. We did talk about Big Luke."

"What did Archie say?"

"He didn't believe me. He got aggressive and asked if we were talking about a well."

"So he was right?"

"Excuse me?"

"Archie. He was right not to believe you?"

Wellington shrugged. "I was not about to get in the middle of a family dispute."

"How was there a family dispute?"

"After about thirty seconds, it was clear that Archie didn't know what Hamish was talking to me about. And I didn't think it was appropriate for me to be the one to tell him."

"Why is that?"

"Because I'm not his brother."

"What else did Archie say?"

"He said that if I was going to talk oil, I needed to talk to the whole family."

"Was he right about that?"

"That's what I was going to find out from Hillside's legal department."

"What did you say to Archie?"

"I told him that me and his brother had a great time at the concert and that I would be happy to take him to the next one."

"What did he say?"

"He said he wasn't interested."

"Then what happened?"

"He was getting pretty mad and I didn't have much interest in talking to him when he was like that and I also didn't want what was clearly a family matter to escalate with me. I told him I'd be happy to talk to him anytime, but that right now, I had to get back to some other guests before they left."

"What did he do?"

"Archie reached out and grabbed me by the arm. I pulled away and said he should really take all this up with his brother. He said that's exactly what I'm going to do and left."

"Which direction did he go?"

"I have no idea."

"So what did you do next?"

"I went and found the other folks I had come there with, made sure they were all good to drive home, and just chatted with them for a little while until the traffic cleared out of the front parking lot. It takes a while after the concert."

"So I understand. What did you do next?"

"Once they were ready to go, I went to my car."

"And where were you parked?"

"In the back lot."

I raised an eyebrow. "I thought that was for employees?"

"And contributors. Hillside Oil is one of the sponsors of the summer concert series, so they give us a couple of parking spaces in the back."

"I see. Did Hamish have the other one?"

"He did."

"So he was your guest of honor that night?"

"He was my guest and I was happy to give him the spot."

"So you went to go to the back lot to leave?"

"I did."

"Did you see Archie?"

Wellington nodded. "Just as I was leaving. I was coming out of the restroom when I saw him walking into the courtyard from the back of the Quarry. I was a little ways away and frankly didn't want to talk to him again, so I avoided him by waiting near the restrooms until he passed, then went along the pathway to the back lot."

"Was there anyone else with you on the pathway to the back lot?"

"I don't remember. I'm sure there was."

"Which?"

"Which what?"

"You don't remember or you're sure there was? We can check the video if you're not sure."

Wellington thought. "I guess I don't remember."

"When you walked along the back path, you would have passed the abandoned stairs?"

"I did."

"Did you see Abby Ackerman when you were there?"

"Absolutely not."

"Why 'absolutely not?'"

"Because if I had, and she was injured, I would've called for help."

"Who said she was injured at that point?"

"Well, you?"

"No, sir, I did not. Do you know what Abby's position on the well lease was?"

"What do you mean?"

"Well, you knew that Mr. and Mrs. Mack were against the well, right?"

"I knew they had been."

"You knew they had turned you down."

"Four years earlier, yes."

"And you knew Archie was against the well?"

"He seemed like it."

"So what about Abby? What did she think of the well?"

"She's not a member of the family."

"No. But she's Hamish's fiancée, so she's the only one whose position on the well actually matters since once she marries Hamish, she gains an ownership interest in his farm."

Wellington's face stayed neutral. "No, I don't know what her position is."

"I want you to assume she's against it."

"Okay."

"If she convinced Hamish not to sign the oil lease, it would cost Hillside Oil a lot of money, wouldn't it?"

Stritch stood. "Objection, Your Honor. Speculation."

"Overruled."

I said it again so the jury wouldn't lose it. "Not getting the lease would cost Hillside Oil a lot of money, wouldn't it?"

Wellington shrugged. "We'd done without it for the previous four years, Mr. Shepherd. I think we would be okay."

"Not getting the lease would cost you a lot of money, wouldn't it?"

"I've been doing fine too."

"So on the way back to your car, you passed the abandoned stairs, right?"

"I mentioned that."

"And you didn't see any sign of Abby Ackerman?"

"I did not."

"Mr. Wellington, I assume it is your testimony that you did not attack Abby Ackerman?"

"Of course I didn't."

I nodded and looked at the red square that was the Mack Farm on the easel. I stared at it until the jury did too. Then I said, "So Mr. Wellington, we've established that you know what the Albion-Scipio is, don't you?"

He scowled. "I do."

"And you know how much gas it's produced, right?"

"Right."

"And you know how much that gas is worth?"

"I do."

"And you made an offer to put a well on Hamish Mack's land?"

"Yes."

"And Abby Ackerman was against putting a well on that land?"

"So you say."

"And you were at the back of the Quarry after the Big Luke concert?"

"I already said that."

"And you were at the abandoned stairs between 11:30 and 12:00 p.m.?"

"We've said all of this."

"I know but we've been talking a while. I just wanted to make sure that was all true."

"It is."

"I don't have any other questions for you right now. Thanks."

Stritch stood. "Mr. Wellington, thank you for taking the time to come and speak with us today."

"Of course."

"You've been very involved in our community, haven't you?"

"Since I moved here eighteen years ago, yes, sir."

"And you moved right here to Dellville, right?"

"Yes sir, that's right."

"You don't live down-state or work in another state, do you?"

"No, sir, I don't. Ohio is another representative's territory."

"I see. And you're involved in a church locally?"

"I am."

"And the Business Association?"

"Yes, sir."

"And I seem to remember you coaching soccer, baseball, and swimming?"

He shrugged, almost shyly. "When you have three kids, you sometimes have to step up."

"And you've been working with landowners here in Ash County and the surrounding areas all that time?"

"Yes, sir. We try to be good partners. We want people to come work with us."

"Now, Mr. Shepherd is a very talented attorney, wouldn't you say?"

"I certainly had that impression."

"Impression. That's a very good word. He asked you some questions there that I think gave the impression that you could've been the one to attack Ms. Ackerman."

Wellington actually looked startled. "Really?"

"Really."

"That's ridiculous."

"I think so, but I'm going to ask you a couple of questions anyway, okay?"

"Sure."

"Mr. Wellington, did you attack Abby Ackerman?"

"Of course not."

"After the concert was over, did you see Abby Ackerman?"

"I did not."

"You said you couldn't remember if you were the only one on the path to the back lot, but you didn't speak to anyone on the way back, did you?"

"I did not."

"So it's fair to assume that you didn't say anything as you passed the abandoned stairs?"

"That is fair."

"So you never said the words 'Albion-Scipio' by the stairs?"

"I didn't speak so I don't see how I could've."

"And you never said the words 'more gas than the Albion-Scipio' by the stairs?"

"I did not, no."

"We were talking about impressions. Mr. Shepherd was trying to give the impression that there was so much oil and money involved in the Mack Farms deal that you might do anything to get it? Is that true?"

"No, of course not."

"In fact, you made an offer to the Macks four years ago, didn't you?"

"I did."

"And you didn't do anything other than call them back from time to time to see if they changed their minds, true?"

"That's absolutely true."

"In fact, there isn't even any indication that a well on the Mack farm would be all that productive, is there?"

Wellington thought for a moment but, rather than look evasive, he looked like a man being careful to give an honest answer. "I don't know that that's exactly true, Mr. Stritch. We wouldn't enter into the deal if we didn't think it could be successful."

"So you mentioned you ran into Archie Mack after the concert, right?"

"I did."

"You hadn't planned on speaking with him, had you?"

"I had not."

"But I got the impression that you were happy to talk to him if he wanted to, right?"

"That's right. But it quickly became clear that Hamish and Archie hadn't spoken and, as I mentioned, I didn't think it was appropriate for me to get in the middle of a family dispute."

"Archie Mack was mad when he spoke to you, wasn't he?"

I stood. "Objection, Your Honor. The witness can't testify to what was in another person's mind."

Stritch raised a hand. "I'll rephrase, Your Honor. Archie Mack yelled at you when he saw you, didn't he?"

"He did raise his voice."

"He grabbed you by the arm, right?"

"He did."

"Did he do anything else like that? Push you in the chest? Bump you?"

"He got close enough that I could feel the spit when he yelled."

"It sounds as though you were able to diffuse the situation, eventually?"

"I was."

"You told Mr. Shepherd that you did not notice which way Archie Mack went after he spoke to you. Do you remember that?"

"I do."

"But you do remember that he was returning from the back of the Quarry, from the area by the abandoned stairs when you went to leave, right?"

Wellington stared at Stritch. "I'm sorry, can you say that again?"

"You're right, that was a bad question. When you left the courtyard to go to your car in the back lot, Archie Mack was coming toward you, wasn't he?"

"He was."

"He was coming from the direction of the abandoned stairs, right?"

"That's right."

"And you avoided him by standing over by the restrooms?"

"True."

"And that would've been around 11:45, 12 o'clock?"

"Somewhere in there. I couldn't swear to the exact time."

Stritch tapped his chin. "Mr. Wellington, did you notice blood on Archie Mack's hand when he came back?"

"You know I couldn't say, Mr. Stritch. It seemed like he was walking pretty fast."

"Like someone who wanted to get away?"

"I can't say that. Like someone who was ready to go maybe."

"And then you went back to your car?"

"Yes."

"Without ever seeing Ms. Ackerman?"

"Exactly."

"Thank you, Mr. Wellington. I have no further questions, Your Honor."

I stood. "Mr. Wellington, Archie Mack didn't threaten you, did he?"

"He did not."

"He didn't push you?"

"He did not."

"He was animated, though, when he talked about his brother Hamish and the well, wasn't he?"

"He was."

"And he was right, wasn't he? The two of you were looking to make a deal behind the family's back, weren't you?"

"I wasn't going behind anyone's back."

"Hamish was though, wasn't he?"

Wellington shrugged. "I don't know that."

I thought. "Mr. Wellington, you were hiding before you went to the back of the Quarry, weren't you?"

He looked confused. "What do you mean?"

"I mean you were hiding so people didn't see you go back there."

"No."

"Tell you what, Olivia, cue up the video."

Olivia clicked and the concession view of the video came up. Wellington was hiding behind the corner of the restrooms.

I used the laser pointer. "That's you right there, isn't it?"

"Yes, but I—"

"—wasn't hiding, right. Run it, Liv."

The video ran.

People moved. Wellington stayed in the corner.

"Seems like you're hiding."

"I didn't want to see Archie. There, you can see Archie coming into the picture right now!"

"A minute or so after you were hiding, yes."

"There, see, now I'm walking by after Archie has passed, just like I said."

"Yes, that's right. You hid until Abby's future brother-in-law had come back. And there you go."

"I was going to my car!"

"Which led you right past the stairs where Abby was found."

Wellington sputtered so that he really didn't say anything. I gestured to Olivia and she stopped the video right when Wellington was at the edge of the frame heading toward the back stairs.

"Mr. Wellington, what is your commission rate per lease?"

"I can't tell you that. It's a trade secret."

"What's your commission rate on a barrel of oil?"

"I can't tell you that."

"What's your commission rate on fifty-nine million barrels of oil?"

Stritch stood. "Objection, Your Honor."

Judge Wesley thought as long as I'd seen her in the case before she said, "Overruled."

"I can't tell you that," said Wellington.

"You get paid a commission rate on cubic feet of natural gas too, don't you?"

"I can't tell you that."

"What's your total commission rate on fifty billion cubic feet of natural gas?"

"I've never had a commission rate on fifty billion cubic feet of natural gas."

"No. I don't suppose you have. What would your commission be on more?"

"What do you mean?"

"What would your commission rate be on more gas than is in the Albion-Scipio?"

Wellington looked furious. Then he said, "I can't tell you that."

"No further questions."

As I sat back down, I saw that Danny had come back in at some point and was right behind us in the first row of the gallery. He motioned for me to come over. I raised my hand and pointed to the judge.

Right on cue, Judge Wesley said, "Members of the jury, that's the morning. Please take a break for lunch and come back in one hour."

We all stood as the jury filed out. Danny waved at me again. I gestured for him to hang on as the jury left. While we waited, I leaned over to Olivia and whispered, "What did you think?"

"The jury is thinking about Wellington more than Stritch would like." Olivia's eyes were inscrutable behind the glasses. "What about you?"

"Too close to call."

She nodded. "I agree."

Once the jury was gone, Judge Wesley left the bench and Olivia and I went over to see what Danny wanted. His face was pale and he seemed a little out of breath, although I thought he'd been there awhile.

"Geez Reddy, you're in worse shape than I thought," said Olivia. "Cade has his work cut out for him."

"What's the matter?" I said.

Danny's face didn't get better, it got worse. He started to speak, stopped, and actually seemed to choke for a moment before he said, "Don't either of you check your phones?"

"The Judge makes us turn them off, you know that," I said. Olivia pulled hers out and powered on.

Danny just shook his head.

"Hey," I said and put my hand on his arm. "What's the matter?"

"He was there," said Danny.

"Who?" I said.

"Where?" said Olivia.

"Professor Timmons. He was there at the Quarry the night of the attack."

44

I looked around. Stritch was gone, but I knew the Judge was right next door, so I kept my voice low. "What are you talking about?"

Danny still seemed to have trouble catching his breath. "I went over to the University like you said and waited at the entrance to the Earth Sciences building. They have assigned parking, so I waited near Professor Timmons's space so I could give him his illustration back."

"He was late and I was worried because I knew you'd already started, but I also knew he'd done us a favor and it seemed important to you that he get it back today."

When he paused, I said, "You did the right thing."

Danny nodded then said, "So finally, a little after eight-thirty, a silver Explorer pulls into his spot and Professor Timmons gets out. So I go over and introduce myself and give him back his illustration and he asks how it went and I said it was going on right now and he just smiles and says good luck and tips the rolled-up map to his head in salute and walks into the building."

I did not sigh or raise my eyebrows or grab Danny by the

shoulders and shake him until he got to the point. Instead, I said, "And?"

"When I got back in my car, I noticed it. His car has a vanity plate—G ROCKS."

Olivia shook her head. "Of course, he does."

Apparently, my head was full of rocks because I wasn't seeing the connection. "Okay?"

"That car was there, in the front lot."

"You just said that, that he was parked in front of the Earth Sciences building."

"No! The front lot of *the Quarry*. The night of the attack!"

I felt a chasm open up in the courtroom floor. "What?"

"You know I've been doing nothing but study that security video."

"Right."

"Well, there's a car that sat there overnight in the lot. Actually, there were a bunch of them. I just figured they belonged to people that had too much to drink or got together and shared rides or, whatever, just came back and got them the next day."

"Sure," said Olivia.

"One of them was a silver SUV with a plate that says 'G ROCKS.'"

Inside, I swore as the chasm grew wider. Outside, I said, "You're sure?"

"Yes," said Danny. "I saw it so many times I was sick of it. I wouldn't have recognized the car at all, but the plate stood out."

"What about him?" said Olivia. "Did you see him?"

Danny shook his head and looked genuinely pained. "I don't know. I've never seen him before today so there's no reason I would have noticed him on the video."

I knew we had the video loaded on the computer to use as an exhibit. "Come on," I said, and the three of us unhooked the laptop from the projection system and turned it toward us.

Danny sat down and began tapping keys as Olivia and I hunched over his shoulder.

I will say this for him, Danny is organized. He had broken out the video by time and usable segments and he clicked right through a series of files until he got to the parking lot footage that he wanted. I glanced at the time stamp. 1:30 a.m., after Kirby had left for the night. Danny was right, there were maybe twenty or thirty cars sitting there, scattered about the lot waiting to be picked up the next morning.

In the second row on the far right side of the camera's view was an Explorer with its license plate facing the camera.

G ROCKS.

I swore. "Does he have kids?"

Olivia's thumbs flurried across her phone. "Facebook," she said to my unasked question. She clicked scrolled and swiped. "Married. Cat lover." She made a face. "Aggressively so. No kids that I see."

"When does he pick up the car?"

"He doesn't," said Danny. "Our video runs through noon the day after the concert and it's still there. We have to get the next one."

"When does the car get there?"

"I have no idea," said Danny.

"Can you find it?"

"Probably. It'll take a little while though."

I nodded. "We need to see him get out and follow him through the video."

"That'll take longer than forty minutes."

The G ROCKS shouted at me from the video screen and I swore again.

"What?" said Danny.

I ground my teeth. "He prepped me for an hour last night."

So I could point the finger at Wellington.

"Let it go," said Olivia. "What's next?"

We had another person to place at the scene. And I was starting to get an idea where he might fit in.

"Where's Cade?" I asked.

"On his way," said Olivia. "He was coming anyway for Archie's bond in case we finished today."

"Send him to the Mack's farm to get Hamish. Have Cade tell Hamish he's still under subpoena and is being recalled to testify."

"Done. Next?"

"Follow Timmons. From a distance! Don't talk to him, just keep an eye on him so that we know where he is if things develop the way I think they might."

"Got it."

"Olivia, I said don't talk to him."

A mirrored stare. "I said, I got it."

"Danny, search the video. Find when he got there so you could see what he was wearing and follow him through."

"That's going to take a while, Nate."

"I know. Set up in the back of the gallery."

He nodded. "What are you gonna do?"

"Buy us time."

$\sim$

I MET with Judge Wesley and Stritch in Judge Wesley's office just before we started for the afternoon session.

"Your Honor, the defense would like to request a brief continuance of the proceedings today."

Judge Wesley raised an eyebrow. "Are you okay, Mr. Shepherd?"

"Yes, Your Honor."

"Family emergency?"

"No, Your Honor."

The raised eyebrow turned into a scowl. "Then why?"

"We learned that there may be a new witness to what happened the night of the incident."

"Who?"

I hesitated. "I'd rather not say at this point, Your Honor. If we're wrong, I don't want to prejudice the Court or the prosecution."

"How long of a continuance are you seeking?"

"Just until Monday."

She looked at Stritch. "I assume you object."

"Absolutely. We're practically done with this case. Mr. Shepherd has had months to prepare. Besides, I have a full docket next week."

"We just became aware of some new information today, Your Honor. We only need a few hours to follow up on it."

"You're going to have to give me more than that if you want this continuance, Mr. Shepherd."

I thought, then said, "There might have been another person at the scene that neither Mr. Stritch nor I knew was there."

Stritch scoffed. I don't know if I knew exactly what that sounded like before that moment, but he definitely did it. He scoffed.

"A one-armed man, maybe?" he said. "Or was it Kaiser Soze?"

"Neither," I said.

"Can you tell me anything else, Mr. Shepherd?" said Judge Wesley.

"Not yet, Your Honor."

"Then your motion is denied. You will proceed with your next witness and if you're out of witnesses, we will move on to closing."

I nodded and we stood. At the door, I turned to Stritch and said, "You know they both did it, right?"

"What?"

"Never mind."

I went out to the counsel table to Danny and Archie and shook my head. "No continuance."

"What do we do?" said Danny.

"Are Abby's friends ready?"

Danny nodded.

"Then we'll put them on and hope that Cade gets here in time with Hamish. I can handle this. You work on the video."

Danny slipped to the back of the courtroom.

Judge Wesley brought the jury in, then said, "Mr. Shepherd, are you prepared to proceed?"

"I am, Your Honor."

"You may call your next witness."

"Your Honor, we call Heather Farrow."

It was one o'clock. Court ended at four-thirty. If Cade couldn't get Hamish back here in time, I had to make the testimony of the three women who went to the concert with Abby last three and a half hours or the case was going to go to the jury.

The first one, Heather, lasted forty minutes and honestly that was a stretch. I could see the jury getting irritated with me for going over the same things with her in different ways and, when Stritch started objecting that my questions had already been asked and answered, I pretty much agreed. But I did it again anyway until the judge directed me to move along and there was nowhere else to go.

The second woman, Kayla Sapowicz, started even worse. It only took twenty minutes before it was clear that, while she had memories of Big Luke that would last a lifetime, we had exhausted every relevant memory she had that was in any way related to the case. I was down to my last topic with her. It was

2:05 p.m. when I asked, "Ms. Sapowicz, did Abby mention her fiancé Hamish at all that night?"

"She did."

"What did she say?"

"Well, early in the evening, she mentioned a couple of times that she wasn't sure what Hamish was doing that night but then, as we were leaving, she saw him and said she was going to catch up with him real quick."

"Did you expect her to return?"

"Not there. We had driven separately, so we were going to meet at HopHeads for a drink after. She told us to go on ahead and she would meet us there."

"Did you leave in the same direction?"

"No. We were parked in front and she had parked in the employee lot in the back."

"Did you wait for her at HopHeads?"

"We did."

"Were you worried when she didn't show up?"

Kayla looked down. "I texted her a couple of times but she didn't answer."

"Did that concern you?"

Kayla shrugged. "She had gone to meet Hamish, so we figured she was...busy."

"I see."

"I felt terrible when I heard later."

"And the last time you saw her that night, she was going to meet her fiancé, Hamish?"

"That's right."

I was out of rope with Kayla. "No further questions, Your Honor."

Stritch looked at me, looked at the clock, then looked back at me, smiled, and said, "I have no questions for this witness, Your Honor."

I only had one witness left, Bonnie Price, and I didn't want to put her on. As Archie's fiancée, she could confirm too many of the circumstantial details—his presence at the concert, the blood on his hand, the history of conflict with Hamish, and worst of all, the lack of an alibi—that would seem all the more damning coming from her. Still, if that was all I had to get us to the weekend, I'd have to risk it.

"Very well, you may step down, Ms. Sapowicz." Judge Wesley looked at the clock and then looked at me. "You may call your next witness, Mr. Shepherd. If you have one."

"Your Honor, the defense calls Bonnie Price."

As Bonnie made her way to the witness stand, Cade opened the courtroom door. He slipped in quietly with Hamish and indicated a place for him to sit. Hamish wasn't dirty, but it was clear that Cade had pulled him from the field—he was wearing a Mack Farms baseball cap, a blue work jacket, jeans, and boots. I saw Hamish make eye contact with his parents and shrug.

I turned back to the judge. "I'm sorry, Your Honor. With apologies to Ms. Price, I'd like to call a different witness. The defense re-calls Hamish Mack to the stand."

Stritch stood. "May we approach, Your Honor?"

Judge Wesley waved us up.

"This is just another delaying tactic, Your Honor," said Stritch. "Mr. Mack has already testified."

I shook my head. "It's not, Your Honor. We're calling Hamish in response to evidence that was put on after he testified and which has relevance to the matter we discussed in chambers. We have a right to re-call him in our case-in-chief."

"You do," said Judge Wesley. "But I also have broad discretion to manage your ability to re-call him."

"I understand, Your Honor."

"You will not repeat his testimony from earlier."

"I understand, Your Honor."

Stritch shook his head. "Your Honor, as I said, this is repetitive—"

Judge Wesley raised her hand. "Did you just hear me say that he will not repeat his testimony from earlier?"

"Yes, Your Honor."

"Then, by definition, it won't be repetitive." She waved her hand, dismissing us back to our tables.

As I walked back to the table, Archie looked at me, his confusion apparent. I waved him closer, bent down and whispered, "When your brother went on casino trips, did he ever go to Dowagiac?"

Archie leaned back and scowled. "Yes. Why?"

I nodded and turned toward the witness stand.

While we had been talking to the judge, Bonnie had sat back down and Hamish had taken his place on the stand. He removed his hat and he smoothed his red hair a couple of times as Judge Wesley said, "Mr. Mack, I would remind you that you are still under oath in this proceeding."

Hamish nodded. "Yes, Your Honor."

"You may proceed, Mr. Shepherd."

"Thank you, Your Honor."

I came around the table and stood directly in front of him. There was only one way that Professor Timmons being at the concert made any sense at all, but I didn't know if Hamish knew about it. I had a hunch and I knew what I had to ask but I had absolutely no idea what the answer was going to be. I believe the Latin term for that kind of question at the end of an attempted murder trial is a nut-cruncher.

"Mr. Mack," I said. "Did you know that Professor Elias Timmons was at Century Quarry the night that Abby was attacked?"

Hamish scowled. "What?"

And that told me all that I needed to know.

Not, "Who the hell is Professor Timmons?"

Not, "What are you talking about?"

Just, "What?"

I nodded. "He was. His car was still in the parking lot the next morning. The one with the G ROCKS license plate."

Hamish turned white. "He told me he wasn't there."

"Where? At the Quarry?"

Hamish nodded.

"You need to answer out loud."

"Yes."

"When did he tell you that he wasn't at the Quarry?"

Hamish's mouth worked, but no sound came out.

"When, Mr. Mack?"

"When we texted."

"That night?"

Hamish nodded.

"You need to answer verbally."

"Yes."

"Did you plan to meet him there?"

"Yes."

"After meeting with Wellington?"

"Yes. I told him it wasn't necessary, but he insisted."

"Because he's been advising you about the potential for oil on your property?"

"Yes."

"How long have you known Professor Timmons?"

"Almost five years."

"Did you meet him at the Diamond Mine?"

"How did you...yes."

"We should explain that to the jury. The Diamond Mine is a casino near Dowagiac, right?"

"It is."

"It offers guided diamond hunts as part of its trip package?"

"Yes."

"And you met Professor Timmons there?"

"Yes."

"Tell me about that."

"He was in our group and knew all about how the mor..."

"Moraines?"

"That's it. How the moraines were formed and why there were diamonds in them. We joked about how I needed to start looking on my farm. A few weeks later, he called."

"About your land?"

"He did. He said he had information that could make me rich."

"What did he want in exchange? A piece?"

Hamish nodded. "Half."

Stritch stood. "Your Honor, we're getting awfully far afield from Ms. Ackerman's assault here."

"I don't know that we are," said Judge Wesley.

"I'll bring it back around, Your Honor," I said. "I take it from what you said earlier that you and Professor Timmons were going to meet at Century Quarry the night of the Big Luke concert."

"We were. I didn't want to, but we were."

"Why did Professor Timmons want to meet then?"

"He wanted to know what Wellington had to say."

"Because you were close to working out a deal?"

"Yes."

"Because you had figured out that drilling for oil is not a farming decision that your parents controlled?"

"That's right."

"Whose idea was it to explore that option?"

Hamish looked down. "Timmons."

"He figured it out?"

"He did."

"Why would you meet at the Quarry?"

"Because there were so many people there that no one would think anything of it if I bumped into a guy and talked to him."

"By no one, you mean your family?"

"Yes."

"Because you wanted to keep it hidden from them?"

"I did."

"But you didn't see Professor Timmons at the Quarry?"

"He didn't show. And then I had my argument with Abby and I left."

"You testified earlier that your argument with Abby was about the well, right?"

"Yes."

"She didn't want you to do it, right?"

"Right."

"She thought it would interfere with organic farming, right?"

"Yes."

"Was it loud?"

Hamish stared at me.

"Hamish, was your argument with Abby loud?"

"Yes." Hamish looked at his brother and then he looked at me. "We yelled."

"And you left?"

"I did."

"And right after you left you got the call from Abby?"

"Yes."

"And so you thought she was okay?"

"I knew she was okay."

"When did you talk to Professor Timmons?"

"We didn't talk. We texted. I sent a text right after I left asking where he was. He answered me two hours later saying he couldn't make it, he'd gotten hung up."

"You left that out of your testimony earlier."

Hamish looked down. "I didn't think it mattered. I thought that Archie had...I didn't think it mattered."

"Mr. Mack, we have video showing that Professor Timmons *did* go to the Quarry that night."

Stritch stood. "Objection, Your Honor. This evidence hasn't been disclosed."

"Yes it has, Your Honor. It's the video we've all been looking at. We just didn't know what his car looked like. We will be able to prove that the silver Explorer with the license plate G ROCKS is registered to Elias Timmons. And that it is in the Century Quarry parking lot at the time of the incident."

"This is in the security video that's been marked as a State Exhibit?" said Judge Wesley.

"It is, Your Honor."

"Overruled."

"Mr. Mack, Professor Timmons was there at Century Quarry on the night your fiancée was attacked after you loudly argued about putting a well on your property. Does that matter to you?"

Hamish's face went the same fiery red as his hair. His jaw clenched, and unclenched, then clenched again before he said, "It certainly does."

"That's all I have, Your Honor."

Before Stritch could stand, Judge Wesley said, "Why don't we take our afternoon break. Members of the jury please come back in fifteen minutes. Counsel, see me in my chambers." Judge Wesley banged the gavel and went back to her office.

I took a deep breath and started to follow her. Then I stopped and did something I came to regret.

I sent Olivia a text. I told her it was Timmons and that she should stay on him.

Then I went into Judge Wesley's office.

45

Judge Wesley sat down heavily. "Why am I just hearing about this now?"

"We just discovered it this morning, Your Honor," I said.

"How can that possibly be?"

"Danny has been scouring the film for weeks, but he had never met Professor Timmons until today, so didn't see him in the video. I'd met him but had never seen his car. Danny saw the car for the first time today and made the connection to the video with the G ROCKS license plate. Then he came to me and told me at the first break."

"And that's why you requested the continuance?"

I nodded.

"Why didn't you just tell me all this then?"

"Because it was still too tenuous to put out there if I was wrong. And I needed confirmation from Hamish or another source."

"And this is all in the video? The video that's already been entered into evidence?"

"The car is. Danny is watching it as we speak to see if we can clearly identify Timmons."

Judge Wesley cocked her head. "Do you know when Timmons left the Quarry?"

"Not yet. The car was there overnight. We don't have the tape for the next day to see when that happened."

"I assume you're going to get it?"

"If Your Honor allows."

"Of course, I'm going to allow it."

Stritch raised a hand. "Your Honor, while this would be an interesting issue for appeal, if that was Mr. Shepherd's last witness, I assume we're proceeding to closing so we can get the jury charged this afternoon?"

"What?" I said.

Stritch shrugged. "You've got your record. The videos and the evidence. It's time to put the issue to the jury."

"Aren't you going to cross-examine Mr. Mack?" said Judge Wesley.

"I've already examined him once. He's confirmed that he received the call from Archie, that Archie was at the place where the attack occurred, and that he assumed at the time that his brother did it. As far as I'm concerned, we have a record in this case and it needs to be sent to the jury."

"You've got the wrong guy, T. Marvin," I said.

"I don't think that's true at all."

Judge Wesley raised her hand. "It's three-thirty on Friday afternoon. Even if you only took fifteen minutes to close, which you won't, we'd have a hard time getting in closing arguments and a jury charge before the end of the day. While I'm not granting counsel's motion for a continuance, I am stopping proceedings for today and letting the jury go home a little early. I'm giving you both the weekend to review the video and run this down. Mr. Stritch, this way you have the whole weekend to prepare your cross-examination of Hamish Mack and incorporate any of this evidence into your case. Mr. Shepherd, if you

obtain additional video or evidence over the weekend, I expect
you to share it with Mr. Stritch that day. The same goes for you,
Mr. Stritch. We will meet at seven-thirty Monday morning to
determine where we are and how we will proceed."

Stritch opened his mouth, Judge Wesley raised her hand,
and he stopped.

"Yes, Your Honor," I said.

We stood.

"I would say have a good weekend, gentlemen, but I prefer
that you have a busy one." Judge Wesley waved a hand in
dismissal. "See you Monday."

We left.

As we went back into the courtroom, T. Marvin and I
stopped. He shook his head. "Danny really only saw the license
plate this morning?"

I nodded. "Touch base once we both have a chance to look at
the video?"

T. Marvin nodded. "Let's talk Sunday morning."

"Sounds good."

"I'm leaning toward proceeding though."

"I understand."

We separated and I looked at the rest of the courtroom.
Archie was standing by the counsel table, waiting. His mother
and Bonnie stood at the rail. Mr. Mack was gone. Hamish sat on
the other side of the gallery, looking forlorn. Cade and Danny
weren't there.

I went to Archie first. I explained that we were done for the
day and that the judge was giving us permission to investigate
over the weekend before deciding what to do Monday.

Archie looked confused. "You mean they're not dismissing
the case?"

"Not yet," I said.

"But you heard what Hamish said! It wasn't me!"

"He didn't exactly say that."

"But—"

I raised my hand. "Don't worry. We're going to get the video evidence together over the weekend. That'll go a long way toward getting a dismissal. Did you know about Timmons?"

Archie shook his head. "I hate gambling. I never went on those trips." He shook his head. "I just want this to be done."

"I understand. We're almost there." I looked at Mrs. Mack. "Where did Mr. Mack go?"

"He had a few words for his son, his other son, and then left. Something about not wanting to add a murder charge to the family list."

"I see. Did you know Hamish was negotiating with Wellington?"

She shook her head. "We really didn't think about it much after we rejected it four years ago. Why wouldn't Hamish tell us this? Why would he let them arrest Archie?"

"Because he didn't know Timmons was there. As far as he was concerned, he had an angry brother right there when his girlfriend was attacked. My guess is once he heard about the blood and the video, he thought that Archie did it. From his perspective, he probably didn't have a reason to think otherwise."

Mrs. Mack looked stricken.

"Do me a favor?"

"What's that, Mr. Shepherd?"

"Keep them away from each other this weekend. Let us sort it out."

Mrs. Mack looked back and forth between her two boys and I got a glimpse of the shrewd, tough farmer who'd kept them in line for years. "I think that's an excellent idea, Mr. Shepherd. Thank you."

I nodded. Since I had called Hamish as a witness that day, I figured it was my job to tell him he could go. I walked over and told him.

"What's going to happen?" he said.

"I don't know yet. Come back Monday morning."

"Okay." His eyes stayed on his mother and his brother. "I didn't know he was there."

"I understand."

"I was sure Archie did it."

"I figured."

"I would never want anything to happen to Abby."

"Sure."

"The oil deal just made so much sense. We would be able to—"

I raised my hand. "You're technically still in the middle of your examination, Hamish. I can't talk to you anymore."

"But I'm telling you that—"

"I'll see you Monday."

He looked exasperated, but he finally nodded and started to walk over to his mom and brother.

"I don't think that's a good idea," I said.

He looked back at me.

"Wait until Monday. Then you'll all know exactly what you're healing from."

He paused there, uncertain. He looked back at his mother and Archie.

The two of them returned his gaze for a moment then turned their backs on him and resumed their conversation.

Hamish twitched, then left.

The last person in the room for me to see was Ronnie Hawkins.

"Abby's not here?" I said.

"Doctor advised against it. And she really didn't want to watch this anymore."

"Have you told her?"

"I haven't been able to get a hold of her since Hamish's testimony. I don't know that it'll change her memory from that night."

"Probably not, but maybe she'll be able to remember some other contact Hamish had with Timmons."

"Maybe." She glanced at the empty witness chair. "There's still some pretty big gaps as to how the attack happened, but it makes more sense than Archie doing it."

"I think so too. We'll see what the video shows."

My phone buzzed. It showed a text message from Danny, which was unusual since he should have been right there in the building.

"Excuse me," I said to Ronnie and opened it.

Get down to security now.

"I'm sorry, I have to go," I said to her. "I'll call you this weekend."

"Talk to you then," she said.

I hustled down the stairs and through the front security desk. Danny was waiting outside the front door.

"Olivia's been hurt," he said.

I stopped. "What happened?"

"She got hit by a car."

"Where?"

"The University parking lot."

"How did you find out?"

"I was standing next to Cade when he got the call."

If I could make the connection to how Olivia had gotten hurt in the University parking lot, then Cade could too. "Shit. When did he leave?"

"Five minutes ago."

"Pack up our stuff and take it to the office. I'll call you."

I didn't wait for an answer as I sprinted to my Jeep. As I pulled out of the lot, I called Cade.

Surprisingly, he answered. "What is it, Shep?" he said.

"What happened?"

"She was injured in the parking lot at the University."

"How did you find out?"

"I'm listed as an emergency contact in her phone. One of the paramedics contacted me."

"A paramedic called? How bad is it?"

"Bad enough that she couldn't use the phone herself."

"Why not?"

"She had a head injury."

"Concussion?"

"Not sure."

"Then what?"

"She got thrown into another car. And hit the right side of her face. Her eye's swollen shut."

I swore.

"Exactly. They're taking her to St. Wendolin's. I'll meet you there." He hung up.

I cursed. Cade wasn't going to St. Wendolin's.

And neither was I.

BONE

46

It was a thirty-minute drive from Dellville to Carrefour on the main highway. I'd be there in twenty. I made calls the whole way.

I called Sheriff Dushane first. I lost precious minutes as his secretary routed me to him. I told him that Cade was on his way to Ohio, that he was speeding, and that he needed to be picked up immediately. He asked me why. I told him. Sheriff Dushane had known Cade for most of his life. He said he would do it and hung up.

Next, I called Danny. I told him to look up where Professor Timmons lived and send it to me. Danny said he would get on it. I told him I needed him to be faster than that and hung up.

I called my mom. I told her Olivia was hurt and on her way to St. Wendolin's. She didn't even pause to say she loved me as she hung up the phone.

I made a call to the Michigan State Police, asked for a particular trooper, and wound up in his voicemail. I left a detailed message about the situation and asked that he follow-up.

The miles ticked by. I was nearing the Ohio border and I still hadn't seen Cade's car or a Sheriff's.

My phone buzzed. A text from Danny with the address. I

loaded it into an app and an Australian woman told me that I was 12 minutes and 8.3 miles from my destination.

I crossed the border into Ohio. Nothing on the side of the road. I called Sheriff Dushane. He answered immediately. No, none of his deputies had seen Cade or stopped him.

I thought about the three men Cade had disarmed. I thought about him casually pounding the MMA wannabe in the gym.

I thought about an injury to Olivia's right eye.

I picked up my phone and made a call I absolutely did not want to make.

~

THE LAST THREE miles were the worst. I had entered an upscale neighborhood in Carrefour, Coral Bluffs, which was exactly as pretentious as it sounds when you consider that there's no ocean in Carrefour and that the neighborhood is utterly flat. It had winding, tree-lined streets, brick walls and iron gates, and— worst of all—a twenty mile an hour speed limit. My Australian guide took me down one street and from there to a lane and then on to a boulevard until I found myself peering past high shrubs that concealed many of the large old homes. Eventually, though, she said that my destination was eight hundred feet ahead up on my right in what turned out to be a cul-de-sac.

I saw a black Expedition turn into the same driveway.

Cade.

I accelerated and shot my Jeep around the curve and past the two brick pillars that marked the long, cement drive. I saw a silver Explorer with the back hatch open parked in front of brick stairs that led into the house. I saw a man with a sport jacket over one arm and a key in the door.

I saw the black Expedition stop right behind the Explorer and the driver's door pop open. Cade got out, took off his sunglasses, and threw them in the front seat of his car. As I slammed on the brakes, he started and turned to face me, standing beside his car like a mountain. He shaded his eyes against the sun as I threw open my door.

A moment later, I saw the flare of recognition in his face, and he turned and ran for the house.

I decided later that it was a good thing that Cade had gotten there first—if he'd been charging me directly, I never would've stood a chance. As it was, though, since he was trying to beat me to the door, the momentum of his charge was directed away from me. I saw Timmons fumble with the lock and get the door open. We were probably fifty feet away from the brick steps when I launched myself and tackled Cade from behind. We both went down in a scraping tumble to the cement.

I knew I had no time. I punched Cade square in the back of the head, right on that bump where the skull meets the neck. Then I dove for his neck and tried to wrap up a chokehold.

I dove too far. Cade let me slip over top of him, then flipped me over his shoulder. As we scrambled to our feet, he hit me square on the side of the head. There was a flash of light and pain as I staggered upright. That was temporary. He hit me with a left hook and then a square right and I went down to my hands and knees.

"Stay down or help me, Shep," he said. "But don't get in my way."

I shook my head, trying to see one of everything again. Then I saw swirling lights and heard a siren blast and the squeal of tires on the driveway. Cade let loose with a roar of anger and pain, lowered his shoulder, and tried to run right over top of me. I put my head down and dove at his legs to tackle him. He blocked it with one arm and punched me in the back of the head with the other. It was like getting hit by a truck. I felt a burning pain shoot down my right arm and my vision went gray.

I heard a voice say, "Freeze, assholes," but Cade kept going, throwing me to the side. So I did what offensive linemen do when they get beat and the linebacker is running free for the quarterback. I spun on the ground and kicked him in the knee.

He went down.

I dove onto his back and held on. I hooked my legs in, wrapped my elbow deep around his neck, and squeezed as hard as I could, trying to choke him out.

I forgot that one of the reasons chokeholds work so well in modern MMA is that there are rules. Cade wasn't bound by any of those. He reached up with one free hand, grabbed a handful of my hair, and pulled. I slipped that way and squeezed harder. He yanked again and I felt myself slipping off.

I heard the same voice say, "I warned you."

Then I heard a crackling and my whole body seized up in pain, and I pretty much lost track of everything for a while.

47

I'm told that it only takes a couple of minutes to recover from being tasered. I can tell you that it felt more like a couple of years. By the time I realized that I was no longer in agonizing pain and could move my limbs, the Chief Detective in Charge of Serious Crimes for Carrefour, Ohio, Mitch Pearson had just put a set of cuffs on Cade and was looking down at me, saying, "Do I need to do the same thing with you, Shepherd, or are you going to behave?"

"No problems here, Officer," I said. I sat up, still on the cement. I wrapped my arms around my knees and found that my suit pants were torn, my jaw hurt, and my right arm burned from my neck to my fingertips. I should have kept an eye on Pearson as he put Cade into his car but, honestly, I was just trying not to throw up.

A second car had arrived behind Pearson. Neighbors were making their way down driveways. I saw Timmons peeking out at us from behind the curtain in his bay window.

Once he had Cade secured in his car, Pearson came back to me and squatted down.

"You want to tell me what this is all about?"

"In your jurisdiction, the man in that house just assaulted Cade's sister and put her in the hospital."

Pearson straightened. "Olivia?"

I nodded.

He scowled.

"There's a concern the attack could've left her blind."

Pearson's expression became truly dark. "You don't say."

"We don't know for sure yet. We haven't seen her. But that's the word."

"Okay."

"You'll also want to talk to Sheriff Dushane."

Pearson cocked his head. "About?"

"There's a high likelihood that the man in there also attempted to commit a murder in Ash County. My guess is that, between you and the Sheriff, you can leverage his crime in your jurisdiction into a confession to the crime in the other one."

Pearson nodded. "And here I thought it was a slow week."

"Oh, and when you talk to Dushane, tell him to call Trooper Stern over at the Michigan State Highway patrol."

"A lot of demands today, Shepherd."

I shrugged. "Do what you want. But Stern's running a cell phone check. My guess is that this guy's phone is going to verify that he was within 1.3 miles of the crime scene."

"That's a pretty broad radius."

"He doesn't know that though."

Pearson looked at the window and the curtain fell back into place. "Who is this interstate criminal?"

I moved my jaw back and forth and learned that was a mistake. "A geology professor."

Pearson stared at me now. "You're shitting me."

"I'm not."

Pearson motioned to two other officers to watch his car, then went to the front door. A woman let him in. A short-time later,

Pearson was leading Timmons out in cuffs. A woman was crying. All in all, it was quite a spectacle.

Once Timmons was loaded, Pearson came back. "You okay to drive?"

I nodded.

He extended a hand and helped me to my feet. Of course, he squeezed my hand as hard as he could but, hey, the guy was trying.

"Thanks for the call, Shepherd. I'll be in touch."

"Wait, you're not taking Cade in too, are you?"

"I assume you're not going to press charges for assault?"

"Of course not."

Pearson nodded. "Then he'll only be looking at misdemeanor trespassing. He should be out in an hour."

"You've got to be kidding."

Pearson shrugged. "Take it up with the prosecutor." Then he climbed into his car and the officers drove away.

It took me longer than I care to admit, but I was eventually able to limp to my car. My arm was still burning as I drove away.

I headed downtown to bail out my friend.

∾

ON SUNDAY NIGHT, Cade and I were sitting in Olivia's hospital room, arguing.

"It was lucky and you know it," said Cade.

"Did you make it up the stairs?" I said.

"Two more seconds and you were done."

"Did you make it up the stairs?"

"Even when you had me by the neck, you couldn't hang on."

"See, because I don't remember you making it up the stairs."

Olivia shifted in her bed. "All I know is, if I got tased by Pearson, I wouldn't be running around bragging about it."

The woman had a point. We both shut up.

There was a knock on the door and we all turned as Sheriff Dushane entered the room. "Hello, Olivia," he said and placed a vase of flowers on her table.

Olivia reached over to the end table and slipped on her half-mirrored glasses. "Hello, Sheriff.

He leaned down and kissed her cheek. "How are you, dear?"

"Good. I feel fine.

"How much longer are they going to keep you?"

"Just until tomorrow. There's no damage. They just wanted to monitor the swelling, all things considered."

"That makes sense. You can't be too careful." He patted her hand. "I'm glad."

"Thanks."

"You're a ways from Dellville, aren't you?" I said.

He did a double take when he saw my face, then pointed at Olivia. "Looks like the two of you should switch places."

I shrugged. "I fell."

"That's what I hear." Sheriff Dushane smiled. "I was just with Mitch Pearson."

"Lucky you," said Cade.

"He did say the two of you had become close lately."

"Very funny."

"I sat in on the interrogation of Eli Timmons."

"How did that go?"

"I think you're going to find that you have a day off coming tomorrow."

"Oh?"

Sheriff Dushane nodded. "I know that you all don't get along with Pearson very well, but he was masterful today. He turned the vehicular assault against Olivia here into leverage about what happened to Abby Ackerman at the Quarry."

"And?"

"And he spilled the whole thing. Turns out Timmons was so anxious about the meeting with Wellington that he couldn't wait and wanted to meet Hamish at the Quarry to find out what happened. Timmons walked right in halfway through the concert and went around to the abandoned stairway knowing he could catch Hamish on the way back to his car and thinking that no one would see them there. So Hamish comes back after the concert, but before Timmons can say anything, Abby catches up to Hamish. She hadn't known that Hamish was going to be there with Wellington and, when she saw them, she puts two and two together and she lights him up about how he can't go behind his family's back and that an oil well doesn't work with the type of wholesome food his family is trying to bring to market. One thing leads to another and Hamish yells at her and he leaves. Timmons is sitting in the bushes and hears the whole thing and he can see his deal evaporating."

"What was his deal?" I asked.

"Oh, right. So you know Hamish met Timmons at the Diamond Mine Casino during a diamond hunt?"

"Yes."

"Apparently, they get to talking about where Hamish's land is and Timmons does research and figures out the Mack farm might be sitting on a huge oil find. Timmons becomes convinced of it and tells Hamish he'll let him in on a secret if he splits it 50-50. Hamish agrees, Timmons tells him, and they pay for ultrasonic testing. That confirms they're on the right track. They both figure it's going to be huge."

"So after Hamish's fight with Abby, Timmons is thinking. Then he hears her talk to Hamish on the phone and he sees his whole deal might be evaporating. So he doesn't even think twice. He comes out of the shadows and tries to get her attention because he wants to convince her to listen to Hamish because he knows what he's doing. Abby's startled though, and she backs up and Timmons watches her tumble head over heels down the stairs until she flips right off it over into the weeds and rocks."

"Timmons panics for a moment but then realizes that Abby is moving and he isn't sure what to do. He hears someone coming and he figures he's going to get blamed, so he hides again. It's Archie and he's angry and he's standing at the top of the stairs yelling at Hamish over the phone. Timmons stays hidden and listens to the rest of Archie's conversation and hears that they're arguing about Abby and the well. Before Archie storms off, Timmons sees him grabbing the rail and realizes it'll prove that Archie was there. And once Archie leaves, he realizes he has an out and that no one knows he was even there."

Sheriff Dushane shrugged. "And I think that's when his thoughts turned. He knew that, even if it was an accident, there's no way Hamish would partner with him if he had hurt his fiancée."

"You got him to admit all this?" I said.

"Most of it. Some of the details he didn't realize he was even admitting. He also might have been under the impression that Pearson would recommend a lighter sentence."

"Pearson won't do that. He can't do that."

"Like I said, he was masterful. So Timmons goes down and he picks up the rock and he tries to finish the job." Sheriff Dushane shook his head. "He had trouble doing it, I think. He kept saying that Albion-Scipio thing like a mantra. Pearson convinced him that we all understood, that it was far too much money to just let go, that anyone else would have done the same. I think one swing was all that he had in him. Fortunately."

"How'd he leave?"

"He climbed the side fence to the Quarry rather than go back through the crowd, walks about half a mile, then catches an Uber over on Stone Street. He went back and picked up the car at one o'clock the next afternoon when the lot was full of swimmers."

I nodded. "That's consistent with what Danny found on the video. It took some time because he was wearing a baseball cap and trying to blend in the crowd, but we saw him slip through the courtyard to the back part of the Quarry about ten o'clock. And then he never came back out."

"I can't believe he admitted all this," said Olivia.

"Like I said, Pearson is good at his job. He's a better interrogator than, oh, let's say an angry gym owner."

"Cade just got carried away," said Olivia.

"I wasn't talking about him."

Olivia stared, then looked down. "Oh, right."

"Confronting a suspect as he gets in his car is never a good idea. Leave it to us next time."

"I was angry. What he did to her...she could've been..." She shrugged.

"I know. Leave it anyway."

"So was it a full confession?" I asked.

"Full enough for your purposes."

"I'll give Archie the good news. I have to call Stritch too."

"I already let Stritch know."

"Before me? I'm hurt."

"He is the prosecutor for my county, Nate. I have to work with him."

"I suppose you do."

Sheriff Dushane put a hand on Cade's massive shoulder. "Well, it's been electrifying, boys."

Cade stared in a way that would have intimidated just about anyone except his pee wee football coach.

Sheriff Dushane smiled. "I mean it. You guys give me a jolt every time I see you."

"Cop humor is the best," I said.

"Amps me up every time." Sheriff Dushane put on his hat, gave Olivia another kiss on the cheek, and made his way out. He paused at the door, looked back at Cade, and said, "That's two." Then he left.

Sheriff Dushane went back a ways with all of us, all the way to grade school, but I had no idea what he was talking about. "What did he mean?"

"Who knows?" said Cade.

Olivia just sat behind her glasses and stared.

I think.

48

On Monday morning, T. Marvin Stritch dismissed the case against Archie. It actually took some convincing; for a few minutes he had some screwball accomplice theory in mind, but eventually he saw the wisdom of accepting the confession of Timmons and closing the case. I think two things put it over the top. First, I told him I'd made the same mistake, that I'd been just as wrong in my conviction that Wellington had done it. Second, I suggested that dismissing a case was not the same as losing it, so his undefeated streak would remain intact. Five months later, Eli Timmons entered a plea for attempted manslaughter, which I imagine Stritch counted as keeping the streak alive. Hard to say.

I talked to Ronnie Hawkins and Abby Ackerman that afternoon and told them the whole story. Abby never did remember any more details about what happened to her that night, but the whole thing spooked her enough, justifiably, that she broke off her engagement with Hamish that same day.

Mr. and Mrs. Mack were at a loss for what to do for a while since their son Hamish was not a criminal, but he wasn't exactly innocent either. It turned out he'd been the one who had orchestrated the crop sabotage. After he had learned about how profitable the well could be from Timmons, Hamish had wanted to make sure their crop yields were high enough that his parents wouldn't be tempted to accept Hillside's offer of a lease for themselves. So he had fertilized the fields and worked night and day to keep them afloat. Mr. and Mrs. Mack were distraught—they couldn't take their land back from Hamish but they also couldn't trust their youngest son anymore when it came to the farm. Eventually, they got their own lawyer and deeded the drilling rights for an oil well on their part of the farm to Peninsula Petroleum, Hillside Oil's biggest competitor.

I'm told Will Wellington put the Macks in touch with the Peninsula folks for no commission. He is, by all accounts, exactly that nice.

It turned out that the drilling pad only took up ten acres, leaving the Macks plenty of land for farming. Mr. and Mrs. Mack, though, wanted no part of the profits. They deeded it all over to Abby. Abby tried to refuse, of course, but Mr. and Mrs. Mack couldn't bear the thought that their son had been such a colossal shithead and sent the payments to a trust in her name.

I heard Abby eventually started donating funds from the trust to support sustainable farming. Later, I guess she teamed up with Big Luke to set up a scholarship for farmers' kids at some university but, I have to admit that, by then, I wasn't paying much attention to the details. I did hear through Ronnie, though, that Abby's hip healed and that she was able to walk normally again, but that the fracture alongside her eye never healed quite right.

It's interesting with clients. Sometimes you keep in touch and other times the case that is the most intense period of their lives is the only time you have any contact with them. I didn't see Archie again for years and I didn't see Hamish again at all, which I suppose shouldn't have surprised me since I really don't spend much time out in the fields of northern Ash County.

As for Cade and Olivia and me, the swelling went down around Olivia's eye and she was allowed to go home from the hospital that Monday without any problems. Cade and I didn't really talk any more about our fight, except that he would sometimes say how easy it was to get out of a rear naked choke and I would occasionally comment on how it's pretty simple to bring down someone much bigger than you...and Olivia would mention that there were times when she wished that her ears had been injured instead of her eye.

Which leaves me to tell you about breakfast.

≈

I SLID INTO THE BOOTH, ignoring Olivia as the waitress came right over.

"One sunny side up hash skillet, please," I said. "With orange juice and coffee."

The waitress smiled and said she'd be right back.

"Check the time," I said.

It was hard to tell if Olivia was amused or irritated as she pulled out her phone, then said, "4:29."

"Ha."

She gave me a little smirk. "You look like shit."

"Feel like it, thank you. You really do this every day?"

"I really do."

"You have issues."

"Doesn't take a law degree to figure that one out."

A carafe of coffee came. I politely declined the cream, then took a gloriously hot sip. "So you're cleared to lead your classes already?"

"I'm not in the hospital."

"That's not what I asked."

"It's the answer though."

"Goodness."

She smiled. "I usually don't have company until my second cup of coffee."

"Well then," I said, and refilled her cup from my carafe. Steam wafted up and left thin trails across her lenses that vanished as soon as they appeared.

A moment later, my personal cast iron skillet appeared with two sunny side up eggs on a bed of hash made from cubed potatoes, peppers, and onions. I hit it with hot sauce, picked up my fork, and said, "Do you want to tell me about it?"

"No." Olivia's bowl of oatmeal and blueberries appeared to need concentration. "How long have you known?"

I shrugged. "A while now."

She nodded. "What gave it away?"

"You know we didn't see each other much for a few years, between law school and life at my old firm?"

"Right."

"When I first started back at the gym, I thought the new glasses were a fashion statement."

She nodded.

"Then it was just little things."

"Like?"

"You don't play softball anymore. You don't spar, only roll. You seem to get headaches when you work on the computer a lot. Dropping out of book club. Getting a bigger TV. No one thing but everything." I pushed my hash around. "Why didn't you tell me?"

She shrugged and said, "There's not much to tell."

"Then it wouldn't have taken long."

Silence.

"Is there any vision in the left eye at all?"

"No."

"What happened?"

Olivia took a bite of oatmeal, then instead of answering me, she said, "You blew out Cade's knee."

I shrugged. "What's a medial collateral ligament among friends."

"You could have done real damage. It could've been his ACL."

"True. And he might have made it to the stairs."

"Why did you do it?"

"Do I have to explain what would have happened if he'd made it to the stairs?"

Olivia looked down for the first time.

I put a little more hot sauce on the hash because, well, you have to sometimes. Then I said, "At the time, all I knew was that your right eye was hurt. And that you were going to need your brother."

"I was fine."

I nodded. "I didn't know that. Neither of us did. Hence…" I shook out a last dash of hot sauce and took a bite.

"So you were saving the support system for the blind woman?"

"No."

Olivia looked up.

"I was saving *a* support system." I shook my head. "Why didn't you tell me?"

Olivia pressed her lips together, then said, "Shep, we've been fine without discussing this. You hire me to investigate cases. I remind you to get your soft ass to the gym. It works out."

When I started to speak, Olivia sighed and looked into the kitchen. "I have enough trouble keeping one over-protective brother at bay. I'm not going to deal with two."

"I wouldn't do that."

"Bullshit. You're doing it now."

"That's what friends do."

"No, Shep, they don't. They respect each other's boundaries."

"Hmm. It wasn't too long ago that my friend had me in the gym every night working things out."

"That was different."

"How?"

"Because it was new for you. You didn't realize what you were going through, and your friend knew better. Your friend, on the other hand, has long since gotten used to her situation."

I nodded and took a few more bites. "You handle it better than Cade."

She smiled. "I used to tell him not to worry about it, that it was more likely that I'd get hit by a car."

"Guess you'll have to retire that one."

"Apparently."

"Is the gym safe?"

She smiled. "I'm more likely to get hurt working for you."

I laughed. "Fair. But the question remains."

"There's a split of opinion."

"Are there any doctors on your side of it?"

"Does it matter?"

"To me."

"A few."

"More on the other?"

She shrugged.

"So you're not going to tell me what caused it?"

"No."

"Is whatever caused it resolved?"

She didn't answer for a while. I thought she wasn't going to until she said, "I don't know yet."

"When will you?"

"I don't know that either."

"You'll come to me if you need help."

She shrugged. "We'll see."

"That wasn't a question, Liv."

"Problems come soon enough without running out to meet them, Shep. I'll handle it when it comes."

I couldn't argue with that.

I swirled the last potato in a tiny smear of hot sauce and paused, then decided that would have to do. I ate the potato, enjoying the burn on the way down, took a sip of coffee and said, "So are you torturing a class this morning?"

"Before the sun comes up," she said, then we finished our coffee, I paid the bill, and we left.

THE NEXT NATE SHEPHERD BOOK

False Oath is the next book in the Nate Shepherd Legal Thriller Series. Click here if you'd like to order it.

FREE SHORT STORY AND NEWSLETTER SIGN-UP

There was a time, when Nate Shepherd was a new prosecutor and Mitch Pearson was a young patrol officer, that they almost got along. Almost.

If you sign up for Michael Stagg's newsletter, you'll receive a free copy of *The Evidence,* a short story about the first case Nate Shepherd and Mitch Pearson ever worked on together. You'll also receive information about new releases from Michael Stagg, discounts, and other author news.

Click here to sign up for the Michael Stagg newsletter or go to https://michaelstagg.com/newsletter/

ABOUT THE AUTHOR

Michael Stagg has been a trial lawyer for more than twenty-five years. He has tried cases to juries and he's won and he's lost and he's argued about it in the court of appeals after. He still practices law so he's writing the Nate Shepherd series under a pen name.

Michael and his wife live in the Midwest. Their sons are grown so time that used to be spent at football games and band concerts now goes to writing. He enjoys sports of all sorts, reading, and grilling, with the order depending on the day.

You can contact him on Facebook or at mikestaggbooks@gmail.com.

ALSO BY MICHAEL STAGG

Lethal Defense

True Intent

Blind Conviction

False Oath

1-24
c mw

Made in the USA
Middletown, DE
06 June 2023

32165406R00246